Thanks,
Finally published!
Enjoy my short
story about my
trip with you
grandfather!
(pages 167-1...
Love,
Cheri

The Guilded Pen

SDWEG
SAN DIEGO
WRITERS AND
EDITORS GUILD

Eighth Edition — 2019

MW00886516

The Guilded Pen, Eighth Edition is a publication of the
San Diego Writers and Editors Guild
P. O. Box 881931
San Diego, CA 92168-1931
www.sdwritersguild.org

The Guilded Pen, Eighth Edition was published by Grey Castle Publishing.
Copies are available on Amazon.com, www.greycastlepublishing.com,
from our website: www.sdwritersguild.org, and www.KDP.com.

Marcia Buompensiero, Managing Editor
Rivkah Sleeth, Editor
Jenna Benson, Editor (Poetry)
Tom Leech, Editor (Poetry)

"First Prize, One Wife" was previously published in *Irreverent Forever*
(2018). Reprinted by permission of Mrs. Betty Feldman and the
publisher, Grey Castle Publishing.

"The Ingénue & the Genie" was previously published in *The Genie Who
Had Wishes of His Own* (2013). Reprinted by permission of the author and
the publisher, Plowshare Media.

Cover design by Grey Castle Publishing with Photo by Caleb George on
Unsplash.

Paperback price $20.00

ISBN: 9781693891137

The Guilded Pen

Eighth Edition — 2019

An anthology of the
San Diego Writers and Editors Guild

iv

Table of Contents

Lost

Found

Found (cont'd)

Still Looking

Dedication

Dave Feldman
1928 – 2019

Dave Feldman roller-skated into the great newsroom in the sky on May 16, 2019. He was born in South Bend, Indiana, on January 7, 1928, and moved with his parents, Irving and Etna (Goodwin) Feldman, to Tucson, Arizona, in 1936. He graduated from the University of Arizona and embarked on a long career as a journalist with stops at the *Douglas Daily Dispatch, Tucson Citizen, Honolulu Star-Bulletin,* and *Stars and Stripes* in Germany. David spent 30 years as a copyeditor at the *San Diego Union Tribune* and taught journalism at the University of Arizona and San Diego State University.

After retiring from the newspaper business, he spent the last decade of his life editing novels and non-fiction books for family, friends, and clients. Dave was the copyeditor for seven issues of the SDWEG anthology, *The Guilded Pen.* At age 90, Dave wrote and published his memoir, *Irreverent Forever*, a lively collection of stories about his adventures and the interesting characters he met throughout his remarkable career. Dave was a staunch supporter of the SDWEG, serving on the board of directors for several terms.

Dave had many passions in life; he loved cars, especially his 1957 Citroën Traction Avant (which he called his "gangster car"), and was an avid roller skater until his doctor made him hang up his skates at age 84. He was a speed skating champion in the Marine Corps but had to decline a professional roller derby contract in Europe when his commanding officer objected. Dave lived a full life surrounded by loving family and friends. He was predeceased by his parents; his sister; Donna Bergheim; his brother, Lewis Feldman; and his beloved children, Greg Feldman and Tracy Shaughnessy. He is survived by his wife of 68 years, Betty Feldman, and numerous nieces and nephews who all fondly recall their uncle who kept the punch lines to his favorite jokes in his shirt pocket.

x

Introduction

Since 2012, the SDWEG has published an anthology for its members. It is, simply put, a collection of poetry, essays, memoir, and imaginative short stories written by our members, which we have categorized as **Lost, Found**, and **Still Looking**.

The categories for submission are specific, but the opportunity for creativity is wide open. Many are real life experiences. Some are humorous. Some are fiction — others are not. Poignant life lessons and personal experiences spanning decades of living are within these pages. All, whether real or imaged, are riveting.

There is no standard to which a writer is expected to adhere other than good grammar, correct sentence structure, a plot that moves forward in some logical way, and characters that are interesting.

Although writing is a singular effort, we need other people to give us their impressions of what we have written. So it is with the anthology. A single piece of work will have had many eyes upon it before final publication.

What makes an anthology valuable to a writer is that it provides a platform to display a small sample of their talent for public viewing. The anthology is a showcase for an author's skill, imagination, and flair for storytelling. Here, authors can try something new, something outside their comfort zone, something beyond their usual genre — and get it out into the universe.

The SDWEG anthology is published for just those reasons. Not many authors have this opportunity. It is one of the many benefits of Guild membership.

— Mardie Schroeder, President
San Diego Writers and Editors Guild

— Marcia Buompensiero
Managing Editor

Acknowledgments

The Guilded Pen, Eighth Edition, 2019 owes its existence to the SDWEG Board of Directors. Their dedication and foresight fostered the creation of a venue to showcase members' works and continue to carry on the mission to support the local writing arts.

Board of Directors 2019
Mardie Schroeder, President
Bob Doublebower, Vice President
Laurie Asher, Secretary
Marcia Buompensiero, Treasurer
Adolpho Sanchez, Membership Chair
Sandra Yeaman, Social Media Manager/Webmaster
Patricia Bossano, Newsletter Editor
Directors-at-Large:
Gered Beeby
Marie DiMercurio
Janet Hafner
Rivkah Sleeth
Penn Wallace
Ken Yaros

———

We are grateful to our editorial review panel who read, critiqued, and edited the submissions. Special thanks and appreciation goes to Laurie Asher, Gered Beeby, Barbara Crothers, Bob Doublebower, Janet Hafner, Richard Peterson, Arthur Raybold, Ken Yaros, Sandra Yeaman, and Christopher Zook.

Marcia Buompensiero, Managing Editor
Rivkah Sleeth, Editor
Jenna Benson, Editor (Poetry)
Tom Leech, Editor (Poetry)

San Diego Writers and Editors Guild

Mission Statement: **Promote, Support, and Encourage the Writing Art for Adults and Youth**

We are a nonprofit local group of writers and editors dedicated to improving our skills and helping others to do the same. Since 1979, the Guild has played an important role in furthering the goals of both novice and accomplished authors. No matter what your writing skill, we can help you get to the next level. Our members come from all over the region in search of support and to share their talents.

Benefits of membership include:
- Monthly meetings with informative speakers
- Marketing Support Group
- Monthly Newsletter (*The Writer's Life*)
- Membership Directory
- Manuscript Review Program
- Opportunity to publish your work in *The Guilded Pen*
- Opportunity to list yourself and your work in the SDWEG Members' Works pages on our website
- Active Website and Social Media Presence
- Access to Online Resources for Writers
- Access to discounted space at the Annual Festival of Books
- Periodic presentation of awards: "The Rhoda Riddell Builders Award" — recognizing efforts to build/expand the Guild; "Special Achievements Awards" — for extraordinary service; and "The Odin Award" — to those who have been major stimulators of the writing arts in San Diego as evidenced by their body of published work.

Guild membership is open to all and guests are welcome to the meetings for a small donation. Visit: www.sdwritersguild.org.

Lost

Lost in Rini

Leon Lazarus

**The first in a collection of short stories describing
a sliver of life in Apartheid era South Africa**

"Listen boeties, my brothers," Lubanzi said, lounging back in
the scruffy reclining office chair. "You can't be scared. This is just
Africa." He looked at Henry earnestly, and then shot me a glance.
"Mapolisa can't stop you whities, they are just cops." He closed
his eyes and let his head relax into the chair, his coarse, densely-
curled black hair, a cushion. The hint of a smile crossed his dark
umber face.

A desk fan in the corner of the tiny student council office
hummed softly, clicking as it changed direction. The bright pink
pages of an underground student publication lifted and fell back
in the passing breeze. Rows of old student magazine covers lined
the walls, papering over cracks and yellow-brown water stains.
Each cover featured photocopied pictures of National Party
politicians, purposefully disfigured with black ink and correction
fluid. Hand-cut galleys of text lay in trays on the desk, an empty
whiskey bottle and an overflowing ashtray served as
paperweights. Here, safe in the foundations of the campus great
hall, we were free to play at creative destruction.

"I don't know about this, Henry," I offered through gritted
teeth. Henry looked back at me; his lips pursed. He strummed a
few random chords on his guitar without finding a song. I thought
he looked cornered. That's how I felt. To get into Rini, we would
have to navigate the back roads and rutted donkey tracks that
crisscrossed the hills behind Grahamstown. Going through the
dusty dongas and ditches was the only way in and out of the
township after dark. The main roads would be closed at the
checkpoints. The cops would be looking for "infiltrators" and
"terrorists" like us after curfew.

"Christ, Lee, we can't leave Lubanzi and Princess stranded here," Henry said, his voice close to a whisper. I wasn't sure if he was trying to convince me or himself, but I nodded.

Princess looked exhausted. Her hair, normally a mass of tight black springs, had been carefully teased and pulled into rows of perfectly formed Bantu knots for the evening. Her attractive round face had a Vaseline sheen, fashionable in the townships of the Eastern Cape. Earlier in the evening, her powerful voice had blown the doors off the Cathcart Arms, her small muscled frame jiving to the music, bringing the audience out of their seats to the dance floor. Now, sitting cross-legged on the floor in the corner, she cradled her chin in her hands, her eyes following the conversation back and forth.

Our office under the great hall became quiet for a few long minutes. The low song of the crickets droned hypnotically from the playing fields that stood between us and the town beyond. This warm summer night felt uniquely South African to me, a strange mix of serene beauty and deeply ingrained paranoia. Despite the state's attempt to stifle dissent, I found the defiance of authority thrilling and gave expression to it through my student journalism and membership in a racially mixed band. I raised hell and made music, suppressing the deeply ingrained fear that it would all end badly in a police cell somewhere.

The government was scary; screw them. Every South African was aware that the Apartheid bureaucracy kept a close watch on its citizenry, especially the scruffy miscreants crossing racial barriers. It was made clear that enjoying the company of a black friend was suspicious and worthy of further investigation. The few who consorted with black women were considered indecent and wicked, obviously a threat to the natural order. The government tapped phones, followed us around, and regularly attended our shows where we would sing "undesirable" songs. Standing on the stage, I could see special branch — the secret police — standing at the bar with a can of Castle Lager in hand. Identified by their cheap pastel Polo knockoffs and knife-edged khakis, they desperately tried to blend in with a cultural landscape they did not fully grasp. Their thick moustaches were styled to resemble the Magnum character on television. Pretoria, the epicenter of bureaucratic power, was known as Moustache city. *Snor City* in its original Afrikaans. Being able to spot these bastards, I came to accept their lurking presence. What the hell. They were paying customers, and the cover charge was ours.

2

I absently glanced out the office door. Across the field, in the dark, there were residences filled with student informants. Usually ex-military guys, they arrived on campus at the beginning of the year and joined groups like the Moderate Students Alliance. I knew their type — infatuated with full-contact rugby, heavy drinking, and fighting. They hated long-haired rabble like me — an enemy of the state. I figured they were all government spies and kept my distance. It was only later I learned the extent to which the anti-apartheid groups on campus had been infiltrated. Being paranoid like everyone else living in a fascist state, I didn't talk much about my activities outside the little office provided for our student publishing projects. On campus, a controversial comment might reach the wrong ears. I held my tongue until I was amongst friends. And even then . . .

It was after midnight. None of the informants would be sober enough to track our movements. How strange it was. Just driving Lubanzi and Princess home was so fraught with danger. They were our friends and bandmates, but legally we couldn't give them a ride! Doing so would require us to traverse a wall of South African police, eighteen-year-old Defense Force servicemen with nervous trigger fingers, campus spies, township gangs, and freedom fighters.

"Lubanzi, you know a safe way in, right?" I hoped he would just say no and opt to remain at my place for the night.

"I've got plans," he grinned. He had an air of indifference to imminent danger that I wished I shared. Of course, he had grown up in a tin shack in Rini township. We had grown up in the white suburbs. He shat in a bucket. We couldn't imagine anything less than clean white porcelain. Henry and I could crank out a workable rendition of Neil Young's "Heart of Gold," but when Lubanzi sang Bob Marley's "Redemption Song," he meant every word, and the audience felt it. Some nights you could see them furtively wiping their eyes.

It was already two in the morning. We had to go soon. I grabbed the car keys and stood up. Lubanzi shot me a toothy grin. The four of us stepped out into the fresh night air, and Princess hugged herself and shivered.

Lubanzi looked up at the blanket of southern stars. "Aweh, let's go."

We set off up the concrete path to the car, the dark outline of the great hall towered behind us. I walked heavily, weighed down by a sense of dread.

3

My Toyota sat alone in the dark parking lot. The little white car with color-coordinated hubcaps had been dubbed the ice cream cone by our fellow students. You could spot it a mile away. It was akin to driving a neon sign flashing the words 'privileged white kid.' Not the best transportation for a furtive excursion into a forbidden settlement but all we had. We piled in.

If we had taken Beaufort Street into the township, we could have been in and out in twenty minutes. Not tonight. We had to take those damned donkey tracks in. We drove past dark shop windows and grids of neat yellow-brick houses with garden gnomes and carports. We passed my little house on the edge of white suburbia, at the end of Seymour Street, where Black and White South Africa met.

A left onto Trollope Street this late at night contravened the Group Areas Act. The car's occupants were silent as we crossed into criminality. With Lubanzi navigating, we took a right turn onto a dusty track around the back of a church hall. We threaded through a clot of hastily constructed tin buildings, bounced along a track broken by deep ruts, up the side of a hill, and into the dark, narrow, winding dust tunnels that cut through the informal settlements.

In the distance, a single pole topped with powerful yellow sodium lamps lit up the center of the settlement. Out here, on the fringes, we felt safe in the dark.

Lubanzi sang Bunny Wailer's "Liberation." Princess, her head resting against the vibrating rear window, gave him a perfect counterpoint on the chorus.

We pushed deeper into the Sun City informal zone in Rini. Here, people lived where they could. A patch of earth and five sheets of corrugated zinc roofing was all one needed to build a home.

"Stop, stop . . . I'm here," said Princess.

I stamped on the brakes, gravel grinding under the wheels as we slid to a halt. She hopped out of the car and ran for the safety of home. I turned and watched the red reflections of my taillamps flicker off gold thread woven into the print of her traditional African dress. She hurried off, disappearing into our dust cloud, up a narrow path between two makeshift buildings.

"Go up there where the road turns," said Lubanzi. He had got us this far without incident. We only had an hour or two before the morning shit-bucket collectors began their rounds. I was

4

anxious to get out before their donkey carts blocked the roads at sunrise.

"Sharp," shouted Lubanzi, as we pulled up alongside his shack. He jumped out and waved us off. Unlike Princess, he strolled casually up the path and out of sight, brushing the dust from his brown trousers and white collared shirt as he walked. We were only too happy to be gone. We drove on, turning right to begin retracing our steps out of the tangle of dirt tracks.

Headlights flashed on in front of us. High beams! Henry and I were temporarily blinded. I stood on my brake pedal. The car slipped sideways and back as it came to a halt on the loose dirt. Seconds later headlights came on behind us. There was nowhere to run – stuck in the ice cream cone on a narrow donkey track.

"Henry, we're going to die, boet!"

"Jesusgoddamchristalmighty . . .," Henry muttered. His straight, brown, waist-length hair and wild beard framed a face drained of all color; his eyes wide in horror.

We could make out figures in greatcoats jumping down from the back of a white bakkie, a pickup truck, in front of us. They had guns. Lots of guns. Long guns. Belgium FNs? Russian AKs? I couldn't be sure. Some sjambok whips and nightsticks. Black men. They could be ANC, local criminals, undercover cops, township police . . . we had no idea.

"Shit," I croaked through suddenly clotted phlegm. "We ran out of luck the minute Lubanzi stepped out of the car."

I became aware of the whooshing of my accelerated heartbeat in my ears. I looked over at Henry, and the terror on his face reflected mine. We were helpless, taken by currents beyond our control. Swept out on a deep undertow. The sinking feeling brought on a wave of nausea.

I heard boots hit the ground and looked in my rearview mirror. Six men stood behind the car. Maybe it was eight. I could see their guns leveled at us.

The grind and snap of a shotgun being racked echoed off the surrounding tin shacks. I thought I heard a safety click.

One of the men ahead of us stepped forward out of the high beams and knocked on my window.

I opened it a crack. "What do you want?"

He leaned in.

"Step out of the car." He spoke with a slow, ominous tone that did not allow for argument.

"*No*. Not until I see some sort of identification."

He looked at me and looked to a figure in the passenger seat of his bakkie. He shouted something in Xhosa, the language of the people in this area. The figure motioned him back. A discussion ensued.

After a few minutes, his face reappeared at my window. "You must get out of the car." This time his rifle, held at waist level, was pointed at my head.

Blood pounded in my temples. "I don't know who you are, and I am not getting out of the car. Show me ID or let me go." I tried desperately to carry an air of authority, even while my body was gripped by a cold terror that vibrated through my fingers and left me fighting for breath.

He stood, shrugged, and called to the truck. An order was shouted back in Xhosa.

I looked at my feet, trying to avoid the blinding headlamps. A flashlight beam ranged across our legs.

A green kitskonstable ID card slammed against my window. Startled, my head turned with a jolt. Township cops.

Henry whispered something indistinct under his breath.

"Dammit," I whispered back, rattled.

I studied the green ID card and nodded my willingness to comply. Township police were rumored to be brutal. Lawless. Henry and I looked at each other with a silent "here goes," and opened our doors. We stepped out into the now chilly morning air. The cloying smell of human feces mixed with the smoke from countless wood fires created a miasma that gave the township its own unique and memorable odor. If oppression had a smell, this would be it.

I needed to piss. I feared I might wet myself.

The cop in the truck stepped out and walked over to us. He had a lapel badge on his coat, an officer.

"You have broken curfew," he said, his voice deeper than I expected. I focused on a small scar that broke the line of his top lip. "You agitators come from town to cause problems here. This is not your township to start shit." He turned to the junior officer. "Put them under arrest. They can drive in convoy."

I tried to understand what that meant. Convoy? What was our destination?

"Get in your car and do what we tell you," the man with the scar said over his shoulder, walking away. The cops, standing in the darkness beyond reach of the headlamps, watched us closely — only their eyes reflecting like predators.

Henry and I returned to the car. Two armed policemen climbed uninvited into the back seat. My fingers trembled on the steering wheel. I felt the muzzle of a gun push into the back of my car seat. Cops quickly clambered onto the load-beds of the two pickup trucks.

I pressed the clutch pedal to the floor with a numb foot. Scraping, I found first gear.

The bakkie in front performed a clumsy six-point turn, township policemen clung to welded side rails as it bucked over a sand berm. We set off, sandwiched in. The ad hoc convoy wound its way through the center of Sun City, under the bright sodium lights on the single enormous pole. Guns remained trained on us from front and back. Every bump in the road felt like our last. Driving a little white car through ditches and across eroded red earth "roads" made the journey seem like a lifetime. Two lifetimes. We finally crossed through the main township checkpoint, passing a fresh-faced teenager in brown fatigues who looked at us the way I imagine a Frenchman would look at a Nazi collaborator. We drove slowly down Beaufort Street, deserted and broken by puddles of yellow light from the streetlamps.

"You can't be scared," I reminded myself, the words repeated over and over.

We pulled up outside the Grahamstown police station, the squeak of our brakes echoed off the colonial era buildings that lined the street. Our passengers clambered out, slinging weapons over their shoulders. The man with the scarred lip approached a clot of on-duty officers. They stood together in the blue light of a single bulb mounted on the red brick above the station entrance. He pointed in our direction and gesticulated, illustrating his report. They appeared to deliberate. When talking became nodding, two policemen, in brass-buttoned, blue uniforms creased to regulation, broke off and walked over. Their spit-shined shoes clicked on the sidewalk.

"Get out of the car now," said Officer Malherbe, his name displayed on a brass name tag pinned to his breast pocket. As he spoke, the township police clambered onto their bakkies. Making a wide U-turn, they roared off in the direction of Rini.

As we were led into the building, a dog in a backyard somewhere barked. Four in the morning in Grahamstown. It was surreal.

Henry and I were shown into a beige room with a dark brown desk. Three square-tube metal chairs with shiny green plastic padding stood at the table. A featureless space designed for interrogations under gently flickering fluorescent tubes. The room was silent but for the tick, tick of brown Christmas beetles trapped in the light fixture.

Detective Pienaar and Officer Malherbe strode into the room, slamming the door behind them. They had our attention. Pienaar threw copies of Errol Moorcroft campaign literature onto the table in front of us, one at a time, as if dealing cards. Moorcroft was our local Democratic Party member of Parliament. I had campaigned for him. Dammit, these had been in the trunk.

"You boys have been up to no good in the township." Pienaar's voice was raised, his words clipped and delivered officiously. He studied our faces for any sign of panic. "Bloody agitators! Communists!" His ears flushed.

"Who else was involved?

"Why are you boys trying to start a war?

"What banned organizations are you working for? The ANC? UDF?"

He fired off his questions in quick succession, hardly waiting for an answer. Our attempt at explanation did not impress him.

"Lies! You boys will sit for a long time, mind you," said Pienaar tapping his finger on the table. He turned and strode out of the room, shaking his head on the way out.

Officer Malherbe lingered in the doorway. "Why was you boys thinking now that you can be in the township with those Kaffirs?" Not waiting to hear an answer, he jogged off after his superior. "These bloody students." His words echoed back down the unadorned hallway.

An officer led us from the room to a hard wood bench, where we waited for dawn and our phone call.

Focused on a small window at the far end of the passage, I noticed the black sky lighten to a dark blue. Malherbe walked from the charge office as the first sounds of traffic drifted in. He motioned us to stand, then turned, and walked back. Henry and I hesitated. I took the first step, unsure of whether we should remain standing or follow the officer. We gingerly entered the front room of the police station. "You can make one phone call." Malherbe pointed to a black payphone bolted to an unvarnished wooden block and mounted on the wall. Henry flipped through the thin phonebook bound to the wall by a zinc chain. He found Merkly, A.

8

Alan Merkly was a highly regarded local lawyer. He had a charming smile and an unerringly polite manner, well-suited to disarming situations like the one we found ourselves in. He also served as the pro bono attorney for errant students and indigent activists.

Henry and I shared the receiver, ears close together. The mouthpiece smelled faintly of beer and vomit. I had a sickening premonition the phone would not work. We were relieved at the sound of a dialing tone. A small victory. A mild panic began to rise after the second ring tone ended. My chest tightened. Would he be home? What if he wasn't? A third ring. As the fourth ring began, Alan picked up. After a polite but rushed greeting, we poured out the entire saga in a breathless back and forth. I heard the crunch of toast; we had disturbed his breakfast. He listened silently to our tumbling and erratic retelling.

We stopped talking, waiting for Alan to tell us it was all going to be okay. There was an unnerving silence. We held our breath. He had no further questions.

"This shouldn't take too long," he said cheerfully, before giving us a polite goodbye. We replaced the receiver, and Malherbe led us back to our bench at the end of the passage. Three rooms down, the phone in the Kommandant's office rang. His door was open, and the sound carried across the cold, wood floors and brick walls.

"Kommandant Viekers here.

"Yes . . . they . . .

"No . . .

"They were arrested in Rini township . . .

"No . . . of course, I am Kommandant in Grahamstown.

"What do you mean that's not our jurisdiction?

"Now look here!

"Yes!

"No!

"Yes!!!!

"OKAY . . .!"

Viekers slammed his phone down.

"MALHERBE!!!!!!"

"Yes, *sir*."

"Give these boys their stuff and let them go!"

"Yes, *sir*."

"And tell them if we catch them in the Township again, they will sit for a long time to think about what they have done!"

9

"Yes, *sir!*" Malherbe led us to the station entrance. "You can go now." His face was pinched.

Henry and I walked away from the building, uncertain of what had just occurred and what would happen next. I expected an accusing shout and the sound of running policemen behind us. Nothing. A few more steps. Still nothing. We reached our unlocked car, parked at the curb of the now bustling street. Passers-by hurried on, unaware of the chain of events that had left us standing in their path at eight in the morning.

Pausing for a moment, I looked back, and the blood rushed from my head. The world spun for a moment. What the hell had just happened? Jesus, others just like me had experienced tragic outcomes in buildings like this around the country. Student leaders found themselves detained for months and years without trial. Activists were sometimes launched out of the highest windows of tall buildings or made to disappear. Henry and I had simply walked out. It was inconceivable. Alan was a goddam magician!

We settled into the ice cream cone with all our possessions except those election pamphlets. They were held as possible evidence. I looked over at Henry, slumped in the passenger seat, his eyes closed. "Coffee," he whispered.

"Coffee," I agreed.

Pressing a button, a stream of water created muddy rivulets of red township dust down the windshield that were swept away in a wiper stroke.

A short time later, perhaps a month or maybe six, we heard that Alan had been shot dead by unknown assailants while in his car. He was on the way home from a fishing trip.

That was Africa. "You can't be scared."

Author's Note: Definitions of Afrikaans words that appear in the story:

Bakkie – Pickup Truck

Boeties – Brothers

Mapolisa - Police

Dongas - Gullies

Sjambok - In South Africa, a long, stiff whip, originally made of rhinoceros hide.

Kaffirs – Derogatory word for Black South Africans. Originally from the Arabic word for non-believer.

10

Kitskonstable ID Card – Special Policeman Identity Card. Normally refers to a newly deputized police officer's identification document. Afrikaans kits ("instant" + konstabel ("constable").

Double Back on Double Black

Paula Earnest

When the weather forecast predicted a dump of fresh snow in the Sierras, I could already picture myself schussing Lindsey-Vonn-style down the powdery white slopes of Heavenly Ski Resort in Lake Tahoe. The skiers, passing above me, sitting two-by-two, thigh-to-thigh in their ski bibs and slick parkas on the chair lifts, would follow me with their eyes as I slalomed the steep terrain in true "Super-G" Olympic alpine ski racing fashion, zig-zagging through gates of flags and poles stuck into the snow like cocktail toothpicks. The National Anthem playing in my head would propel me to record speeds of 90 mph as I carved the course, shouldered into my razor turns, and flew over five-foot moguls. I would blind the cheering fans of snow bunnies and bombers who whistled and hooted as I flashed past them in my neon lime green ski jacket and skin-tight, blue luge leggings.

"Just look at that girl go! What style, what grace!"

Suspended on guts and air, I would race through the finish line in gold medal time, landing a perfect parallel stop that hailed the crowd with a rooster tail of snow. Such was my fantasy. Such was my moment of fame.

But some of us were never meant to wear gold, or silver, or even bronze for that matter. In fact, some of us should have just set our starry eyes on enjoying the white stuff that marshmallows are made of instead of trying to slay a white monster rising out of the ground. Some of us should have our heads examined. What was I thinking when I looked out from behind my iridescent ski goggles and up at that blizzardly taunting behemoth and boldly raised my stabbing poles sky high shouting, "Is that all you got?"

The gloves were off, and the challenge was mine to defend.

When the chairlift briefly stopped to unload me onto the top of "Mount Olympus," a place meant only for gods, or demons and the insane, it wasn't exactly regret that I felt. It was sheer terror. The gun to your head, heart-pounding, no-air, can't-breathe, I'm-dying kind of terror that froze me in my ski tracks. Only the

13

clouds that enveloped me on this hellish hill seemed to take pity on my plight.

The sheer drop-off in front of me spun my stomach into an alley-oop. Gold medal panic, for sure. I stood staring as if an ice sculpture, aware of each expert skier boldly vanishing over the edge, plummeting down into the mouth of the mountain – lemmings, each and every one of them. The ridge line between the top life-saving lip of the mountain and the plunging white sheet of death dropping off it was a hair's difference. A blink and it would all be over. One step forward on my waxy runners would end it all. What oxygen there was in the thin air evaporated in that terrifying moment. I gasped imagining my lime green ski jacket impaled on the jagged rocks below, my scattered bloody bones speared like red icicles into the mountain's white flesh.

No, never in a million years would I ski down into the bowels of that beast. Not for a gazillion-trillion-dollars would I dare cross over that ledge that separated life from death. And not a snowplow nor stem Christie could save my sorry ass if fate pushed me over that double black diamond cliff. There was nothing black nor shiny about this precipice.

Besides, what kind of run name is "The Fingers" anyway? Although, I do have one digit I could raise for this unforgiving slope. It should have been called, "Perdition Peak" or "Last Rites Ridge." If only I had brought my pocket Bible with me should I career off this iceberg. But who was I kidding? No Hail Mary could save my soul from a fall into this snowy pit of hell.

So, I did what any sane person in this split-decision moment would do when prayers go unanswered. I bent over, unclipped my ski bindings, stepped out of my narrow skis that would have happily downhill-raced me to my death, picked them up like two hobo sticks slung over my shoulder, and retreated – white flag waving. I clomped my way back toward the chairlift in my monster boots, skis and poles off, and pleaded with the lift operator for a ride down. My ensuing sobs, frozen tears, and uncontrollable shaking would seal the sympathetic deal and melt him into a pile of sentimental slush as he listened to the tale of my horrific fate should I attempt to ski down that god-awful hill.

My performance was Oscar worthy. With the chairlift now stopped, and a mile of not-so-patient skiers stuck swinging on their windblown chairs waiting, my wooly operator loaded me onto my chair of shame. Hiding in plain sight, lit up in lime green, I was carried solo down the sheered-off mountainside, fake

14

limping into the arms of the glaring, non-cheering crowd below. There were no whistles, nor hoots, nor applause as I passed all the Bode Miller wannabees ascending the expert-only mountain. They were one with the gods. They had no need for prayers.

Regrets? Sure. Buying that damn screaming-green jacket. If only I had worn white that day. No one ever wants to double back on a double black. No one.

English 101*

Irene Flynn

I thought
in a different English than yours:
my words
floating from my lips
like beautiful, gliding birds.
Their music the same in form and shape
as you would know.
But, my intent,
however dutifully conceived,
perceived with foreign dialect
and muddled definition.

Such are the dangers
of this too familiar language —
assuming that you understood
as I thought you should.

Yet you thought
in a different English than I
and my diligent words,
like brilliantly feathered birds,
lay wounded and could not fly.

(*substitute your mother tongue.)

The Ingénue & the Genie

Margaret Harmon

There was once a girl named Roxanne who wanted so desperately to be a success that she could barely close her eyes at night to sleep. She watched celebrity shows and practiced being interviewed alone in her room. In her high school yearbook, the prediction under her senior photo read "She'll be famous."

As a college freshman, she majored in American Literature to write the Great American Novel and wrote two short stories that were published. But when she saw three movies in one weekend and realized that nobody's reading anymore — it's all about visuals, she changed her major to drama. During her sophomore year, a boyfriend convinced her to major in physics because she was really good in math, and beautiful women physicists grab headlines. But it took a lot more work to be *great* at physics than to be *good* at it. As a junior, she became an accounting major to make a fortune on Wall Street, but trying to never make a mistake limited her creativity. She switched to physical education to be a personal trainer in Hollywood so she could make hands-on contacts with stars, but when the novelty wore off, her classes were boring.

Interning at a New York publishing company after graduation, Roxanne spent her spare time in antique shops, searching through costume jewelry cases to find real gold, platinum, and gems that had been mislabeled. One day, in a shop with particularly interesting faux ruby brooches and wannabe emerald rings, she moved an ancient clay oil lamp off a glass case full of Art Nouveau rings and pendants. To avoid scratching the glass, she put the heavy lamp on the floor. So people wouldn't trip over it, she slid it between two bookcases. It barely fit; she had to force it with her foot.

The Art Nouveau pieces were exquisite. As she peered through the glass at a possible genuine emerald ring, she saw, swirling from between the bookcases, a mist coagulating into a human form. Within moments, it became a slender genie with a jeweled turban.

Roxanne looked around. She was alone except for the shopkeeper waxing an armoire on the opposite side of the store.

The genie smiled and straightened his turban. "Three wishes," he said. "Anything you want."

Her heart pounded. Was this perfect or what? She swallowed hard. "*Anything?*"

The genie nodded. "That's my job."

Roxanne smiled. "I want to be a success."

"Okay." He rubbed his hands together. "As what?"

She opened her mouth . . . then closed it again. She inhaled. And let her breath out. "Which will be better—a film director making smash hit movies that elucidate current philosophical contradictions or the inventor of a vaccine to prevent the Ebola virus? The vaccine is more idealistic, but I'd have to support my lab with soft money."

The genie shook his head. "I don't choose. Only grant." He smiled encouragement and crossed his arms. "This is opportunity, not necessity." He waited.

She thought until her eyes bulged.

He looked at a grandfather clock ticking near the door. "I think this shop is closing pretty soon."

Roxanne's face reddened, and tears filled her eyes.

"I'm granting you three wishes," the genie said. "Whatever you want, and you're—"

"I know." She ran her fingers through her hair. "It's just that whenever I see someone succeeding at something I could do, I stop what I'm doing and start what she's doing. I'll never succeed if I keep changing directions like this. Even talented people—"

"True," the genie interrupted. "But they're closing."

"Can you get back in there so I can carry you home on the subway? I don't think you can ride dressed in just that."

The genie frowned. "All right. But hurry. He's locking the door."

Roxanne ran to the shop owner and bought the crusty lamp. Outside in the damp air she bent over it and pretended to cough so she could whisper, "We'll be home in half an hour; I'll tell you when it's safe to come out again." On the subway, her eyes darted as she pressured herself to choose what she should succeed as.

In her tiny third-floor apartment, she set the lamp on the dining table beside her only window and called into the spout, "We're home. You can come out."

20

Nothing.

She called again, her stomach knotting. Had she lost her chance? Her greatest chance in the world to succeed and she'd wasted it? She shook the lamp. Turned it upside down. Tried to pull the lid off. She rubbed it.

The genie rose from the spout. "Ah yes. Your first wish is to succeed at what you'll tell me."

She took a deep breath and squeezed her eyes shut.

"Ready?" the genie asked.

"Almost," she said.

He nodded and began humming something ancient.

Roxanne paced the floor and pep-talked herself. "What am I *best* at? But this is a magic wish so I can choose *anything*, right?" She turned to the genie. "I can, can't I — wish anything I want, whether I'm gifted at it or not?"

"Certainly." He closed his eyes, swaying to the rhythm of his humming.

"Then I should go for fame and fortune. I want to be the most famous singer in the world — who earns the most money."

He opened his eyes. "Religious chanting or opera or — what type of music is popular now?"

"Oh, why not opera? But I hate opera! It's ridiculous and . . ." As she flung her arms, despising opera, she knocked the lamp from the table and out the window to the concrete below, where it shattered into a thousand pieces that bounced and rolled until cars ran over some and people walked on others, crushing them into the sidewalk and street.

Roxanne leaned out her window as mist rose from the gutter, floated gently toward the river, and joined a fog bank.

21

Lost at Sea

Janice Coy

Today was no different than most of the spring. A thick layer of beach fog masked the sun until just before sunset. After a brief reveal, the sun slid below the clouds, burning them away with fiery rays that tinged their underbellies in brilliant shades of orange, gold, and pink. The locals had a name for the annoying daily fog—May Gray—and they always hoped the dreary mess would dissipate before it became June Gloom. On days like today, all of Agave Beach seemed dismal. Even the waves didn't look inviting to swimmers. The ocean temperature rarely climbed above the low 60s this time of year. Beach goers walked or jogged along the water's edge; some surfers switched to their spring wetsuits. The only ones wearing bathing suits were tourists. Some ran into the Pacific Ocean shrieking, but mostly those were children.

After sunset, the clouds snuck back as gray cotton puffs. But as the night wore on, it looked like someone—tired of the sun's concealment—ripped a hole in the clouds for the moon. It shone through the tear bright as a newly skinned knee, lighting the waves—highlighting each frothy breaker, so the foam glowed iridescent. The beach was deserted, long hours past the time scuba divers emerged from the ocean and humped their dripping gear to their cars. Gerald and his Chihuahua mix, Baby, had the sand all to themselves.

Gerald kicked off his left Reebok first. The shoe sailed from his bare foot, twirled, and plopped onto the sand. Gerald didn't believe in shoelaces, never had. They restricted his foot's freedom. He barely tolerated shoes. Now, he laughed at his shoe, stuck there in the sand, going nowhere, his mirth bubbling up through his chest and snorting out his nose. The second shoe got no air and crashed, but Gerald had already lost interest. His chapped lips were puckered on the mouth of a clear bottle. His hand caressed its body, tilting it upwards, draining the final clear drops. When he couldn't get anymore, he gently shook the bottle. No point in getting rough. He had a faint memory of treating a woman in a similar fashion, and he smacked the bottle's bottom with a loving open palm. The woman had squirmed, but the bottle provided nothing. Gerald squinted, pressing his right eye at the bottle's opening. Empty.

Gerald dangled the container in his fingers. The suck and pull of the waves on the sand gave him an idea. He would hurl the bottle into the ocean. He flung back his arm, then stilled. Maybe he should write a note to Jaye first. Explain why he stole her tequila, roll the paper up, and shove it into the bottle. He imagined a tourist snorkeling in the cove and discovering the bottle twined in a wad of kelp. He guffawed thinking of the tourist's sputtering face—his sunburned ears, his reddened eyes stinging from the shallow layer of saltwater sloshing in his snorkel mask.

"Gotta pen, Baby?" Gerald hooted with laughter. "Paper?"

The little dog at Gerald's heels was silent; her raspy breath a whisper between the sets of waves slapping the beach. Gerald pretended to search the folds of skin at the mutt's neck for paper and pen. He checked behind the dog's oversized ears. Gerald doubled over. The dog's stoic stance sent him into peals of hilarity. He fell over onto the sand, kicking his bare feet and windmilling his arms as if he were making a snow angel. He took a last shuddering gasp. Baby licked his face. Gerald scratched behind her donkey-like ears. The sand was cold; summer was another month away.

Jaye's fuzzy, disappointed face seemed to materialize on the moon. She frowned at Gerald lying on the sand. Not only did he steal her tequila, a gift from a grateful customer, but he fell off the wagon. Fell hard. He was sober two months. Hated every single goddamn second of it. The pot was medicinal. Jaye understood that. He carried a creased doctor's note for his bum knee. But the tequila—he had no excuse.

Jaye put the full bottle in the bottom drawer of her desk at the kayak and surf shop just yesterday. A tourist bought it for her in Mexico, said it was made of one hundred percent agave. Gerald couldn't remember if there was a worm at the bottom. Maybe it was too nice of a bottle. He didn't remember swallowing a worm. He rubbed his stomach hoping the worm, if there had been one, was still enjoying its tequila bath. Jaye always said she wanted to visit Mexico. The country was no more than twenty miles away. But as long as he knew Jaye, she never got around to crossing the

24

border. She said her Spanish needed improving. And something about getting a passport.

"Aw shit," Gerald rubbed his bristly chin. "A man's gotta be free." He sat up, wiggled his toes in the sand. "Jaye knows that."

She was young. She would learn soon enough she couldn't save everyone.

Gerald staggered to his feet, holding the empty bottle by its neck. He spun the bottle in great slow arcs at first. But gradually his arm picked up speed until the bottle gyrated in wild circles around his head. He felt like a circus performer. One last giant swing and he flung the bottle into the ocean. The bottle bobbed for a few seconds. A wave struck it, and the bottle tumbled through the surf. Soon, the bottle washed up on the sand where the water nudged against it. The bottle was stuck until the tide came in. Gerald shook his head. A stuck bottle was no good. He and Baby trotted to where it lay — still intact.

Gerald grabbed the bottle. His head spun from bending over and standing up again. He wobbled on the sand until the beach and water stopped revolving around him. Baby danced around his heels, avoiding Gerald's large bare feet. This time, he would do it right. He would throw the bottle out beyond the reach of the waves. Gerald leaned back on his right leg; his toes gripped the sand. He bent his left leg in front of him, like he'd seen many pro baseball pitchers do. He wound up the bottle and sent it hurtling out over the waves. It landed with a splash he could see from the shore, quickly filled with water and sank.

Gerald pointed his chin to the moon and puckered his lips again. He howled and hooted at his success, his breath misting like a stream of cigarette smoke. Earlier in the night, he threw away the rubber band that twisted his graying hair into a low bun. Now, he shook his hair so it writhed with him. Baby flitted around him, lifting her paws as if she detested the sand, darting in every so often to nip at Gerald's ankles and remind him of her presence.

"You wanna dance!" Gerald picked his knees up in a jig. He began whirling around Baby, faster and faster, until his hair lifted off his shoulders, strands whipping his eyes.

Soon, he felt as if his jacket was smothering him, and he stumbled and weaved as he struggled out of first one sleeve then another. Baby did her best to keep out of his way. The discarded jacket landed in a heap on her head, and she managed to wiggle out from underneath it just as Gerald spun into the shallows of an encroaching wave.

25

The moon or Jaye's face — the details were fuzzy — made a path on the surface of the water, and it seemed to Gerald the path beckoned. He spun closer to the ocean, stumbled into a hole and now a rush of water soaked the thighs of his jeans.

Baby patrolled the water's edge. She never got a paw wet except by accident. Her barks drew Gerald's attention. Was she warning him? He turned to look at the agitated dog. A small wave slapped his butt while he was considering Baby's opinion and he lost his balance. The back of his head hit with a heavy splash, a mix of water and sand poured across his face and into his nose. He coughed and spluttered tasting salt. His t-shirt and jeans were soaked. The water retreated, but a wet touch lingered on his neck; a bunch of seaweed bumped against his shoulder. Gerald knelt in the sand. He draped the slimy plant like a scarf around his neck.

"High fashion, Baby!"

Baby paced and barked just out of the water's reach.

Another water surge pulsed around Gerald's waist, pushing Baby further back onto the beach. The tide was coming in. Gerald flopped onto his stomach and allowed the wave's retreat to pull him along. Soon, he was deep enough to swim. He rolled onto his back so the moon was on his face. He squinted at its brightness. The ends of the seaweed trailed behind him, sometimes getting caught in his hair.

When he was young, Gerald created a swim stroke. He called it froggie style — borrowing the arm movement from the backstroke, the legs from the breaststroke. He thought the stroke pure genius. His father would shout at him from the pool deck. "Pick a friggin' stroke. Do the goddamn freestyle." Gerald pretended he couldn't hear with the water in his ears. He would close his eyes so he couldn't see his father's red face or the way his Adam's apple grew like a bad tumor when he yelled. The pool was one of the few places he could escape his father's disappointment. He hadn't swum in a pool since he left home at eighteen — more than forty years ago — to wander and work odd jobs. The whole experience of swimming in a concrete enclosure was too confining. Nothing like swimming in the open ocean.

Gerald swam the froggie style now. His jeans were heavy — dragging on his legs — and he wished he left them on the beach with his shoes and jacket. He supposed he could wiggle out of them now, but why bother? He was in the zone; he could do the froggie stroke for hours. That was the magic of it. Harmoniously flowing with the water instead of fighting it with flailing arms, tiring kicks and sideways breaths that always seemed to draw more water than air.

He only flipped onto his stomach when he needed to dive under a wave, but soon he was beyond the break and he happily floated on his back up and over the swells. The water didn't feel cold. He smiled thinking he was like a frickin tourist, but it was probably the tequila keeping him warm.

If he lifted his head, he could see the moonlit path shining beyond him. He believed it could take him all the way to Hawaii. He imagined washing up on a warm, white sand beach. A bikini clad woman greeting him with a lei.

Jaye would be mad he swam away. The ocean stopped her from going further than she wanted; it hemmed her in. She said she didn't care. Only another freedom seeker like Gerald would know she was lying.

All those years, all those people. Gerald didn't know why he let Jaye get under his skin. Maybe it was his age. He felt more tired lately. He found himself thinking about the old homestead, his imagination smoothing the edges off the truth of his upbringing. He knew at fourteen his father hated him. But the passage of decades made the memories hazy. He had never been a father, at least no one claimed to be his child. But Jaye. She would look at him, and he would think he could be her father.

Gerald ran his tongue around the circle of his salt-crusted lips. He stopped moving his arms long enough to finger the kelp clinging to his neck. He popped one of the little air pods on the seaweed and thought about heading back. But the shore, his jacket and his shoes seemed so far away he could hardly remember what they looked like. Kind of like the old house where he grew up. Sometimes he thought it was a small ranch with a patch of lawn, but then he remembered the swimming pool and figured the house must be bigger than his memories.

By now, the ocean currents had carried him beyond the point that protected the cove. Baby was a speck. Her opinion no longer relevant, Gerald felt like he was soaring outside time and space. He looked but couldn't distinguish the horizon. He lost track of the land, the cliffs where the cormorants nested, and the rocks where the sea lions sacked out every day and barked whenever they felt like it.

He was so tiny really. What did he have to show for his life on the road? His relentless pursuit of freedom? His body was an insignificant dot in the vastness of the water engulfing him.

27

Gerald began to cry; his tears slow at first, trickling down his cheeks and merging seamlessly with the water. Then, his shoulders shook and he forgot about his froggie stroke. His legs dropped below the water's surface, his feet dangled. His jeans felt like rocks.

And just like that he was drifting ever so slowly down, down, down. His slack body taking on water like the empty tequila bottle with its open mouth. He was in the oblivion of darkness when a black shape began to circle his splayed arms and legs.

Empty Nest

Paula Earnest

It was there, between the carelessly stacked pile of
decayed cedar logs and chopped sumac branches
that the rat revealed herself to me.

A tangled mess of garden tools
(weathered rake, broken-handled shovel, twisted garden hose and
mud-caked trowel)
stood guard over the dubious woody structure — new home to my
gray squatter.

First appearing as piece of dull pewter — stone-shaped — wedged
between the wood,
she startled at hearing me (her dart-dash retreat revealing her
cover).

Over the next days, I felt her presence each time I visited the
woodpile:
scuffled sounds shifting under the shelter of twigs and twisted
vines.
I stood and listened as she tunneled through narrow gaps and
crevices of
dried bark, splintered pine, and mulched debris.
Her fingerlike whiskers navigated haphazard stick runways.
Her hungry teeth gnawed wood pulp, burrowing through weeds
and fallen leaves —
soft bedding for her awaiting nest.
Between the braided branches laced within the logs, this mother
rat made claim:
a birthing room for her offspring due any day.

The second, and last time I spied the thin line of her naked tail,
I thought—a tiny twig.
But then saw two pink paws, like star-shaped pearls.
I hoped to greet the rat who had so cleverly eluded me in our
hide-and-seek game.
My booted foot inched forward as cautionary fair warning
to the den dweller within the wood-layered maze.
But the rat did not jump or scoot.
Her paws and tail remained rooted there.
I watched. Waited. Was she scared?
No—Betrayed instead by her firewood home.
Silenced by the toppled roof that pinned her in.
Once shielding life, but now her tomb.

I gently moved the arm-length branch that had buttressed the
wooden walls
sheltering the gray recluse for three short weeks,
protecting her from the stalking Siamese, red-tailed hawk, and me.
Lifeless now—Her onyx eye that looked ahead but could not see.
Could not know.
How a single shift could end a mother's life
and lay barren her empty nest.

Ropa Vieja*

Irene Flynn

I am tired of other people's passion —

Passion worn like yesterday's old fashions.

Fed to the surrounding crowds

Like an overdue feast

When in fact they are but yesterday's leftovers:

Not enough to clothe for warmth;

Hardly enough to nourish or sustain.

I take my own and carry them like rations.

*Spanish translation: "old clothes"; a Cuban dish.

Phone Numbers

Valerie E. Looper

I am a gambler. I don't bet on trivia, like a mere paycheck, but every now and then, I will place a real bet. One time I took a risk and lost my phone numbers.

I was three years out of college, working as a chemist, and driving those Houston roads to work. It had taken me a year to learn how to drive in that traffic on I-45. On a good day, no fewer than three people tried to kill me on my way home. The city boomed in the early 80s, when it seemed like half the population of Michigan had moved to Texas in search of opportunity.

My father had taught me how to drive. He said, "Drive the speed of the traffic, baby. When you drive on the highway and have trucks on either side of you, you will feel boxed in. Your instinct will be to slow down; you must not do that. You risk having somebody hit you from behind."

At the time, there was a huge advertising campaign to lower the speed limit to 55 mph in order to save gas. I had been trained to obey all traffic laws; but my father was telling me that driving 55 — in heavy traffic averaging 15 mph faster — invited an accident. Of course, I parroted back to him the Driver's Ed lesson stating that a driver who rear-ends another is at fault.

He just shot me the sideways look he reserves for foolishness, and said, "If you get rear-ended, fault won't matter. Drive so that people don't have to avoid you."

He told the truth.

In Houston, the traffic ran close, the speed limit was a suggestion, the work trucks would make a new lane on the shoulder in the morning, and nobody used their turn signals for changing lanes. Accidents were frequent.

I spent a while practicing to keep my foot off the brake. I played auto hockey, scoring myself on how many cars I passed, and how many passed me. After a few months, I stopped getting excited and learned how to watch the flow of cars, especially that ripple of taillights that might mean a potential pile-up. Getting

33

excited or nervous in that environment is dangerous.

I adapted well to the Houston freeways until I became temporarily unfit to drive.

I was pregnant, and I'd already had three or four fainting spells. I had not wholly fainted or fallen yet, and they did not last long. They had nothing to do with stress or heavy activity. I could be doing something ordinary, like standing in my boss's office talking to his secretary about a schedule and suddenly see grey icicles around my field of vision. I would have time to sit down and take some deep breaths, and it would clear. So far nothing had happened, but I knew I had no business driving home.

My company was very helpful. They had a van pool and offered it to me. All I had to do was make a short drive along a low-speed back road to get to the first stop. I asked my husband, Bill, to drive me to the van stop. He said no; he would not even try to figure out how much extra time it would add to his commute.

I sat in my car, one morning a few weeks later, looking at my seat belt, with my belly flopped over it. My mind could see the film they'd shown us in driver's ed class, in an effort to get us to use the shoulder straps; and, I knew very well what a lap belt alone does in an accident — it scrapes along the hip bones and up into the abdomen as the body is flung forward. It can burst a full bladder, end a pregnancy. Wearing the lap belt alone could kill my son-to-be. Sure, I had the shoulder belt, but the cars at that time were made by pin-headed men who thought that every driver was at least five foot five. I was five foot nothing, and the shoulder belt laid across my neck. If I were hit from the side, that belt could kill me. I had never used it because it was dangerous to me. That meant using only the lap belt laying ominously across my hips and, now, below my full, still-growing belly.

I unhooked the belt, and said silently, "Lord, you can take him, but you'll have to go through me." It felt weighty to set the belt aside. I was one of the first few drivers who was trained to use a seat belt from the start.

~

A day or two after making that decision, I woke up in a chair in a hallway. Bill, my husband, was seated next to me. I confronted a deep, dark mystery. I did not know where I was or how I got there, and, I had a suspicion of something I did not want to know. I looked down and saw a small swelling in my stomach. I touched it, and it did not hurt. Out of somewhere dangerous, I asked him, "Am I pregnant?"

34

He said, "You're fine, everything is fine."

I went somewhere cloudy.

I woke up propped in a bed. Some woman with a hard face asked me what seemed like extremely stupid questions. "Do you know where you are?"

For some reason I found that question vastly provoking. "No," I said. "I presume I am in a hospital."

"What day is it?"

Again, I answered out of deep annoyance. "I don't know — September, October."

She did not quit. "Who is President?"

Oh. That question initiated a little, cold trickle of fear to run down my back, because I had no idea. I knew I should know the answer. I hunted for an answer and finally, guessed wildly, "Jimmy Carter?" Then, I felt an upwelling of dense black suspicion. So, I cautiously asked my own question. "Am I pregnant?"

She answered, "You are six months pregnant. You and the baby are fine."

I went somewhere cloudy.

I woke up in an ordinary hospital room that had open curtains framing a sunny view of green grass and a lacy mesquite tree. I turned, with some difficulty by pulling on the bed rail, to see a small closet. I saw my work shoes, caked with mud and grass clippings, on the floor in front of it. The shoes caught and held my attention, because those shoes don't get dirty. I could not recall how the mud and grass got onto them.

I noticed that I felt stiff, but not hurt. I explored myself; and, underneath the patterned hospital gown, I found big bruises on my right arm and upper right leg, a stiff shoulder, and a slow-moving neck. When I ran my fingertips across my neck, something crusty came loose. I saw that my fingernails came away with dried blood.

Underneath my exploring fingers, my hair was full of something dry and hard like paint. High up on the back of my head, I found stubble where long hair used to be, as well as a long row of something that had to be stitches. I could not remember getting the stitches, and nothing hurt. It should have hurt.

I pushed down the rail and got out of the bed — sliding off the edge because it was far too high — stepped on cold linoleum and opened the closet door. I found my purse but none of my clothes. My coat was missing. I wondered why I knew that my coat was missing, and yet I had no idea why my shoes were dirty. The shoes sat there on the floor, proof that I had been walking somewhere muddy — that I could not recall.

~

Bill would later tell me that he had been with me that morning, as I waited for admittance to the hospital. I had given the EMTs both my work phone number and his — but both were out-of-date because we'd each switched jobs in the last few months. Our former co-workers had contacted our friends at our current jobs.

Bill had taken my raincoat to the cleaners because it was covered with blood. He'd seen the car, which had been totaled. He would tell me the stick shift was bent 90 degrees, and that the interior had been drenched with blood. My head had hit the post on the passenger side. He had seen my footprints in the ditch with the car. I had run off the road and hit a culvert.

The investigators said I had failed to make a curve, possibly because I had seen my own headlights reflected in a plate glass living-room window. I don't remember any of this, but I have driven that route since then and seen my headlights reflected back to me from a window. A short time after that, the highway department would put up caution signs around that curve, and one big sign to interfere with the view of that window.

~

I had lost six months of memory. In that moment, at the hospital, looking at the closet that did not have my clothes and coat, I was alone with questions and mysteries and suspicion.

She was back, frown in place, and asking unnerving questions, again. "Do you know where you are?"

This question gave me a flash of annoyance, and I answered in huge irritation, "No, I think this is a hospital." How was I supposed to know this? I decided to guess: "Clear Lake."

"What day is it?"

"I am not sure."

"Who is President?"

"Ronald Reagan." I knew that last was right. Then I had to ask something I did not really want to know. Out of dread and suspicion, I asked, "Am I pregnant?"

"Yes, you are six months pregnant, and you and the baby are fine."

I collapsed in relief, tainted by suspicion of something I did not dare examine. I did not know whether I had heard that answer

36

or made it up.

~

This time, she did not just appear in front of me. I saw her walk in through the door, a nurse in a neat, white uniform with a tense frown, now familiar to me from, what I suddenly recalled, were several conversations. She had been asking me diagnostic questions, and I had been giving her alarming answers. *Diagnostic.* The word reverberated in my mind because it had not been in my grasp, for a while, and now it was back. I thought I knew what she was going to say.

She asked me the date. This time, instead of taking instant offense, I told her I wasn't sure, but the month was November, after Halloween and before Thanksgiving.

She asked me who was President, and I grinned and said "Jimmy Carter. Reagan has been elected but has not yet taken office."

I switched back to her earlier question. "This must be the third or fourth week in November, because it is not Thanksgiving, yet." I felt as proud as a kid who had won a spelling bee.

And then that tense, suspicious feeling came welling up.

With stinging eyes, I accused, "And you are going to tell me that I am pregnant, right?" Even to me, my voice sounded harsh, a ragged mixture of command and plea and fear.

That plain woman's face lit up like an angel. She said, "You are six months pregnant, and you and the baby are fine."

She did not ask me any more questions, and I no longer needed to ask mine.

~

I have not relied on my memory for phone numbers since then. I still do not recall the events of that day, until sometime late in the afternoon. I had gambled and lost a chunk of memory. However, my first son is now a brown-eyed handsome man, fit and cheerful as any mother could wish.

It was worth it.

Discontent with Contentment

Amy Wall

Oh contentment, I invited you in. I didn't know you personally, but it seemed that everyone else did. I *now* know that wasn't true. Even though I thought they did, my friends didn't know you.

I asked you in to clean my skeletal closet. You did. You removed the bones one by one as every year passed, until my closet was free of them — and spacious again — and empty. That is what you left me.

I welcomed you to support my maturity — to rid me of the drama I was creating. Decades passed. You coached me to walk away when I needed to. You encouraged me to avoid negativity. I did. No more drama. You gave me an outlet, transforming drama into story.

Oh contentment, you inspired me to take the higher road. You instructed me to use unpleasant circumstances to define myself, using my reaction to negativity as a way to hold my chin up high with the grace of a dancer. I started to like myself through becoming a better person. You stripped away pain from difficulties and turned them into lessons.

I was angry. You instructed me to breathe. You took my hand over paper and guided me to write. The anger went away with every stroke of the pencil. You dragged the anger out, like a drunk being pulled out of a bar at closing. Anger left, the last patron for the day.

I hiked mountains, fostered friendships new and old. I hugged my children and kissed my husband. I sought gratitude for my belongings, did yoga, breathed deeply, and smiled and laughed. Then you came knocking. You pounded on the door until I answered. I had to invite you in after all you had done. Damn you for coming in. You came in, grabbed her, and walked out as though I owed you some kind of payment for all you did. You had to remove her didn't you. Oh contentment, you had to take her away . . . ripped clean from my soul. No goodbyes. You took away the one thing that carried me through all these years — *my muse.*

Syndrome

Jenna Benson

Gone so soon –

my light has faded blue,

gently transitions to gray,

until the last glimmering light dissipates.

I look down at my outstretched arm

and strain to close my fingers into a fist.

I lower it,

and with it goes my will.

You're gone,

vanished;

and in trying to fathom this wide-open wound,

you have shattered everything I thought I knew.

It's as if your presence was a perfect lie:

exquisitely crafted,

you had me believing every line.

Tears fall –

I am no longer cognizant

of the pools collecting in my palms.

I will never see you again:

the pit of my being knows this.

The Nuclear Option

Gered Beeby

"We trained hard ... but it seemed every time we were beginning to form up into teams we would be reorganized. I was to learn later in life that we tend to meet any new situation by reorganizing and a wonderful method it can be for creating the illusion of progress while producing confusion, inefficiency, and demoralization."
    Misattributed to Petronius Arbiter (c. 27-66 AD)
    Roman writer during the reign of Emperor Nero

"Man who cannot find ass with either hand has no need of toilet paper."
                    Corrupted saying of Confucius
                            Origin: Unknown

Memoir Chapter 12 –

San Onofre Surfing Beach
San Onofre Nuclear Generating Station (aka SONGS)
Corporate America
The Stroke-of-Brilliance Manager
Nuclear Regulatory Commission (NRC)
Culture Problem
Loophole Engineering
Botched Designs
The Emperor Has No Clothes
Major Nuclear Accident
Permanent SONGS Shutdown
                        ~

Both quotes above are frauds. For these memoirs, I have tried to select meaningful thoughts as keynote touchstones for each chapter. Most are chosen with noble sentiments that reflect an important theme for that particular episode. But what happens when your most poignant take-home memory is one of sad contempt? Read on.

As mentioned in the previous chapter, in mid-year 1985, I made a major career change. Departing employment as an engineer with the County of San Diego, I accepted a job as a construction manager at one of the most visible nuclear generating stations in the country. The twin containment domes of the San Onofre Nuclear Generating Station (SONGS) sit on the west side of Interstate 5 near San Clemente at the northern border of San Diego County. Technically, the domes are designated SONGS Units 2 and 3. The much earlier and smaller SONGS Unit 1 is to the north, but often escapes notice in comparison to the other two.

Given its proximity to such a major roadway, SONGS may just be the most recognizable nuclear plant in the world. Nuclear opponents may well decry why it was ever built there in the first place. After all, the site also sits on a known seismic fault zone, which is troublingly close to huge population areas of Orange County, as well as Los Angeles and San Diego. Needless to say, the site employed thousands of technically oriented people. I was one of those.

Some appropriate decision-making did occur. Being close to the areas it serves is wise from a power transmission standpoint. More fundamentally, from a pure technical aspect, is the matter of waste heat disposal. All electrical power plants, including nuclear-fired ones, are basically steam-turbine power plants that operate under the Basic Steam Cycle. An essential phase of the cycle is removing and dissipating low-end or "bottom cycle" heat to extract maximum power during the full steam cycle. For SONGS that heat sink is obvious — the Pacific Ocean.

SONGS is truly gigantic. I learned that early on from indoctrination courses and simply touring the site on my own. Walls of the domes are four feet thick at the base. These walls taper to somewhat thinner cross-sections at the top. Overall, they are designed to withstand a postulated and very violent steam explosion of the core primary system due to extreme overheating. Note that this would not constitute a "nuclear" explosion from the fuel material itself. The fuel is low-enrichment uranium that could never produce a nuclear yield such as bomb-grade uranium. But it can produce plenty of power.

The numbers become staggering. 1000-plus megawatts *per unit* are all but meaningless to most people. This translates to well

44

over 1,000,000 homes being provided electrical power needs year after year after year. The immense step-up transformers that send this high-voltage electrical energy out to the transmission grid weigh in at 500 tons each, over one million pounds. Many of us had the chance to see one get moved off-site for replacement. I lost count of the number of wheels on the multitiered trailer that supported this monster on the access road.

One of the more interesting facts I learned concerned the main steam turbines on the outside, seaward deck. Rotating machinery like large turbines need support from main horizontal journal bearings. Placed over 100 feet apart, the extreme end bearings for San Onofre turbines required an unusual adjustment. During periodic maintenance, the end-bearing sleeves are replaced, but must include some microscopic, angular shimming. The reason is surprising. Across 100 feet of distance, the angle of the Earth's gravity as it pulls straight downward to the center of our planet varies ever so slightly. This angular change, minute as it is, needs to be addressed to alleviate premature bearing wear from the off-angle direction of the weight.

Here, then, comes my eventual concern and problem and, at times, disgust for the whole SONGS environment. The terms I list at the beginning of this chapter create a kind of capsule summary. Each term identifies a worsening degradation into an ultimate failure and collapse. The shift shows my initial optimism and hope, but the eventual descent into despair. This Greek tragedy played out—complete with unbridled hubris over a period of some decades. My direct observation encompassed just over ten years.

This all began when I accepted a job as a construction manager within the group that oversaw design-change construction projects. Many might question why take on work of this kind in 1985 for power plants that had recently been completed. Both Units 2 and 3 had concluded initial power runs and were producing power for the vast electrical grid of the Southern California Edison (SCE) empire. True, the main work was done, but with any large [read: huge] installation, there are always modifications, reworks, and new design features that need to be added. Each construction manager in this group had several projects they would oversee.

Our role was chiefly as client representative for SCE with the physical work mostly being carried out by the resident construction mavens of the Bechtel Corporation. Sometimes independent contractors got hired, but, by and large, Bechtel held premier status. After all, they had been a major player in the early days of nuclear technology development in the United States. So, they did the work, while we in the oversight business kept track of their actions and communicated project status, usually on a daily basis.

All of this went on swimmingly for about a year, until I came face-to-face with the realities of corporate America. The construction group needed to be disestablished. No organization can help profits when large numbers of excess personnel remain on staff. As a relatively new hire and one of the few licensed professional engineers around and as a regular SCE employee rather than a contract engineer, I believed my position was secure. Think again, pal. Demand for profit plays few favorites.

Nonetheless, there were other openings on-site where someone like me could fit. Quality Assurance (QA) loomed up and eventually did work. The head manager was a fellow Civil Engineer, and we got along fine. I was assigned to a specialized group whose purpose was to attempt to predict where quality problems may occur. Interesting. How does one go about discovering a problem event when the event has not yet happened?

Some within the traditional QA structure thought this effort was a lost cause. Nearly all other endeavors within QA dealt with carrying out performance-based audits of whether procedures were being followed. Talk about dull — necessary, but dull. And linked with QA was QC (Quality Control). They were the inspectors who verified whether these necessary checks were actually done. Dull compounded with dull.

For my own part I made the best of it. Much of this trends analysis was review of incident reports at other nuclear plants nationwide. In general, this work came under the definition of "Quality Engineering." During this period, I was sent by SCE to Rochester Institute of Technology (RIT) in upstate New York for a one-week course on the subject. Most of this consisted of statistical analysis, and how data can be collected that may yield insight into where problems might be brewing. At least, that was the concept.

Back at SONGS, this became a hard sell. Few seemed to know what our mini group was doing, and even fewer had any concept of why this was being pursued in the first place. Eventually I was able to produce some data and whizbang statistical graphics that tried to show problem areas. But what this mostly produced was

46

resentment. Sure enough, things got reorganized. The lead engineer retired and moved out of state. I was shifted into a more traditional QA role.

So many of my colleagues were perfectly content to remain in their comfort zones with tasks they had repeated year after year. Ambition seemed a scarce commodity. This syndrome did not escape notice by the on-site Nuclear Regulatory Commission (NRC) staff. These officials get assigned to plants nationwide to evaluate nuclear safety compliance. In essence, NRC people would much prefer to have nuclear licensees such as Southern California Edison perform this vigorous oversight on their own. Dream on.

By now, I had survived three years at the SONGS site. More and more, as a seasoned veteran, it became apparent that higher management seemed reluctant to enforce important requirements. More specifically, they wanted no investigations that produced findings with an adverse impact on profits. Indeed, "enforce" was categorized as a dirty word by the new QA Manager. (By the way, the previous QA Manager had moved on to other duties. Churning of organizational leaders within Corporate America is not a new phenomenon.) We, along with other SCE investigative groups, were supposed to suggest and advise, not enforce. About this time, I coined my own perspective on the abbreviation "QA" and felt it should stand for "Questioning Attitude." One of my QA cohorts actually said a kind of prayer on my behalf. My approach was notably career-limiting. But, for me, this exemplified what NRC reports had, for years, dubbed a "culture problem" at SONGS.

Curiously, I ended up more proficient in this job than anyone anticipated, including me. One example was a case where we were evaluating closure of documents known as Non-Conformance Reports (NCRs). Thousands of these NCRs get issued each year for any number of discrepant conditions at nuclear plants. Most of these needed to be closed prior to a unit's restart after a refueling shutdown. One of these reports identified certain paper-trace readouts for control rod drop tests at old Unit 1. Details get complicated but, in essence, the traces failed to show the proper shape to confirm compliance. The NCR closure statement claimed an instrument adjustment had fixed it.

Well, guess what? I augured deeper and found the newer, corrected trace—which was duly recorded, but buried—had not changed. Evidently QA auditors like me had rarely if ever bored into technical issues like this. Further, the engineer who closed the NCR had also persuaded the responsible QC inspector to sign off on the report without ever examining the revised traces. Not good. No fix had ever been done. This constituted falsification of an official document. The upshot was that I issued two Corrective Action Reports (CARs), one to the testing group and one to the QC organization. These were heavy hits and were taken seriously. Rumor has it at least one person got reprimanded to the point of "reassignment to other duties" — read "fired." I even gained a left-handed compliment by the QA Manager. I had become "Mister Destructor." I was almost a techno version of Dirty Harry. Moreover, this episode got touted to NRC staff as an example of effective QA oversight. Swell.

By this time, the importance of technological expertise among oversight groups had taken hold. We all had the opportunity to get grilled by a board of savvy managers who wanted to assess knowledge levels of oversight and inspection staff. The end result was good — for me. One of these managers was expanding the newly established Nuclear Safety Group (NSG) and was moving this group from the Edison engineering facility in Orange County to on-site SONGS. Transfer was welcome. I had escaped QA.

By 1990, I was a five-year practitioner at San Onofre, and the change seemed a *de facto* promotion. NSG's mission was to discover problems before they happened; reminiscent of duties I had coped with earlier at QA. Only this time, the examination processes were far more institutionalized and industry relevant.

The design-change process at SONGS was getting much more scrutiny. Years before, an embarrassment occurred involving the air-start mechanism for the Units 2 and 3 emergency diesel generators. These are enormous generators powered by equally enormous train locomotive diesel engines. Compressed air was the method of choice for starting these beasts. Air pressure starting would be available even when there was no electrical power on site. The whole point of these machines was to supply the power vital safety equipment needed should all site power be lost.

Earlier, some stroke-of-brilliance designer observed that compressed dry nitrogen would be a better substitute for air. Compressed nitrogen is somewhat easier to handle and is less likely to be corrosive. This design change went through a conventional review cycle and was installed. But wait. After many attempts the engines would not start. Eventually, someone decided this design-change needed a second look.

Something different was afoot. The compressed air did not operate a conventional air-start motor, which would crank the engine like the electric starter motor on an automobile. Instead, these huge engines started by synchronized porting of compressed air to each cylinder. This would mimic the initial combustion action and roll the engines until the diesel combustion process took over inside the cylinders. But more importantly, the compressed atmospheric *air* contains about 20% oxygen, which can burn. Pure dry nitrogen, in contrast, can never support ignition nor allow an internal combustion engine to start. Someone working this air-start design change clearly did not understand the physical nature of the device they were trying to improve.

These past few paragraphs may seem lengthy to illustrate a point. True enough. This foul-up got fixed — quickly and quietly. I only learned of this episode through grapevine talk from colleagues who had worked at SONGS years before me. Nobody wants to expose their shortcomings, which is universal in any human society. Also, people may claim they want constructive criticism, but rarely welcome it. Much further, these same folks will go to great lengths to trivialize the effects of such errors, or even deny they ever occurred in the first place This reaction puts any internal review-type group at serious odds with the ruling officials for the power plant. Megawatt output and corresponding cash inflow kept things going after all. NRC staff made numerous observations on this lack of intellectual honesty over the years.

All this sustained my growing distrust. Along this path, I added a new term to my technical lexicon — Loophole Engineering. This slang and degenerate term evades a detailed definition, at least in the academic sense. For the right-thinking professionals at SONGS, it meant disgust over the tendency for some technical gurus to play along with a preconceived conclusion in order to appease the boss. Too often, the results turned on an exception that was allowed in the legal framework of a standard. These technicalities too often were not known factors founded in science or other accepted experience within the engineering profession. Fortunately, these instances were few, but cobblestones like these might well pave the road to hell.

So, what is an ethical person to do?

You keep on working and make the best of it. Away from the nuclear plant, I remained a caring parent, but was confronted with an incipient disaster that could end any marriage, as it eventually did mine. No matter what the future events, our family needed income. At this point, I will invoke the foresight of Kipling, "That is another story." And that story will unfold in a forthcoming chapter of these memoirs.

Meanwhile, the job at SONGS had taken on a more interesting perspective. In addition to design review, much of what the Nuclear Safety Group did centered on a process known as Probabilistic Risk Analysis (PRA). This is an elaborate assessment of the kind of problems and their likelihood of occurring during any given evolution that would involve complex systems. Of necessity, these analyses required elaborate computer programs that could process large gulps of data inputs and yield a quantifiable probability. Typical inputs would be things like "What is the chance that a motor-operated valve might fail to function during any given hour?" Based on a mass of industry records, these values came to be known. This same reasoning could apply to other types of devices, sensors, or even static components — such as rupture of a piping weld in a critical safety system.

Once mashed together, these thousands of facts, or best guesses, calculate an overall probability of success, or worse, failure of an outcome. All this becomes very geek-like and I will not go into much more detail. For the most part, these machinations, at best, give you a general tendency of what to expect. NRC officials would not allow any nuclear plant to operate strictly on PRA results. Real-world influences always intervened. Ultimately, the most powerful influence was obvious — human action. No matter how elegant the guesswork, safety of anything eventually depends on people doing the right thing at the right time. This translates into procedures and, sometimes, individual courage.

In the course of this somewhat respected discipline, come some intriguing outcomes. First, there are boundaries. We learned about a published analysis done at another nuclear plant that reported such and such a device or system was so reliable it would not fail in 10 quadrillion hours. Wait a minute. That duration exceeds one trillion years, far longer than the age of the known universe! Nothing will ever be that safe. Allegedly, that analysis got reworked.

Also, there are limits at the other end. Critics of the nuclear industry would propose possible accidents, then complain about

50

how plant officials had failed to design for them. Early on, the NRC addressed such concerns. Consider a postulated meteorite impact at SONGS. Recall the mile-wide meteor crater near Winslow, Arizona, east of Flagstaff. A cataclysm of this magnitude is physically possible, but the odds are nil. Consequently, risks from remote chances like these were classified as "Non-Credible." In more recent politically correct times, the term *force majeure* is the terminology of choice. We no longer wish to label such events as acts of God.

Still, Probabilistic Risk Analysis can produce interesting guidelines. However, that is about as far as things can go. Let us face it—work, anywhere, is mostly uninteresting. I did get a temporary assignment to the SCE engineering complex in Orange County. This was an opportunity to work with some "real" engineering projects. But as years went on, NSG spent more time with detailed scrutiny of plant drawings and circuitry designs. These item-per-item efforts tried to identify possible high-risk evolutions during plant refueling shutdowns. One of these bothered me.

Refueling is a complex evolution for nuclear plants. All of these over-20-foot-long fuel bundles inside the reactor core need to be moved. Some get removed, since their life has "burned out" and need to go into storage inside the Spent Fuel Pool. Other partially used bundles get shuffled into new locations inside the core. Additionally, some brand-new unused fuels get added to the core. And these bundles, except the new ones, must be kept underwater at all times because these spent and partially used bundles, once irradiated, get hot—and stay hot due to internal decay heat generation. Further, if exposed to air, they would be sources of high gamma radiation. A person so exposed would receive a lethal dose in a matter of minutes.

During some subsequences, massive refueling water drain-down was only prevented by deep, U-shaped bladder seals in the Spent Fuel Pool gates. The pneumatic inflation system for these seals was not robust. One worker verified this system was about the same as using automotive heater hoses. In my world, this posed too great a risk of drain-down and consequent exposure of spent fuel bundles at certain times in the upcoming refueling outage. My draft report outlined these concerns. These findings never got published.

Coincidentally, during refueling outages, various support groups, such as NSG, would cross-train into some other groups that may have needed more manpower. At this juncture, I got assigned back to construction management. Nonnuclear water piping in the main steam, turbine cycle was thinning out too quickly. Sections of these 20-inch-diameter pipes needed to be replaced at various points. My role was back-shift manager — all well and good — at least for now.

But a specter was looming. Downsizing. This word sounded more pleasant than the tire-meets-the-road term used on the street — layoffs. By now, it was obvious that I asked lots of questions. By mid-year 1995, I was past fifty in age and, despite some good standing professionally, things were not looking good. In some fairness, however, the severance package was quite generous. Supposedly, some long-standing staff members at SONGS actually volunteered for it. If it was not a golden handshake, it was at least a silver one. And further, why would anyone want to stay where they were not wanted?

For me, these future prospects were still underwhelming. At home, the bills needed to get paid, and the likelihood of quick reemployment seemed limited. But an opportunity of sorts did come forth. NRC rules dictated that departing nuclear staff got an exit interview. Here is where I first expressed my concern, outside of SONGS, that safety was not as safe as it should be. NRC officials certainly get their fill of sour grapes from former employees. But my case was apparently more compelling.

A few weeks after leaving, I was notified at home that investigators from NRC headquarters wanted my sworn statements about SONGS. We did this in a La Jolla motel suite that served as temporary offices for the NRC people. I related my concerns about the fuel handling system and, more generally, about the prevailing attitude among senior staff about soft-pedaling safety issues. Their confrontational approach toward NRC at most levels had been known for many years. This syndrome was well entrenched. My pitch to NRC that day was that they would not listen and could not be trained. No single issue could prove much of anything. The collective picture was problematic. My thoughts were that, sooner or later, there would be a disaster. In no way could I predict what actually did happen.

Connecting these proverbial dots proved elusive. Concluding comments from my interview showed that no provable "smoking gun" was there. But, at least I said my piece, and the investigators took the time to listen. If any immediate changes got implemented at SONGS, it was never shared with me.

52

~

Let us "Fast Forward" about a decade and a half. Much had moved along by then. I had even retired, a couple times over.

At SONGS, a much-anticipated repair was finally underway. Inside the big domes, the sixty-foot-high steam generators were being replaced—two for each unit, four in all. These are giant heat exchangers that form a boundary between the reactor system "Primary" cooling water and the outside turbine system "Secondary" water. Thousands of tubes made giant U-shapes inside these "non-fired pressure vessels." Most would call them boilers. Erosion and wall thinning of these heat transfer tubes had been a chronic problem. Boilers were to be replaced that included some internal reconfigurations, which constituted a major design change.

Some of the following discussions reflect my own speculations about what happened next. History shows these new boilers worked—for a while. Scarcely more than a few years after these expensive installations, SONGS experienced the most significant accident that had ever occurred at the site. One of the new boilers experienced a Primary-to-Secondary rupture leak. This was possibly due to wear because of excessive vibration within the tube bundle.

Much of the fallout has been emotional rather than radiological. Quick action by the operators initiated shutdown and kept the actual ejection of radioactive material out to the atmosphere minimal. Still, this was inexcusable.

Looking back to when the partially redesigned boilers were conceived, the new internal configuration of tubes, bundle stabilizers, and baffles should have received a full-blown design analysis. These tests often involve physical mock-up trial runs to verify tube erosion, vibration, and a host of other parameters under operating conditions. And these get expensive. For a long story made short, the analytical review ended up being an abridged process. SONGS management convinced NRC staff this limited review was sufficient. The Loophole Engineers scored an initial victory—but it was a Pyrrhic one.

All wishful thinking and excuses aside, this was a major foul-up to the tune of over a billion dollars. I, for one, do not believe such a goof can be dismissed as "just one of those things" during the course of doing business. The SONGS crowd had committed one of the unforgivable sins of nuclear technology. They had operated their plant in an Unanalyzed Condition.

How did this happen? Believing SCE was as autocratic as before, my sense is that nobody was able or willing to tell the Emperor he had no clothes. The new boilers were designed with more tubes than the original, thus allowing greater heat transfer into the Secondary steam system and thus greater power. Motive for more power output may have worked into this equation.

Black eyes got distributed all around, including to NRC people. The Feds were probably not interested in SCE's plea to allow operation of the as-yet undamaged plant under reduced power to gain some payback from their investment. Both plants were ordered permanently shut down.

In the aftermath, what can be said? Will a detailed failure analysis of the SONGS boiler tube rupture(s) ever be known? Maybe. Will steam generator designs get refined to prevent accidents like this? Maybe. Is any study in the works that may address the symptoms and possible cures for the "San Onofre Syndrome?" Maybe.

For now, the domes at San Onofre sit as a kind of monument. They remain mute evidence of the consequences of ambition and self-righteous arrogance. Enough already.

Missing You in the Morning

Marty Eberhardt

Sun lights the curtains,

The furnace roars, in this, the coldest hour.

The dog's toenails click on the wooden floor.

He knows I'll put on the kettle,

Then let him out.

I open the door to the sweet smell of grasses

Wet from a cool night rain.

The mourning doves coo my contentment

Marred by a missing sound:

Your gentle snore.

Where's the Money?

Mardie Schroeder

Problem: How do you get the equivalent of $15,000 out of Italy when you're only allowed to take the equivalent of $200 in lire?

What if you don't know the exact amount of money you have in the bank because there are no monthly statements to show you? You must guess the amount. If you ask to take out all your money and to close the account, you will have to explain why to a manager.

Solution: You go to the bank on lunch hour and ask to withdraw $15,000 in lire from your account prepared to say you are buying a condo and need a cash deposit. They give it to you. You put it in your big purse and walk six blocks in three-inch heels to your job, resisting the urge to look behind to see who has followed you. Oh, the discipline it takes to not look behind you.

Problem: How do you change lire into dollars?

Solution: You find people who need lire in exchange for a check for American dollars. Not easy, but eventually you do it. Of course, there is no way to know if these checks are legitimate, is there?

Problem: What bank do you send the checks to in San Diego?

Solution: You go to a different Italian bank and get the address of a San Diego bank. They give you the address of a Bank of America on Cañon Street. You mail the checks to a Bank of America on Cañon Street explaining in a letter that you will arrive in November and will identify yourself when you get there.

Problem: You arrive in San Diego and discover there is no Bank of America on Cañon Street. There is no bank period on Cañon Street.

Solution: You go to the post office on Midway, show the letter to the teller, and ask where the letter may have been delivered. He looks at the address on the letter. "It probably would be returned to Italy because this is a Canadian zip code." You're in a panic.

You have no money and don't even want to think of it being lost if it was returned to Italy.

You call a Bank of America branch and ask if they received a letter with checks in it and they say, "No."

You go downtown to the main post office and show the letter to another teller. He tells you the same thing and suggests you go to the Bank of America downtown.

You go to that bank and ask to see the manager. She calls a branch on Rosecrans Street and speaks to a manager there. Eventually she hangs up and turns to you. "Your checks are at the Rosecrans branch and they are waiting for you to come in and identify yourself."

You do what any grown up woman would do — you burst into tears.

Now you know how to get money out of Italy. However, there still is a problem. You still have money in a bank in Rome, but you don't know how much.

Solution anyone?

Lessons from My Little Brother

Sandra Yeaman

My brother Brian was the youngest child in the family by four minutes. His twin, Bruce, arrived first. Until Bruce's arrival, Mom thought she had been carrying her planned fifth, and final, child. Brian upended many of my parents' plans.

I was ten when the twins were born.

The twins arrived a month earlier than expected. Mom and Dad didn't have two names picked out, so their initial birth certificates listed them as Baby Boy #1 and Baby Boy #2. They were also both underweight and had to remain in the hospital until they could tip the scales at five pounds. Brian was bigger, so he came home first.

By then, I had waited three weeks for a baby to come home, and I was tired of waiting. Because he came home first, Brian became my baby. I volunteered to feed him, to change his diapers, to bathe him. And because I was ten, and probably because she knew the workload would soon double, Mom let me.

Bruce came home two weeks later. Everyone around me ooh'ed and ah'ed about how cute both boys were, and I admit Bruce was cute then and has grown into a handsome man. But then, in my heart, I knew Brian was cuter.

For the first year Mom fed one baby, and I fed the other. Mom changed one diaper, and I changed the other. When they cried, Mom picked up one, and I picked up the other. By the end of the year, I was no longer volunteering to help, but I accepted my role as mother-in-training.

The two boys were very different. Brian was blond. Bruce's hair was the more typical dishwater blond that we in Minnesota considered brunette. Brian not only started out bigger, he grew to be both taller and heavier than Bruce. In fact, as Brian grew, we began calling him our teddy bear because he loved to encircle us in bear hugs, sometimes to mark that he was happy, sometimes when he was sad, and sometimes when he just felt like it.

Once through high school, Brian attended the local technical school and became an electrician, while Bruce went off to university and became a computer engineer. At the conclusion of their educational paths, Brian stayed in our hometown to work. Bruce moved away to a larger city.

I left home on my journey into the world before the boys reached their teens. I missed watching them grow into adulthood. But the connection I felt with Brian remained strong.

When he asked me for advice about getting married, I had already gone through one marriage and a divorce, so I told him if he had any doubts he should wait. So he waited. His girlfriend at the time, Lori, blamed me for breaking them up.

Ten years later, when he married for the first time, he insisted they schedule the wedding when I would be home, something that only happened once every year or two. Perhaps he should have waited that time, too, since that marriage lasted only a few months, though without it, we wouldn't have his son, Corey, in our family.

After another ten years, he did marry Lori. Because of the smiles her presence brought to his face, I was absolutely delighted that they didn't let the intervening years interfere with their future. In addition, Lori brought her sons, Eric and Alex, to the family. And together, Brian and Lori created Megan.

Brian never wanted to play a game unless he could find a way to cheat. It was no fun to play by the rules, he told us. Watching us to see if we caught him cheating, that was Brian's fun. But I watched him teach his son, Corey, how important it was to follow the rules. Brian had been caught breaking the bigger rules of life and knew the consequences. He wanted to save his son the trouble.

Brian always seemed to find the perfect gift for me at the holidays, something that made me think he knew me better than any of my other siblings did. A collapsible pair of scissors that I could carry with me on my world travels was one of my favorites.

In 2010, when he was 51, Brian went to the emergency room at the end of the long Labor Day weekend because he just couldn't shake a cough and cold. Instead of issuing him a prescription and sending him home, the doctors checked him into the hospital after diagnosing him with acute myeloid leukemia. He never left the hospital.

Eleven weeks later, we lost Brian. But during those eleven weeks, my siblings and I agree that Brian shared three gifts with us, three lessons on living.

First, Brian reminded us of the importance of saying thank you. I watched Brian thank everyone who came in contact with him while in the hospital. He thanked each of us in the family when we arrived and again when we left his room. But we weren't the only ones he thanked.

Part of his treatment involved being placed into a state of artificial paralysis for two weeks. This treatment left him partially paralyzed even when the artificial inducement ended. For this reason, he often had to ask for help: to adjust a pillow, to shift his position in his bed, to cover both of his feet with the blanket. Whenever he asked for help, he always thanked the helper.

When the doctors came into the room to discuss what he should expect next, or the nurses came in to give him a shot, or a CNA or physical therapist came in to twist and shift his body to prevent muscle contractions, even when the news was depressing or he knew those treatments would be painful, he always thanked them.

Second, Brian reminded us of the importance of saying I love you. I watched Brian openly and warmly tell those who came to see him that he loved them. It was no surprise that he would tell his wife, his children, his siblings, and Dad that he loved us. But because I lived far from him, I hadn't realized how big his world was, how large his family-by-choice was. During my visits, I met Brian's neighbors, his coworkers, and his friends.

And although the opening in his throat, where his trache tube had been, prevented him from speaking above a whisper, he found ways to be sure each visitor knew he loved them. Sometimes it was just a touch or a whisper. Sometimes he asked Bruce to help him spell out the message using a board with the alphabet on it. Bruce would run a pen along the alphabet and watch for Brian to nod when he reached the right letter. It took only a few letters to figure out what he meant to say.

Finally, Brian reminded us of the comfort of small things including both laughter and something cold to drink. One Sunday evening after the nurse gave him a shot, she asked if he wanted anything else. He asked her to change the TV channel to the one with the Minnesota Vikings game. She told him the hospital didn't carry that premium channel.

"Well then, I'm out of here," he whispered loud enough for her to hear. Brian wanted to be sure no one left his room without at least a smile.

Brian couldn't eat or drink because the paralysis affected his ability to swallow, resulting in a risk of food or liquid getting into his lungs. One set of tubes delivered food and water while another set removed waste products. Every time a doctor or nurse asked him if he needed anything, he asked for a drink of cold water, something he knew they wouldn't give him. It was a sure way for him to get a laugh.

In the last week of his life, Brian asked Bruce to give the eulogy at the funeral and suggested we place a pitcher of ice water on each table at the reception afterwards. We honored both wishes. When we get together as a family, we toast Brian with ice water.

We lost our brother, our baby brother, almost ten years ago. But those final lessons, those final three gifts, will remain with me for a lifetime.

The Night Marchers

Yvonne Nelson Perry

Boom . . . Boom . . . Boom.

I hear the Night Marchers coming.

Low *pahu* thuds fill the windless night. The dirge-like sound of the drums, like rolling thunder, echoes down through the narrow valley to the ocean.

The sea churns around me. I stumble out of it and sink to my knees on the beach. The moon behind me, bright as polished bone, throws my crouching shadow across the hard-packed sand. With head bowed, I wait.

Tutu told me stories about these ghost warriors and their followers. Although my grandmother never lied to me, I didn't believe her tales about the Night Marchers. Until now.

For most of my eighty years, I have lived on this isolated sweep of beach. Before coming to this place of my ancestors, my wife, Mahina, and I lived in a village on the other side of the island. We had a small house with a vegetable garden surrounding it. We even grew our own *taro* to make *poi*. We never wanted more than we had.

Then, *Kua*, the shark god, sent a great white *mano* to take away our girl child. That day, my daughter and I dove off my outrigger for a swim along the shore. As we swam back to the canoe, the fin of a *mano* cut me off from Noelani. Before I could get to her, the shark snatched her.

It had her body in its huge mouth when I grabbed her and tried to pull her free. Then, its jaws clamped shut and bit Noelani in half. It swallowed half of my child, then yanked the other half away from me and disappeared.

Stunned, I treaded water in a circle of my child's blood.

Gone. My sweet, sweet baby girl. Only six-years-old.

My daughter never made a sound, but the screams of her mother, running up and down the beach, remain with me still.

63

From that time on, my wife would not let me fish or swim in the ocean. She lived in fear of *Kua*, the shark god, who could change his shape at will. She seldom left the house. At night, we slept holding hands. Years later, we had a son, but for only twenty years. A war took Kahala away. He lies in some foreign field far from home.

Mahina died soon after that. For a long, long time, I tended her, tangled up in her sad memories, lost from me forever.

Now I live in a shack by the sea. The reef here drops off into deep water, good for fishing. The rocky ridge above me is barren, except for *kolea* nests. The nearby valley is filled with *kukui* trees that give me oil for my lanterns. Mango trees and giant fern fronds provide more food. The sea, the cliff and the valley feed me.

Boom . . . Boom . . . Boom.

Their drums grow louder.

Old Hawaiians say, if you look directly at the Night Marchers, they will kill you. Now, they pause on the ridge above the beach. I rise and stare up at them. Wearing *koa* wood helmets, *tapa* loincloths and yellow feather capes, some of them raise long spears over their heads. The heavy lances can pierce a man's face and explode out the back of his skull. When their victim falls, the spear pins him to the earth.

Boom . . . Boom . . . Boom.

Out of the mist they come, marching six abreast. Two carry torches, two beat *pahu*, two carry spears. Their feet never touch the ground.

I stand in their path, an old man ready to die.

They don't look at me.

They pass me by.

Boom . . . Boom . . . Boom.

A single ghost warrior, at the rear of the Night Marchers, stops in front of me.

He is Kahala.

I look directly into his eyes and feel the weight of my years lifted.

As I step forward to embrace my son, he points to the women and children behind him. I see my wife, Mahina, and my daughter, Noelani. Both smiling at me, both whole. I fall into step between them and we stride out behind Kahala.

Our feet do not touch the ground.

We are the Night Marchers.

Boom . . . Boom . . . Boom.

64

~

Ku`u ka luhi, ua maka.
He, who leaves his wearied mind
and body behind, is at peace.
- Old Hawaiian proverb

Celestial

Jenna Benson

Contrasting
shapes and colors
painted on the inside of my eyes.

Running through the constellations,
dreaming only of fantasy lands.

Resurrect the stars
and shape a new galaxy out of me with their dust.
Wrap your arms around Jupiter,
rest your fingertips gently on my skin.
Stare into the black hole in front of you
and try not to jump.

We thought we were the sun,
all that ever mattered.

The space between us now is lightyears.
We are all unformed piles of stardust.
We've forgotten our most favorite memories,
and laughed in the face of the past.

Where the ends met

the edges ignited,

releasing us from this world.

The light is ripped away,

leaving us here in the most comforting darkness.

Anniversary

Elizabeth Duris

We met in the most unusual way. It was on the red eye from LA to New York City. I was just coming off the unbelievable experience of having an interview with Twyla Tharp in her Los Angeles dance office. We had spread my sketches over her conference table. She liked my designs. Could I free my calendar to join her team in costume and set design for the *Oklahoma!* revival? I had only been living in New York six months, so freeing my calendar was one of the easier tasks. Freeing myself from a two-year relationship would take the greater doing. But it was time. We realized we were losing oxygen, so we both stepped back to take a breath.

The year was 1984. Yes, that famous *1984* of George Orwell. The LA Summer Olympics. The 1984 of Madonna, Prince, and Michael J. I was 26.

He was a free-lance writer covering the exciting LA sports scene. Young Jerry Brown, Governor Moonbeam, had just completed his term, and his predecessor, Ronald Reagan, was now in the White House. Tom had just landed a new assignment which took him to New York, then on to DC, to begin a stint as speech writer with the Reagan administration.

As Tom and I buckled our seat belts, we were both trying to come off cloud nine in our careers. It took little time to eschew sleep in favor of the five-hour conversation that led to our first date, our three-month engagement, and our wedding in the Adirondacks shortly after my birthday.

The years following were so exciting for both of us. By 1995, I had moved on to join Zandra Rhodes, newly arrived from Britain where she had designed for Lady Diana. She was about to unleash her colorful bolt of design and explosive creative spirit on the opera and musical scenes in the US. By now, Tom had moved on to the Clinton administration, where he was now head speech writer. This meant we were bicoastal in our careers, but because of the nature of our work, we both could operate conveniently from our Connecticut home.

Now the boys are grown and off on their own. Ben chose to follow his father's lead in political speech writing; Ted is currently comedy writer for his hero and mentor, Seth Myers. We are grandparents of two little girls.

This is how it could have happened. This is how I would have fashioned it were I the Master Cylinder, were I the Prime Mover. This idyll would have been my life had leukemia not stilled my blood vessels and taken my life on May 4, 1964.

My name is Karen. Today is my anniversary.

And So Went My Youth

Kelly Bargabos

Have you seen my youth? She was last seen wearing skinny jeans, a T-shirt with no bra, and flat shoes. She has a full head of hair, before the hundreds of thousands of strands were lost on the bathroom floor, the color still a natural shade of brownish-blonde.

She escaped when I wasn't looking—like my virginity so many years ago, when too many beers loosened my grip, and it slipped through my fingers in an instant; lost to some boy on a night I barely remember. Surprised it was that easy.

The money in my 401k disappeared a few years ago while I was sleeping. I've watched the blackjack dealer scoop up my chips with grace and ambivalence. I've pulled the arm at the twenty-five-cent slot. The machine threw me a party as my money disappeared with the lucky sevens, diamonds, and hearts rolling and flashing to innocent melodies.

The down payment on my condo may never be seen again, despite my in-depth analysis and number crunching of interest rates and real estate values. But there wasn't a formula or spreadsheet that would tell me that in two years the real estate bubble would burst, and values would crash—bottom out to their lowest in twenty years. I didn't calculate that we wouldn't flip it fast enough and, in the blink of an eye, we would have a condo in Florida gathering dust, worth half of what we owed the bank. There were no red flag warnings to tell us that we would have to hold on to this condo and wait for the value to climb back to pre-bubble levels, and that no one knew how long this would take.

No analysis told me that ten years after that, our marriage bubble would burst and crash, bottom out. And, after all the dividing of assets and the painful, tortured disjoining of our lives, this condo in Florida would be the only thing left in both our names, still waiting for the market to recover, so we could sell at that profit we were promised so long ago, and go our separate ways.

I lost my faith once, blaming God for a heartbreak He didn't cause but let happen on his watch. We didn't speak for months, which turned into years. I was sure I'd never find that faith again. It turned up one day, as suddenly as it had left, and I realized He was never gone.

Some things fade slowly from our sight, like the water tower outside my bedroom window. The name of the factory that was once here had been emblazoned with fresh, dark letters on its battleship-gray torso. The tower stood guard on strong legs while the workers came every morning and punched their card, forging things we no longer use, leaving their sweat on the factory floor, waiting for the whistle to end the day — while the sun and the rain and the snow and the wind and the days wore the letters on the tower down to a ghost of what they once were.

And so went my youth.

Lost in the Capital of China

Dora Klinova

It just happened that I decided to be brave. Such a decision came to me—not the first time in my life. About a quarter of century ago I had the same urge. Even stronger. It made me escape from the falling apart Soviet Union and run to America. Did I ever feel upset that I made that decision? Oh, no, I was proud of myself, enjoying for many years the blue sky of blissful California. Then I decided that California was extremely nice, but it was not the end of the world for me. I visited Paris and Rio de Janeiro, Australia and Tahiti, crossed Panama Canal, etc., but I never have been to China and Japan. I felt that these parts of the world desperately needed my investigation. Life goes by, years run, and, without going to China and Japan, my life is not complete.

This idea silently was cooking in my head. Then I decided to share this idea with my husband. He was not so happy about this. His mind works differently than mine. China and Japan were not a big priority in his life. But if the woman wants, what is the man supposed to do? Just to be smart enough and obey, without any complaints. Complaints spoil the fun.

So, I found a good travel offer: a cruise from Hong Kong to Tokyo. We decided to stay in Hong Kong for three days before the cruise started. Running away from a noisy and crowded Hong Kong, we found a hotel in peaceful Lantau Island that is about half hour away from Hong Kong by ferry.

We packed our suitcases and flew from Los Angeles to Hong Kong. It was a sixteen-hour flight. Sitting for sixteen hours in airplane's narrow seat, I felt like a mummy in sarcophagus. I counted this flight as two for one—the first and the last one! Never do it again.

Our three days in Hong Kong went fast, and finally, we appeared at our gorgeous Holland America Westerdam ship. Next day, the ship brought us to Shanghai.

Before departure, I spent a few weeks with my computer trying to find the best excursions at the ports of our cruise. Did I do a good job? No. I do not think that it is possible to choose a tour using their descriptions. But we got a nice touch of China in Shanghai.

The most unforgettable incident happened in Beijing, the capital of China. Our ship docked in Tianjin. This port is located about three and a half hours bus drive from Beijing. Certainly, we couldn't miss the capital of China and bought the tour to Summer Palace in Beijing. The tour guide, Tony, a short young man, talked to us for three-and-a-half hours telling us perhaps everything he had learned about China, and finally we appeared at the Summer Palace.

It is impossible to imagine the amount of people at the square of this Palace; to understand it you must come to China. It seemed to me that half of entire population of China was at this time at this Palace. There were hundreds of guides who kept their flags high above their heads, ruling the crowd. Everybody ran, being afraid to lose their guide.

I was smart enough to equip myself with a walker to save my back from the crowd. Two of us, my walker and me, were not able to find enough space in the narrow and uneven cobbled walkways of this huge square. Maneuvering with my walker, I lost my husband, Tony, and our group. Soon I understood that it was absolutely impossible to reach them in this huge moving mass of people.

I lost my group. I lost my husband. I was worried about him, hoping that he would stay with the group, not trying to find me by himself. Our passports were on the ship. They gave us only the copies of our passports. I carried both of the copies in my purse. If he leaves the group and he is also lost, he will be without identification papers. I hoped he carried his American driver license.

Can you imagine? It was already about 5 p.m. We were supposed to go back to the ship to Tianjin, driving three and a half hours in the bus, and I was in the middle of this giant moving anthill of people. I tried to talk to any one of the guides, but they didn't speak English and couldn't stop for a second, being afraid to lose their group. Nobody spoke English!

I became scared. In the middle of this unbelievable crowd of people from all over the world, I felt so lonely and so lost. Everybody ran. Nobody paid attention to me.

I started to yell. "Help! Help! Help!"

Finally, a policeman came to me and, without any word, directed me to follow him. He also did not speak English. I did not have another choice and obeyed. We walked more than a half hour under hot sun until he brought me, exhausted, to the police station. Nobody spoke English there either. They put me in the corner and forgot about me. I patiently waited, then started to yell. "English! English! English!"

A man came in. He knew English, like I did Japanese. But somehow, he understood me. He asked me where I am staying in Beijing. I said that I am from the Holland America ship that is docked in Tianjin. He did not know what means Holland America. I felt that he also did not know what means Tianjin. He couldn't understand how I appeared in Beijing coming from Tianjin. "By bus," I said. He asked me the telephone number of the bus driver. I did not know it certainly. He asked me the phone number of Holland America. I also did not know it and asked him to look at Google Internet. He did not know what means Google and Internet. I felt that I am talking to a dummy.

Can you imagine? The Police Department in one of the main attractions of the capital of China with thousands of foreign tourists and visitors did not have Internet!

I asked to call somebody else for Internet. No, it was impossible for him.

I said, "Put me in the car, let us go to the Entrance and find the bus!"

"Here there are seven entrances. Where is your bus located?"

Ridiculous question! I decided to leave this police station. He did not let me. I was arrested! Scared to death, I started to yell loudly, banging the table with my fists. "American Embassy! American Embassy!"

He did not pay attention.

I came to the opened door and started to yell as loud as I could into the street. "American Embassy! Help! American Embassy! Help!"

Now he became more active. He did not want a scandal with American Embassy. I was too noisy a woman for him. He called somewhere a few times, and then explained to me, "Your guide lost you. He cannot come back without you. He will come to us. He must!"

No, I did not believe him. I did not believe a word this dummy said to me. I was not able to wait. I chose the moment when he did not look at me to run away. He ran after me. And outside — oh, such a surprise! My husband, with my group and our guide Tony, was approaching the police department!

I was found. I was saved! Hip, Hip Hurrah!

California February

Marty Eberhardt

Little shoots of green,

The promise of flowers,

But above

The great oaks crack open

At their curves.

Other branches, already fallen,

Lie like huge wooden snakes

Beneath brown pines.

Dry needles salt the green sprouts.

This year's winter,

Mud-brown, gray-skied, flooded,

Will yield fireworks of poppies,

Purple symphonies of lupines and shooting stars,

Conventions of butterflies and moths.

But there is no return

For those whose roots

Need more

Than one anomalous year.

Some wild lilacs

Will soon burst blue with honey-smell

Midst their neighbor shrubs,

Dry, leafless, lost.

We will sing the spring

As the birds do,

But as we celebrate each new bloom,

Each Canterbury bell, each dark peony

Nodding beneath an oak,

We must raise our eyes to that dead tree,

See it,

Know there may be more,

For one wet winter

Will not deter the expected march

Of drought.

Lost

Peggy Hinaekian

Nora stood at the open window of her bedroom, gazing at the ocean. The swishing of waves rippling along the shore calmed her anger — somewhat. She held a plush red rose, and the sweet fragrance boosted her morale.

The bastard had gone back to his wife. Yes, Richard had gone back to his wife.

She took off the 18-karat gold bracelet he had given her for her birthday. Its inscription — her name on one side and birthdate on the other — was a painful reminder of his betrayal. She threw it in her nightstand drawer and banged it shut, cursing as she did so. She hated the "f" word, but she used it. She used it twice. It liberated her.

Nora vowed to take her revenge. She had to plan it carefully, though. She should take her time and not be hasty about it, which she was always prone to do. Only then would she feel exonerated. She was going to have the last word. She looked at herself in the mirror and liked what she saw. She was certainly better looking than that wife of his with her puffy fish-mouth lips and fake silicone boobs.

"This is not the end," she told herself, feeling confident. She was sure things would happen. Not even a wife would take from her the man she loved.

"You are being absurd," her best friend, Ella, told her when she met her for coffee at their favorite café.

"That filthy rich bitch will never let him go. She has him in her well-manicured claws and, from what you have told me, he likes money a lot, more than he likes you, I bet."

"But he told me he loved me," Nora said, "and he planned on getting a divorce, soon."

"And you believed him. I didn't know you were that naive. Forget about him, he is not worth your efforts. Concentrate on finding another guy, an unmarried one, a divorced one maybe, but without kids. Kids would complicate your life, and there is

79

always the ex-wife to deal with, if she has not remarried. Look around, I am sure you will fall in love again. You always do — always with the wrong guy, though. Try to choose wisely next time."

"I can't forget about him. It is easy for you to say, but I do love him. I can't believe he left me. Do you think I have lost him? I'm shattered. I don't think I can live without him. I can't deal with this loss."

"Love, love, what does it mean? You are too romantic. You fall in love too easily. You think you love him because he is not available. Don't be so melodramatic, my dear. You'll live. I can assure you."

Nora pondered over Ella's last statement, but she did not agree. She had a plan. An infallible one. He was not lost to her. She was going to get him back.

She punched in some numbers on her cell phone.

"A Better You Cosmetic Surgery," the cheery voice announced. "How may we help you?"

Songs of a Life — Meg

Robert Gilberg

August 10, 2018 — A friend is dying. She's been dying for the last two-and-a-half years of pancreatic cancer. She's fought it with everything she has — her strength and courage, disbelief, denial and refusal, her great sense of humor, help from her husband, her dog and cats, and scores of friends. But nothing stops this disease, and living longer than two and half years is beyond unusual. She knows when I visit and enter her room that I'm there, but nothing much more transpires. She tips the corners of her mouth up when I kiss her on the forehead as I leave, and I wonder how many more days . . . It's close now.

She loves music and movies and has been my go-to source for actors, actresses, and movie titles when I couldn't remember them. It's useless to debate movie trivia with her and my wife; they know everything.

But music is a different story; she knows a lot, but I know more. It's always been fun to play name-that-tune with her. We'd race to see how few notes were played in order for one of us to name the tune first. We could get some tunes in only two or three notes. Or even one — the first ring of the cowbell at the start of The Stones' *Honky Tonk Women.* But we had to identify the performer(s) as well, or it didn't count.

I know pre-eighties music best, but she has the post-seventies, hands down, over me. It's because of our age difference, and the generation that separates us; but she even did well with the pre-eighties. I know the jazz and big band era music she knows little about — but she always loved it when I played the great tunes. I taught her about piano wizards like Errol Garner, Teddy Wilson, George Shearing, and the masters of big bands, such as Duke Ellington and Count Basie.

She loved listening to my Pandora piano jazz station, *Misty Radio,* over a glass of wine and snacks in early evening hours. Another Pandora station I created, *In a Mellow Tone Radio,* focused on soft big band music that works well in the same ways. Most of the tunes are old mellow jazz standards from the 30s and 40s, many of which she, surprisingly, knew. That's because of her father who played them around home. It surprised her to find I knew her father's music — even though I'm from a younger generation. But anyone who followed jazz in the 50s and 60s would know that the modern jazz players of that era didn't abandon the music of the great composers who preceded them.

Today, I wonder if any music is playing in her mind as she drifts, hour by hour, toward the end. I know I'd want to be listening to the tunes of my life in those last hours. Hauling a bunch of CDs over to her house to play DJ for her crossed my mind more than once, but since she never speaks now, I don't know what would be right. Guessing seems too risky; what if I picked things that just don't work for her at this time? I'd never want to add to her agony.

It's too bad we never think of these things while there is still time do something about it. Playing recordings of loved music from one's life might be as beneficial as medicines and care from home helpers in those final hours. What could be better to quiet the rage against a life-ending disease than hearing favorites at the time when peace seems the most important thing?

Music underscores and colors the important events of many people's lives. It does mine, and I'm sure it does Meg's, too. It's like a calendar, but with melodies rather than dates. Associating the best times and friends of one's life with a favorite tune in a peaceful environment could be better than the strongest painkillers doctors can prescribe.

~

August 19, 2018 — Meg died a few days after I started and, then, suspended this little essay. Her death was just a few hours after Aretha died — also of pancreatic cancer. It could even have been the same day, but we'll never know. It happened during the night. I think Meg would be happy going into the next world with Aretha; they were both rockers. I can imagine the two, boogying along a yellow brick path, bright smiles on their faces.

I didn't know where to go with this piece before tonight. But I do now; I'm making my deathbed music list today. And I know Meg well enough to think it would have worked for her too, although that's too late. My music will be a mix of instrumental versions of original artists' creations, performed by classically trained stringed-instrument musicians.

Instrumental-only versions can offer a way for the listener's imagination to run free, substituting personal thoughts and feelings that could be suppressed when vocalists are singing. Voices and lyrics can get in the way — by being too rough, or too trivial, or slightly off one's moment — not allowing the listener to have his/her own intimacy with the music. And, the truth is, many times, melody and rhythm are more important than lyrics, which may well be the case in the final hours. String quartets or trios, that get it, can deliver the same syncopation and musical emotion as the original vocal-based songs, allowing the listener more ease and freedom. One could even imagine being a vocalist, fronting great musicians, silently singing on the way to the next world.

Isn't that a better way to go out — instead of TV commercials, the trivia of game shows, or the numbing repetition of cable news droning on in the background? There is one important rule to be kept in mind when creating the list — the songs must stick to the original musical themes and emotions, not watered-down shopping mall or elevator pablum.

It's just a beginning with, I hope, years to finish — as I review the music of my life, working through jazz, folk and folk-rock, blues, maybe a little country, and more. I know these would work for Meg, and I'm going to play them now.

Meg, if you are listening . . .

~

My list — but only a start:

Imagine	John Lennon
Layla, (extended piano coda)	Eric Clapton, Derek and the Dominos
Will the Circle Be Unbroken (Traditional)	Carter-Cash Family, Nitty Gritty Dirt Band
Mr. Tambourine Man	Bob Dylan
Whiter Shade of Pale	Procul Harum
Into the Mystic	Van Morrison
Stairway to Heaven	Led Zepplin
Wild Horses	Rolling Stones
Wish You Were Here	Pink Floyd
Beethoven's Five Secrets	The Piano Guys
The Long and Winding Road	The Beatles
Fields of Gold	Sting
Misty	Errol Garner
I Say a Little Prayer for You	Franklin, Warwick (with Aretha's vocals)

83

Fallen Hero

Lawrence Carleton

Harry's is a dimly lit place just a short walking distance from the base from which it derives most of its business. They go there in groups or meet up with friends, but you can be left alone if you want to be. That night, 14 February 2019, Jake Earl Huggins wanted to be. He sat at the end of the bar, nursing a beer and thinking.

"Rosie turned out okay," he remembered. "Taggert gave her The Talk, the way he knows how, and in the end she caved." That had been a couple of years ago.

Jake had gone on to serve in Kandahar, and he'd come back with recommendations. He had modified a handheld scanning device to rapidly detect concealed weapons at a distance. It had proved useful in surprising circumstances. If he re-upped, he'd probably get a promotion.

Good old Taggert. He'd done for Jake what he'd done for other guys under his command. "Look, Rosie," he'd have laid it out for her, "do you really want to ruin Jake's career? He's a good soldier, and he's got a family. And think of yourself: you'll become known as a troublemaker. You won't advance, and they'll stick you with the worst assignments."

In the end, Rosie accepted an early discharge, but qualified for benefits.

"Back then we knew how to do it," Jake thought. "Why couldn't it be like that now with Liz?"

Elizabeth Martinet worked in the same office with him at the base. He saw her every day. Tall, built, blue eyes, sexy smile — when she smiled. Liz was beautiful without trying. In fact, she didn't try. She was all business. She never reacted to his jokes.

After a while he'd started visualizing her in a bikini, then later, he modified his scanning device to image her as buck-naked. She never caught on to what he was doing.

Then came that Sunday night.

The guys had cut out early to catch a movie, but it sounded like a chick flick, so he'd stayed at Harry's. In walked Liz with two of her friends. She stopped to ask him how he was doing – he looked a little down – then caught up with her friends at a nearby table.

On the TV over the bar, the baseball game ended, the Tigers beat the Twins.

Closing time.

Liz and her friends got up. As they passed him, he asked her for a favor.

"I'm kind of in bad shape, Liz. Sort of lost count. Can you help me get back to the base?"

He was pretending to be worse than he really was, of course. He let her catch him a few times as he wobbled to his barracks. "Stairs," he mumbled, looking up and down the flight. "I'll take it from here. Thanks for the help. I can crawl up."

"That's okay," she replied. I'll steady you. Which door?"

"The second. Thanks."

He knew that his quarters would be empty that night. As soon as they got the door opened, he grabbed her, carried her to his bed, and had at her. This was going well. She was confused and struggling but hadn't thought to scream. Then, right when he was just getting to the good part, she somehow managed to get her left foot up against his chest and pushed him off.

"Bitch," he muttered, and leaned into her again. He never saw that right leg coming. A hard foot to his neck knocked him cold.

When he came to, she was gone, and he was a crumpled mess on the floor at the end of his bed. "It was consensual," he rehearsed as he cleaned up.

It didn't take long for Jake to hear from Taggert.

As soon as he entered Taggert's office, his boss let him have it.

"Do you know who you assaulted?"

Jake mumbled.

"Consensual my ass. She uploaded pictures of your sorry self to the Cloud. Doesn't look like she agreed to anything but knocking the crap out of you."

Jake didn't know what to say.

"Ever heard of Bob Martinet? *Congressman* Bob Martinet? On the main House committee that oversees the military? Elizabeth's his daughter. She's following in her daddy's footsteps. In a way that's lucky for you. She doesn't want to waste her time on this. She just wants you gone."

86

Jake couldn't believe this. Was he getting The Talk? He was. Guys don't get The Talk. He could hear Taggert's words, as though from a distance. This wasn't happening.

"Here's the deal. You don't reenlist; you don't get any medals. I give you a desk job away from her, and you keep a good distance from her until your time is up. Then you go quietly. You get to retire with the usual benefits. That's to show mercy on your family, God help them. Elizabeth originally wanted to impose a reduction in rank."

So here he sat again, tonight, at Harry's, alone at his spot at the end of the bar, nursing another beer. Thinking the same thoughts over and over. He'd have to tell his wife something, and pretty soon at that. What could he say that she would trust and not suspect? How would he provide for his wife and daughter, who believed in him, without telling them why he couldn't stay in the service?

The waiter tapped him on the shoulder. Jake looked up with sad, empty eyes.

"Closing time," the man said. "Time to go."

Jake paid up with his credit card. He stared past the waiter, at nothing in particular. He steadied himself against the bar as he rose from his stool. He turned toward the exit and mumbled, "I know."

Good-bye, Mikey — and Thank You!

Ken Yaros

There's scarcely an American generation that hasn't been touched by war. Still, no civilian is prepared for it. We've all seen movies depicting shooting and violence. Some have read books on war and consider themselves armchair experts on historical battles.

Hollywood does a credible job presenting every type of conflict from sniper fire to a nuclear explosion. We watch, unscathed.

But when *you* find yourself ensnared in a vortex of mayhem, your life changes forever. Some display physical scars. But most injuries are unseen. Through military ceremonies, parades, and national holidays we honor the many who have served our country.

Perhaps the best way to fully appreciate their sacrifice is through sharing personal accounts from individuals we've put in harm's way.

Fortunately, most of us will never experience warfare. For the unaffected, it is difficult to appreciate why so many have served and continue to volunteer. Nearly every combat veteran can tell you a story of a soon-to-be-forgotten hero. This is such a story.

~

In less than a minute after deplaning at Cam Ranh Bay, Vietnam, in July 1969, I knew I had entered a new world. The terminal, a converted dingy hangar, confined a youthful horde of humanity, civilian and military. A cacophony of figures garbed in everything from heavy flak jackets to Hawaiian shirts, milled around waiting for flights or new assignments.

The next day, I left for Tuy Hoa Air Force Base, my new assignment for a year. That afternoon, I unpacked and received an M16 and a .38 S&W. The next morning, I was to be ready for work by seven a.m. Introductions were brief, orientation nearly nonexistent, my appointment book already set up for six days a week, nine hours a day. I was one of three staff dentists with the rank of captain.

Tuy Hoa AFB, named after the adjacent town, protected one of the most unspoiled beaches on the South China Sea. A majestic mountain range rose about ten miles to the west, framing an idyllic coastal fishing village and vacation destination for locals. I saw it as deceptively beautiful, totally out of character for a war zone.

The July sun turned our base into a sauna with afternoon temperatures of 105 degrees accompanied by 90 percent humidity. More than once I was tempted to shave my head.

Tuy Hoa AFB, a.k.a. "grandmother's place," usually felt safe. Our biggest challenges were boredom, monotony, and isolation. We were well protected, not because we were so valuable, but because our F-100s and C-119s were. Our perimeter was nearly impenetrable.

Unless they mounted a full-on rocket attack, the Viet Cong would not be able to get through our fences. Even so, we were on constant alert.

The dental clinic took up a small wing of the hospital, a one-story, modular affair — self-contained and air-conditioned. Our modest ten-bed facility supported the Air Force reconnaissance mission in coastal Viet Nam. Seldom were our beds filled with casualties.

~

One Saturday, in mid-April 1970, Major Jim Nelson, the hospital commander, invited us dentists to a birthday barbecue the next day behind the hospital. Being the senior chief flight surgeon, even on a small base, was prestigious, so we felt honored that he invited us. At about five feet, nine inches tall, and of slender build, he had the appearance of a much younger person. Despite his superior rank, he prided himself on being one of us.

"Look, guys," he said, "I was able to trade for a twenty-pound bag of dehydrated shrimp, which is now in the immunization refrigerator rehydrating. I got hamburgers and hotdogs. If you bring some soda and beer, we'll have a few laughs. We have two birthdays to celebrate in the hospital. Besides, I'm throwing my own bon voyage. I'm leaving for R&R in Hawaii next Thursday. Joining my wife."

It didn't take much convincing to get a small group of corpsmen together since nothing was going on anyway. The base commander had banned our most popular weekend sport, volleyball, due to accidents. Volleyball caused more significant

90

injuries which needed medical care than all activities on or off the base. Up to that day.

By noon about twenty GIs, mostly from the hospital, had convened on the small patio behind the dispensary. One of the corpsmen brought a *Playboy* magazine which received lots of attention.

Major Nelson gave the okay to light the charcoal in the rusted half barrel we used for a barbecue grill. Sodas were brought out. We stood around talking about the major's R&R and razzing one of the corpsmen about his birthday.

Around 12:15 Nelson received a call on his mobile hospital phone.

Crackle. "Tuy Hoa hospital?"

Nelson dived for the phone. *Crackle.* "This is Tuy Hoa. Over."

Crackle. "Tuy Hoa, this is Dusty forty-three. I'm three clicks [kilometers] north of Nha Trang, [another Air Force base about 40 miles south of us]. Heard you have some shrimp?"

Nelson, normally chatty, mumbled, "Yeah. Over."

Crackle. "Tuy Hoa, we got something I think you'd like. We got five gallons of Dolly Madison chocolate ice cream on DI [dry ice] for *our* birthday boy here and we're looking for a party. Are you interested? Over."

"Dusty, that's fine. What's your ETA?"

Crackle. "Tuy Hoa, we can be there in ten minutes give or take. Over."

"Roger. We'll have the dogs and shrimp ready."

We decided to take what we could inside. Food on the grill was pushed aside and covered. The chopper landing on the helipad nearby would blow sand everywhere. So, we went inside and waited. Nelson stood looking through the hospital's rear glass doors for their arrival.

Sure enough, the Huey chopper soon appeared as a dot in the sky. A few moments later it landed with a roar in a storm of sandy bits. After shutdown, the two-man flight crew and two medics jumped out, slipped off their flak jackets, and met us on the patio.

Captain John Anderson, the pilot, made the introductions. The arrivals were all smiles and appeared well groomed, for Army forces—cleanly shaven, hair combed, and wearing fresh uniforms. We found out later they had just attended chapel services.

One of the medics lugged a large steaming box. I assumed it was the chocolate ice cream, a rare treat for us. We brushed the sand off the picnic tables and resumed preparing for our barbecue.

The chopper crew had left Cam Ranh Bay that morning, before they had time for anything but black coffee. Anderson said they were starving as he shoved the cardboard box under a picnic table. Vapor swirled around it while the hotdogs and hamburgers sizzled on the grill. Thick white smoke rose from the grill.

It had been left to get too hot while we waited for the helicopter to arrive.

Two hospital corpsmen cursed as they sprayed water on the grill to attempt to control the overheated coals, while the rest of us sat at the picnic tables to get acquainted with our guests.

"Hey, where are the &##*^ shrimp?" The major moaned. "That may be the only food edible by the looks of things!"

"Coming right up, sir," yelled a corpsman who left the table and headed inside.

I sat next to a tall, chatty, youthful three-striper medic from Little Rock, his handsome face tanned and weathered by the sun.

"Hi, I'm Michael D. Stoneworth, Jr.," he said with a Southern drawl. "My friends call me Mikey. Michael seems too formal around here." He reached for my hand.

I introduced myself, and we chatted for a few minutes. Mikey had reenlisted for a second tour, not unusual for medics.

"Yep, just ninety days left and I'm out of here. Actually going home." He smiled.

He had a fiancée, Rebecca, and wrote to her daily. He spoke about his goal of attending nursing school in Arkansas where he had already been accepted. He was too shy to mention he was the birthday boy Captain Anderson spoke about.

~

We sat looking toward the smoking barbecue drum when —

Crackle. "Dusty forty-three, can you read?" a voice blasted out.

Captain Anderson grabbed his phone, "Forty-three here. Over."

"Forty-three, we just received a mayday from two soldiers injured in a Jeep accident about ten clicks northwest of your position." The voice barked coordinates. "Can you respond? Over."

"Can do. We're shut down now but can be there in fifteen minutes. Over."

"Roger. Report as soon as you arrive."

"Roger. Out," Anderson shouted.

His crew jumped up, grabbed their jackets and raced toward

92

the aircraft.

We heard Captain Anderson and his copilot quickly go through their preflight as we left the patio once again for the safety of the dispensary. The helo's rotors started slowly, but sand soon began flying everywhere.

Sergeant Mikey stood in the opening and sent us a MASH-type salute as they took flight and rotated to leave. In a minute we were outside again surveying the mess. The hot dogs and burgers were scorched — inedible.

"We likely won't be seeing those boys again," Nelson said. "I guess it's time for the shrimp. Nothing around this goddamned place ever works as planned."

We brought out the rest of the beer, soda, and chips and grabbed plates of shrimp.

A medic who considered himself a gourmet produced a cocktail sauce with ketchup and pepper.

We got to talking about *our* birthday boys again and what plans they had made to celebrate the day, really a joke since nothing was going on. One of the sergeants came up with ridiculous suggestions for us to go surfing or to join a safari which brought us all to laughter.

Major Nelson showed us pictures of the hotel he would be staying at in Waikiki and spoke about how he had arranged to fly out of Saigon.

Crackle. "Tuy Hoa Hospital?"

Nelson grabbed his phone. "This is Tuy Hoa. Over."

"Dusty forty-three. Two seriously wounded. ETA nine minutes."

Crackle.

[Unintelligible].

We were surprised that they were bringing two Army grunts to an Air Force hospital. We quickly got into emergency mode.

"All right," Nelson shouted. "It's time for you feather merchants [visitors] to leave and leave now. We've got work to do."

We put two stretchers into the hallway and turned on lights and operating room equipment. We opened trauma kits and positioned them next to the operating tables. Nelson split us into two groups. Corpsmen pulled plasma bottles from the closet. X-ray techs checked the developing fluids and loaded cassettes. We were able to muster about fifteen medical personnel. Since we continually trained for emergencies, we were prepared.

93

There was nothing to be done now but to stay inside until needed. In the military, you can spend a lot of time waiting, thinking. It's nothing like the movies. You get to conjure every conceivable outcome, knowing nothing is certain.

We assembled in that same hallway by the glass doors, standing nearly motionless, but for our breathing and an occasional whisper or cough. I could feel my heart pounding, my jaw tightening. It would be only minutes before we would be called to maybe save a life. I wondered how we would perform. Certainly, it could be our ultimate challenge.

I tried to focus on the positives I could see, willing hands, good equipment, great doctors. In a few minutes we could see the familiar blip of a helicopter slowly growing.

This chopper flew erratically, trailing black smoke.

Crackle. "Tuy Hoa?"

"Tuy Hoa here!" Nelson replied from the patio.

"Tuy Hoa, prepare for possible emergency landing. Will attempt to put down behind the hospital. Fire on board. Two wounded. One nonresponsive. ETA one minute. Out."

I could now clearly see smoke pouring out the tail.

Nelson came inside and grabbed the base telephone.

"Fire Suppression! This is Major Nelson at the hospital helipad. Need immediate assistance. Incoming chopper landing in less than one minute with onboard fire. Do you copy?"

"Roger, Hospital. This is Fire. We will be on site in three minutes. Stay away so we can get in."

Crackle. "Tuy Hoa, this is Captain Anderson. Do you read me?"

"Ten four, Captain. You're almost home!"

As the bird approached the field behind the hospital, I saw that Captain Anderson had to fly nearly sideways at times to control his craft. He made a wide circle around the hospital. That's when I noticed a gaping hole in the tail section. The Huey landed hard in the dirt about 200 feet from the hospital, sending up a great cloud of smoke and grit.

When the aircraft hit, I heard a loud groaning of metal bending against its will.

The tail section had smashed into the ground, but the landing struts did their job. A pair of legs hung from the open doorway.

I saw the fire trucks, sirens wailing, lights twirling, several blocks away.

"Screw Fire," Major Nelson shouted. "Let's get 'em in."

We threw open the glass doors of the hospital and ran toward the burning helicopter as the rotor blades slowed. Our peaceful day of celebration had turned into a chaotic nightmare. I paid little attention to the fire trucks racing to us. We had never practiced for a fire rescue.

Sergeant Mikey, unconscious on the floor of the chopper, was handed down and placed on a stretcher.

Nelson remained on the ground. Another flight surgeon jumped into the aircraft to help shift the copilot onto a stretcher.

Before we could transport the men, white sticky foam soaked us and the helicopter. The helo morphed into a giant dripping metal grasshopper. Captain Anderson and the second flight surgeon emerged from the site looking as though they had fallen into a vat of shaving cream.

"Move, move, move," Major Nelson barked. "Let's get them triaged."

Once inside the surgery unit, corpsmen handed us towels and helped us out of our soaked clothes and into scrub tops. All the while Nelson pulled more equipment closer for us to use. We either worked with the major or talked to him daily, but never saw him like this. He took control, giving our group confidence to handle an unusual trauma case, rare for our tiny Air Force hospital. I felt tense, but upbeat, thinking somehow everything would turn out okay.

Nelson assigned six corpsmen and one flight surgeon to care for the copilot. Eight corpsmen, one female nurse, and I would stay with Sergeant Mikey. The major would assume responsibility there. Only a thin white curtain separated the two operating rooms.

Major Nelson barked orders. "Vitals! Start saline IV. Hook up cardiac monitor."

I helped cut off Mikey's clothes and remove his boots, leaving only his dog tags, underpants, and socks. A corpsman wrapped a blood pressure cuff around his upper left arm.

We affixed EKG leads to his chest and legs. Almost immediately stats came in. "No blood pressure."

Nelson yelled, "Faint pulse, respiration zero. Start CPR! Ready epinephrine. Bag him."

Sticky blood filled Mikey's mouth. It appeared he had bitten his tongue. I wiped it clean and placed an *S* tube to open his airway. He offered no resistance.

At the same time, medical technicians looked for signs of

injuries and reported them aloud as they uncovered them: "Bullet wound to neck, no exit wound, bullet wounds to both legs, bullet wound through lower back and exiting through upper abdomen, no bleeding of consequence." The head nurse mechanically repeated these findings every couple of minutes, as though none of us had already heard them.

"Corpsman," Nelson bellowed, "another unit of blood and two more of plasma, quick!"

Meanwhile, on the other side of the curtain, just feet from where I stood, I could hear corpsmen talking to the copilot who wanted a cigarette.

"Flesh wound to upper left arm with through and through," the surgeon said. "Gunshot wound to upper left pelvis area. No exit wound visible. Blood pressure 112 over 60 and falling; profuse hemorrhaging from left hip; large hematoma and contusion mid scapula. Probable internal bleeding. Start an IV and get him to x-ray to see where the hell the bullets are."

Seconds later, the curtain separating us bulged towards us as they rolled the copilot into the hallway and to x-ray. Later the flight surgeon announced the grim news. "Splintered pelvis will need immediate opening and debridement of the wound. Let's get that goddamned bleeder!"

Within minutes the copilot had been returned and I could hear the anesthesia machine hissing and the clicking of instruments indicating the operation was underway.

Later, I heard the flight surgeon. "Let the record show that a pin and two screws were placed, major bullet fragments located and removed. Clean him up and dress the wounds. He's one lucky hombre. Tell Captain Anderson we think he's going to make it."

In our surgery we worked to get Mikey's body to react. His heart was not responding to our CPR efforts, neither to the epinephrine nor several rounds of the defibrillator. He had shown some slight signs of life in the beginning, but our final efforts would have to be extraordinary if we were to be successful. By now a dozen of us hovered over him, each in turn trying to get him to respond.

Chaplain Don Davis had been called to the crowded surgery. His nickname was Mr. Optimistic. Davis, an ex-football lineman, never displayed a negative attitude, even when he faced personal tragedy. He'd just say, "I'm going to let Jesus carry this one."

Davis had one more request that day. He came to the head of Mikey's table, gripped both sides of it, leaned way over, and spoke softly into Mikey's ear. "Michael, take a breath. Michael, please take a breath. You can do it, son. Michael, open your eyes. We need you to open your eyes. You're doing great, young man."

We paused for a moment hoping maybe Davis could do what we weren't able to.

Major Nelson wanted to attempt one last procedure to help Mikey. He would massage Mikey's heart trying to stimulate it to beat. Nelson grasped a large surgical knife. With two cuts he incised a ten-inch opening just below the rib cage. I stood at the table a couple of feet away, unable to divert my eyes, barely able to breathe.

Nelson pushed his hand well past his wrist, into the chest cavity.

I looked in disbelief.

One of the nurses couldn't contain her emotions any longer. She quietly left the table and walked a few feet into the hallway, leaned against the wall and slid down to the floor.

She had likely concluded Mikey was gone.

Five minutes later, at 2:15 p.m., Major Nelson straightened, looked around the room, and noted the time.

"That's it," Nelson said. "It's over. Let's close and prepare the body for transport."

He bent over Mikey, squeezed his shoulder. "Sorry, pal. We did our best."

Nelson turned, stripped off his gloves and mask, threw them into the trash, and walked out as though no one else were in the room.

The fight for Mikey's life had taken under an hour. The whole afternoon left me shaken and in denial. In less than two hours we went from a lazy Sunday of celebration to a reminder of what this war was about for many thousands.

There would soon be tears and hugs and bloodied instruments thrown with a clank into the sink. Several corpsmen went out to smoke. Others, blood-splashed, hung around in the hall in no hurry to clean themselves up. Time slowed. Minutes and seconds were no longer precious. Our battle, our hero, had been lost.

Chaplain Davis, smoking cigarettes outside with some of the corpsmen, waited around for an hour. He kept telling us how proud he was of us and that Sergeant Mikey got the best care possible. His words were of little consolation. We knew we failed. Three cruddy dime-sized chunks of metal took the life of one of us whose only purpose nine thousand miles from his home was to save lives.

Mikey's body lay on the now-darkened table just a few feet from me. Words were beyond most of us. So, we moved to the next phase of cleaning up as if on automatic pilot.

At the same time, barely twelve feet away, yet in another world, I knew that the upbeat corpsmen, some still unaware of the final events next door, smiled as the copilot's blood pressure returned to normal with the help of a saline drip and a transfusion. The surgery had proceeded as hoped. Their patient would soon be in his hospital bed.

Nelson left to go to his tiny office. He would have four hours of paperwork to complete. We heard him slowly pecking away on his manual typewriter as he filled out the necessary forms in triplicate detailing Mikey's last hour.

I helped put Mikey's clothes, keys, and wallet — with pictures of his family and his beloved fiancée — into a heavy cardboard box, unhooked his short tag, and sent it to Nelson. I placed the other one in his mouth, following protocol, and looped the chain around his neck.

By the time I was ready to leave, we had washed his body, combed his hair, and covered him to his shoulders with a green hospital sheet. He looked peaceful, almost angelic. The lines on his face eased, his youthful appearance again recognizable. As we prepared to leave, we said our goodbyes in our own way — some out loud, some silently. All I could think of was, *you'll soon be home with those who love you the most.*

I was pretty sure he would have liked to hear that.

Sergeant Michael D. Stoneworth, Jr.'s personal articles would be logged and placed into a lockable box to be returned to his family.

Early the next morning, a team from Cam Ranh Bay arrived to strip the chopper of any usable equipment, finishing by early afternoon. A dump truck carried the burned-out remnants of the tail section to the scrap yard. A large crane carted off the shrapnel-ridden remainder of the aircraft. Forty-three would never save another life.

Afterward, a dozen men raked the dirt and picked up any fragments from the aircraft. When they finished, I could see little evidence of the crash from the day before. I heard someone had taken the box containing the chocolate ice cream and placed it into the hospital freezer. Monday evening, a transportation detachment came for Mikey. His remains would be back in the US by Tuesday evening and at his home for interment on Thursday, the day Major Nelson was to leave for R&R.

That same night, Captain Anderson met us outside Nelson's office to tell us what happened.

"We flew into a Viet Cong trap," Anderson said. "Somehow they acquired a mobile phone and called in an emergency. They staged a Jeep accident with cadavers dressed in US uniforms. We circled the burning Jeep. It looked serious, so we went in quickly, which was a mistake. As we landed, Mikey jumped out and was shot. My copilot ran to him and carried him back to the bird. They had us surrounded.

"Then a gook threw a grenade at the chopper, lifting it off the left skid, leaving us with a hydraulic leak and a massive hole in the tail. We couldn't hear. It was a nightmare. I had no way to even know if you heard our mayday."

Anderson and his remaining corpsman left Tuesday, catching a flight with another Dusty.

Wednesday afternoon, Nelson requested all of us who were on duty the preceding Sunday to come to his office at 1900 hours. He wanted to thank us for our efforts, which, he said, "were beyond anything" he had seen in twenty years being a doctor. He spoke softly. His voice cracked more than once, forcing him to stop. He said he wanted to read a teletype from the copilot recuperating at Cam Ranh Bay, also thanking us for all we had done and to add something about Mikey.

They discovered that in dying, Mikey saved the copilot. Doctors at the hospital in Cam Ranh had discovered that the hematoma and contusion the copilot suffered were from a bullet that passed through Mikey's chest, and ricocheted under the copilot's flak jacket, ending in the skin between his shoulder blades. This occurred while he carried Mikey back to the helicopter. If not for Mikey, he too would have suffered a mortal wound.

Major Nelson then turned the meeting over to Chaplain Davis to say a few words to help us deal with the tragedy. He offered a prayer of thanks for Mikey's life and all the folks who put their lives on the line every day. Then he asked for a minute of silence.

Nelson followed with a statement to read. Through the base commander's office, they had been in touch with Mikey's parents, telling them that Mikey died a true hero. They said they were glad Mikey was with friends when he died. By the time the reading ended, I found myself biting my lip.

When the mess cooks heard that Mikey's crew brought chocolate ice cream as a gift, they prepared a memorial cake with a Dusty helicopter 43 depicted on top to be served with the chocolate ice cream that Mikey helped deliver. Some of us started to walk out.

"Not so fast, people," Nelson said. "This is our way to honor Sergeant Stoneworth, even knowing him as briefly as we did. I think this is what he would have wanted."

We shared the cake and ice cream.

~

Epilogue: America's Loss

The Vietnam War was the longest armed conflict we had ever endured. We lost nearly 60,000 Americans. Five times as many were severely injured. Our military involvement began in 1962 and ended in 1973. During that time, the Huey (helicopter) crews served our forces in many capacities. The Dustys, short for dust offs as they were affectionately called, were marked with a big red cross on the nose. Crews helped to transport thousands of wounded and evacuated untold others from harm's way. Many insiders have verified that Dusty crews were in battlefield conditions every day of flying, carried little armor, and only light arms for protection.

Many crews flew three or more sorties daily. Few Americans, then or now, understood the degree of danger they faced. The attrition rate was high, but it never deterred them from flying. Sergeant Mikey was in good company — a compassionate group of skilled, courageous young men who repeatedly flew into danger to help their fellow soldiers.

100

Lost Love

Olga Singer

I yearn to write, and words fail me. I have stories to share, and the flow of storytelling evades me. My patience is running thin — what to do? I release the need to write, and yet it continues to nag at me — how do I respond?

I am sitting in the beauty of Puerto Vallarta, Mexico. My eyes wander outside to the magnificent view where ocean meets sky.

The days here are long, and yet, they are passing rather quickly — too quickly. I want to make time stop, hold it still, rewind it, and follow the sun as it rises once again to greet the day, gently tapping the leaves and waking the birds. I want to sit in the cool breeze of the setting sun and watch the crescent moon slowly appear in the indigo sky above.

I close my eyes. I can feel him sitting close to me and lightly brushing my arm with his fingers. My mind is playing tricks on me. I am sure my senses are heightened, and I can breathe in his smoky scent. The one I fell in love with. Why did he have to leave? He never got to experience this special place. He was tied to a job he seemed to love more than he loved me.

I guess you could say his arms are the only other place I ever felt truly at home. There are times, like when I come here to Puerto Vallarta, where I can reach out and bring him to me. Feel his strong arms wrapping themselves around my shoulders and hear his throaty laugh as he nestles his face in the crook of my neck. And then, just like that, the spell is broken, and he is gone.

This is my third night here, and the crescent moon is once again high above, calling to me. Easier to see him here in the almost black of night than it is to brush him away. I want to feel him here beside me in the quiet, mixed in with the sounds of the night jungle. He is far away now, somewhere I can never reach him. And yet, he is as close as my heart will allow him to be. *Why did you leave me so many years ago?* I whisper to the breeze, knowing the answer will never come.

Broken Dreams

Diana Avery Amsden

I opened the box on my closet floor,

Found the dark green velvet I bought in Boston sixty years ago,

Planning to make a dress to appeal to you,

A pink silk rose nestled in the sweetheart neckline.

Inspired by Manet's painting of a girl behind the bar at the Folies

Bergère.

I stood on a busy street corner,

Bereft to see how many people were not you.

The happiest hours of my life were spent in your presence,

Listening to you speak, watching you move,

Like a sunflower following the sun.

In the bottom of the box,

A package never opened:

The iconic J. Peterman duster

I bought decades ago for you,

A romantic outdoorsman, gentleman, and scholar.

When you were alive,

Wherever you were,

I felt an invisible magnetic cord connecting us,

Abdomen to abdomen.

I no longer sense it —

Yet — life is like electricity, a form of energy —

Convertible with matter ($E=MC^2$) —

And matter can be neither created nor destroyed —

You are *somewhere* — *WHERE* are you?

You are still more important to me than anything else!

I sense a void in this lonely world,

This barren sunless world,

A void that would have been filled by the child

You and I should have conceived.

My womanhood was wasted, my life's purpose left undone.

Was it too late when we met?

I lay the coat back in the box,

Lay the fabric on top,

Mementos of what never happened,

Mementos of broken dreams.

And Then They Were Gone

Marcia Buompensiero

As told to me by Joe Zottolo Bonpensiero

There were only three men who really knew what happened aboard the *Calabria* that day in January 1939, five days after the *Calabria* and her crew of six sailed from San Diego Bay, past Point Loma, and headed south to fish Mexican waters. Marco Zottolo was the Captain of the *Calabria,* and Leonard Torre and Carlo Gimanco were two of his crewmen.

~

Marco Zottolo hailed from Mazara Del Vallo, Sicily, by way of St. Louis, Missouri. Lack of an ocean in St. Louis was most likely the cause for the family's move to San Diego, California.

The Zottolos were a close-knit happy family. Marco and his wife, Marianne, had four sons and two daughters. Their lives were simple. They would gather around the kitchen table, tell stories, sing songs, and drink a little *Vino da Tavola* (table wine). The women tended the house, while the men went down to the sea to fish to support the family. They were old-school Sicilian-Greek fishermen with saltwater running through their veins.

In 1939, the nation, like a sick dog, bowed its head and whimpered in distress. The national unemployment was 19 percent with jobs almost nonexistent and tough to find. The government was trying to avert another depression looming on the horizon. A new federal wage bill was passed with a surprising minimum wage of 25 cents per hour. Marco would say of the times, "You couldn't live on minimum wage, but it's a start."

Marco and his family of nine had a modest three-bedroom home on State Street, in the Italian ghetto area of San Diego known as Little Italy. It was a few blocks up from the waterfront and where the majority of local Italians and Sicilians lived.

Luckily, a large family gave the Zottolo's an economic edge as they worked and saved together. After Marianne met an untimely death, the result of a virus, the family struggled on with her memory uppermost in their minds. Working for the common good was their custom, and they pooled their money to buy a fishing boat. The vessel they bought was named the *Calabria,* after a small town at the "toe" of Italy that faced Sicily. The *Calabria* was a solid economic bond, which could see them through the tough times and feed the family. As a man whose life was built on positive values and happy family, Marco only thought of a future filled with hope. Even after Marianne's death, he was not one to delve into life's dark side.

One late January morning, Mary, Marco's eldest daughter, scurried about the kitchen as she did each morning, preparing a simple Sicilian breakfast of toast and café latte for her father and her husband, Joe Asaro. Always appreciative of her gentle ways, her father would often say, "*Dio* has sent me you, to remind me of your mama." In turn, Mary nodded in respect, happy to please her father, joining the two at the table. The three were early risers, and it was a pleasant time of readying herself in anticipation of the hectic on-coming rush.

Soon her brothers, Dominic and Frankie, and her own children, Serafina, Marianne, Angelina, and Anthony, would descend hungrily. Joe, Marco's eldest son and my father, lived with his wife, my mom Amanda, in a nearby apartment. Every morning, he would walk to his father's house for breakfast.

That morning over their lattes, Marco said, "I've been thinking we should ready the boat to go out soon. In several days it will be February, and we have come to enjoy the beach too much. It is time to get back to work. If we leave soon, we might be lucky and bring in a good catch before the prices start to fall."

"That sounds reasonable, Papa," Joe said. "I have a son coming in May. When my brothers, the bums, get up, we'll give them the good news and they can tell their girlfriends goodbye for a while." Both men laughed.

Shortly thereafter, Vito, Dominic, and Frankie showed up at the table, still groggy.

"Good morning," Marco said. "I guess you had a bad night. Too much vino, eh? Well, not to worry. Your brother and I have decided we'll make it better for you. We leave the day after tomorrow for Baja. I'm planning for a weeklong voyage."

After breakfast, Joe told his brothers to ready the *Calabria* for the trip.

The boys iced down the hold for the provisions bought from Busy Bee Market. The plan was to be gone by ten. As a small fishing boat, about forty feet long, the *Calabria* had a crew of six: Marco; his sons, Joe, Dominic, and Frankie; and crewmen, Leonard Torre and Carlo Gimanco. They departed on schedule.

Four days passed slowly as they headed south to the fishing grounds, and, although the fishing hadn't been what they had hoped, they caught enough fish to pay expenses and for replacement provisions. But they consumed more than they had anticipated.

On day five, the weather turned foul, and Dominic, the "papered" skipper, recommended they take refuge in the normally tranquil bay of Colonet, in Baja, Mexico. They entered the bay just before dark and slept reasonably well, until winds increased, and the bay became choppy. The morning brought calmer weather.

Marco's sons wanted to go ashore for some reason. It may have been to replenish provisions, or to pick up repair materials for minor mechanical problems in need of a quick fix, or to simply barter cigarettes to the locals for lobsters. Marco wasn't keen on it. He warned his sons against going ashore in the unpredictable weather. However, the boys decided to go anyway. They dropped the skiff and headed off. With luck, determination, and Joe on the oars, they made it to land.

Ashore, they walked to the Mexican store, about a half-mile inland and up the cliffs of Colonet. After making their purchases, they headed back to the skiff and found the winds had increased with a vengeance during their short time ashore. Angry black clouds belched rain into their faces as they tramped down the path to where they had secured the skiff. Although odds of beating nature and getting back to the *Calabria* looked slim, the daring brothers were determined.

With the pride of youth, they would test nature one more time.

The shore-bought provisions were secured in the skiff, and Frankie moved to the bow, since he was the lightest. With Dominic pushing from the stern and Joe shoving from the side, the skiff rushed into the water, meeting the outgoing currents. Joe settled into the center bench, grabbed the oars, and maneuvered the skiff through the surf, then Dominic clambered aboard.

An agreeable wave flung the skiff up and into the surf like a toy boat. The sea continued to cast them about, as water squalls overcame team efforts, and Joe plied muscle and sinew to the oars. A maniacal riptide seesawed the water round the boat, as swirling waves buffeted its sides. Undercurrents, like the tentacles of an octopus, groped and tugged, pulling the skiff deeper into the tumultuous caldron of the bay. The rain continued to pelt and blind them. The three did all they could to hang on. They cursed nature's gods and bellowed at the tide. The skiff heaved and bucked like a wild mustang on the open range.

Finally, the tide shifted and moved them closer to the *Calabria*. The boys could see their father aboard the boat.

From the deck of the *Calabria*, Marco frantically yelled instructions to his sons and watched, as hope resurfaced. For a moment, he thought they would make it.

Suddenly, a malevolent wave came out of nowhere. It crashed down on the skiff's bow. Frankie was violently ejected overboard. Then, the skiff buckled, lifted again, and crashed down on the flailing boy — knocking him unconscious.

Helpless, Marco watched in horror as Frankie floated face down in the water.

Panicked, Joe and Dominic rushed forward, leaning over to grab Frankie — just as another mountainous wave slammed the skiff, casting both men overboard. They gasped for air in reaction to the cold shock of water, but the raging sea around them showed no mercy. Both men gulped enough water to fill their lungs. In those final moments, Marco watched as Joe clutched Frankie's collar in a desperate attempt to save him. He could imagine Joe's last thoughts as he floated near Dominic's drowned body must have been — *never let go . . . never . . . let . . . go.*

Marco's frantic yells stopped as he took in the horror of his drowned sons. Tears stung his eyes; rage filled his heart. His boys never had a chance.

~

The next day, the Mexican and US Coast Guard found Dominic floating near the overturned skiff; Joe had washed up on the shore about six miles down the beach.

On February 7, 1939, the *Calabria* chugged into San Diego Bay with her flag at half-mast. On the ice below were two of Marco Zottolo's sons — Joe and Dominic. Frankie was never found.

I was born in May that year, the only remnant of Marco's eldest boy. Marco was able to bounce me on his knee and carry me to the wharf on the bay, but he was never the same. He wore black as he openly grieved. Two years later, he died. Some say, he didn't have the will to live and died of a broken heart.

~

On a grassy knoll, at Holy Cross Cemetery in San Diego, stands a monument to three young fishermen. Two of them were my uncles. One was my father. When I find myself in a quandary over life's challenges, and I think that the options appear too bitter to bear, I weigh those challenges against those my grandfather endured and gain perspective.

This is the story that Marco, my grandfather, told his family and friends. It was passed down to me. As one of the few remaining grandsons of Marco and the only son of Joe Zottolo, I often reflect on this tale of loss.
—Joe Zottolo Bonpensiero

NOTES

— **Joe Zottolo Bonpensiero**, Lt. Col/USAF Ret. and former member of the SDWEG, passed away in 2017. This is one of the many stories he told about his fishing family and their life on the seas. His published works: *Niputi* (about his notorious Mafia uncle), *Chocolate Moon* (more stories about his early fishing days); and *Dinner in Happy Valley* (hair-raising tales of his tour of duty in Vietnam) are still selling regularly.

— About the different spellings of the family surname: "Bonpensiero" was the ancestral name first recorded in the official municipal records in Santa Flavia, a province of Palermo, Sicily and county seat for the region. Over time, generations of hand-written notations in the old Sicilian language on birth records by midwives resulted in two different spellings: BOMpensiero and BUOMpensiero." The errors were never corrected.

Bracing for Change

Olga Singer

January 2017 was quickly approaching. And now, here she stood, once again, bracing for the change. Every four years, she has to adjust to someone new or, sometimes, continue on with the same. It's been this way for as long as she can remember.

As 2016 came to a close, she found herself saddened and scared for her future. The last eight years had been blessed with hope. Hope and anticipation for change, for acceptance of a new, better way of living life. But that was eight years ago. There was so much to look forward to back then. Hope, excitement, and good — really good — things could be felt in every corner of her world.

As the landscape of her inner world changed and the push and pull of her light and dark side fought for attention, she soon found herself getting lost. And it happened ever so slowly. Too slowly for her to notice it happening until it was too late, and she was truly lost. Her radiance had been dimmed.

Someone new was about to take his place beside her. He, with his crass words, his blown-up ego, and his constant tweets, was about to take her hand and lead her through the next four years of . . . *what*? She isn't sure. She is convinced it will be a disaster. He is a leader like no other she has ever seen.

She is made up of many colors. On any given day, she can be found wrapping her arms around the many immigrants landing on her shores seeking a better life in her protective embrace.

On other days, the falling rain, the harsh climate of her waters, the rough terrain of her land can pound the life out of her many inhabitants.

On bright days when the warmth of the sun shines, her people can be found frolicking on the beaches or in parks sprinkled throughout her beautiful land.

Now, on the cusp of 2017, she sits and waits as the new someone, the someone many don't support, takes the seat most important in her world, to guide her through the next four years.

111

She would rather have a woman, one with compassion — not afraid to show vulnerability and emotion — taking her by the hand and leading her through true change. But alas, that is not to be. Her world is not quite ready for that . . . but it's coming, she can feel it. It's coming.

With her eyes to the heavens and her feet firmly planted on the earth, she stands tall. She is the voice of her forefathers and all the men and women who have come before her.

She is America!

All Is Not Lost ... Yet

Janice Coy

An agitated rattlesnake appeared one spring morning in

the bicycle path gutter,

trapped between the freeway and the dirt hills, scraped of cover

for

the construction of million-dollar homes.

A fat diamondback ready to strike at

the calves of unsuspecting cyclists, like us.

Another rider tried to warn us as

we drew near the reptile, but

he was gone before we understood his wild gestures, his shouted

words

were muddled by the wind.

Round a corner, we saw the snake squirming

angry on the cement and bits of gravel like

someone who doesn't understand why life

changes or how fears can drive you mad.

We stopped by the fence, a strip of woven wires meant to protect

us from

the traffic hurtling by on the other side.

We felt safe there, believing

we were beyond the reach of the creature's poison.

We took pictures and then we rode on, complacent,

thinking the snake had nothing to do

with us. But

we were wrong.

The embittered serpent slithered down our street and

settled in our neighborhood.

We unearthed the shovel we last saw rusting in

the garage; now, we're watching for

our chance to sever the

snake's head.

Found

Beijing Moonlight

Michael J. McMahon

It had been a long day and darkness was descending. With the last of the seedlings in the shallow water of the paddy field, Li Xiu Ying straightened up and massaged the ache and tiredness in her lower back. She had not eaten since her brother Liu Wei had brought her a meal of rice and vegetables at noon and hunger pangs were beginning to sound from her swollen belly. But the pangs did not get in the way of the pride she felt in the work she had done. She had always been a strong girl, well respected for the amount of work she could get through in a day, whether planting or harvesting. Even with the child kicking and announcing its presence throughout, she could do the work of several of the other women in the village. They all knew it too and reluctantly said so. Yes, they all admitted that Li Xiu Ying was head and shoulders above them all.

Now, as she looked down from the heights of the soaking fields, she could see the city in the distance, baking in the yellow smog with only the occasional hint of a structure peeking through. She had been there only twice in her short life and found it unappealing. The people pushed and shoved and rode their bicycles straight at her or forced the exhaust of their Honda bikes down her throat. No, it wasn't for her. If the fields weren't as free as they had been, she at least had room to move in the still clear air.

Liu Wei sat cross-legged before the wok on the fire in the middle of the packed earthen floor. Anticipation prompted him to begin preparations for the evening meal. Anticipation, like an inner clock, needs schooling, and the movement of the sun and moon. He had left the work in the paddy field to return and make ready. As she entered, the bamboo framed hut that was their home, though open to the elements, smelled strongly of garlic and onions. He had added both to the oil in the wok and was stirring with a metal soup ladle, sautéing them lightly before adding the red pepper, celery and ginger. The steamed bream, a gift their aunt Li Jing had brought earlier in the day, lay on a platter beside the fire to keep warm.

Li Xiu Ying loved his cooking. He was better at it than anything else he did. She didn't mind if he left the planting early to return and prepare their food. It was the great joy in their life. They could do without all luxuries but not without their food. Most of what they earned was spent on it. She had wondered if the emotion that made him angry all the time was the same one that made him such a good cook. There was never an answer to this. Probably because there were too many other unanswered questions.

"Is it finished?" he asked. When she had replied that it was done, he shook the vegetables in the wok and said, "Good."

She watched him finish the meal off with a flurry by pouring scalding cooking oil and soy over the fish to make it crisp up. The crackle made her even more hungry. She could already taste the skin. It was her favorite part of the fish. On this day of all days, when the planting was done and Li Jing had brought it to honor the time-old tradition.

It was not easily come by, involving a lengthy walk for the woman, all the way early in the morning to the fishing village of Huailai to the east. But Li Jing had the good blood in abundance and trial-some though the trip might be, she put her nose to the wind and got on with it. It did not pay to grumble, it got in the way of so much else.

And there were other things to grumble about. Things like the incident in the mine in Shanxi province that had taken the lives of her husband and brother, the father of Li Xiu Ying and Liu Wei. She had loved both dearly. She could overlook their foibles and in-discrepancies and see only the good in them. For they were good men who wanted only the best for all those around them. Wasn't that why they had gone to Shanxi to work in the mine in the first place? To earn the money so they might build proper homes for them all? Homes with maybe a stove fueled by gas and electricity to light the night. Homes built of concrete to ward off the cold or cool the hot summer sun. With a courtyard at the front and a line to hang the dripping clothes from.

But all that was lost now. Like so much else. The men had succumbed when the meager bracing collapsed under the weight of ten thousand tons of coal. They and twenty-two others. Pushed to their limits below the unforgiving, suffocating dense clumps of the black mineral that had taken a million years to compose and

118

only seconds to take their lives away. And with their lives was gone the dream of a home like those owned by the coal moguls in the city. Homes built of indestructible concrete blocks and paid for with the money saved from bracing unfit to hold up even the smallest of collapses.

Yes, it was all gone now. Never to return. Leaving them only the small comforts. The comfort found in the piece of fish crackling on the platter, savoring the deliciousness of the skin. And if that was all there was to savor, so be it.

There was nothing to be savored from Liu Wei's anger. It had festered since the day he had gone to the city with Li Jing to see if it was possible to retrieve the bodies of the men from the depths of the mine. But, of course, it was not possible. To find them under the mass of solid decomposition was asking for a miracle, and the mine owners did not believe in miracles. They believed in common sense and the Yuan currency. This they only believed in. This and the uninterrupted production of the black diamond dug out from deep in the earth. So, a new seam would be dug, the twenty-four committed to their grave, soon to be forgotten by all but those who loved them.

They had left the sixteen-year-old Li Xiu Ying alone while on their endeavors in the city. She too had taken the news hard as well she might. Her father had doted on her, calling her age-old affectionate terms like "his little orchid." For truly she was an orchid. Young men eyed her. Older men too, but they were living in the past if they thought themselves to be contenders in the contest to embrace the orchid in a loving way. In the full bloom of her youth, Li Xiu Ying enjoyed the admiration. And if Liu Wei felt resentment, he did not show it. She was his only sibling and he understood. He understood his own value to the household because that was a value of heritage. Li Xiu Ying would have been married off and the head of the new household at the side of the hill with a sturdy house and courtyard built from the efforts of their father in the mines. But none of this was to be.

He watched her devour the fish and vegetables, picking the skin and flesh from the fish on the platter with her chopsticks while piling vegetables into one of the small decorative bowls from a set they'd had in the family for as long as anyone could remember. Li Jing said she thought the collection had belonged to their grandmother, but she wasn't sure, and Liu Wei didn't care who they'd belonged to just so long as they lasted because he didn't want to go to the expense of replacing them.

119

And as he watched her with her swollen belly he cared even less about the bowls and their origin. So what if they ended up in pieces? That swelling would cost more than it would to replace a few broken bits of porcelain. She had really done it. No sooner had she been left alone than she had gone and lain with someone whose name she would not divulge to him. No matter how hard he pushed her, all she would say was he had brought sweet won tons with bananas and almonds and cinnamon and they had lain on the packed floor and she wasn't even sure what had happened. Was that all she had to say? Yes, that was all she had to say, and now could he please leave her alone.

When she finished her meal, fatigue began to come over her. She got up from the floor and made her way to her makeshift bed behind the curtain. It did not shut him out completely, but it was better than being under his angry glare all the time. She lay down on the hard wooden surface and pulled her blanket close. There were stirrings within her. Uncomfortable stirrings and sharp pains. A few here, a few there. Feelings of fright began to enter her mind.

The closest she had come to witnessing a birth was the day Wang Yong called to her to come and assist him while he birthed his water buffalo in the pen at the back of his own bamboo hut. He hadn't really wanted assistance. He had done it many times before with his own and other people's animals, but he said he always liked company on these occasions, and she was the only one about. She watched with curiosity and fascination as he helped the buffalo ease the newborn into the world by pulling on its legs with a piece of rope, only to see it plop out in what seemed like an elongated bubble onto the dried leaves he had used as bedding. It had all seemed so easy. The mother appeared not in the least exhausted despite her ordeal. This was the same water buffalo Liu Wei had used year after year to pull the plow prior to the planting. She was old now and chances were, she would not last too much longer.

But who knew? Who knew anything anymore? There were no certainties. When her father and uncle had left to work in the mines in Shanxi province everything had seemed so certain. They would return with wealth in their pockets and all would be well. Now, there were no certainties left. Only the cruel bitter taste of a new life emerging into a very uncertain world. Li Xiu Ying was glad when sleep overcame her.

120

Today would bring a modicum of peace and rest, what with the planting completed. The sun shone through the open gaps in the bamboo and sent a warmth across her. She had woken with fright on realizing its presence, and this persisted for a few moments. Her customary early rise had sent her mind into mild confusion. Shouldn't she be "up and doing" as her father used to say? It was, after all, another working day and there was usually no respite from it.

Outside she could hear the muffled voices of Liu Wei and Li Jing. It was a morning voice. The sound, whether muffled or loud, that had a beginning to it. It was recognizable as a morning sound that seemed to carry into eternity. Fear again came over her. What could they be discussing? She lay still on the hardness of her makeshift bed and strained to hear. But even the lightness of the morning sound failed to reach her ears. She waited until she heard what she was sure were the footsteps of Li Jing retreating to her hut before attempting to rise.

It was a heavy and laborious rise, made all the more so by the movement in her belly. When she got to her feet and pulled the curtain back, Liu Wei had entered and seated himself as always, cross-legged before the minimal fire and the wok. He had a bowl in his hands and was throwing the contents into the pan.

"There will be no work for you today. Li Jing says you must rest. She brought you a milk pudding."

She was grateful for the news. Her body was still in recovery from the arduous task of completing the planting the day before, and the idea of a day's rest was appealing. She retired to the back of the hut, down to the pit, a deep hole in the ground lined with rocks, dug by and shared by all. It helped to relieve the pressure on her belly a little. When she returned Liu Wei had placed the one chair they had in close proximity to the cooking. It was a good chair. Better than anyone else's. Their father had procured it from somewhere, but he never said where. "I came across it," he had said. They all agreed it should be left at that. She sat in comfort before the fire and watched as he heated the pudding, stirring gently.

How lucky she was to have Li Jing in her life. The woman had sacrificed so much since the men had departed. She brought food out as if from a magic cauldron in ancient times when the people broke their backs in the fields with not a tool or water buffalo in sight, or so the stories went. The luscious smell of the cardamom and her favored cinnamon had already begun to fill her nostrils.

121

Liu Wei ladled the entire hot contents back into the bowl and bade her eat. There were carrots and nuts and fruit in the milk, and it tasted so rich.

She wondered had Li Jing finagled the milk and cream from Wang Dong and his buffalo. She could see it now. The woman standing before the belligerent man and telling him not to be so cheap with his possessions and to learn how to share. He, arguing his own case by telling her she was an interfering old cow with a worse temper than any water buffalo he'd ever had and to get away from him. But Li Jing was always relentless. It had been her survival tool, and she never let go. She got the milk and cream to make the pudding, and Li Xiu Ying devoured it. When she finished her meal, Liu Wei said he must return the bowl to Li Jing, and he had other things to attend to. He did not specify what those other things were. His thoughts were not made of milk and cream, fit to be shared.

He left her in the comfort of the chair and the birds chirping. The happiness of the birds. Where did they get it from? If she had envied anything in her life it was the sound of the nightingale. To hear it sing unseen, its song echoing across the sky. She had found one while still a child walking the road to Taipan with her mother and father. It was fluttering helplessly on the dirt path. She had picked it up and asked her mother what they could do to help it. Her mother had told her it was nearing its end of days and to place it in the bushes by the side of the road so it might expire in peace. She stroked its orange and yellow chest and placed it among the foliage. It would always be there for her; her mother had said. To help her when times were too hard. She must open her heart to it, and it would come.

Was it a lie? Was it something her mother had said to quell her own fears? Was she paving the way for the day when she herself would not be there for Li Xiu Ying? Time would tell, and there was not so much of it at that. Her mother had succumbed to the tuberculosis quicker than even she could have imagined. They had left it too late to make the journey into the clinic and the help she needed. By then the poison in her lungs had rendered her terminal. Others were struck down too by the infectious disease but had gotten to it in time from seeing the plight of her mother, the sacrificial lamb dressed in herbs and ancient remedies. The herbalist at the clinic had said she may have gotten it from drinking tainted buffalo milk, but it was only a guess. Some things are all guesswork he had said, and things are what the heavens

122

deem them to be. His guesswork did not extend to the taint in the air she breathed when an infected old man in Taipan happened to cough next to her. Now her mother had joined the nightingale and its sweet song of love and freedom.

It was evening before Liu Wei returned. He seemed all of a fuddle and ill at ease with himself, rummaging here and there, pacing about the hut that presented little opportunity to rummage and pace about. He filled the gaps between the bamboo sticks with leaves and trampled the already packed earth with his feet. He set and reset the kindling beneath the wok for what seemed the hundredth time, ensuring that not a twig was out of place. Observing him, she lost track of the amount of time he spent in these activities, but time mattered nothing when the contractions started.

~

She wished for some relief from the harshness of the boards beneath her but there was none to be had. Her head was in the lap of Li Jing, and it offered some comfort at least. Wang Yong's wife had come to assist. She'd had no children of her own, but she too had seen the buffalo birthing and felt she knew the procedure well enough to take control even if there was little to take control of. Li Xiu Ying responded to the odd encouragement in the classic expectancy of the peasantry. To bear with it in silence. This she had been told by a wizened woman from the lower end of the valley whose ministration was more of a superior scolding than a gentle voice of understanding. But Li Xiu Ying had taken it to heart and resolved to heed the woman's stern behests. She let out no cries. In the same way as she had observed the silent buffalo, she committed herself to her own torturous experience until a girl child appeared, crying its way into the stillness of the night.

Liu Wei stood outside the hut and heard the plaintive cry. It pierced his ears. He entered in time to see Wang Fong's wife cut the umbilical cord and wrap the infant in calico cloth. She handed the child into his terrified hands. Li Xiu Ying caught his wild and defiant eyes in her own for only the briefest of moments. He gripped the calico parcel, and as quickly as he had entered, he left. With her head still in the lap of Li Ying, and the child's cries resounding in her ears, Li Xiu Ying looked up into her face for explanation. Her eyes filling with tears, Li Ying could only murmur "It's for the best." She had no more resolutions. No more milk and cream. All had already been resolved. Liu Wei had taken the newborn, and neither Li Xiu Ying nor anyone else would ever see it again.

~

It was the small hours of the morning before she found the strength to rise from her bed and pull the curtain back. Liu Wei was seated in the only chair and appeared to be drunk. He was incoherent to her. She walked past him and out into the cool air. It refreshed her in the same way as the sweet won tons with bananas and nuts and dates flavored with cinnamon Wang Fong's wife had fed her to lift her spirits and quell her hunger. Wang Fong's wife had told her they were her specialty. Nobody made them better, and she would sacrifice a lot to afford the ingredients. Wang Fong himself insisted on her making them often his craving was so bad. She laughed when she said he was "a devil for them" and hid her embarrassed chuckling behind her palm. This Li Xiu Ying remembered as she made her way up the slight incline to the paddy field.

It would be a few hours yet before the sun came up and the birds begin to sing with the new dawn. As she stood barefoot on the elevated ground of the sodden field, she could see the lights of the city far off in the distance, drenched by smog in the light of the moon. She wished she could hear the sound of the nightingale. The one she had held in her hand and placed among the bushes. The one her mother had said would be there for her forever. She strained to hear it. It was out there somewhere. Surely it would come to her now. Now when she needed it to cling to. She could hear her mother's voice. She must open her heart to it, and it would come.

It was faint at first. A whispered note on the clear air, pandering to the still of the night. She was unsure if she had even heard it. A barely perceptible tweet, like the flick of a finger striking a large gong. She waited, straining to hear it again. When the second note sounded, the moment made her glad. She could hear it as plainly as her mother's voice. There was no doubting it. Then notes flittered across the dark sky in an endless song of hope and love and freedom. It was her nightingale. Sounding out from who knew where. Its song bringing a smile to her face, taming the desolation and turmoil in her mind.

Shedding tears through her smile as silently as she had endured the birthing, hearing her mother's voice in the wondrous song of the nightingale, Li Xiu Ying stood and stared at the sad and lonely glare of the Beijing moonlight.

Author's Notes: What is LOST and FOUND? Hope.

No Blinders

Gary Winters

There must be something that compels us to write. Why do we do it? Then there are those of us who must be photojournalists, which further complicates things because it is often more difficult to obtain a good photo to go with an article than it is to write the article. And what reward do we get? A tiny credit clinging to the side of the photograph no one notices.

The media I write for often ignore the photos that accompany the articles. This is a downright shame because the article and the photo complement each other. This bothers me.

Are my photographs not good enough? Am I doing something wrong? Do I not have the eye I think I have? What do I have to do to find out?

I entered a photography contest, that's what.

I holed up on my favorite bar stool in San Felipe and waited for the local padre to lead the children's parade around town. They do this every evening at dusk for the twelve days before Christmas in honor of the Patron Saint of Mexico, the Virgin of Guadalupe. At sunset I could hear them coming, children filling the street next to the malecón, the sea wall.

I strolled out with my Canon SureShot in my hip pocket and managed to climb up on a chair without falling off. The passing padre was striding along with purpose all right, gazing not at me, but out to sea. The moment was passing with the back of his head in my lens. The clouds were shifting, the light failing, the chair wobbling. I clicked. The puny built-in flash was enough to get the padre to turn his head toward the light for an instant. I snapped it.

In the foreground a mother held an infant in her arms making sure the child was part of the parade. A boy in the front of the parade held up a banner that read Bless Our Homes. The children were focused on the march like little attending angels.

I enlarged the photograph so the faces would show up and submitted it to the California State Mid-Winter Fair. This was my first foray into the world of competitive photography. The fourth

127

premium went to yours truly.

Now I know why we do it. It's for the money. My prize was $5.

I Found It

Frank Primiano

In the 70s and 80s, a ubiquitous bumper sticker appeared. It was yellow with three words in bold, black letters: "I Found It." My friends and I were uncertain but reckoned it might have something to do with religion.

One evening, during my daily walk, I saw a man washing a car that proclaimed on its bumper — "I Found It." Maybe he could tell me its meaning.

We exchanged pleasantries. The man appeared rational for a potential fundamentalist zealot. I pointed to the sticker and asked, "What, exactly, did you find?"

He answered without blinking. "My wife's G-spot."

Ah-ha. It did refer to a religious experience.

Baby Weight

Erik C. Martin

Tammy pulled the stack of mail out of the box. A pale, pink envelope stuck out from the bills and ads — the invitation to Margaret's baby shower.

"Oh hell."

Like when Grandma Betty had died, the sting was no less for knowing it was coming.

"The Mommy Club claims another one."

And Margaret had been the last friend that Tammy had actually liked. Now, she'd be stuck hanging out with sad Sally Smith or Wendy-Who-LOVES-Dancing-With-The-Stars.

She slammed shut the mailbox door and jiggled out the key. Her phone began to play Billy Joel's *We Didn't Start The Fire*. The name on the screen read Paula, but the photo was a toddler with cake on his face.

Tammy's friendship with Paula had effectively ended three years ago when Aiden was born. Since then, things had devolved into Facebook likes and the occasional text message. This was the first phone call in more than six months.

"Hello?"

"Sweeetie! It's Paula! I just got Margaret's baby shower invitation. Did yours come yet?"

"Uh huh. I'm holding it." She fumbled with her house key and managed to get the door open.

"Isn't it great? I'm so excited for her. I know it was hard for her and Dan to get pregnant. They've been trying for so long."

"Uh huh."

Her apartment was stifling. First day of September and it was the hottest day of the year, nearly one hundred degrees along the coast. Tammy didn't have air conditioning.

"Have you looked at the gift registry yet? I'd be happy to help you pick something out. If you need help."

"No. I literally just got the mail."

"Honey! She's been registered at Babies 'R' Us for a month! If you wait, the good stuff will all be gone."

Tammy placed her workbag on a dining room chair. The bag

tipped over dumping out her empty Hogwarts travel mug, Heat Miser lunch box, a thick file, and a *Vanity Fair*; on the cover was a picture of Serena Williams, naked and pregnant.

"I don't know. I might just send some Pampers and a fruit basket or something. I'm not sure I can make it."

"What are you saying? You have to come!"

"I hate playing all those games. That one where you eat chocolate poop out of a diaper?" She shuddered.

"They're candy bars. I think I understand. You're upset because it hasn't happened to you yet. Tammy, it isn't too late. You're young still."

"Thirty-five."

"Tons of women wait until their thirties. What's the hold up? Does Jason still have cold feet? If I were you, I'd throw out his X-Box and tell him to grow up."

"What? No! God, it's hot today." She opened her sliding door and turned on a fan. "It's a mutual thing. Neither one of us thinks we're ready for that."

"Are you kidding? You'd be a great mom! No one is ever ready. You just have to do it."

"We can't really afford a baby," she protested.

"Ha! And I can? You make do. You sacrifice. It is the greatest thing you will ever do, trust me."

Tammy grabbed a marvelously cold bottle of chardonnay from the fridge. She cradled her phone between her ear and shoulder and dug through the drawer where she kept her wine key.

"Umm, that's great for you. I don't think it's for me though."

"What are you talking about?"

Pop!

She poured straw-colored liquid to the rim of her wineglass.

"I don't want to have kids. I never did. I'm tired of pretending that I do. I'm sick of the looks of pity that I get from women who have kids when I tell them I don't—like I'm a failure. It's bullshit. I made a choice not to have children. I've worked not to have children."

The other end of the line was very quiet for a moment.

Then, "So what . . . am I some kind of asshole?"

"What? No!"

"No. That's what you're saying. That I'm an idiot for having a kid."

"That isn't what I said. But I feel like *I'd* be an idiot if *I* had a

132

kid . . . if I let myself be brainwashed by all the crap the media puts out."

"What are you talking about?"

"You know, like the hundred movies they make every year. The couple says they don't want kids, then, surprise, they get pregnant in the next scene, spend forty-five minutes debating, have the baby, and it turns out to be the greatest thing ever."

"It is."

"It's a lie."

"Screw you! You have problems!"

Tammy drank down a mouthful of the fruity chardonnay. She smiled.

"I do. But I'm not compounding them with children."

"You need help!" Paula hung up

Tammy took another sip, loving how the cold wine warmed her insides. She picked up the pink envelope that had caused her so much stress only ten minutes before. She held it tightly and ripped it in half. Into the trash it went.

She called Jason.

"Hey, let's go out for dinner tonight . . ."

First Prize, One Wife

Dave Feldman

Among the many exploits of my rocky career, I was a speed skater.

Not a great roller skater, but good enough to place third in the California state championships in San Francisco, back in 1947. And I had an offer to tour Europe with a Roller Derby team, but I was in the Marines, and they thought poorly of the idea.

The bronze medal in the state competition proved nice, but by roller skating, I really won first prize in something else: My bride of many years.

The skating rink, out at the beach in San Francisco, was well below the Cliff House but short of the amusement park. A tall, slim girl, generally at the rink on weekends with her sister, wanted to learn to speed skate. I took one look and knew I should be her teacher. I volunteered and gave her a few tips. Her name: Betty Whiteley. She had high cheekbones and lustrous blue-green eyes. Long ago, a lesser-known gorgeous Italian actress named Alida Valli made the big screen in *The Third Man.* Well, Betty looked like her prettier, younger sister.

At the rink, well before she would date me, I asked for her address in Redwood City. "It's 118 Avocado Street," she said. Not true. Her address, I later learned, was 419 Manzanita. There is no Avocado Street in Redwood City.

Nevertheless, I persisted.

Our first date, we spent walking along Geary Street, counting the beer cans chucked into the gutters by inebriates. Our second date, we went to the movies. I should remember the film playing, but I spent most of the time slyly admiring her.

Back at the rink, the management held races on most nights. I entered a men's race one Thursday night, came in second. Then, in a surprise because they hadn't done it before, they held a race just for servicemen. I ducked into the men's room, took off my long-sleeved sports shirt, and went onto the floor wearing my Marine shirt, complete with corporal's stripes on the sleeves.

I finished second in that race, too.

Betty skated over and started giving me hell. "What do you mean, pretending to be a Marine just so you could skate in another race?"

"I am a Marine," I said hesitantly.

"No, you're not. I'd have never dated you if I knew you were a Marine, or even a sailor. My folks and I wouldn't have allowed it."

"It's true. I am a Marine."

"You lied to me," she said,

"No, I just didn't ever tell you. Until now."

Her anger lasted another ten minutes. Then she decided that since we'd already had two dates, it might be too late to back out.

She was hooked. I was hooked.

~

After working and living in San Francisco, she was staying in Redwood City with her parents. It was June of 1948.

I was stationed at Alameda Naval Air Station, across the bay. After we started dating, we established a routine. I had every other night off, which meant taking the bus to Oakland, the train across the Bay Bridge to San Francisco, and a Greyhound bus twenty-five miles south to Redwood City. We would sit outside in her dad's old Hupmobile and neck (but nothing more), and fall asleep until 4 a.m. An alarm clock would awaken us, and I'd jog to the Greyhound bus station and reverse the trip back to Alameda, arriving at 6:50 a.m. when I wasn't due until 7:00.

That September, my Marine days ended. I returned to Tucson and the University of Arizona. Betty stayed in Redwood City. But on three-day holiday weekends, I would borrow one of my dad's automobiles off his small used-car lot and drive the 900 miles, nonstop, to see my intended.

Sometimes, on my way home, she would accompany me as far as Los Angeles. At that time, the road from Bakersfield over the mountains to Los Angeles became known as "Suicide Alley" because it had three lanes. One in each direction, and a middle lane for passing, if you had the guts. We started up the Grapevine, its name for the part closest to Bakersfield, and it began to snow. Being a desert rat, I'd never driven in snow before. But I knew to drive slowly.

I kept it at a steady ten miles an hour. Unfortunately, a car ahead of me puttered along at a steady five miles an hour. I pulled out gingerly to pass. Our car spun around twice, then headed for a deep ditch. I think it would have been a ten-foot drop.

136

Betty believed it to be twenty feet, although with time it's become thirty feet. Miraculously, we hit a stone mileage marker — they came along every mile — and bounced back onto the highway. The only casualty: the 1937 Buick's front end. Betty and I were grateful; my dad much less so.

My final year at college in Arizona, Betty came down from San Francisco and got a job at the university's admissions office.

Our necking, relatively innocent, continued. The day after I graduated, I married the most beautiful girl in Tucson. One who hated the desert but loved me.

She has endured Douglas, Arizona, which is twenty miles beyond the end of the world, and eleven years in Tucson.

In high school, although Betty always made the honor roll, she would skip the dull classes and go in to San Francisco to watch the United Nations being formed. Now she's up on the news, talks back to TV pundits who disagree with her, and drives her husband bonkers with her crossword-puzzle questions about sports.

Did we argue and fight and threaten to leave for good and always? Of course. That's what married folks do. But making up is better.

Betty is a traveler. She could live out of a suitcase, provided she could find a Laundromat. Europe was her kind of place — a wonderland for travel, and that we did. She fell in love with Seville, Spain, when she and the kids spent six months there because of son Greg's health.

When it became time to put Greg and Tracy in college, and Germany didn't have anything for them, I had to tug and push Betty and Greg back across the ocean. Tracy and I were looking forward to life in America.

~

It took five different colleges and a number of years — in Germany, Arizona and California — but Betty collected her BA in anthropology. She then excelled at her eighteen years with Child Protective Services, a heart-wrenching job if there ever was one. She did her best at helping medically fragile children, but finally left when it became clear that the children's best interests were not always being served.

Then she became a knowledgeable, helpful travel agent.

I often call her by the initials, BW, which stand for Beautiful Wife. She retorts that they are merely her initials from before marriage. And I must report that she has the most acute hearing of

137

anyone I have ever encountered. Betty can hear a cockroach pass gas at forty paces.

Somehow, she has worked magic because many decades later, she is still the most beautiful girl in town, not Tucson, of course, but San Diego. I admit to being biased about her beauty, but what about this: A perfect stranger, seeing us walk out of a local restaurant, said to me: "Does your wife know you're out with a younger woman?"

I rest my case.

Lost in the Fog

Arthur Raybold

My brother, Richard, loved planes, horses, and boats. He would have to wait until after he graduated from high school in 1945 and joined the Army Air Corps before he could learn to fly. Until then, our dad had a friend, Jockey Jarvis, who owned a horse farm, where my brother cleaned the stables on the weekends, so he could ride horses for free.

Rather than playing football and baseball for his high school, Richard preferred making money, working in Hutchinson's Bookstore in New Bedford, Massachusetts, after school. With his earnings, he saved enough money to buy a used sailboat, with a centerboard and one mast. At 15, he was proud to be the owner of a sailboat.

He and our dad built a rudder. Our dad found a used sail, which he was able to trim to fit the boat. When the boat was ready to sail, they lofted it on to the top of Dad's car and drove it to the Hathaway Machinery Company in Fairhaven, where Josh Hathaway said they could leave it tied up to one of his many docks.

Richard loved sailing around the draggers — the fishing boats that fished with nets dragging along the bottom of the ocean — avoiding them as they came in and out of New Bedford Harbor. He especially loved the winter mornings, when all the lines were frozen, and the sun made spectacular designs on the boats. One afternoon, he noticed the fog was rapidly moving in from the ocean. He jerked the rudder a bit too hard, and the pin connecting the rudder to the stern popped out. He was in the center of the harbor, halfway between New Bedford and Fairhaven, and he had lost control of the boat.

What can I do? he thought. *Lower the sail and slow the boat down?*

The boat slowed, as it continued towards New Bedford. Richard looked west and spotted Palmer Island — six acres, with nothing on it but the WNBH radio tower.

Palmer would be good to land in, with its light on the top of the tower, he thought.

He guessed it was about 5 p.m. It was already twilight and getting darker. He could not see land on either side. He used his right hand to paddle the tiny sailboat towards Palmer Island, with the help of the light from the tower.

~

When Richard hadn't returned, Mom called Dad and told him to call the Coast Guard, while she would call their good friend, Frank Leary. He had a speedboat and might be able to search for Richard. She also called Josh Hathaway and asked if he could help. The little boat still had not returned to its Hathaway spot.

~

Richard's centerboard hit some rocks one hundred yards short of Palmer. He was able to exit his craft and swim to shore.

Lucky me, he thought. *I can find plenty of firewood.*

Richard was able to gather all kinds of wood at the high tide line. He remembered he had brought his prized Zippo lighter with him for just such an occasion. Soon, he had a blaze going and he kept feeding the fire.

I bet Mom called Dr. Leary, he thought, *and he's out there now, looking for me.*

It was so peaceful, with the fire lighting up his territory. He concentrated on staying awake. Suddenly, he began to see a light coming towards him very slowly. It was too small to be the Coast Guard. It had to be Dr. Leary.

~

"Richard, it's Dr. Leary. Can you walk or paddle out here?"

"Yes, Doctor. Thanks for looking for me."

Richard moved towards the spotlight, picking his way carefully over the rocks. "I hope you didn't have to leave the operating room to find me?"

"I did, but this is more fun than delivering babies."

Courage

Sarah Faxon

He had wanted to be a centaur for Halloween. Instead, he was dressed in a white hospital gown with tubes sticking out of his arms. It wasn't so bad this time around, Adam thought. He could see out a window from his bed and wasn't stuck around the other side of the boring ol' curtain like last time.

Twilight was approaching and soon every kid in town would be scouring front porches, hollering "trick or treat," while he would be stuck in bed. The other lions and soldiers, dinosaurs and knights, would busy themselves sorting out chocolates from peppermints, sours from those dreadful pennies, and toffees from the rest of the pile.

Little Adam would not be able to partake in sorting his candy into a little mountain range this year, but that was all right. The pretty nurse who was always smiling had told him that this would be it. The last of the treatments. He had endured enough tricks for one little boy and from now on, he would be finding nothing but treats.

"Adam," the nurse had said as she began his treatment, "after tonight, you could be a centaur, a king, an astronaut, anything you dream, because you've already fought a dragon and lived to tell the tale."

She told him that he would leave the hospital with the best treat of all—the courage he had found within. Most grown-ups had yet to find this courage within themselves.

Marty & Rose

Bob Doublebower

You just couldn't beat the Santa Ana River this time of day, Marty thought. An hour after it rose, the sun would peek out from behind the Honda dealership on the other side and glint off the two feet of water meandering between its grey concrete banks. Marty sat high up on the sloped west bank, at the edge of a wide dirt patch in front of the bridge abutment. It had been a wet spring, bringing water to the river, but, as Marty peeked to the south, out from under the highway girders, he saw only blue sky today.

Eighty or so other souls, alone and in pairs, dissembled lives assembled, took up various sections of the dirt swath. An argument broke out somewhere behind him, and Marty turned to watch. Eddy, his neighbor from three tents over, liked to call himself The Edge when his eyes got wilder than usual, for reasons known only to Eddy. He was getting into it with some Mexican guy Marty had never seen before. People come and go. They were loud, with lots of pointing, but it didn't look like there was going to be a fight. Crap. Marty turned back to the river. He tried to focus. Holding the sides of his head helped. To be productive, today needed a Plan.

Around the end of rush hour, he'd hike up Orangewood with his sign under his arm and swing around the back of Jimmy's Donut Hole right after the breakfast rush. If he timed it right, and the clean-up guy wasn't a prick, he could catch the scraps en route to the dumpster, rather than after. A good day begins with a good breakfast. That done, he'd head on down State College to the freeway ramp.

Marty had come to believe that the a.m. and p.m. rush hour were not good times for panhandling. Too many angry trucks with too many angry radios blaring. The drivers would glare at him out their side windows, seeing him, in the moment, as the embodiment of the vitriol in which they stewed. The midday crowd was much better. People running errands, more laid back, picking up kids from soccer. More NPR and Kenny Loggins. They were the ones who rolled down their windows and smiled. He'd been a can hauler in the past, but the recycle business wasn't what it used to be.

Marty got up and walked back to his campsite. He didn't have a tent. Didn't need one, as far as he could see. The freeway overhead kept off the rain. What he did have, though, was a 12-foot section of snow fence (thank you CalTrans) that made a neat, three-sided space that he called his. Marty looked down at his earthly possessions.

Time to stash. The trick to not getting ripped off was to make it all unnoticeable. Nothing shiny showing. Funny how people had a measure of respect for an unremarkable bedroll. That's why he gave back the space blanket Social Services had given him. Too shiny. He rolled his camp stove, along with his impressive collection of butane lighters (yeah, he was that guy) in a dirty brown towel. His ragged checkerboard from the 99 Cent store lay flat under his ground cloth. Time was he could beat most anyone here, but the checkers themselves, well, they'd gone missing a while back. Other things — utensils, a radio with no batteries, a beat-up Thomas Guide — likewise disappeared under his bedroll. Last of all, he took from the snow fence, a small framed photograph. The glass showed the streaks left by a dirty thumb wiping off the dust. The picture showed a woman and a young boy. This he looked at for a long moment, then wrapped it in his other tee shirt, and pushed it to the bottom of a nondescript backpack.

Stashing didn't take all that long, and the tires on the roadway above still didn't have that 50-mph sound. Perfect time for today's first beer. He looked around, suddenly self-conscious, then bent to rummage in that same backpack, coming up with a tall, silvery can. Panhandling did provide some of life's smaller pleasures.

But it wasn't those 24 oz. Steel Reserves that lapped up the mortgage money, was it Marty? It wasn't days on a bender that crashed the drywall business, was it? It was getting washed away in those turbulent currents of the Texas Hold-Em river. So many times. He'd gotten the bug, and the bug had gotten him.

He popped the top, closed his eyes, and took a long pull. When he opened his eyes, The Edge was standing beside him.

"You believe 'dat sum'bitch? Come in here askin' me if I wanna move downtown! Where? Where the hell downtown? What about my dog? What about my stuff?"

144

"Where was he from?" Marty asked. "City, County, or do-gooder?" He tried to remember ever seeing Eddy with a dog and couldn't.

"City, I think. Hell, how should I know? Why now? We h'ain't seen them peckerheads for months! You seen downtown, lately?"

Marty offered The Edge a pull from the can and said, "Dunno. Baseball season's starting, I think. Maybe that's it." The giant halo over Angels Stadium loomed to the northwest.

The Edge narrowed his eyes as he handed back the can. "When's the last roust you heard of?"

Marty wasn't good at remembering things, and he sure didn't want to start the day this way. Being upset in the morning could last all day. He had a Plan, he remembered, and yakking about city policy with The Edge wasn't part of it.

"Jeez, man." He peered into the can and wiggled it. "I met an old woman with a parakeet a few weeks back said they been chased out up near the park. Didn't say which park." Marty drank down half of what was left in the tallboy. Now, if he stayed quiet, maybe Eddy would leave. After about a minute, it worked.

Soon enough, it came time to pick a sign, and head out. Veteran though he was, the well-worn "homeless vet" sign seemed to have less effect on the midday crowd. Couldn't figure why. He picked instead his newer and crisper "God Bless You for the Help" sign, done in ecclesiastical purple and gold magic marker, on white. Magic, indeed.

So-armed, and his stuff stashed, he slicked back his hair and headed for Jimmy's.

~

Not much could ruin Rose Candelero's day. Her daughter's twelfth birthday was coming up, and it pushed aside all of life's other little struggles. Like making the rent. Like the cable bill. Like having to take this extra work shift. She could have stewed, too, about no response yet from Celia's dad, but she didn't. The bus dropped her off a block away from the Sanitation Department's Hill Avenue station. This wasn't trash day in Hill Ave's district. Something else was up. In the locker room, Rose sucked in her gut to get one more belt hole as she squeezed into her green work pants. Out in the back lot, buses lined up.

"Somethin' goin' on today?" Rose asked her supervisor. He had lined up his squad of 10 in the briefing room. Instead of an answer, she got handed a clear plastic bag with a zipper. Oh crap. She'd seen this before—the hazmat pack. White paper suit (well, it

145

felt like paper), booties, face mask, and about a dozen pair of blue gloves. Gonna be messy. The squad sat down and waited.

Rose turned to Gabby. "Heard anything?" Gabby usually knew stuff even before the supervisors. She had a knack for it.

"Nothin' official, but I saw a 10-wheeler dump truck hauling a bobcat out on the street. We don't get that just every day."

"Great. Sounds special," Rose said in a tone as flat as a freeway through two hairpins gripped in her teeth. She pulled her black hair back into a bun, then slumped back on the bench and waited.

~

Marty decided to knock off early today. It had been a pretty good haul, so far. He counted $17 and 50 cents, three holy cards emblazoned with the Blessed Mother, and four copies of *The Watchtower*. Someone had also given him a book on spiritual healing which he threw in the bushes. He didn't read much these days. Breakfast had stuck with him pretty well 'til now, but soon he'd be hungry again. He headed back to camp.

Marty didn't think much of it when he saw Margaret with her yappy dog walking up Holland Street. He was still about a half mile from the overpass. People wandered all the time. Then he saw Charlie and Gus. They'd been campers longer than he and rarely left together, fearing for their stuff. Marty walked on a few more blocks, and the human trickle had become a small stream. Nobody made eye contact. The clang of a loading operation and the hum of a big diesel faintly ricocheted off the concrete riverbank. Two young black guys in camo pants, vets most likely, pedaled by on rusty bikes. Marty started to worry, not sure why, and walked a little faster. Now every block had people on it. Some he knew, most he didn't. Finally, about a block out, he saw Eddy.

"Yo, Eddy, where you headed?" Marty yelled.

Eddy's head snapped around, first left, then right, until he caught sight of Marty.

"They rousted us, man," Eddy called back. His voice crackled with panic. "They came in around noon and said we had to go. Go where?" He emphasized the "where."

To Marty, seeing was believing, so he hurried to the overpass, and scrambled down under the girders.

The dirt swath was bare.

Off to the north side, a big dump truck sat idling, while a little pissant bobcat scooped large black plastic bags into it. Sanitation workers from the City, about half a dozen of them, stood around

146

talking to a few of the stragglers. A pile of white coveralls sat heaped off to the side.

Marty went numb. This had been his home for over a year. Could he still watch the river in the morning? Where was everybody going? Where was his snow fence? Where was his stuff, and . . . Oh my God . . . Where was his backpack — with the picture? He began to wander about aimlessly, getting more rattled, trying to put it all together. He saw a sanitation worker leave a group nearby and he walked up to her.

"Where's my stuff?" he blurted out.

Rose turned and looked at him. This was not her first roust, and the human toll never sat well with her. But a job was a job.

"All personal belongings, except dangerous and contraband items, are in those bags being loaded over there," said Rose, trying her best to sound like a paragraph in this morning's directive. "You'll have an opportunity to retrieve your belongings at the storage facility."

Marty just stared at her, confused. "I don't have a storage facility. Can't I just go get my stuff off the truck? Shouldn't be too hard to find, there's a backpack, kinda tan, and a snow fence." Of the fifty or so black bags in the dump truck, Marty's backpack, in one of them, did not stand out.

"I'm sorry, sir, you can't do that. All those bags are in the custody of the Dept. of Sanitation, until we can check them over." Of course, they weren't actually, but to have a crowd swarming over the truck did not sound like a good end to the day.

Rose had long since gotten used to getting yelled at, cursed at, and threatened during these operations, and it's at this point that it usually happened.

But Marty just stood there. If he'd been able to make a move in any meaningful direction, he would have. None seemed meaningful. Instead, a feeling like rising water began building behind the bridge of his nose.

He didn't yell. He spoke softly. "The backpack . . . I got a picture . . ."

Long delay.

"My boy . . ."

It had been a long day for Rose. She wanted nothing more than to clock out, go home, and smoke a bowl. Day done. But at that moment, something tiny began to yield inside her. Always she had stood firm in the face of the pleadings, the anger, and the lost looks, but it tired her.

147

"What boy?" she asked, although she really already knew.

Marty looked past her to the river beyond, no longer in the moment.

The yielding inside her edged closer to collapse. Rose shifted gears.

"We take all this stuff down to Hill St. The idea is to sort through it, but that doesn't always happen. If it's not retrieved in seven days, we toss it."

Marty came back to the conversation. *What did that mean? Toss it? Toss it where? Where's Hill St.? How far is that?*

He said, "I only know the streets up around here. You know, where I been."

Rose dug into her back pocket and handed Marty a motel voucher, good for a week.

"Here, take this. It's for the Starland over on Chapman. At least it's a place to sleep 'til you get your bedroll back."

"There's a backpack, too," Marty called after Rose, as she turned and walked toward the crew bus.

He'd been to the Starland before. Nestled between a Speedee Oil Change and another likewise run-down motel, it had managed to stay on the City's voucher list, that not being a high bar to clear. He still had his sign, but the day for panhandling had passed. He started walking. *Seven days,* he kept saying to himself. He trudged into the motel lobby as the sun set over the cargo cranes of Long Beach.

"Hi, Hector," he called, waving his voucher in the air.

Hector looked up from behind his thick glass enclosure.

"Hey, hom', where you been? Long time."

"Around. You know. No. 8 still available?" Marty asked. "Is the puke gone?"

"Yeah, yeah, man. That was gone months ago. The girl came in just this past Tuesday. We're in good shape."

Marty handed over the wrinkled voucher, and Hector slipped a key on a plastic fob under the glass.

"You be here all week, Marty?" He nodded and turned for the door. On the way out, he stopped and turned back.

"Hey, Hector, you know where Hill St. is?"

Hector frowned and slowly shook his head side to side. "New one on me, hom'."

Marty remembered his Thomas Guide, but couldn't remember where it was.

~

148

Rose Candelero slept a peaceful night, unlike some others after a roust. Sometimes she couldn't shake the abuse she'd absorbed for a day or two. That guy, what was his name? Marty? She'd written his name on the voucher receipt. He looked so . . . wounded . . . but so restrained in his misery. That thing that had bent within her, that tiny seed of empathy, had spread through her, and the reward had been a good night's sleep. Today was her day off, and she had a party to plan.

~

Marty got back to work the next day, this time over on the 57. On his way there, he ran into the camo vets on their bikes. Each balanced a big bag of cans.

"Nope. Heard 'a Hill St. but couldn't say where the hell it is. What town's it in?"

Marty had no answer for that and walked on. *Six days.*

~

Celia Candelero came home from school early two days later. They'd let her go to help her mom set up for her party. She loved that kind of thing. There were streamers and balloons, and the table set for eight of her friends. She got to help make the tres leche cake.

But throughout the day, an undercurrent of sadness built within Rose. Sooner or later Celia would ask, and Rose had no answer but the truth. Later, as the cake cooled on a rack, and the last of the name cards stood at their places, Celia asked.

"Heard from Daddy?"

Inside, Rose crumbled. But outside, she had to be strong.

"No, not yet, Angel. Maybe he's out of town." OK, maybe not the whole truth.

That evening, Rose thought for a long while about kids and daddies. About the bond and the need. And she thought about that unshakeable small kernel of love she still felt for Celia's dad, and this confused her to no end.

~

Marty went about his usual days—Starland to Jimmy's to the offramp and back to Starland, but, through it all, he felt like a ghost. He didn't have his stuff, and that made him feel like half a person. But, worse, he didn't have his picture. It anchored him, as it had through all the bad years. He didn't walk these days, as much as he drifted.

Early Saturday morning, five days after the roust, Hector banged on the door of No. 8.

149

"Hey, Marty. You got a call."

Marty scrambled from bed, put on the one shoe he could find, and followed Hector to the office.

Marty gripped the phone like it was an unknown object. "Hello?"

"Marty? Marty, this is Rose, from back last Monday. I gave you the voucher. Remember?"

It began to come into focus. "Yeah. Yeah. Hi."

"Marty, did you ever get your stuff? I still see that big pile of bags in our yard. Not many folks have showed up. You plannin' on coming down?"

"Yeah, I plan to, but nobody I know knows where it is."

"Well, I know. Hey, I'm off tomorrow. Why don't you hang out at the Starland till about ten? Can you do that?"

"Sure."

Without further chitchat, Rose hung up.

Marty stared at the phone, then hung up and asked Hector for a rubber band. He wrapped this around his index finger to remind himself. 10 o'clock.

Next morning, Marty sat on his bed, rolling the rubber band off and on his finger. He heard a car pull up, then a knock. He crammed himself into Rose's battered Corolla, and they headed south, past donut shops and diners he had never seen.

"We're not really supposed to come in on Sundays, but I told my supe I had paperwork to catch up," Rose said to ease the awkward silence.

Marty stared out the side window. *Man, this is a big goddamn city.*

Finally there, Rose rolled down the car window for the security guard. She didn't say a word — she just pointed to the looming bag pile and then to her passenger. She parked next to a small side entrance and said to Marty, "Wait here."

She disappeared inside, then came out dressed in her hazmat gear. The Department of Sanitation had its rules. Together they walked to the pile. It was now much bigger, owing to another roust just this past Thursday. Together they unstacked, shoved, lifted, threw, and kicked bags this way and that. Not all were open, but some were. Marty felt sure he'd know his when he saw it.

Two hours of this had cut a pretty good path into the middle of the pile. Marty worked like a man on a mission, but Rose began to wonder if this was all futile.

150

Then Marty saw something that gave his heart wings. Sticking out of a dusty, ripped trash bag, at the very bottom of the pile, he saw four inches of CalTrans snow fence.

They walked back to the Corolla. Rose had taken off her hazmat suit and bundled it under her arm. Marty clutched to his chest a dirty tan backpack.

Commitment

Candace George Conradi

last night i married my Self
   this morning i awakened pregnant with possibility

in the darkness of my dream
   i could see forever
   receptive, waiting patiently
   hiding nothing

shame, sadness, regret
   pure joy, success, memories
   all layered parts, but not me
   life experiences exposed

i saw her in the distance
   the "me" i had forsaken
   and moving toward her
   my heart softened

she was calm, present, beautiful
   she had never left
   but had waited for my return

153

choosing her

    no longer frightened by false evidence appearing real

    no resistance, no option

    to what was, is, or might be

only awareness

    i thanked my body

    one hand to my heart, the other to my belly

    and celebrated the miracle of life

The Loudest Voice

Robyn Bennett

I imagine I was always writing. Twaddle it was, too.
But better far write twaddle or anything, anything,
than nothing at all. —Katherine Mansfield

I stepped into my favorite place: a bookshop. Those new-book smells sent tingles up my spine. Just like when you're in love.

I ran my hand over the covers of the books—shiny, bright, new things. *The 18th Abduction,* James Patterson. Again? Doesn't he ever sleep? *It Devours*, from the author of *Welcome to Night Vale*—a book I had recently read and loved. *Essential New Zealand Short Stories* by Owen Marshall, the critically acclaimed writer of short stories.

Critically acclaimed.

A persistent dream. Could I? Dare I?

One foot in dream world, the other leading me past the book bargain bin (where the books that don't sell go) and outside to the seat in Seymour Square overlooking the flower beds of summer blast color—marigolds, ranunculi, pansies, and pink sweet peas.

The sky, a cornflower blue like the palest of sapphires, stretched out forever.

Sitting down on the wooden seat, I whispered, "I'm going to write a book."

"You're going to do *what*?" my Inner Voice asked.

"Write a book."

"Ha. Why?" Inner Voice hid pretend surprise.

"Because I've always wanted to, and I have an idea for a story."

"What are you going to write about that hasn't already been written?"

It was a good question.

"Well, true. But if that was true, then why are bookshops filled with books?" I asked.

"People want to read. They must read," Inner Voice said, like the Dalai Lama of Books. "What writing experience do you have?"

"English was my favorite subject at school, and I make up stories all the time."

"That's a good start. What writing courses have you done?"

I stared at the dirt. "Um. None."

A long pause.

"So how would you start writing?" Inner Voice asked.

"There's a model that everyone follows. It divides a story up into three acts, and then you break that down further into an inciting incident, plot points, dark night of the soul, the climax, and then the resolution."

"It sounds like you know what you're talking about."

"Not really." Doubt crept into my voice. "What if I break the writing rules?"

"Rules were made to be broken. Wasn't it Somerset Maugham who said there are three rules around writing, but nobody knows what they are. You know the best advice from Stephen King?"

"Yeah. You learn best by reading a lot and writing a lot, and the most valuable lessons of all are the ones you teach yourself."

"Are you going to look for a publisher?" The Inner Voice pitched higher. "It's very hard to get published. You'll end up being rejected and rejected and rejected."

"Like J. K. Rowling?"

"Yeah. She was rejected 12 times." It came out sounding like it was a badge of honor.

Two teenaged girls walked past, giggling. One grasped a book in her hand. I recognized the heavy tome and animated cover — *Harry Potter and The Philosopher's Stone.* Coincidence?

I sighed in time with the wind. "I'm not sure I could handle rejection. I know my work will never be good enough to be accepted by a publisher."

A helpful suggestion came from the Inner Voice. "You could self-publish."

"Self-publishing has a bad rap."

"Not necessarily. It's up to self-pubbies to be professional and produce the same quality of work as traditionalists."

"If I took the self-pub route, I could get my book published faster."

"Much faster. *Fifty Shades of Grey* started as a self-published book, and look what happened to that." Inner Voice was turning helpful.

156

"Aha. Book sequels and a movie."

"See, you never know what might happen."

I focused on a yellow carnation. "Next, you'll be suggesting someone who has a piglet will name it after one of my characters."

Inner Voice laughed.

"I still don't know. I'll end up comparing myself to other authors." *Doubt, doubt, doubt.*

"And you should. That way you'll get to be a better writer."

"I still think people will think I took the easier road by self-publishing and that I'm really no good."

"Pff! Let people think what they want."

"So, with my limited expertise, you think I should still have a go?" I squeaked.

"Absolutely. Then you'll be able to say, 'I wrote a book,' and smugly smile when other people say that's what they've always wanted to do and never do."

I smiled. My thoughts were formulating.

Inner Voice was back. "What genre are you going to write?"

"Romance."

"Who reads romance these days?"

Okay, Inner Voice. You don't have to shout.

A couple walked through the square, hand in hand. "I researched. It's the world's biggest selling genre. Besides, we all need love. It makes the world go around."

Inner Voice frowned. "I dunno know . . . Romance . . . Some people view romance as chick lit and not as sophisticated as literary fiction."

"That's what I want to write. So, I'll write what I know rather than what I don't know. And what I enjoy writing."

"That makes sense."

Another pause.

Inner Voice was relentless. "What will you do on days you have self-doubt?"

"Look at all the inspirational quotes I've put up on my Pinterest board."

"Like what?"

"Rob Bignell said, 'You are a writer the moment you start writing, not when you've sold your first book.'"

"What about Sylvia Plath's quote? 'The worst enemy to creativity is self-doubt.'"

"Or from Louis L'Amour: 'Start writing no matter what. The water does not flow until the faucet is turned on.'"

157

"How often are you going to write?" Inner Voice asked.

"I'll write for a minimum of an hour a day."

"Aim for 2,000 words a day."

"Word counts don't work for me."

"Then do what works for you. And eliminate distractions." Inner Voice was sparkling.

"Eliminate my cat? I don't think so."

There would be challenges.

I squashed Inner Voice.

I stood up, breathed in and out, and set off for home.

~

I stared at the first blank page of my clean, fresh, and wordless notebook, a pen poised in my hand.

My mind was blank too.

Nothing.

The seeds of the story that had been simmering away barely raised its head. My characters were misty, vague. I needed to pull them out, rescue them. They have a story. It must be told. My hero and heroine will fall in love.

I wrote a sentence, then two, then three. I was underway!

A page was filled.

I read back over the page.

Cross out, cross out. Add, add, add. Write, write, write.

This is good. I've made a start. The characters are coming alive.

I'm happy. I'm writing. And chapter one is done.

But as I read over chapter one, it all seemed so amateurish.

"I sometimes fear my writing is too plain and simple. Other writers seem to write with an amazing variety of words," I said.

"Ah, but Stephen King advises to write in plain English and use the first words that come to mind," Inner Voice reassured.

I looked back over my work. "I think I've done that, but I'm torn. It's probably a load of nonsense."

"At least you wrote something. You can't edit a blank page."

Oh, wise Inner Voice.

"I looked over my notes on how to write a great first chapter."

"That's brilliant. See, even though you've not done any writing courses, you've researched and you're learning."

"Yip. Even if I have to keep rewriting the first chapter a million times. God, I just wish it wasn't taking so long. This is a classic example of you don't know what you don't know."

~

Blood. Sweat. Tears. So, it's a cliché, but it's true.

158

Nine rewrites.

Eighteen months later.

Inner Voice was with me. Every. Step. Of. The. Way. With every word. Encouraging me, teasing me, pushing me. We cussed at each other. We laughed at light bulb moments. Cried when it all seemed too much.

And then with my new writing, editing and self-publishing skills, my first book was published.

One of the proudest days of my life.

"You did it," Inner Voice said, a warm self-satisfied voice.

"Yeah, I did."

"Now life can get back to normal."

"There is no normal for a writer." *OMG, I'm a writer.*

Inner Voice and I were quiet for just a moment.

"You know," I said. "I have an idea for another story."

Inner Voice just smiled.

Diego and the Orphan

Sally Eckberg

I woke up when I heard Mom calling, "Diego, do you want to go for a walk?" After all the rain, both of us were happy to take our morning walk on a bright sunny day. We had only gone two blocks when we passed an alleyway. I heard a mewing sound coming from a trash can that had been tipped over. I pulled at the leash until Mom let me go directly to the trash can.

I knew she heard the sound also because she immediately bent over to look inside the can. Some papers and rags moved, and we heard the sound again. A tiny white paw pushed out of the trash. I pulled out a rag while Mom pushed some papers aside. There it was. The sound we heard was coming from a small puppy. I could see that the pup had a few black spots when Mom picked the little guy up.

We went straight home where Mom called the vet. Then the three of us hurried to the car. The little pup turned out to be a female. Mom wrapped her in a small blanket and placed her right next to me. The pup snuggled into my chest and I put both of my front legs around her. We drove to the vet's office.

I had to wait in the car while Mom took the puppy in to see the vet. She returned one short nap later. We took the puppy home and Mom fed her some food from the vet. Shen then placed her next to me again and cautioned me, "Take care of the baby now."

A week later, the pup was sliding around on the floor, stepping in her food dish, spilling the water bowl, and getting stuck behind furniture. Not to mention the small puddles that seemed to follow her everywhere. It was then that Mom named her Misanthropy. A few more weeks went by, and Misanthropy grew stronger and more playful. Lucy came over, and we spent many hours playing with the pup.

As Misanthropy grew stronger, she also acquired many more black spots on her white coat. She was definitely not a Doberman like Lucy and me. Mom and Dad decided to give her a nickname,

161

Pebbles. At that point, it was determined that the puppy was a Dalmatian.

I just could not imagine anyone throwing a cute little pup like Pebbles into a trash can. One day, I asked her if she remembered anything about that time. She told me she just remembered yelling and someone grabbing her and throwing her into the trash can. It was scary and she was afraid. I told Pebbles not to worry anymore because Lucy and I loved her, and so did Mom and Dad. She was in a safe place now.

Presidio Park: How We Got a Fun Park For Free

Tom Leech

There was this hill, nothing fancy about it,
Though it was a good spot to view the near valley,
And over there was a wandering river
That made it a fun place to wander and dally.

Tribes of many names over the centuries
Had made this hill their village and gathering spot,
As history researchers in more current years,
Were able to learn from many a dug-up plot.

Here's where the Spaniards set up their mission,
With a padre named Serra the key to the ground,
Then they moved it east for an important cause,
That's where enough water could be much better found.

Others soon arrived here and left many marks,
Mormon brigades who marched over 2,000 miles,
Sailors from American boats in the bay,
Plus a skipper named Stockton whose name marks the files.

The landscape was much like those nearby hillsides,
Until a businessman with a big store downtown,
A civic leader who'd run twice for mayor,
Saw it and said "Why's this not a park of renown?"

So George opened his wallet and bought the place,
Then found special nature designers to employ,
Creating meadows, orchards, foliage and such,
To make a real beauty for people to enjoy.

To tie in the hillside's historical links
He re-built that same mission from its past era,
And made a museum of major acclaim,
Named after that Padre Junipero Serra.

Then in 1929 the businessman
Gave this to us as a community landmark,
And made it a place the public could call theirs,
With the relevant name of Presidio Park.

Should you want to make a real-life connection
And receive a memorable and personal lift,
Go visit his home next to Balboa Park,
And say "Thank you, George Marston, for your special gift."

The Real Mother

Mardie Schroeder

"I always knew I was adopted," Lenore told me. "It's no big deal. My father was an officer. He was stationed overseas when he and my mother applied to adopt a child. My mother loves to tell the story that I was fussing when I was brought in to see her, but the minute I was in her arms I quieted down."

"It wasn't until I graduated from high school and was preparing to go out of state to university that I looked through the family's official papers for needed documents. It was then I discovered that not only was I adopted but I was an illegitimate child."

"That must have been a shock," I said.

It took many years of wondering about her biological mother and father before she had an opportunity to act. While driving around Mission Valley, an ad came on the radio about finding lost persons. This was her chance. She called the number given and spoke to the person about her quest, giving the woman the information she had. She learned her search would take her to Germany and that she had to pay $200 in euros to begin the process.

A few days later, her German intermediary relayed that she had found records about her mother in a small township in southern Germany called Garmisch. Apparently, every time someone moved, the Germans recorded where and when. Who knew the Germans kept such meticulous records?

Lenore was on her way. First stop, Munich. She went to a farm where her newfound aunties lived.

"Not a day has gone by that we haven't thought about you," they said. They showed her baby pictures.

She was surprised at how much she resembled other family members. She spent several hours touring the farm and talking to relatives she hadn't known about. "It was so heartening to have this kind of reunion," she told me. "They really welcomed me with open arms."

The next stop was to see her mother. "I was so excited to meet my birth mother, particularly after receiving such a welcome from my aunties," she said.

The meeting lasted about ten minutes. "My mother never asked one question about me or my life. She was unwilling to give me the father's name, if she even knew it."

Lenore did, however, meet a foster brother she didn't know she had. He filled in a bit of her history. She had lived a short while with his family. She had been left with a sitter while the family was at a wedding. When they returned, they learned that officials had come and taken her away to be with her new adoptive parents.

The saddest part for me was to hear that her mother would never know what a bright, charming, capable person she had brought into the world. She would never learn of Lenore's business success, her brilliance (she is a Mensa), or her love of tennis.

It's hard to believe that, after Lenore waited so long to finally make the voyage to meet her mother and to have such a negative and unwelcoming experience with her, she could still say, "It's okay. It's no big deal."

166

Shark Island

Cheryl Lendvay

The needle on the fuel gauge, bobbing on empty, demanded our attention. My radio distress calls of "Mayday, mayday, mayday," roused no interest from anyone within the broadcast range. As the sun sank into the horizon over the Sea of Cortez, Jack, my dad, flew the little Cessna 182 at five hundred feet. I was his copilot. Four of us desperately searched out the windows of the airplane for level, solid ground. Even a beach would do.

"Look, Cheri, that might be a landing strip over there on that island," Dad said, pointing across the water.

"Uh, I don't know, Dad. I don't see it," I replied, as my heart started to race.

"Well, kid, I think we gotta go for it," he said matter-of-factly. And we did.

Once we began our low flight across the expanse of sea, there was no turning back. The sky darkening, and the landmass even darker, we approached the island. Dad banked the Cessna to the right and glided it toward the earth. At last I had a glimpse of what I hoped to be a landing strip.

"Dad, looks like you were right," I said in a calm, cool voice, internally shouting with joy and relief.

Kerplunk. He set the Cessna down on the hard-packed ground. The fuel gauge on empty, we coasted to a stop. We were now on a dirt landing strip in total darkness, out in the middle of nowhere

What island was this? I knew we were somewhere off the west coast of "Old Mexico," which is how Dad referred to the country of Mexico, but we had no idea where we were. We were lost.

It wasn't supposed to happen like this. It was Christmas break from school, and we were fleeing the chilly rains of northern California. Dad spontaneously planned a few days of warm, balmy weather on the pristine beaches of Puerto Vallarta, Mexico. A few years earlier, movie stars, Richard Burton, Ava Gardner, and Elizabeth Taylor, put the obscure fishing village on the map. Richard and Ava filmed *The Night of the Iguana* there, and

167

Elizabeth Taylor joined Richard during the filming. The affair made the cover of all the tabloid magazines. It sounded so exotic.

Near the end of our first day of flying, Dad, impatient to get to our destination, decided to take a short cut. To heck with that bothersome-official-flight plan he had filed back in the United States. "You guys see those railroad tracks down there?" he said, as he tilted the plane to the left so everyone could get a better view. "I think we're better off following them. We'll cut off a heck of lot of miles." He rambled on. "Since we can't fly at night in Old Mexico, we should get as far as we can."

"Yeah, Dad, but we're scheduled to land in Hermosillo," I reminded him.

He wasn't the least bit phased. "Then we'd still be about six hundred miles from Puerto Vallarta."

Unfortunately, I hadn't been able to persuade this pilot-in-command to stick to our flight plan, even if I was an eighteen-year-old adult, and his copilot.

So here we sat . . . my younger sister, Cathy, bored to be on this trip — worse yet — with family members, her boyfriend, John — with us only because Cathy was there, Dad, and me. We were alone in the pitch-black night, sitting upright and rigid in a cramped, fuel-less Cessna. It was so quiet I could hear everyone's heart pounding.

Then we saw the headlights of a vehicle heading toward us.

Through the darkness, we watched the lights of the vehicle bounce up and down, back and forth, as it made its way toward us across the rugged terrain. Peering over the back of the front seat Cathy asked, "Who in the heck could that be?"

I wondered myself. *Mexican soldiers, hippy campers, drug smugglers?*

We braced ourselves for what or who we would face in just a matter of minutes.

As the vehicle approached us, Dad switched on the landing lights, and we saw an open-topped jeep, four-wheel drive. At the wheel appeared to be a man wearing a wide brimmed hat. We sat motionless in the Cessna.

The man brought his jeep to a halt, left the engine running, grabbed a large flashlight, and stepped out. With the landing lights, beaming headlights of his jeep, and the streaming light of his flashlight, we could now see the driver, a rather short, stout, dark-skinned man. A giant smile on his face, he shouted, "Hola, hola," as he waved his free hand at us.

168

Well . . . he seemed friendly enough.

Dad popped open the door on his left side of the Cessna and hopped to the ground. "Cathy and John, stay right here," he directed, as he motioned for me to get out with him.

I was the only one in our group who spoke beginning conversational Spanish. (*Donde esta el bano, por favor?* Where is the bathroom please?) Oh, how I now wished I had gotten a better grade in that class! But who in their wildest imagination would have ever dreamed I would end up in this spot with the Spanish language being the most important ingredient in our immediate future?

Our new friend seemed overjoyed to see us, laughing and smiling and rattling off in rapid-fire Spanish. None of us could understand a word he said. We were like aliens who had dropped from the sky. Then I felt Dad nudge me forward, evidently to try to explain why were there.

"*No tenemos gasolena por el avion,*" I muttered, or something like that.

The man's eyes widened. It seemed like I had managed to get across our message that we didn't have any gasoline left in our airplane.

"*No problema, no problema.*" He motioned for us to come with him by first gesturing to himself and then to his jeep.

By this time, Cathy and John had descended from the Cessna, and we gathered around our new friend. Nodding my head, "*Si, si, si,*" I acknowledged I understood we were going to go with him. I pointed to the airplane and made hand movements like I was carrying suitcases.

Our friend's head bobbed up and down. He fully comprehended.

The four of us started to remove a few small bags from the luggage compartment of the Cessna. *What was the minimum amount we needed to take with us?* I thought, as I rummaged through our motley assortment of bags. *Where were we? Where were we going, and how long would we be gone?*

Right in the middle of all the commotion was our friend whistling and singing as he arranged our bags into the back of his jeep.

Once our baggage was loaded, Dad walked back to the Cessna and locked the doors. Then we all clambered into the dusty jeep. I, the official language translator, was in the front seat, perched next to our friend. Dad, Cathy, and John squeezed into the back seat.

169

After grinding the jeep into gear, it lurched forward, and off we headed into the darkness.

Rocking back and forth and jerking up and down, the jeep traversed the rugged landscape. Brush scrapped along its metal sides, and small branches occasionally slapped us in our faces as we motored through the darkness. Only the headlights of the vehicle and the moonlit sky shed any light on our destiny. We were at the mercy of our new friend.

I didn't have a sense of where we were. I have always needed to know where I was positioned in time and place. Looking up at the star-filled sky, I could only lament I had no training in celestial navigation. Glancing back over my left shoulder, I could see Dad. With his eyes closed and a wide grin on his face, he appeared not to have a worry in the world. He looked like he was in his element, savoring this adventure. Cathy and John, snuggled closely together, relishing the romantic moment . . . as if we were on a midnight hayride through the hills of Sonoma County.

The reality was . . . we were lost. We were forging through the night—on an unknown island, with a total stranger, who didn't speak our language and was at the wheel of a dusty, topless four-wheel drive. This was our immediate situation. What could we do but make the best of these impossible circumstances?

After what felt like an eternity, our friend shifted the jeep into low gear. Descending a steep slope, he suddenly brought it, with its weary passengers, to a stop.

What? Why? Where were we now?

After the dust settled, I could see the headlights of the jeep were shining on a shed made of sticks. "*Bueno!*" our friend declared with a gigantic smile on his face.

We had arrived.

"*Un momento*," he said, as he held his palm in the air, indicating we were to stay where we were. He left the engine of the jeep running with the headlights shining onto the wood stick structure. As he climbed out, he took his flashlight with him and disappeared into the dwelling. Moments later, he emerged with a lit kerosene lantern held high in the air.

When he signaled to us by lifting his free hand upward, we immediately scrambled out of the jeep. We each grabbed our own bags out of the back. (Cathy and I, being teenagers, had remembered to bring our all-important makeup kits.)

Following our leader, we ducked our heads as we entered what we now assumed was our friend's place of establishment. As

170

I peered around inside, I noted the main section was one room, with a single bed, a dirt floor, and a few items of clothing hanging from nails in the studs of the makeshift walls. Tidy. The kitchen area was outside, which seemed to me to be a good idea. Stacked stones were arranged to form what I considered to be a barbecue pit-type cooking appliance. Dad was nodding his head in complete satisfaction with our overnight accommodations. Our host began moving in circles pointing here and there. Cathy and I would take the bed in the main house, and Dad and John would join our host sleeping on the ground in the outdoor kitchen. More kerosene lanterns were lit until the abode and kitchen were aglow with dappled light.

"*Tienes hambre?*" our host asked, with his dark eyes shining in the glow of a lantern and a wide smile on his face.

"*Si como no,*" I think I might have said. *Boy, were my Spanish skills really coming in handy now!* Yes, of course, we were hungry.

With that, he spun on his heel, went directly into the open-air kitchen, and began assembling sticks and dried grass to start a fire in the barbecue pit. Smaller pieces of cut tree limbs, like those from which the walls of the dwelling were made, were added to the burgeoning flames until a nice crackling, full-fledged fire was ablaze. The moist night air filled with smoke and the smell of burning wood. He set a grill over the flame and, from a corner, brought out a large heavy pot. Using both his hands to lift the pot, he heaved it on top of the grill. He let out a chuckle, seeming to be pleased.

Taking a flashlight, I wandered away from the kitchen and looked around to become more familiar with what I hoped to be our temporary housing arrangements. I noted that everything we needed was actually there. A large ceramic container held water, and an outhouse and a make-shift shower were off in the distance. There was even a small mirror hanging from a nail in a stud — most likely for his shaving. But it would also be essential to Cathy and me for our morning makeup application and hair styling.

Before too long, the pot on the grill, filled with water and various ingredients, was boiling, and our dinner was ready. Bustling around the kitchen, our host gathered a mismatched assortment of bowls and spoons. He ladled out the steaming stew — one bowl for each of us, full of beans, some kind of meat, and a nice hot broth — and served with corn tortillas. Wrapped in scratchy wool blankets provided by our host, we gathered close to the fire and made ourselves comfortable on the ground, hot bowls

171

of stew in hand.

Smiling at one another, we nodded to show our contentment. When I looked at Dad and saw the gleam in his eyes, I got the feeling he couldn't have been happier. Being lost didn't seem to bother him one iota. It appeared to me our host was satisfied too. He had rescued us in the darkness at the end of the landing strip, was sheltering us from the cold, damp, night air, and was feeding us from his personal stash of food. He was our serendipitous savior.

Who was this hospitable man? What was he doing on this island? Was he all alone? Thinking about him being alone here on this island, I began to worry. *How were we going to get off this island?* Oh, and by the way . . . *Where exactly are we?*

We were about to find out.

Lost and in a desperate situation, the ability to speak fluent Spanish mattered not. The spoken word went out the window, so to speak, and something more basic kicked in. Communication happened, and we learned a lot.

Our host, friend, savior's name was Alfonso. Using sloweddown Spanish, facial expressions, and hand gestures, he explained to us he lived alone on *Isla Tiburon*, or, as I translated, Shark Island. The waters surrounding the island were rich with sea life and teeming with sharks, over one hundred different species, including great whites. The island had once been inhabited by the Seri Indians who were believed to be cannibals. Now, the island was designated a nature reserve, and Alfonso was the sole caretaker. Using a sharp, pointed stick, he drew a map in the dirt and showed us where we were on the island.

"*Que animales estan aqui?*" I asked, wanting to know what other animals to look out for.

He told us the Mexican government had placed a number of pronghorn antelope on the island, and it was his job to oversee the project and monitor the well-being of the herd. There were also coyotes and several different kinds of birds on the island, but not much else. Every day he talked with his headquarters in Hermosillo by way of shortwave radio. Then, he showed us a generator he could crank up for additional power.

And so, our evacuation plans began to develop. Alfonso used the shortwave radio to contact a *compadre* in Hermosillo, who relayed our situation to the airport authorities. We were officially "missing in action." Hermosillo had been our destination and refueling point in our original, discarded flight plan.

"*Si, si,*" Alfonso assured his contact, our plane would arrive sometime tomorrow.

Really?

It was late, everyone was exhausted from the day's misadventure. We "bedded down" for the night, as they say in cowboy movies. Tomorrow was another day.

The next morning after a breakfast of scrambled eggs and more corn tortillas (and no time for Cathy and me to apply our makeup nor style our hair), we found ourselves back at the end of the landing strip. We huddled together shivering in the cold, foggy, marine air—our bags clustered around our ankles.

Dad stepped forward, unlocked the Cessna, got in, and fired up the single engine. Alfonso and John stood nearby, ready for action, while Cathy and I held all our baggage in place. Even with the propeller whipping wind around us, we heard Dad shout, "There still seems to be some fuel left! The gauge isn't exactly on empty."

He shut off the engine and slid down out of the airplane. He was frowning, rubbing his whiskery chin with his hand, and looked to be in thoughtful contemplation. "Alfonso, *cuantos* miles is Hermosillo from *aqui?*" Dad asked, in his expanding Spanish.

"*Es mas o menos ciento treinta y nueve kilometers,*" Alfonso said, as he scratched the number 139 in the dirt, as if to ensure Dad understood how many kilometers to Hermosillo.

John quickly calculated the kilometers to be about eighty-six miles. Eighty-six miles from Isla Tiburon to Hermosillo . . . or so.

How were we going to get our airplane off this island, back to the mainland, and land it at the airport in Hermosillo with so little fuel in its tank?

"We're gonna have to lighten our load," John said, as if reading my mind.

Yes, we all agreed. He was right. We needed to take everything out of the airplane that wasn't essential so it would use less fuel flying to Hermosillo. We all began unloading the remaining suitcases, jugs of water, magazines—every tiny bit or scrap of anything that weighed even an ounce. Alfonso jumped in to help us pile it all off to the side of the landing strip.

We stood back and sized up the airplane.

What else could be done?

Then Dad motioned to John and Alfonso to join him. They put their heads together for a few seconds, nodded. Alfonso headed to his jeep and pulled out what appeared to be a toolbox.

Looking at one another, Cathy and I wondered what the heck they were talking about?

Once back at the airplane, the three men quickly went into action with wrenches, pliers and who knows what else. They had the doors of the Cessna open and were removing the two rear seats out of it.

What? Now what?

Everything started happening way too fast. A few quick words of explanation tumbled out of Dad's mouth. I thought I heard him say words like, "Don't worry, we'll be back, you'll be fine, I love you girls." And then he kissed us both on the forehead, turned away, and jogged toward the airplane. Before we knew what had happened, Dad and John were seated in the two remaining seats in the front of the Cessna and the doors slammed shut.

Dad shouted, "Clear!"

In a daze, Cathy and I, with Alfonso close by, stepped back and away as the propeller started whirling. The plane spun in place, then turned toward the runway. It picked up speed and lifted off halfway down the airstrip. We stood motionless and watched it as it banked and headed east over the shark-filled sea toward the mainland.

With the fog now cleared, we squinted into the bright morning sky. I kept my eyes focused on the little plane until it was just a speck in the air. Thankfully, it was still in the air!

Cathy and I looked at each other. We were left behind on Shark Island — Isla Tiburon — and feeling very lost. "What happened?" she squealed. We turned to look at Alfonso who was standing among aircraft seats, a toolbox, suitcases, duffel bags, and a pile of other miscellaneous articles. He was smiling from ear to ear.

My sister and I were very close in age, only fourteen months apart, but we were never really very close. Cathy aggravated me, and I bugged her. Until today. Now, we were like two peas in a pod, and we had each other's back — in the true sense of the word. "What are we gonna do?" she whispered, jerking her head sideways toward Alfonso.

Alfonso, speaking very slowly and in his most simplistic Spanish, explained that he had a lot of work to do. "*Tengo mucho trabajo.*" He had to check on the antelope and drive around the island. He motioned for us to join him.

So, we three piled into his jeep and headed off over the hills and around the island. Occasionally, he would stop, get out, check a post in the ground, inspect a fenced area, or take out his huge black binoculars and slowly scan the landscape. Alfonso seemed to be a jovial man with an easy smile and helpful to a fault. At times, he would burst into singing a Mexican folk song like "*Adelita*."

Once, while driving through some tall grass, we came upon a dead antelope. This caught his attention immediately, and suddenly he was strictly business. He leapt out of the jeep and thoroughly examined the carcass.

"What do you think he's looking for?" Cathy asked me.

"Probably cause of death, visible wounds, I suppose."

We watched as he measured the legs, torso, and neck, checked the teeth, and made notes on a spiral pad. Shaking his head, he made a tsking sound as he climbed back into the jeep.

Onward we ventured. The sky was crystal blue. The sun, bright. And the air, fresh with the smell of the sea. In the cool breeze, Cathy and I shivered a bit, and we each pulled our cable knit sweaters tighter around us. The landscape was full of tall, waving grass, rolling hills, and a few short trees with an abundance of underbrush. It was absolutely quiet, except for the sound of the jeep's engine, an occasional cry of a sea bird . . . or Alfonso's singing. This is how we spent the morning — the three of us scouting the island and looking at scattered herds of antelope.

Nagging in the back of my mind and in the pit of my stomach, I wondered and worried whether Dad and John had made it to Hermosillo. Or had they plunged into the shark-filled Sea of Cortez? I kept my eyes peeled for the sight of the Cessna overhead, my ears straining to hear the sound of its engine.

It wasn't until mid-afternoon that my efforts were rewarded. We heard the engine first. Then we saw her. Circling above the island was the Cessna, with Dad and John onboard.

Dad must have spotted us on the ground as he tipped the wings of the little plane and headed toward the landing strip. We did too, with Alfonso driving like he was at the wheel of a Formula One high-performance machine. I clutched the side of the jeep and Cathy hung on for dear life as dust billowed all around us. We made it to the landing strip just in time to see the Cessna touch down.

"Yahoo!" Cathy and I bellowed in unison.

"*Aiyiiyiiyiii*." Alfonso called out at the top of his lungs.

We were all so happy and relieved! I guess we had tried to

175

keep our worry and concerns from each other. So, jointly, our joy just exploded!

Once the plane came to a halt, Dad and John tumbled out. Alfonso showed up with his toolbox. The men struggled to fit the seats back into the airplane, then secured them tightly. Our bags were situated into the luggage compartment, and all the small items were crammed into the tiny compartments inside the plane. An hour later, everything had been put in place.

After hearty handshakes, hugs, lots of smiles, and even a few tears from Alfonso, we were ready to go.

"*Hasta luego,*" he called out as we climbed into the Cessna.

"See you later," we responded in kind and began strapping ourselves in for taxi and takeoff.

With the Cessna full of fuel and the four of us onboard, Dad turned to me as I fastened my shoulder harness in the copilot's seat. "This is your flight, Cheri."

Taking over the controls, I taxied the Cessna to the end of the airstrip. Turning into the wind, I gave it full throttle. The Cessna rolled down the runway, picked up speed, and lifted off the ground. I banked, turning the nose of the aircraft east, then south toward Puerto Vallarta. As we looked down from the sky, we saw Alfonso waving his hat in the air for all of us to see.

We had been lost. Found and rescued by Alfonso. Now, we were leaving him behind, alone on *Isla Tiburon*.

Now, as pilot in command, I was sticking to our flight plan. Next stop, *Ciudad Obregon* for the night and refueling. Final destination, Puerto Vallarta.

Over the drone of the single engine, I shouted, "Hey guys! Do you think Alfonso was a Seri Indian?"

"I don't know about that," Dad said. "But, Cheri, he sure wanted your hand in marriage!" We all laughed at his joke.

Was he joking? I was never quite sure. Whether he was or not, I will always be grateful for everything he did for us. Thank you, Alfonso, and go with God.

Muchas gracias, Alfonso, y vaya con dios.

A Thesis Defense

Frank Primiano

The train started with a jolt. Those passengers still standing caught themselves as they were pitched backwards. Overcompensating, they took several steps to regain their balance before seating themselves for their commute.

A latecomer staggered along the aisle, a dance partner of the swaying train. Near the rear of the car a hand shot into the air. The man attached to it pointed at the empty seat beside him. The straggler smiled with recognition and continued toward him.

"Hey, Roscoe," the seated man's voice boomed, "find any more dead bodies?" Conversations among nearby passengers ceased.

"That's some way to greet a friend you haven't seen in five months," Roscoe Morse said. His briefcase slid to the floor between his feet as his slender, six-foot frame dropped into the seat next to Dave Nagy. They shook hands.

"Sorry to disappoint you," Roscoe said, "but, nope, found just the one reported in the newspapers." To his relief, this admission appeared to dampen the interest of most of their fellow riders. A few nosies, however, didn't attempt to mask their eavesdropping. "How ya doin'?"

"Same ol' shit. Workin', commutin', domestic crap," Dave said, his Brooks Brothers suit straining to contain him. "You'll find out when you get hitched."

"At the rate I'm going, that won't be until after Eisenhower gets reelected."

"Yeah, you're too busy discoverin' corpses." Dave said, chuckling. "So, what happened? All I know is what I heard on the news."

"What's to tell? My brother, Steve, and I came across a piece of a body. The cops did the rest."

"Come on. There's gotta be more."

Roscoe shrugged, removed his cap, and stroked his sandy blonde crew cut. "Okay. You ever been crabbing?"

177

"Nope."

"I hadn't either before this summer. Steve and I were hangin' out the week before I had to leave for Arizona to do my research. I was bitching about my three months comin' up in the desert. He said why not spend some time near water before I go. I don't know where he got the idea, but he said we could try crabbing. He'd never done it before, but thought it might be interesting, a challenge. So, we drove to the shore and found a place that rented boats, motors and crabbin' equipment."

"What equipment?"

"A string with a weight, a net on a pole, a bucket, and some bait, for each of us. After a quick lesson on catching crabs, the rental guy pointed us to the marshes along the bay where the water's only a few feet deep. He said that's the place the crabs are. So, we putt-putted over there."

"How'd he say to catch 'em?"

"The little bastards are supposed to grab onto the bait — pieces of fish tied to the string. You feel a tug when they do this. So, you slowly pull up the string, and when you can see the crab, you scoop it up with the net and dump it into the bucket."

"Sounds easy," Dave said.

"It's not. We used our oars to sneak up on a likely spot and lowered our strings into the water . . . and waited . . . and sweated . . . and swatted . . . bugs."

In the midst of this narration, the train stopped at the next station. Commuters jostled each other.

"Damn," Dave said, looking toward the front of the car.

"What's up?" Roscoe asked.

"See that woman who just got on? Standing beside the conductor."

"The one with the shopping bags and the raggedy clothes?"

"Yeah."

"She some sort of bum?"

"Yep, and a psycho. She goes through the train begging until the conductor catches her. You know she's nearby from her BO. She panhandles downtown, too. I've seen her."

"How's she a psycho?"

"She picks pockets. The conductor nabbed her once, and she went unstable on him, screaming, yelling, punching. Cops came. She disappeared for a while, probably in jail or a mental hospital."

"Then I'm glad I won't be taking the train," Roscoe said. "My hours'll be too irregular, working on my thesis. I'm getting a parking permit today, so I'll be driving. I leave your lady to you."

The train resumed its journey. Smiling, Dave said, "Look, the conductor's making her go forward, probably somewhere he can keep an eye on her." Audible sighs from nearby betrayed a shared relief at her exit. "So, finish your story."

"Right. We'd waited long enough without feeling a tug. We decided to check our bait. Mine was mangled. Something had torn at it. I'd missed when the crab attacked my hunk of fish. So, from then on, if we felt *anything*, we pulled up. The crabs were supposed to hold onto the bait and not let go. But they kept falling off before they got close to the surface, before we could net them."

"Ha! They're no dummies," Dave said.

"True. So, we decided not to wait until we pulled them up. As soon as we felt anything, we shoved the net to the bottom and scooped before they could fall off."

"Did that work?"

"Sort of. I felt something. Steve manned the net and dug up a load of muck that he dumped into the boat. In the slime was a small, wriggling crab.

"Steve got the next tug. I grabbed the net and brought up just glop and seaweed."

The train pulled into another station. Dave said, "Next stop is yours. You better hurry with the story."

"Okay. So, Steve had another nibble. I plunged the net into the water. It came up with half the bay's bottom in it but no visible crabs. And worse, the boat was filling with runny piles of crap.

"We decided to tidy up a little. I used the net like a shovel. As I pushed it all into a heap and lifted, Steve said, 'Holy shit'."

Dave asked, "Why'd he say that?"

Roscoe spoke above the noise of the moving train. "Because, in that oozing, brown slop was a crab."

"Good for you."

"Yeah, 'good for me.' Problem was that it wasn't alone. It was clinging to a hand."

"A hand?"

"Mostly pale bones, but with a few slivers of meat and strands of sinew holding them together."

Two people in front of them and the man across the aisle leaned in, providing Roscoe an unwanted audience. Dave said, "'Holy shit' is right. What'd ya do?"

"I jumped back from it and nearly capsized the boat. Steve threw up over the side. We had to get the police. I rammed the net pole, handle first, into the water, as deep as it would go into the mud, as a marker. We crossed our fingers it wouldn't come loose. I kicked in the ol' Evinrude and set a speed record to the dock."

"What'd the rental guy say when he saw the hand?"

"That idiot? He fumed at his messed-up boat. Said we'd have to clean it, and return his net, or he'd keep our deposit. Steve argued with him while I phoned for the cops."

"What'd *they* do?"

"Sent a squad car, then an ambulance and two detectives. After quizzing us, they called for divers."

"Were there reporters? I bet it was exciting."

"It should have been, but I was worried about our deposit. You know the rest. The divers turned up more body parts, mostly bones — the crabs had been very efficient stripping them. The feet and lower legs weren't found. The cops figured they're imbedded in a washtub of cement out in the bay."

Dave said, "The news mentioned it might be some gangster."

"Yeah. A detective told me that was the assumption they were working under. But after all this time, since the summer, they still haven't made a positive ID."

The train's wheels screeched. They were a half mile of curved track from Roscoe's stop near the university. He stood, grasping the handles of his briefcase. Its aged leather squealed under the stress of its contents. "Maybe, if I can take a night off, we can get the guys together for a card game."

"That'd be great," Dave said. "In the meantime, keep on the lookout for more body parts."

~

"Hey, Roscoe, found any other dead bodies?"

Several passengers stopped what they were doing to look at the tall figure in a hooded car coat and scarf taking a seat beside the man in the fur-lined parka who had called to him. The train was already rolling.

"That's some way to greet a friend you haven't seen in four weeks." Roscoe said, removing his earmuffs and gloves. He wiped condensation and melting snow from his glasses.

"Why're you taking the train?" Dave asked. "I thought you're driving to school while you finish your research."

"Car's in the shop. I figured I could be a slave to the train's schedule for one day. Anyway, the snow's supposed to get worse this afternoon. Now I won't have to drive home in it." He leaned back and settled his briefcase on his lap. "So, how you been?"

180

Dave said, "I'm okay, workin' my eight hours. What're you puttin' in, like twelve?"

"Some days more than that, even weekends. And, no, no more bodies."

"Too bad. Just when I thought you had a fallback career with the cops if your research didn't pan out."

"Don't say that, man, even kidding. I've put too much time and effort into this." Roscoe clutched his briefcase to his chest. "My first draft's in here. It better fly. I don't have the energy to repeat all that work."

"Don't worry. You'll do okay. Just remember to tell the police, again, when you find another body." Dave chuckled.

The train slowed. Roscoe looked around. "Hey, isn't this where your girlfriend gets on?"

"Who?" Dave said, scowling.

"You know. That beggar lady you pointed out last time I saw you."

"Oh, yeah. You remembered."

"How could I not after your description of her exploits?"

"Well, she and I haven't crossed paths much. Rarely works this car."

"Why don't you report her when she does?"

"And get on her shit list? I told you she's nuts. You never know what she'll do. She kept hounding one guy who complained, until he quit riding this train."

"Then why not just give her some change to get rid of her?"

"That's the worst thing. She comes back for more when she sees you again. Just ignore her, if you can tolerate the smell. And don't, under any circumstances, make eye contact with her."

"Uh-oh. There she is," Roscoe said. "Looks like she isn't heading back here. Now all you have to worry about is your ride home tonight."

"I been lucky. She takes a different train than mine in the evening. I've run into her then only a few times. And she sat the whole way. Her feet were probably sore. She's none too young as far as I can gauge."

They watched the woman, under the stare of the conductor, disappear into the car ahead.

~

Roscoe boarded the last train that evening. He had his thesis in his briefcase. He'd work on it later if he could stay awake. The long nights and early mornings were catching up with him. This

181

ride home was a chance for a nap.

The flurries of the morning had become a full-blown snowstorm by the time he left his office. He thanked whichever gods were listening that he didn't have to drive in it.

Not paying attention, he landed in the smoking car. As the train lurched from the station, the smell wafted to him through the cigarette haze. It was the kind of nauseating stink that, once you got it on you, took forever to get rid of.

Most seats were empty, including the ones beside and facing him. He sneaked glances at the other passengers. Casually, he turned to scan behind. There she was, three rows back, puffing away, and, *Oh, God,* she caught him looking at her.

He faced forward a little too quickly and slid down, so his head didn't show above the seat back. What was he worried about? If she approached him, he'd give her some coins and she'd go away. *I won't be on this train again for who knows how long. She won't get another chance to bother me.*

He was too exhausted to keep thinking about the woman. But the odor, even with the smoke partially masking it, was sickening. He raised his window a crack. The gusting air blew the smell away. But it was frigid and accompanied by the occasional snowflake.

He pulled his hood over his forehead and folded his arms on his chest with his gloved hands thrust into his arm pits. His coat tails and briefcase on his lap kept his legs warm. In less than a minute he drifted off.

Roscoe stirred at the first stop as several people got off. The same for the next. At the third station he was still comatose when the train jerked to a halt. The shuffling of feet, and people bumping into his seat, partially roused him, but his eyes remained closed under his hood. His dreaming ceased, however, when his lap began to chill. He opened one eye and looked.

His briefcase was gone.

In an instant he was fully awake and on his feet. An odor, best described as that of rotting flesh, hung in the air. His eyes searched the group making its way to the front of the car. In the throng was the beggar. She held two shopping bags with one hand. From the other hung Roscoe's briefcase.

My thesis.

"Stop her. That woman," he shouted, "she stole my briefcase."

Several people turned toward him, unsure what he was yelling about. Others swore as the woman shouldered past. Still screaming, Roscoe ran toward the front of the car. Passengers blocked his way.

Valuable seconds lost, he leaped onto the snow-blanketed platform. *This is the woman's stop.* He looked both ways but didn't see her. The departing commuters streamed toward the station house and the stairs to street level. Their footprints blended, forming a wide path to the left.

To his right, a lone set of prints went off the end of the platform, past the rear of the train, and beside the tracks. He chased those, heedless of the ties protruding from the tracks and the possibility of a sprained ankle, or worse. Through the falling snow, a shadow moved beyond the bridge the train had just passed under.

My work. All my work.

The footprints were clear in the drifts despite the darkness in this gully through which the tracks ran. Stumbling footfalls and grunts sounded ahead. He was gaining on her.

Without warning, the footprints abruptly disappeared. Roscoe stopped. Everything was quiet. No street noises. No train noises. Just his heavy breathing. But wait. Was that only *his* breathing? He fought to hold his breath. The wheezing continued, from beyond the underbrush to his left. Snow had been knocked off the branches. She had jumped into the bushes. He followed. Her gasps were louder. His nose ran, but he could still taste her stench. She was nearby.

Roscoe pushed through shrubs into a clearing. Backed against a tree was the woman, stooped forward. She was a troll protecting its territory. Her paper bags lay at her feet. Both hands were pressed against her sides. One held Roscoe's briefcase by its handles.

Roscoe said, "Give me that."

She struggled for breath. "Not . . . a . . . chance. The way you want it back . . . must be something valuable inside. You gonna have to buy it from me." She slumped forward even more and coughed.

"Listen, lady. I'm a student. I don't have any money. Anyway, I wouldn't give it to you. You're a thief."

"I am what I am . . . but you not getting this . . . unless you pay up."

They faced each other, neither making a move or saying a word, separated by a curtain of falling snow and clouds of breath.

Roscoe considered the situation. *Maybe I should humor her; see if*

183

she'll take the money I have on me. He slipped off a glove and reached into his pocket. Ninety-six cents. Not even a dollar. He had no bills in his wallet. He took a step forward with his bare hand outstretched.

"Here, take this. It's all I have."

The woman straightened and pressed against the tree. "What? Change? I get more for just the empty briefcase. You think I stupid?"

"No, I don't think you're stupid. You can keep the briefcase. Just give me the papers inside. Nobody'll give you anything for them anyway."

"No thanks. I think I get better deal if I keep everything."

Roscoe made a decision. He rushed toward the woman intending to grab the briefcase. Anticipating this, she extended her right hand. Roscoe skidded to a stop. The silhouette of a large knife stood out against the white background.

"Come near me, I slit you."

"What the hell're you doing, lady? Somebody could get hurt."

"Yep, and it gonna be you." Her breathing was less labored. *Dave was right. She is crazy.*

Roscoe stood assessing his new predicament. This was her territory. Besides her odor, he sensed the smoke of a wood fire. Was it from a house above the gully, or was it from a campfire farther down the tracks where other beggars lived? Ones who would come if she screamed? He didn't want to find out. Whatever he was going to do, he had to do it now.

He put his glove back on, scooped up a handful of wet snow and packed it into a softball-sized lump. Standing no more than ten feet from her, he cocked his arm so she could see what he was up to. He threw directly at her head. She ducked to the side. The snowball pounded into the tree and shattered, showering her with snow chunks.

In his follow-through, Roscoe sprang forward and grabbed the briefcase with both hands, one on each side, and pulled. Although the snowball's impact distracted the woman from Roscoe's attack, her fingers remained locked on the handles. Off balance, she lashed out with the knife.

Roscoe raised the briefcase as a shield, its movement impeded by the weight and strength of the woman's arm. The knife slashed leather.

He yanked again. The woman, regaining her balance, made another thrust. As before, the briefcase took the brunt of the blow.

184

Shit, this bitch might get me.

Roscoe kicked at the woman's legs. He slipped. The kick missed. The knife arced past his knee. As long as he held onto the briefcase and pulled on it when the woman lunged, he could block the knife or make her miss altogether . . . he hoped.

Both were panting. Conditioning was becoming a factor. Roscoe, much taller than the woman, but probably not outweighing her, was on an adrenaline high that compensated for his sedentary lifestyle and lack of rest. But he knew he couldn't last much longer. The woman, despite her apparent age and smoking, appeared to have gotten her second wind and was becoming more aggressive.

Decision time again. This manuscript was his whole life, but was it worth losing fingers for, or worse? It would set him back months, but he could rewrite it if he had to. *Maybe I should concede. But I have it in my hands. How to get her to let go . . .?*

The woman swung again. That was too close. Time to retreat.

About to release his grip on his thesis, he glanced over his shoulder and saw *it* through the falling snow . . . hanging from a drainpipe protruding from the bank of the gully . . . a long, thick, pointed, ice stalactite.

Roscoe dodged the next thrust. He glanced at the icicle again . . . and decided. Backing toward the pipe, he pulled in that direction, dragging her with him. It was a tug-of-war, with the briefcase between them.

"Lady, let me have my bag and we can both walk away from this."

"Not a chance, college boy. You leave, you tell police I have knife. No. You a dead man. I chop you up good. Then nobody finds you 'til next spring. Maybe never."

God, this lunatic wants to kill me.

The woman lunged. Roscoe jumped to the side, jerking the leather case, matador-style. She stumbled past him. He let go with one hand and grabbed the icicle, breaking it off at its base.

He now had a weapon of his own.

~

"Hey, Roscoe, find any more body parts?" Dave Nagy chuckled at his own joke. Roscoe Morse slumped onto the seat beside him.

"Don't you think that's getting a little old?"

"I guess so," Dave conceded. He studied his buddy. "Man, you look like shit, and smell like it, too. It's as bad as that beggar

185

lady. Are you feeling okay?"

Roscoe looked at him through half-closed eyes. "That's some way to greet a friend you haven't seen since yesterday."

"Yeah. . . yesterday. What are you doing on the train two days in a row?"

"Car's still in the shop . . . until the snow lets up."

"And what happened to your briefcase there?" Although Roscoe held it to his chest with his arms crossed over it, several gashes were visible in the damp leather.

"I, uh, slipped and dropped it in front of a snowplow. It got kinda mangled and, uh, shoved into a stinky sewer. I had to, uh, reach in and fish it out. And since you asked, no, I'm not feeling my best today. I didn't get much sleep last night."

As he spoke, Roscoe gripped his briefcase more tightly. "And I've decided not to tell the police again if I know where pieces of a body are . . . or even a whole body."

The Girl Who Hit Like A Man

Syd Love

Wilmer Paulson sometimes felt like he had been born on a tennis court, had lived his whole life on one, and would die on one, a demise he did not happily anticipate but which he accepted without complaint. Of course, he had not forgotten his four years in the army during World War II when he often couldn't get to his tennis racquet. However, he spent that period Stateside and enjoyed long stretches conducting physical education classes and in his free time giving lessons to paying officers he afterwards regularly subdued, often 6-0, 6-0.

So, Wilmer lived much of his military duty immersed in, dominated by, and thriving on tennis. He also gave lessons to enlisted men. He didn't charge them.

Wilmer felt as though he could have been a star on the tennis circuit had the war not come along just two years after he graduated from college and had embarked on a promising tennis career. But Wilmer realized he represented only one grain of sand on the beach comprising millions of men and women the war thwarted, damaged, or destroyed. He seldom complained about his lame leg, injured in an automobile accident that could have happened even without the war. Still he often longed for what might have been.

He recognized that the military made an instructor out of him. Wilmer relished the role. On the day the army discharged him after hostilities ended, Wilmer Paulson determined to develop a champion. He would live his shattered dream through that person.

After teaching for several years at clubs throughout the county and accepting a continual river of students — young and old, male and female, promising and woeful and often exasperating — he decided to hunt treasure on the public courts of San Diego. He now trained the talented thoroughbred he long sought and who, he hoped, would lead his stable into a golden era.

"Let's take a break, Monica," he said across the net to the young blonde he'd been watching practice serves. "I'll buy."

Monica Conover joined him, and they left the court to seek the shade of a Monterey pine in front of the Morley Field clubhouse, where she sat on a bench. Wilmer slipped coins into the machine nearby and returned with cans of orange soda pop for each. He sat beside her.

"Your serve looked sharp," Wilmer said.

Monica nodded, sipped her drink. "I love that high bounce."

"You're nearly there with it. Then you mix the high-bouncing kick serve with the flat serve down the middle, and you'll have your opponent off balance and cross-eyed."

She laughed.

"After you catch your breath," Wilmer said, "we'll work on your net game, then hit some ground strokes."

"We could play a set."

"Not today. My leg's acting up."

"Your leg's always acting up when I want to play a set." She poked him softly with her elbow. "Come on. Just one friendly set."

"The last time we played 'just one friendly set' you nearly whipped me."

"I don't call losing 3-6 nearly whipping you."

"It was closer than the score sounds, and you know it." Wilmer finished his soda.

"All right," she said. "Tomorrow then."

"My dear, you are a relentless foe."

~

Wilmer Paulson worked part time at the clubhouse taking reservations, restringing racquets, selling T-shirts and tennis balls, giving advice, and occasionally signing up a new student. He had worked full time until acquiring so many clients the clubhouse duties interfered with his teaching. Though the complex of courts and clubhouse was public, Wilmer, by common consent, had a court assigned exclusively for his classes. In exchange, he always enrolled at least one youth he did not ask payment from. That youngster now was Monica Conover.

Wilmer had discovered her on a summer afternoon just after her tenth birthday, pigtailed and skinny, freckled and awkward, wearing cutoff jeans and white T-shirt and the most-battered tennis shoes Wilmer had ever seen not dangling from power lines. The way her pigtails bounced and twirled as she incessantly used a warped wooden racquet to pound a dirty white ball against the backboard near the concrete courts told Wilmer she gave herself a thorough workout.

As he watched from the shade of a eucalyptus, the girl switched the racquet from her right hand to her left and hit just as well that way. Wilmer reached several conclusions: *She's unschooled, ambidextrous. She's driven. She's poor. And she has vast potential.* He approached and smiled.

"You're going to bust that backboard into splinters."

This time when the ball rebounded, she popped it up with the racquet, caught it with her free hand, and smiled up at him. "Yeah. My mom made me quit hitting against the garage door."

"I would think so. I was twice your age before I could hit that hard."

She laughed, and they introduced themselves.

"I know who you are," Monica said.

"How's that? I've never noticed you in the clubhouse when I'm

188

there."

"I've seen you play. You could beat anyone here if your leg didn't slow you down."

So, she's a critic too. But she's right. "Then you probably know I give lessons. Would you like instruction?"

"We can't afford it."

"I wouldn't charge. It's called pro bono."

"What does that mean?"

"It's a payback to make up for all the fees I take from others."

"What's the catch?"

"No catch, young lady. I do not lie nor cheat."

"Hmmm. Maybe I'll ask my mom."

"Let's go to the clubhouse and phone her right now." Along the way they neared a trash can. "Throw that ball away."

Monica looked into the container. "There's a bunch of good balls in there."

"They're well used. Grab a couple for serving practice and leave yours."

Wilmer watched Monica retrieve one, look around as though not wanting to be caught stealing, and pocket it. But she kept hers.

"Mom's a waitress at The Pancake House in North Park," Monica said. "Works split shifts and might have already headed that way."

"When will she be home?"

"After ten."

"What do you do for dinner?"

"I fix it. Then I eat it."

Monica's mother didn't answer the phone.

"What's on the early dinner menu at The Pancake House?" Wilmer said.

~

The hostess knew Monica from previous visits, smiled at the arrivals, and directed them to her mother's serving area, where Monica handled the introductions. She and Wilmer ordered cheeseburgers with onions. Wilmer's wife, Alice, summoned from her job running Adlai Stevenson's campaign office in San Diego County, requested decaf and a croissant.

"Gotta go back to work in a bit," Alice said. "We can't coast, so many people like Ike."

Debbie Conover, saying she could take a short break, joined them. Wilmer explained his plan, liked the rapport between Monica and her mother, knew his wife saw it too, would approve of Wilmer's taking charge of the girl's tennis career if that's what resulted.

"We live near this tennis complex," Alice told Monica. "On the nights your mom works you would come home with Wilmer for dinner with us. If it's dark, one of us would drive you home afterwards."

"That's too much," Debbie Conover said.

"It's part of our contract," Wilmer said.

"What contract? You said you wouldn't charge."

"My word. A handshake."

Debbie sounded "Hmmm" the way Monica had and added, "Look, it's nice. You folks are swell. But you're talking charity. We can't accept. I have a job. The tips are good. Monica is more help to me every day."

"Monica is a candidate to become a wonderful tennis player, perhaps a champion. She can still help out at home. Lessons don't last all day, and I have other students. When school's in session, after classes is enough. A few hours on Saturday, Sundays off if she wants."

"Wilmer often takes on a student for free," Alice said. "He is a wonderful coach. I've never heard him talk about a young person's potential the way he described Monica. We'll watch out for her, both of us."

"It's just so much, what you're offering."

"Wilmer says Monica might be that future big star he's always looked for."

"What do you think, Monica?" Debbie looked at the wall clock.

"It would be fun to play every day. Maybe by high school I could try out for a team."

Alice stood, tapped her red, white, and blue lapel button, *Adlai Is For You in '52*, and grabbed her purse. "You folks hash it out." She kissed Wilmer's cheek, shook hands with Debbie and Monica, and left.

They continued talking, mother and daughter mainly. Talk of a Mr. Conover did not enter the conversation. Wilmer looked from Monica to Debbie, back to Monica, to Debbie again. Finally, she hugged her daughter, kissed her cheek, and stood. "Nice to have met you, Coach." They shook hands. "Please keep her away from my garage door."

~

Wilmer held firm. He and Monica volleyed for half an hour and now sat in the shade in front of the clubhouse to wind down and chat before she rode her bicycle home. Her tennis dress, white and comfortable, fitted well, looked good on her. Monica had reached her permanent height of two inches over five feet, shoulders broadened, her form filled and rounded from toes to topknot. She had discarded her pigtails in favor of a medium-length ponytail, and she used the best racquets, which Wilmer furnished with a locker in the clubhouse. Alice kept Monica in tennis attire and shoes, plus a supply of white bill caps with *Monica* embroidered on them in blue, a gap in the back for her ponytail.

Wilmer and Monica talked as coach and student, as father and daughter, as best friends.

"You could still use more racquet-head speed on your forehand, get a higher bounce."

"I'll work on it."

"And you shouldn't slice so many backhands."

"You do."

"That's because I'm *old* school."

190

"Remember you promised we could play a set tomorrow."

"I did not promise. Besides, you need to hit with kids around your age. They're fast like you and will give you a more realistic game."

"I've already played every kid my age."

"And vanquished them. You are a regular assassin."

She giggled. "Some were boys. Wilmer, I want to play in the national Girls' 15s."

"You're only twelve."

"Doesn't matter. And you know it."

"You're still too young."

"Am not."

"Honey, I don't want to rush you. If you didn't do well — not necessarily lose but get beaten badly — that wouldn't be good for you mentally."

"What if I played well, maybe even won?"

"That would also be bad for you mentally."

"How could that be?"

"Your ego. And it's already as big as the clubhouse."

"Is not."

She's right. Usually is. Never met a young player that good and yet so humble. "Just kidding, Monica. Look, I'm ready to take a break, but you could practice serving, and I could watch from the bench. It's an hour before my next student."

"It's rather warm on this midsummer day, sire."

"Heaven forbid Her Majesty is discomfited."

"A bit, my lord."

"That will pass. Now hie thee out there and slug 'em."

"Yes, maestro." She laughed and jumped up.

"Serve some left-handed. And tomorrow when we rally, hit some with that hand too. It's a skill that comes in handy when you're chasing a backhand you can't quite reach and can switch to your left. I've done it a few times, but never with your touch."

"Will do. And if I broke my right arm I could still play."

"Why did you switch anyway? You say you're a natural lefty."

"Everyone I watched played right-handed. So I thought I should too."

"Now you look natural from the right."

"I think I like it better."

Twenty minutes later when Monica finished serving and started home, Wilmer, wanting to sit in a cushioned chair, entered the clubhouse where he found a letter awaiting him. He opened it with interest, read with disgust, reread it with dismay and anxiety.

~

"I don't blame you for being upset." Alice set down her glass of Pinot Grigio, picked up the letter. "Like an agent, trying to steal your client." She set the letter aside. "I'm sorry, Honey. What are you going to tell

191

him?"

"You mean before I give him directions to Hell?" Wilmer refilled their glasses. They cherished this nightly session of wine sipping and chatting before dinner, though lately they often had to skip it because of Alice's election commitment. And Wilmer Paulson did not enjoy this night's gathering.

"He probably wouldn't be interested," Alice said, "if he knew she didn't have money."

"Not this vulture. He'd find a way to profit."

"And there are the others." Alice sipped her wine.

"What others?"

"A couple of men have called for you. No names I recognized. They tried to pump me for information."

"What did you tell them?"

"The same thing you're going to tell this guy." Alice tapped the letter on the coffee table.

Wilmer leaned back, stretched his legs, held his glass on his stomach. "I knew word would get out. But I still don't like it. I suppose they've been hanging around watching her."

"Honey, you couldn't expect to keep Monica a secret, the way she hits. And she whips everybody who challenges her."

Wilmer nodded. "Yet, she isn't arrogant, just self-confident."

"I wish I could have hit like her. Would you have taken me on?"

"No."

"Why not? I had potential, number one on our college team. And my folks had money."

"You're too pretty. I would have had other plans for you."

"Satyr."

Wilmer laughed, quickly became somber. "I don't want to lose this girl."

"You won't. She's family. We're family. Her mom too."

"Monica wants to enter the national Girls' 15s."

"She's too young."

"I mentioned that."

"You can stop her."

"I'm not so sure. That girl could debate Lincoln and Douglas at the same time."

~

Two days later at practice Monica arrived late. Wilmer noticed her lack of animation, her brow in a crease, her mouth a pout. She hugged him and turned away.

Wilmer waited a few beats and tapped her shoulder.

Monica turned slowly, sniffling, looking up at him. He took her hand and led her to the bench in front of the clubhouse. She sniffled again, blurted her misery.

"Mom's new boyfriend wants to take over as my coach."

192

Wilmer sucked in a deep breath, let it out slowly, stretched his legs in front of him, looked straight ahead.

"He says he knows a lot of important people in sports and politics. And he'll help me go right to the top."

"Does he know there's no money in tennis? Just expenses if you're good enough? That the best you'll do is win a few silver plates? Something to put the turkey on at Thanksgiving?"

"I told him. He says there are other ways we can make money."

"Like what?"

"He didn't say."

"What does your mother think?"

"She's happy. He promised her a new car right away."

"And what do you say?"

With the back of her hand Monica wiped her nose. "He promised me a new car too as soon as I'm old enough."

"And you said?"

"We told him we had a contract with you. He asked to see it, so we told him we didn't have it in writing. He laughed." Monica turned into Wilmer and sobbed.

~

Monica practiced early the next day, and Wilmer took her home to talk with her mother before Debbie Conover left for work. Her boyfriend rose from the couch, and she introduced them. *Debbie doesn't know what she's doing. 'Duke Monroe'? He's like no coach I ever heard of. This guy's a fraud. Enough jewelry to choke Lady Godiva's horse. Sounds like a New Jersey gambler.*

They talked for a few minutes, Monica frowning, unspeaking in a rocker across the room, Debbie smiling and nodding on the couch beside her boyfriend, Wilmer seated nearby.

"Monica's doing great," Wilmer said, "coming along just fine." He knew he sounded feeble.

"She'll do even greater with my friend coaching her."

"But, Debbie, he . . . we . . ."

"I know all about you," Duke Monroe said. "I've checked you out. You've never coached anyone who made it to the top. And you yourself aren't any hotshot, never were."

"I held a fairly high ranking before the war." *Why defend myself to this ape?*

"Ages ago, mister."

"And so, I coach and don't compete anymore. I don't have to hit like Pancho González as long as Monica does." *I'm getting out of here.* "Debbie, please think carefully about this."

~

After two weeks oppressed by the dread of possibly losing Monica as a student, and Alice's talking with Debbie proving fruitless, Wilmer regained his spirit and hopes the day Monica, arriving for practice, smiled

193

and trotted up to him.

"Duke's gone," Monica announced.

"Your mom kill him?"

Monica laughed. "Kicked him out. He said her new car had to wait until I won the Girls' 15s. Showed us an old Lincoln Zephyr that coughed and moaned and cried for paint."

They enjoyed a vibrant practice session, and afterwards Wilmer agreed to play a set. He had to employ every lob, drop shot, soft chip, and looping forehand in his armory in order to win.

"Any luck at all and I'd have skunked you, Wilmer Paulson."

"My dear, this gimpy older man is unskunkable."

They laughed and hugged and walked to the clubhouse.

Efforts continued by other coaches to take over Monica's training. Team Wilmer laughed them off, also rejected challenges from boys wanting to see if Monica played as well as hearsay declared. But they allowed the next male challenger the privilege of finding out for himself.

"J. Desmond Updike III," he announced in his approach to Monica and Wilmer resting on the pine-shaded bench in front of the clubhouse. "You may have heard of me."

Wilmer stretched his legs, crossed his arms. He saw Monica's inquiring look.

"My serve," the boy said. "My hundred-mile-an-hour serve." Challenging, almost taunting, he stepped closer to Monica. "So this is the blue-eyed blonde girl who hits like a man."

"What do you want, Jay? Monica has to get back to practice."

"That's just my first initial. Call me Desmond. I thought the girl would be bigger."

"I'm big enough."

Wilmer liked the challenge in her response.

"Hey," Desmond said. "Don't get mad. I just thought we might hit a few. I'll take it easy with you."

Wilmer saw a red-haired youth a little older than Monica, several inches taller, smirking, confident, egotistic, tinted obnoxious. He toted a new racquet bag and wore white tennis sweater and pants with spiffy canvas tennis shoes. His cap, monogrammed, said *Beach and Tennis Club*.

"Aren't there any girls at your club you can beat up on?" Wilmer said. "Or boys?"

"They asked me to stay—I'm staying away temporarily. Change of scene and all."

"What do you think, Monica?" Wilmer drew in his legs, placed his hands on his knees.

"It's up to you, Coach."

That's what I like to hear. "He'll be faster than me. Hit with him if you'd like."

"I'd much rather play a couple of sets," Desmond said.

"All right. They'll give you a locker in the clubhouse." Wilmer motioned toward it. "Get a can of balls and charge it to my account."

When the boy moved out of hearing, Monica said, "You gave in easily."

"He's on a mission. The original J. Desmond Updike is his grandfather. Owns the Beach and Tennis Club. You know how some rich kids are. The old man runs a tight ship, might have banned the boy for acting up or cheating or something. Or maybe not. The kid's father is the pro there and not a bad one. My guess is the boy's here to spy without being so obvious like the others have been, some in street clothes, studying you from the stands."

"So, he reports to his father, like a scout, and his dad might want to coach me?"

"I can guarantee you he'll want to. I'm surprised we didn't hear from him earlier."

"Maybe this one will be able to afford a new car." Monica laughed and stood.

"Let's have some fun. Play him left-handed. If he's too tough for you, switch."

"So you want me to skunk him if I can."

"That would be lovely, yes. Here he comes."

The challenger, in costlier shoes than before and wearing matching headband and wristband, joined them. He smiled and strutted while they walked to the battleground.

Desmond won the right to serve first.

Wilmer doubted his serves reached 100 miles an hour, though they sizzled.

Monica's sizzled more, her ground strokes too. She skunked him, did so left-handed.

"I got off balance, confused, playing a lefty." J. Desmond Updike III, taking deep breaths, sat on a bench to rest. "Otherwise . . . but it's true. She does hit like a man."

"You should see her play right-handed," Wilmer told him.

"Huh? I don't think I want to. Hey, you're kidding, aren't you?"

Debbie Conover heard from the boy's father as well as from several more men wanting to assume Monica's tutelage. Debbie spurned them, kept on driving her old Studebaker.

Monica continued to defeat all challengers, often demoralizing them, finally cajoled Wilmer into letting her, just short of her thirteenth birthday, enter the national Girls' 15s competition. She won it. The local newspapers published her picture on the front page, mentioned Wilmer twice.

Almost immediately Monica began pestering Wilmer to let her enter the Girls' 16s.

"Honey, let's wait until you're at least fifteen."

Monica laughed. "What for?"

How I Found the First Americans in My Life

Dora Klinova

It was the year 1990. The Cold War was over. The Soviet Union started to fall apart; it was a mess in the country. Jews were once again allowed to emigrate; the rest of the citizens envied and hated them. They blamed the Jews for everything. The Jews were always the guilty ones. Period.

The Soviet Government desperately needed foreign currency and welcomed tourists, especially from America. Little by little, the Americans started to come. Their curiosity about mysterious Russia was much stronger than their fear of those unpredictable communists. I seriously started to think about emigration and tried to find any avenue to meet some Americans and communicate with them.

I lived in Odessa, a beautiful resort on the Black Sea with a high level of culture. An old prestigious International Hotel named "The Red Hotel" was secured and protected, and only for foreigners, mostly Americans. For us, the average Odessa's citizens, The Red Hotel was a no-no territory. We were not permitted to put our nose inside.

Americans, who visited Odessa and stayed at The Red Hotel, were unreachable. There was no way for us to meet with them. But the Americans refused this isolation. They wanted to communicate with Odessa's people.

As it is said, if you seek, you will find.

One day, I was introduced to the director of the committee who organized the leisure time for the American groups in Odessa. Their program itinerary scheduled one evening with an Odessa family including a dinner at their home. It looked like a protest to the invisible wall that the Soviet security system had built around Americans. This dinner was a challenge to the Odessa tourist committee. They had to find a trustworthy family to host the Americans for an entire evening and leave them alone.

197

The director courted me (or pretended doing this) perhaps waiting to see if he could safely introduce American tourists to me. He found that I was an excellent cook. Despite many suspicious looks cast my way, he finally decided that I would not shoot or bite the Americans. He said, "American tourists want to spend an evening with an Odessa family. Would you like to prepare a nice dinner and invite a couple of Americans to your place?"

The only family I had at that time was my handicapped 83-year-old Aunt Rachel who lived with me. I laughed. "Do you think they will be interested in meeting Rachel?"

"You will be great by yourself."

"I barely speak English," I said.

"Don't worry, they have a translator."

"OK, I will do it. Would you like to come as well?"

"No, no, they won't like any officials at the dinner. They want to feel free."

~

The Americans' itinerary provided three hours to dine with a Soviet family on Tuesday, from 6 to 9 p.m. When I agreed to this adventure, the director informed me that he would be sending me not two, but six Americans plus a translator.

I burst into laughter.

"Why are you laughing?" he asked.

"You made your job simpler. It would take a lot of your time to find another trustworthy Odessa family. It is easier for you to send a whole bunch of Americans to my place, isn't it?" I teased him.

"You are too sharp." He laughed.

"Don't worry, I can handle it. I will greet all of them," I said.

I was permitted to invite some of my friends. The leisure program would pay for the dinner expenses.

"My God," I thought. "I have to put together a whole party."

The director called me. "Please serve the dinner with three crystals."

"What does it mean?" I asked.

"One crystal for wine, the second for brandy, the third for water or juice."

"What?" I asked him. "No. You make these three crystals at your fancy hotel. I will do it more simply. It is my home and my rules. OK?"

"OK. You are the boss."

198

I laughed. They are really crazy about Americans. Three crystals! Funny expression. I will remember it.

~

My mind played ping-pong with the idea of making this dinner. I should prepare an outstanding dinner. I must show these Americans what it means to have dinner in a Russian family. Why Russian? No, I am not Russian. I am a Jew. I will prepare Jewish food. I will tell them that I am a Jew.

Should I invite some of my friends? Yes, it would be a good idea. No, it wouldn't. Who needs to know that I expect guests from America? Personal contacts with Americans were not welcomed.

To have Americans at my home and not to tell anybody? To keep this secret?

Impossible! I wanted the entire world to know it! Tuesday? Not a good day. I worked and usually came back home at 6:30 p.m. To prepare the dinner a day or two before, on Sunday? No, the food must be fresh. I needed a day off on Tuesday.

My boss was also a Jew. All Soviet Jews secretly cherished an emigration dream. My boss studied English, pretending that he needed it for his dissertation.

In the morning I came to his desk.

"May I invite you to my place for a dinner on Tuesday?" I asked.

He looked at me with surprise. We had never socialized before.

I explained. "I will be having a group from America over for a dinner. Would you be interested?"

His eyes sparkled with interest.

"Yes, perhaps."

"You are welcome to come with your wife."

"I am sure she will be pleased." He looked at the calendar. "Oh, I cannot. Unfortunately, it is my daughter's birthday. But if you need, take Tuesday off. We will pay you for this day."

Great! This is what I needed.

I invited a couple of my Jewish friends in order to share the Americans with them.

It was September — the blessed time in Odessa. The Market had all one could want of fruits and vegetables. I bought the best and started creating wonders in my kitchen.

My aunt came to the kitchen with her crutches.

"What is going on here?"she asked.

199

"We will have special guests," I replied.

"How many?"

"Seven."

"Why are they special?"

"They are from America."

"I do not remember that you have American friends. Did you ever meet them before?"

"No."

"Are you crazy? Don't you know that all Americans are gangsters? Do you want to bring to our home seven bandits?"

"Who told you this rubbish?" I asked my aunt.

"You work, work, work. You don't know what is going on in the world. I know. I watch TV. I read newspapers. You must immediately stop doing anything for them."

She yelled at me, banging on the floor with her crutches.

"You are tired; go to the balcony and rest," I told her.

"I am not tired!" She raised her voice.

"OK, your crutches are tired. You will break the floor. Go to the balcony! Relax. I will talk to you later."

"You don't listen to me! I categorically forbid you to open the door to these bandits. They are all bandits!" She pointed her finger into my face and left to the balcony loudly crying.

I worked hard for a few hours. To the accompaniment of my aunt's crying, I prepared a great dinner. Aunt Rachel dramatically refused to eat lunch. She walked into her room and slammed the door. Near 6 p.m., I asked her to change from her robe to a nice dress.

My aunt yelled. "No! You are a stubborn donkey. I don't want to see you and your darned Americans!"

At 6 p.m., my guests arrived. Kind smiling faces. They introduced themselves: Florence and Irwin Blickstein from Boca Raton, Florida; Adrian and Rosemary Pinto from Norwich, Vermont; Virginia Foote from Tucson, Arizona; and, Ida Fowler from El Paso, Texas.

They were a part of a senior group of medical professionals. Delighted to come to my home, they looked in amazement at the table covered with a colorful abundance of food.

"How could you find so much food?" they asked. "The shelves at your stores are empty."

"In my refrigerator," I joked.

They couldn't believe that I had prepared everything myself.

I announced, "This is not a Russian home; it is a Jewish home.

I am a Jew. I want you to enjoy Jewish food. I live with my old aunt, but she doesn't speak English and asked to excuse herself. She has decided to stay in her room."

Irwin said, "We are also Jews. Does she speak Yiddish?"

"Yes, she does."

"Can I talk to her?"

"I hope so."

We came to Rachel's room. Irwin started to talk to her. I left them alone.

In a few minutes my Aunt called me. "Where is my lipstick? I need a mirror and my best blue dress. I will come to the dinner."

Three hours flew by like three minutes. We laughed and talked, talked and laughed, and sang Jewish songs. They sang to Aunt Rachel "A Yiddisher Mama."

Who cared that my English was poor?

At nine p.m., the bus driver knocked on the door.

"We must go. This is the best time we have had on this trip. We would like for you to come and join us at the Red Hotel tomorrow at lunchtime. We will be there, and we will wait for you."

"I am not allowed to enter The Red Hotel," I said.

"Don't worry. We will take care of it," they insisted.

The next day I brought them a gift—a beautifully illustrated book about Odessa. Our meeting was short; their schedule was very tight. I left with my hands full of souvenirs. Perhaps they expressed their excitement about the evening in my home to the tour administration. I was placed on the top list as the Odessa family to greet Americans. Every two weeks a different group of Americans came to Odessa. I made two more dinners and met another twelve Americans. Then America discontinued this program. It was not a pleasure for the tourists to see depressed people and empty store shelves.

In 1992, I immigrated to America. I called some people who visited my home in Odessa.

One couple from Seattle, Zelma and Erwin Kremen, came to see me in 1994.

Florence and Irwin Blickstein often telephoned me from Boca Raton, Florida. Irwin talked to Rachel for hours in Yiddish.

Rachel died in 2001. Florence and Irwin Blickstein passed away in 2004.

My boss, Eric Edelberg, lives in New York now.

All American names in this story are real.

~

I met these first American people in 1990 in Ukraine. Today is 2019. Twenty-nine years passed. Twenty-nine long, short as a blink, saturated, and meaningful years. Now I am an American myself. I live in wonderful San Diego, enjoying beautiful blue sky of California. Something unbelievable had happened to me in America. America gave me inspiration and made me a writer. America gave me a Merit Award for my poetry. My three books, written in English that is not my native language, are over the world now. One of my books is translated into Japanese! America gave me so much!

I bow to you, in honor, America!

The Living Dream

Sarah Faxon

It was beginning to sprinkle, but the lighthouse continued to call to her. She had waited twenty years to see this island and would not insult her dreams by being chased off by a bit of rain.

The confines of life back home had restricted her for far too long. Life had taken her through many unexpected turns—all away from this, away from her call to the emerald isle. She knew that she was supposed to travel the world, to see and taste it all, but seeing her husband's dreams realized came first. After fourteen years of supporting him came the cascading divorce-sea. When light on the horizon at last began to shine out from that tempest, her mother drew ill and the rest of her coffers went to providing and caring for her.

Through it all, the call of the uilleann pipes and the bodhran drums sang her to sleep. The tune, rhythmic and patient, told her that someday the rolling hills of Ireland would be hers.

Awake and unchained, this was her time, and she was going to see as much of the island as she possibly could.

The drops were cool falling upon her smiling cheeks. The sensation helped to remind her that this was real. The thought delighted her as she walked down an uneven stone path littered with sheep. The ewes baaed at her and nibbled on her wrists as she wove through their flock, continuing on her journey.

Passing through the jumble of sheep, the lighthouse, tall and majestic, rose directly above her now. Being this near to the edge of the cliffs, she could smell the sea that sprayed up from the rocky beach below. It did not seem possible, but her smile extended all the more as she ran her ungloved hand across the cool, stone edifice of a sailor's beacon.

The "No Trespassing" chain strewn across the entrance was quickly stepped over as she bounded inside the abandoned building. What was an adventure without a bit of mischief?

Winding her way up the thin tower, she giggled delightedly to think that, in wandering away from her tour group, she had accidentally discovered such a gem. The tour group she traveled with had been a good deal. Flight, food, board, and booze were all included, but the rigid structure and stuffy buses were not for her anymore. There was too much lift in her sails to follow someone else's course now. It tickled her to think that she, a woman who had spent most of her life ruled by the demands of others, had found her strength at last on the banks of the Irish sea.

Reaching the top, she inhaled the crisp air of the eastern coast blowing through a window, broken by time. Gulls sang in the distance, and she could clearly see the grey, turning waters below. She did not know which was greater — the view, or feeling like a real-life Indiana Jones.

All the problems she had at home, all the drama of her past — all of it was gone, lost to the sea. All that mattered now, as she inhaled deeply and freely, was that she was finally living her dreams.

Am I My Brother's Keeper?

Elizabeth Duris

It was not an unusual 6 a.m. to wake up to find one of my cats sitting on my chest, staring directly into my face, waiting for me to clear the cobwebs of interrupted sleep to welcome him.

What was unusual was his persistence. Customarily he would finish the stare down, figure I had cried uncle and that he had won. Then he would bound off to the bathroom to pull down towels, dump the wastebasket, or climb into the tub to challenge the drain plug to a rematch.

But not today. Today Lucca hung back, waiting for me to climb out of bed in search of coffee. He hung at my heels, shadowing me like a bad rash. He began making strange sounds, not a full meow, but a more plaintive, soft mew, mew. "What do you want, Lucca? Banana? Okay, banana." Usually it's Lunah who is the morning banana-beggar, but he was nowhere in sight.

I refreshed their water, refilled their cat food bowl, and attended to the daily litter box cleaning. But Lucca was not a happy camper this morning, no matter what we were doing. "What's wrong? Why are you crying? Why did you nip at my leg? What do you want? Where's Lunah?" Yes, where is Lunah? By now we had been up long enough to have Lunah start playing the bully, edging out Lucca at the banana ritual, nudging him at the food dish, or pushing him aside at the water trough.

Lunah is the smaller of my two adult Ragdolls. He has the face of an angel, lavender markings, soft blue eyes, and a delicate, gentle, almost feminine look about him. Lucca is considerably larger, has a masculine face, and appears to be a formidable force with his sable and seal point markings. Make no mistake, however. Lunah is the street-savvy, in-your-face bad boy in our house. Do not be fooled by first impressions. He is the quintessential escape artist, slyly maneuvering himself at any door for a possible taste of the unexplored freedom beyond. Coyotes be damned.

By now Lucca was figure-eighting my legs wherever I went. The sad mewing continued. Finally, I asked my husband, "Have you seen Lunah this morning?" When he said he hadn't, I questioned him about any possible opened door. "No" to that also, so I started a room-to-room search. Was Lunah sick somewhere? Had he eaten something? Had he choked on one of his stolen waste basket treats? Had he possibly escaped, sight unseen, and now lies dead outside, a victim of that wretched coyote?

Had Lucca all this time been calling me to action? "Find my brother. Go get my brother. My brother is not here. Find him." At long last I reached the far end of the house, checked the laundry room and the back bath where Lunah likes to sit looking out of the window. No Lunah anywhere.

As a last resort, I unlocked and opened the garage door. Out bounded a very hungry and thirsty Lunah. He had been locked there in the dark garage all night! My husband's nightly watchman routine included checking all doors. Lunah somehow managed to escape into the garage in the process. Hopefully, lesson learned. With Lunah the Streetfighter, I'm not entirely sure.

And "Yes," meows big brother Lucca, "I am my brother's keeper."

An A-Musing Find

Melody A. Kramer

She's been missing for months. My muse. I'm sure she's lying on a beach somewhere, soaking up the sunshine, sipping a margarita—rocks, no salt. The bitch! No advance request for vacation, not even a post-it note to advise me of her whereabouts. Shameful! I'd fire her if I could. Sadly, I've found no replacement for her . . . yet.

Stella is the inspiration for everything I've ever written. However, she's fickle and unreliable, and I've had it! She's got to go, or come back, whichever. I'm not that picky anymore. I've got stuff to write.

I sit with my pen and paper contemplating my options. I think I need to find a new writing muse, maybe not a replacement but a temp, you know, like any other business handles employee absences. I certainly need a more reliable muse. Even a lesser muse with staying power would be better than intermittent flashes of genius from a frequently vacationing muse, right?

I'm thinking I want a male muse this time, sort of a Greek-god-looking, guardian-angel–without-wings, Cheetos-eating type of guy. He would be laid back and self-confident with a razor-like wit, never pushy, just present and supportive, focusing his baby blues on me from time to time saying, "You know you can do this, just write." Then he would grab another Cheeto and quietly crunch while checking his text messages. Every now and then he would look over at me and a small smile of pride would appear on his face as he would watch my frenzied, messy handwriting of an article or the next chapter of my upcoming book. Vacations? He'll come along with me on mine.

Oh, yeah, it's time to find a new muse!

Ninety-nine resumes later, mission accomplished. Out with the old; in with the new. Stella is out, Adonis is in.

Funny thing about vacationing muses, though, they don't care if they get fired. I sent Stella her walking papers, via text, email, and a post-it note delivered to her poolside in Bermuda. (I was right. She was sipping a margarita at the time.) She didn't get mad. In truth, it would have been a little affirming of me as an author if she had. All she did was send me a text. "good luck with your next book" it said without elaboration or punctuation. No exclamation point, no smiley emoji, no sense she was actually wishing me well. Instead it seemed to be more of a raised middle finger daring me to write anything worthwhile without her ever present guidance. Sorry, Stella, but my own middle finger is busy typing my next bit of genius prose. "Good luck getting another writer to muse over" I am too busy to text back.

Meanwhile, I have inked the deal with my new muse, Adonis, and, I've got to say, this relationship is already showing promise. "My dearest," he leans over and whispers in my ear, confident, and rightly so, that flirting with me will get him everywhere. "My dearest, do not rush. Inspiration is born of a relaxed mind and spirit. Words will come when your mind is in the right place."

I know he's right, but it's tough to get my mind in the right place. I still have to earn a living, often frantically typing out a plethora of meaningless words to meet work deadlines, words that do not fill my soul or move my spirit. It affirms the truth of what he said. Anyone can produce mere words, but words with meaning take a lot more than the assembling of consecutive letters like some careless game of Scrabble.

I gaze over at Adonis, comfortably resting against a nearby Grecian pillar that only he and I can see, crunching on Cheetos again. "Write epic stuff," he says. "Are you in an epic space yet?" I feel the tense muscles in my shoulders, the queasy feeling in my stomach, thinking about all of today's tedious deadlines. "No, not yet," I respond, "but soon." I turn to my keyboard anyway and start typing. "What are you writing, my dear?" Adonis queries. "Nothing much, but I'm feeling inspired." I wink and return to my keyboard.

1958

Chloe Kerns Edge

I was hiding on the back bank just below the lawn, out of sight with my boyfriend, Lee Flores. My dad hated him. Lee had black curly hair, he was thin—about 5′8″—and he had nice brown eyes. He wore thick black-framed glasses which he took off to read.

He said, "You don't have to take this shit."

"I don't?" It was the first time in my life that I had any idea that the beatings my brother and I took from my dad could be any other way.

I'd been playing with my gray kitty who followed me everywhere—telling Lee about my broken ribs, showing him bruises on my arms when he'd said it. I was letting it sink in. I had never not known being beaten. I had always been beaten—since before I could talk.

"Pre-verbal experience" they would say in the shrink's office. Now I realize that my dad had the battered-child syndrome; back then, the words, "child abuse" and "battered child" hadn't been coined yet. It was discipline, "spare the rod and spoil the child" discipline. Only my dad couldn't stop once he got started. He had to pound and pound and then kick until we couldn't move. Then he'd stomp away, and I would crawl or scurry, depending on how badly I was wounded, to my closet to hide.

I told myself stories about why it happened—that I'd been put into the wrong family at birth. Later I believed that the reason I was always getting it was because I was bad. Around twelve years old, I got really mad about it and fought back—yelling hatred at my father, screaming accusations before the inevitable pounding began.

I was angry, and I was twisted by then. I had told the Sunday school teacher at Christ Lutheran Church that my dad was beating me. Her eyes got big, and she said, "Oh, no!" She acted like she'd do something about it, but she never did. Finally, I got up my nerve to tell the vice principal at Pacific Beach Junior High School what was happening to my brother and me at home. I thought for sure someone would at least go talk to my father, but nothing ever happened. No one even tried to protect us. That messed me up.

It was as though my brother and I were in our own war—only it wasn't always going on. The battles erupted out of clear blue sky while we were all having fun with our dad. He was big and his hands were huge. He had an overpowering presence. His hair was dark brown, and he had green eyes behind the glasses. He could make up stories and poems, and he sang the best songs. So sometimes right in the middle of the fun he would snap, and a beating would begin.

Usually these insane outbursts occurred when my mom wasn't home. Sometimes she was there, though. Her brown eyes would flash fear, and then her yelling would add conflict to the violence my dad was creating. "Bill! Stop, Bill!" Like it would do any good—like he could stop—even if he wanted to.

My mom was 5'6" with brown curly hair, a Roman nose and kind brown eyes. She was Black Irish, as they say, and she had olive skin. She would die for us, she had said, but she could never stop him. He just yelled and cussed and pounded or threw me across the room to crumble against the piano, or better, the couch. Sometimes if I stayed down, he'd leave, but if I was mad and got back up, he'd finish me off until I couldn't move. Then, I'd get to my closet somehow. A few times, my mom came to get me out of the closet. She'd say that my dad loved me very much, he cared about me so much, and that's why he lost his temper. I never figured that out. It would have been better if she'd never said it.

After I was grown up, I realized my dad was an alcoholic; my mother's dad was an alcoholic, and she was just trying to "fix" her family. Years later, I realized that in the 1940s, no one knew about Post Traumatic Stress Disorder. My dad had been a Major in the Marine Corps stationed in Germany during World War II, and who knows what heinous things he had seen over there.

Out on the back bank, we had to whisper. Lee had snuck up from the street below because I wasn't allowed to see him. What Lee meant by "You don't have to take this shit" is that I could run away from home with him. I had heard of kids running away, but I didn't know anyone who had. I had no idea it was illegal. I had not thought of consequences. I was thinking of one thing only. My rule. I had to be a virgin when I got married, and I could not break that rule. That was why I was scared of running away with my boyfriend. He said we could sleep at our friend's houses.

So, I made a decision that would change my life forever. I snuck in the house, got my toothbrush and comb and a jacket, and I walked away from it all. We were gone for eleven days. During that time, Officer Shaw, the juvenile officer, stopped me on the sidewalk on Diamond Street and asked me if I'd seen the Kerns girl. I said that she was in my gym class, but I hadn't seen her this week. He showed me a picture of myself. He said her mom was really worried, and if I saw her, I should tell her so. I said I would. I walked away from his police car thinking he was too dumb to drive.

We were busted in somebody's garage where we'd been staying for an afternoon. We were taken to Juvenile Hall on Meadowlark in separate cars. They took me into some rooms called "receiving," checked me out, told me to take a shower with lice shampoo, and gave me an ugly dress. I don't know what happened to Lee, but I was put in with the big girls because I was "developed for my age." I was fourteen, and they were all sixteen, seventeen and eighteen.

I was assigned a room and told to read some rules in there. A matron with a lot of keys came and took me into the day room. In one corner were female police officers at an enclosed desk. Diagonally across the room were some stud broads, mostly big. All around the room, girls were sitting in chairs, seeming to be waiting for something. There was one pretty girl sitting a couple of chairs from the cop's station who was crying. She had blue eyes and long brown hair. One of the big girls said from across the room, "Shut up, bitch!" But the girl kept crying. The big girl got up and came across the room. We couldn't see them, but she had razors between her third and fourth fingers, both hands. She went straight for the pretty girl's face and slashed from outside the eyes to the corners of her mouth, straight down her cheeks.

I made up my mind right then. I don't cry.

Very shortly, some big men came running and took both girls out—the bloody girl on a stretcher and the big girl in handcuffs. This was my first hour in Juvenile Hall. Days went by, and we didn't see either of them again.

No one beat me. It was the first time in my life that I was safe. I learned how to hot-wire a car with the shiny side of a gum wrapper (theoretically), and I was shown how to smoke pot. They used a pencil to demonstrate and made me practice for the day that I would smoke my first marijuana in the shower. It was a roach and I got high from it. I learned about relationships that

211

girls have with girls and I realized that it was possible to have sex with a girl and still count as a virgin. Things were looking up for me. I was labeled an uncontrollable minor, a juvenile delinquent, and a runaway.

On Sunday, my mom and dad came to visit me, and I stood on a table, so I was taller than he, and told my father to leave. Of course, I was reprimanded and told to get down, but juvie was the first home of my own. I was counted. I fit in. The decision to run away began a drug run that would last a quarter of a century, land me in a mental institution, and turn me into a felon.

The decision about not going all the way with Lee was a very good one because my father pressed charges against him for statutory rape. I insisted on being checked and the charges were dropped.

Before all this happened, I had been the Student Council vice president, elected by the ninth grade. I had been the captain of the Pacific Beach pom-pom corps and enjoyed my share of popularity. When I came back to school, very few kids wanted to know me.

I learned that if you get your sense of self from others, they can also take it away. I was forever released from the mainstream. Now I was free to find and think for myself.

Uncle Hamilton's Stories

C.H. "Scott" Currier

Three children exited the northern Virginia plantation's once stately mansion and walked through knee-high weeds toward a small cabin and dilapidated barn. Now, in post-Civil War 1869, such properties were struggling to survive.

Spencer, fourteen and the oldest of the trio, said, "You're fibbin', George Fry. I got a shiny new nickel that says there's no way you and your sister lived in a cave for four years."

Ten-year-old Mary Fry kicked at the boy's leg. "No northerner calls my brother a liar, Spencer Otis. We did too live in a cave during the war, and we'll prove it."

Thirteen-year-old George smiled and said, "A fool and his money. I'll take that bet." The boys shook hands.

Spencer pointed toward a field. "I thought slavery was over. What're those Negroes doing out there?"

"They're sharecroppers, farmin' the land. The money from whatever sells is divided between them and my Pa," George said. "Not much to share these days. Times are tough."

Reaching the cabin, the children clomped and scraped mud from their shoes as they climbed the steps to its weathered porch. Their breath was visible in the chill air as George rapped on the hand-hewn door and shouted, "Uncle, it's George and Mary." He turned to Spencer. "He lives here alone."

"C'mon." A man's deep, gravelly voice boomed from inside. George pushed the door.

"Best leave that open. It's a might smoky in here," the man said softer. He sat at a small table on which lay a horse collar he was repairing. Leaning back in his chair, he tamped tobacco into his briar pipe with arthritic fingers. His eyes shone white, contrasting with his ebony skin.

Mary Fry hugged the old man and kissed him on the cheek. "Good mornin', Uncle Hamilton."

He looked at the trio. "Seems like you brung a friend today." His smile deepened the wrinkles around his eyes.

213

"Yes, Uncle. This is Spencer Otis. He just moved here from New York City."

George nudged the boy with his elbow. "Ah, hello, sir," Spencer said, as he looked around the spartan room.

"That's okay. You just call me Uncle. To what do I owe de pleasure of y'all?"

George said, "Uncle, Spencer doesn't believe what we did durin' the war, and Mary and I want you to tell him all about it."

"Hmm, well now, I is kinda busy. I still gots to fix this here collar, muck de stalls an' feed de horses."

"What if we feed the horses and clean the barn? Would you tell the story?" George looked at his sister and Spencer. They nodded.

Uncle Hamilton pursed his lips and scratched the gray stubble on his chin. "Well, I guess you got me in a corner of de coop. Okay, pull off your shoes an' jump on de bed an' I'll git to tellin'."

The old man set the horse collar on the floor, lit his pipe, and gazed through the open door. The children arranged themselves on the mattress. At last, he took a deep breath, turned in his chair, and looked at Spencer.

"When de war broke out, eight years ago, de Colonel, these young'uns' pa, called me up to de big house. Missus Fry, their mama'd been feelin' poorly for a right smart spell. De Colonel said how I'd been with de family on this plantation for purt-near forty years and that he and his oldest son, Jack, had got to go to Bull Run to fight de war. De Colonel said he was goin' to leave everything on de farm for me to take care of. I was to go up and see de Missus every mornin' and sort of talk things over. De Colonel, he got out a bunch of keys and showed me what they all fit. There was a mess of them too: de smokehouse, de seed house, de silver closet, and de key to de safe in de cellar where all de money was put.

"While we was standin' there jawin', a soldier come ridin' up with de summons for de war, and we had to get de Colonel and Jack ready. They both had an extra horse and a boy to take care of them and keep their boots shined. Jack had taught me to read and write some and know about money. They said they'd write us as soon as they got anywhere they could.

"Jack was just a-rarin' to go get at those Yankees, but de Colonel, he was a friend of General Bob Lee, and they was thinkin' this war's gonna let loose de devil on everyone."

214

Hamilton stood, grimacing, and shuffled to the river-rock fireplace to warm his hands. "Nobody but you two children slept that night," he said, speaking to George and Mary. "All de rest of us just cried and prayed. De next mornin' after we sent de Colonel and Jack on their way, I went up to see de Missus, and I hardly knowed her. Her eyes was all red and her cheeks all hollow like she ain't eaten nothin' for a month.

"Next day she had de fever. My woman, Jennie, knowed a lot about healin' and such. She tried everything she could, but nothin' took."

"Why didn't you just go get a doctor? Anybody'd do that," Spencer said.

Hamilton shook his head and raised his voice. "Course we tried to get a doctor. But there weren't none to be had. They was all up at Bull Run." Hamilton grumbled under his breath as he returned to sit at the table.

George glared at Spencer.

"Well, how was I to know?" Spencer said, as he crossed his arms tight over his chest.

Hamilton continued. "Three mornin's later when I went up, I find Jennie kneelin' by de side of de bed and de Missus' head on her shoulder. Jennie pointed me to kneel by her, and de Missus reached over and took my hand. She said, 'Please take care of my babies, won't you?' and just went to sleep. About ten o'clock, she was gone."

Mary turned her head and buried it in her brother's shoulder. "I wish I could remember her."

George said, "I know, Sis."

Spencer, scowling, wormed himself off the horsehair mattress, and said to George. "I thought we were going to hear about a cave, not all this other stuff. Heck, there wasn't no cave, was there?"

George jumped off the bed and faced Spencer, while pumping his fists. "Tell him, Uncle. Tell him 'bout the roost."

Uncle Hamilton reached into the pocket of his dungarees for a metal flask. He pulled the cork, smiled, and took a long swig. "Now, don't you two get your hackles up. Mr. Spencer, you sit down by de door and cool off. I'll get to that cave story soon enough. George, put some more wood on de fire, then you sit where you was. I'm about to tell y'all about de Yankee Army that purt-near caught us."

The two boys exchanged hard looks but did as Uncle said.

215

"Next day we had de buryin'. All de colored folks around de country was there, for they all loved Missus Fry, and not many white folks was there because most of de men went to de war and de white women went south to be safe.

"Jennie and me talked everything over. De soldiers was gettin' mighty biggity, and there was sure a lot of them. We was gettin' some pay for de cattle and feed we was sellin', but then a Bluecoat tried to catch one of de girls down back of de barn. Some of our boys heard her holler and let loose Jack's bulldog. When that Yankee got over de fence, he left most of his clothes and a chunk of meat."

The old man stood, put both hands on his bottom, arched his back and howled. He chuckled as he sat.

All three children roared with laughter.

"We saw trouble comin' and, with both you Fry children on our hands, we figgered we'd better hide out. We put most of de money and de Missus' jewels under de big oak at de edge of de soapstone quarry. Then we took some of de pictures and furniture to de old cabin down in de hoop pole forest, north of Mt. Vernon.

"I reasoned no matter where we found ourselves, I'd need to do some huntin', so I picked out a rifle that belonged to de Colonel. Jennie shook her head and told me that if a slave was caught with a gun, there'd be big trouble. She said to bring Jack's bow and arrows, so that's what I did."

Uncle Hamilton knocked the doddle out of his pipe and repacked the bowl from a stained leather pouch. He relit the pipe and blew a smoke ring across the room in Mary's direction. She giggled as she put her finger through the middle before the circle fell apart.

The old man continued. "I got de field hands together and told them what de Missus had told me before she passed: that they could stay in their cabins or go away, just like they wanted, but be back when de war was over.

"On a gray afternoon, Jennie and I hitched de mares, Mazie and Maud, to de covered wagon and started out. Jennie held you, Miss Mary, in her arms and sat with George in de back. We was goin' to see a moonshiner that knew about a place where runaways went to in de Shenandoah mountains. We was told he lived off de Luray Pike.

"On de second night, it came on to thunderin' and lightnin' and de wind a-blowin' down trees all around. Those old mares was mighty nervous, but we struck de pike and started up. It

216

weren't long before there was sure one big lightnin' that purt-near blinded me. But Jennie, from de back of de wagon, said, 'Hamilton, there's a whole parcel of soldiers right up there in de road, and they's comin' this way.' I quick drove into de bushes, and we all held our breath. They was so close, we could smell de sweat off their horse's backs. Thank de good Lord, there weren't no more lightnin' till they got past.

"Soon we saw de road to de camp of that moonshiner. We stopped in de trees, and we all fell asleep, glad to be off de pike.

"By sunrise, I was wakin' up that man in his little cabin. He said his name was Abraham Jones. He told me about a cave called de 'Roost' where de runaway slaves go. It was up Nigger Run and was hard to get to because there weren't no trails. We'd have to wade de creek and climb some waterfalls, but once there, we'd be safe.

"I give Abraham a ten-dollar gold piece and asked him to bring us two bags of meal, a side of bacon, and a bag of salt with all de news of de war in de fall before de snowin' starts and he agreed.

"We followed an old lumber trail for another day until we got to de ford at Nigger Run. There was a grassy clearin' beside de stream where we could hide de horses, so I tied a bunch of vines to trees and made a fence so de mares couldn't run off. We unhitched de two after puttin' de wagon deep in de woods, then turned them out into that pasture.

"Jennie took both you children and the Good Book we brung. I loaded up what I could carry, and we started up. Because of de rainin', de run was about fifteen feet wide and about three feet deep with de water rushin' over smooth rocks and mighty hard walkin'. It took all day, but we made de Roost before sundown."

Hamilton stood, stretched his back and took another swig from the flask.

"It was a big cave and inside there weren't no sign of critters except where a bear had been sleepin' some time back. But outside there was a mess of tracks: deer, coon, turkey, and a lot I couldn't figure out what they was. I built a fire in de firepit inside de cave that de runaways used, and de smoke went right up through a crack in de roof.

"After Jennie looked at those tracks a while, she said to me, 'Hamilton, we is got to build a cabin in that cave, so no varments is goin' to get at my babies.'

217

"Course I agreed. Jennie was de biggest-hearted woman in Virginia and always thinkin', so when she said anythin', everybody, from the Colonel down, would say, 'I reckon you is right, Jennie.'

"I had to go back to de ford to get the rest of our belongin's. By Saturday night I had everything up. Sunday, after some Bible schoolin', Jennie showed me about her thoughts on de cabin. All de walls'd be as tall as de ceilin', maybe eight or ten feet. It'd have two sides pokin' out from de back of de cave to de front and be about as wide. There'd be a wall to shut de front with a door in de middle and a window on each side."

"Jennie showed me how to make windows out of rabbit skins soaked in turkey grease," George said.

Hamilton nodded. "She was sure smart like that. Then she took me out in de woods, to de pines, and showed me a bunch of poles. She'd taken that ax and hatchet and trimmed them while I was bringin' up all de supplies. De poles was for de cabin walls, and for a pen outside that could keep you two safe.

"It took about two weeks to build de pen and de cabin but when we was done, Jenny said, 'Now I can sleep cause Mr. Bear ain't gonna get at my babies.' Course no bear was gonna get you two no-how without gettin' through her and me first.

"After that, I took some salt and spent a day lookin' up a spot for a deer lick. I found one on de side of de mountain. I put down my salt about fifty feet from a bunch of scrub pine. I didn't say nothin' to Jennie cause I 'lowed to get ahead of her just once.

"One day when de wind was right, I took de bow and arrows and went over to check my salt lick. I hadn't got in de scrub before there was a young buck standin' with his head down. I put an arrow in his side, right back of his front leg. He gave one jump and landed on his side. I gutted him and toted him down de hill.

"When I got back, Jennie smiled all over. She had most of de meat cut up in strips and hung in de sun and de hide scraped and wrapped up in salt before sunset. She said, 'Hamilton, I want two more deer like this one to make clothes for us all.' It was getting late enough in de year, so de fur was good, and I set a lot of snares and most every night got a coon or maybe some other varmint, and I got one more deer."

Mary said to Spencer, "She made us mittens and pants from all those animals."

Spencer asked, "Uncle, what about the horses?"

218

"Oh, every week I'd go see 'bout Maud and Mazie and check de fence. Once when I got back, these children was a-cryin' and Jennie, lyin' down, was so hot you could fry eggs on her forehead. De pain in her misery was so bad she couldn't hardly stand. She said, 'Hamilton, boil some herbs in a pot of water.' I did. She drank some and I wrapped her in blankets.

"Toward mornin' I took those blankets off and they was wet like mop rags. De next day she began to feel better, but, Lordy, that old woman sure had Hamilton scared." He rocked in his chair and wiped his forehead with his sleeve.

George said, "Oh yeah. We were afraid she was dyin' for sure. Remember, Mary?"

"Sort of, but I don't want to think about Jennie like that. Uncle, you ain't told us the bear story for a long time and I want to hear it again."

"I was just gettin' to de bee tree Jennie found."

"Oh, that's a good story. Uncle, tell that one, then the bear story."

"Okay, Sweetie. Well, long in de fall before it got cold, a tree behind de cave got blowed down and was lyin' there with roots stickin' up and branches settin' on de ground. Bees was comin' and goin' from a crack in de trunk. I got me a whole pile of wet chips and lit a fire that sure put out a lot of smoke to stupefy de hive. Then I chopped a big hole where de bees was and there was enough honey to fill a barrel. I'd take a big comb and smoke it 'till they'd all drop off and give it to Jennie. After she had all she could tote, I closed de hole so de bees don't freeze come winter.

"One mornin' a bear, smellin' honey, woke us up tryin' to tear de chinks out between de poles that made de sides of our cabin. Jennie and I struck de floor on de same tick, went through de door and there he was, standin' higher than a man, with his mouth open big enough to toss in a basket of corn. I got an arrow in him just as Jennie hit him right between de eyes with de ax. It warn't long before I was taken his hide off and we had meat for de winter. That's de rug in de Colonel's bedroom."

Spencer, looking up at George wide eyed, asked, "Is that all true?"

"Sure is."

"Dang."

Uncle Hamilton took an ember from the fire with tongs and relit his pipe.

219

He said, "That moonshiner, Abraham, come up about then. He brung us a bag of corn meal, and one of salt, and a slab of bacon, and tells us de war's a funny business. 'First, both sides'd fight, and one of them would run off. Then, soon as de other side got rested, they'd run off, too. Then they'd come together again, and de Yanks'd run off behind a hill and get their boots shined and their hair brushed. Then they was ready to fight some more and there was General Bob Lee waitin' for them. A lot of those soldiers was getting hurt but neither side was, what you might call, gettin' licked.'

"I thanked him for de news and vittles then asked, 'How long you been moonshinin', Abraham?'

"He said, 'All my life, I guess. My daddy was one of George Washington's slaves. They was all made free when he passed. My daddy learn't whiskey makin' from de president, I reckon. Then he teached me. He also teached me prospectin' in these hills. That's why I knowed about de Roost.'

"Then I asked him, 'What was your daddy's name?'

"He said, 'Willie Jones; he passed about ten years ago.'

"I said, 'I knowed your daddy. We was young'uns together at Mt. Vernon. That's when I got sold to de Colonel's pappy. Seems I just missed out on bein' a free man myself. I still thinks about that sometimes." Hamilton sighed and shook his head.

"De next summer slipped along easy and soon Abraham was up again. He said Stonewall Jackson'd been kilt and Bob Lee'd gone up north to show de Yankees a good army, but it didn't look like anyone was gettin' whupped."

Hamilton looked at George, "I recollect I made you a bow and arrow just your size for your birthday that year."

"You sure did, Uncle."

"And I showed you how to shoot, and one day you brung home a partridge hit smack in de head. Jennie was so proud; you couldn't hardly talk to her."

George nodded, grinning.

Hamilton continued. "Abraham come up again de next spring. Said President Lincoln freed all de slaves and he was gonna give them each a patch of land and a mule. Our Abraham said de slaves was all singin' a new song.

'Ol' Jeff he say he hang us,
If he can find us armed.
It's a mighty big thing,

But we ain't much alarmed.
He's got first to catch us.
Before de way is clear,
And dat's what's de matter
With de Nigger volunteer.'

"Jennie didn't say nothin' till after he was gone. Then she said, 'Hamilton, how many of them fools is goin' to get along with no master and no Missus to look out for them and give them a proper burial?'

"I never told her, but to my thinkin', there's nothin' in this life or de next like de feelin' of bein' free."

Mary slid off the bed and climbed onto Uncle Hamilton's lap. "I don't understand, Uncle. Didn't Daddy always treat you good?"

"Mostly, but not his daddy. I guess you're old enough to know. Hop down honey."

Hamilton stood and with difficulty, pulled his shirt over his head revealing scars crisscrossing his back.

Spencer gasped. Mary, standing with her hands covering her mouth, began to tear.

"Now, Miss Mary, no need to cry. They don't hurt me no more."

George sighed. "I remember seein' those when we lived at the roost. Was that from my grandfather?"

"No, sir, it was from your pa, de Colonel."

George and Mary looked at each other in disbelief.

"Your grandpappy stood there and forced your daddy to whip us when he was still a young man. He didn't take to it like some do. Said it made him sick." He turned to Spencer. "When these young'uns' grandpappy passed on, de Colonel was at West Point where most of de cadets was talkin' against slavery. When he come back, he knowed to treat us better."

Spencer cocked his head and with one eye nearly closed, asked the old man, "But what you said about freedom, wasn't it right there for the taking? I mean, you could have escaped when you were at the cave."

"Fact was, we knowed that runaways was bein' hunted down and brought back for de bounty; even up north. Anyways, Jennie and I was gettin' too old to start our lives over. But mostly we'd made a promise to de Colonel's wife, and you don't never break a promise."

221

Spencer replied under his breath, "Huh."

Hamilton continued while putting on his shirt. "When Abraham come again de next spring, he said General Grant done took hold of de Yankee Army, and there weren't goin' to be no more runnin' away. They had to just keep on fightin' even if they was licked.

"A year later, Abraham come up again and told us de war is over. General Grant'd taken Lee's army and he reckons it's safe for us to go. I looked at de side wall of de cave and it was full of scratches. I asked you, George, how long we been there."

George smirked at Spencer. "I'd been keeping count: three years, nine months and ten days. Now pay our wager." Spencer stood, dug in his pocket for the nickel, then slapped it into George's outstretched hand.

Mary said, "But that's not the end of the story. Uncle, keep goin'."

"Okay. Jennie took your brother by de hand and with you on her shoulders, started down de run. Me and Abraham took de rest of what we wanted, got to de ford and hitched up Mazie and Maud. We gave Abraham our thanks, and he headed back to his camp. In three days, we was home.

"De Colonel was there, in bed, but Jack'd been kilt and we couldn't hardly console you two.

"Some Negra woman we didn't recognize was waitin' there, too. We looked at her and she at us. Then she smiled and we knowed. It was our girl, Lucy. She'd been sold by de Colonel's pappy to a plantation down south when she was only seven years old. She was over forty and made a beeline back to us when de war was over. Jennie screamed, and Lucy and I had to hold her up. Den we all hugged and cried for I don't know how long.

"When we looked in on de Colonel, you children said you didn't hardly know him.

"He was so thin and yellow dat neither Jennie or I expected him to get well again.

"Jennie and Lucy nursed him like they would a child. Soon, they had de Colonel sittin' on de porch in a big chair. He'd just sit there for hours starin' out at nothin'.

"Four of de hands had returned to their cabins so I bought some mules and got de plows goin', but we couldn't get de Colonel to take no notice. He had rid back from de war on his horse, Blackie. We got that horse fat and slick. I brought him and another horse around one mornin' and asked de Colonel if he

222

wouldn't ride de place with me. He kind of brightened, and I helped him get in de saddle. We rode for about an hour. After that, he used to ride every mornin', but he said, 'Hamilton, you saved de place, you run it and I'll pay you.'

"One day, about a year after de war was over, Jennie took sick and de Colonel said, 'Hamilton, you and Lucy take care of Jennie. George and I'll run the plantation.'

"It sure was a big help havin' my Lucy there because Jennie was just worn out, I reckon. We had big doctors from Richmond and Washington come by, but they couldn't do nothin'.

"Jennie lived about another month. We buried her on a knoll overlookin' de plantation. De whole county, white and black, was there to help put her away."

Tears ran down the old man's face. "Well, those're my stories."

Mary and George, crying, hugged him as he sat. Spencer, sniffling, put on his shoes and walked to the barn. Soon the two Fry children joined him. Without uttering a word, they completed Uncle Hamilton's chores as promised.

~

"Hey, Dad, you still working on those memoirs? President Roosevelt's Fireside Chat will be on the radio in five minutes."

George Fry stood. He placed both hands on his lower back and groaned. His Bright's Disease was getting worse. He looked at the scribbling on the unlined paper. Some days he could barely read his own handwriting. "Be there soon, son. Just finishing for the day."

He picked up the time-tarnished 1869 nickel from next to his pad and tucked it carefully in his pocket.

The Dove and the Balloon

Robyn Bennett and Bob Boze

Nina stepped out onto the balcony of her apartment and her face lit up with a smile. It was another stunning San Diego day — clear, sunny, a perfect 75 degrees with barely a breeze. She looked up, and her smile grew even bigger as she took in the beauty of the Pacific Ocean, off in the distance the Coronado Islands. To her left, she could see the hills in another country, Mexico. One in particular, the one with the big hills, had become her favorite. She didn't know its name, but had dreamed of having a house on top of one of those hills and was sure it was the best place in the world to build a house.

To say Nina loved where she lived would be the understatement of the century. A short three blocks north of the US-Mexican border, her apartment faced west, toward the ocean. The beautiful view aside, it also had some of the most spectacular sunsets anyone had ever seen.

Just as she took a sip of her coffee, Dove landed on the railing of her balcony. "Dove!" she cried out.

Dove let out a "Coo, coo" and danced along the railing, sidestepping first to the right, then returning left to the same spot in front of her.

"You are such a hoot," she told him. "Oops, sorry, owls hoot. You're such a coo, Dove," she corrected. She had tried to think of a very cutesy name for him when he'd first landed on her railing, but nothing sounded right. Nothing she came up with was "him." But, every time she used the word "dove," she was sure he tilted his head, looked into her eyes and cooed. And so, "Dove" it was. A name that was now special to both of them.

Dove and Nina were best friends. She had been training him (she thought he was a he) for months. Each morning, she would start her day on the balcony with a cup of coffee, some bird treats, a plate of the best bird food she could find, and a trinket or two. Each morning she would throw a trinket out into the air above the courtyard below her balcony, and Dove would give chase. It took

225

a few weeks for him to figure out he was supposed to catch the trinket and bring it back, so, at first, most of them ended up in the courtyard below.

Finally though, he caught on and snagged whatever she threw in midair and brought it back to her. That earned him a bird treat each time and a plate of gourmet bird food at the end of each training session. Now, the two of them would start each day off on the balcony; Nina sipping her coffee and throwing things for Dove to retrieve, Dove retrieving them, being handfed his treat, and the two of them laughing and cooing until Nina had to shower and head off to work while Dove went wherever doves go.

Nina loved starting her day off with Dove, her only true friend here. Likely her only boyfriend too, if she thought about it. Yeah, another Saturday morning with no one but Dove to share it, and the weekend, with.

Her love life was a big fat zero. Deliberate at first, but now, months after moving to San Diego, she was sure she had a sign around her neck that read "Decent Men — Danger — Stay Clear." She'd gone to parties, even hung out with her fellow medical center workers at "after work get-togethers," but soon realized decent guys were almost extinct. Most of the men she'd met were no better than the one she'd dumped and run here to get away from. *Hum, wonder if Dove would follow me to the convent if I became a nun? Got the celibate part down, and bringing my own dove might even earn me some kind of special prayer sessions or something.*

"Time for another cup of coffee, Dove. Don't go away. I'll be right back," she told him as she headed back into the apartment. Dove cooed, as if to say, "Okay."

~

Ben stood in line at the border crossing. "I can't believe this line," he mumbled to the stranger in front of him. "Gets longer and longer every Saturday."

"Si, you expect privileges, Gringo?" the guy said without turning around.

A slight breeze came up and the bright red heart-shaped helium filled balloon that Ben was holding smacked the guy in the back of the head. "Lo siento . . . Sorry," Ben said.

"Si," the guy snapped through gritted teeth, still not turning around.

Several seconds went by and the guy finally turned. The balloon caught his eye and he smiled.

"For you uh . . . novia?"

226

Ben chuckled. His Spanish sucked but at least he knew what *novia* meant. "No, no novia. No girlfriend. For my *hermana* . . . my sister." He wished he'd had a novia, but living in Mexico and barely speaking Spanish had proved to be a major handicap when trying to date.

"Si." The guy turned back around just as the line finally started to move.

For several months now, Ben had been working in Mexico, in a small medical clinic just across the border. The clinic helped the homeless, those who had no insurance or very little money. He had gone there when he found out more and more Americans were crossing the border for medical services . . . services they couldn't afford in the US — services open to those of both countries.

When he told her that he was moving across the border for a while, Ben's girlfriend, now his "ex-novia," had pitched a major hissy fit and left him. No matter how hard he tried to explain that more than half of his patients were Americans, she'd still called him a traitor to his country and told him to stay on *his* side of the border, the south or Mexico side. And he'd pretty much done that, until today, his sister's birthday.

He reached the ID checkpoint and showed his US passport to the border agent. The agent looked at the balloon and smiled. "Girlfriend?" he asked Ben.

"Nope, sister's birthday."

"Tell her happy birthday from the border agents."

"Thanks, I will," Ben answered, returning the agent's smile.

Ben crossed the border marker on the walkway, stepped aside, set his backpack down, and bent over to put his passport back in the backpack. With the balloon's string in one hand and his passport in the other, Ben tried to undo the flap on the backpack. But the balloon kept floating in front of him and blocking his vision. Frustrated, he loosely wrapped the balloon's string around one of the backpack's shoulder straps so he could see to unbuckle the flap.

As he pulled the flap open, the balloon's string slipped from around the shoulder strap and gently floated upward. By the time he saw the end of the string heading skyward, it was too late. The balloon was now twenty feet off the ground and floating gently into the US.

Watching the balloon float away, Ben shook his head. "How could you be so stupid? Helium balloons rise, you dummy," he mumbled. As he watched it move further away, he realized that the balloon seemed to be floating in the same direction he needed to go. Better yet, it didn't seem to be going any higher, just hovering about 20 feet off the ground and floating, floating in the same direction as his sister's apartment complex.

He started following the balloon at a quick pace and then started running. Just as he was almost directly under it, a slight breeze came up and the balloon made a right turn, right where he would have turned to get to his sister's apartment! *Weird!*

~

Her refilled coffee cup in hand, Nina looked up, just in time to see Dove take off from the railing. By the time she reached the door, Dove was back on the railing with a bright-red, heart-shaped balloon floating in slow circles about a foot above his head. Nina followed the string from the balloon down to Dove's beak. "Aw, Dove, you shouldn't have!"

Just then, there was a knock on the door.

"Be right back," she said to Dove. *I really need to get some friends, I'm talking to a dove,* she thought as she headed for the front door. Peering through the peep hole she saw a bright smile attached to what appeared to be a very handsome face.

Easing the door open a few inches, her eyes locked with the most beautiful deep-sea, blue eyes she had ever seen. "Yes, can I help you?"

Through the door opening, Ben found one sparkling hazel eye peeking at him. "Um . . . I'm . . . I'm sorry to bother you, ma'am, but a dove took my balloon, and he landed on your patio," he stammered.

Ah, that's where the balloon came from, Nina thought, as she opened the door wider and realized he was even cuter than she'd first thought. "Are you accusing my dove of stealing your balloon?" she asked, unable keep from teasing him, or staring at him.

"Uh, your dove? As in . . . your dove?"

Nina couldn't help but snicker. "Yes, my dove. As in 'I trained him.' At least, I think it's a him."

The smile in her eyes clearly told Ben he was being teased. *Ha, two can play at this game!* "So, you taught him to steal balloons, did you?"

"Not steal . . . catch. And yours is the first balloon he's had a chance to steal . . . uh, catch." She didn't know why, but something told her to keep teasing him. "You should take better

228

care of your balloons. You need to keep them leashed and under your control at all times. We do have balloon leash laws you know."

He liked her, she was funny, spunky and mesmerizing. Her smile lit up her face and continued into her eyes, where flakes of gold sparkled against the dark brown background.

Guilt began to sink in as Nina watched him stare at her. Returning his stare with a big smile, she felt compelled to confess, "I'm sorry, I didn't mean to tease you. When I saw Dove — that's his name, Dove — with the balloon, I thought he'd gone and 'borrowed' it for me. We were just having a discussion about not liberating balloons when you knocked."

"I, uh . . ." Ben stopped. He couldn't think of what to say.

"Just a minute. I'll go get your balloon," Nina said. Walking out onto the balcony, she eased the string from Dove's beak and smiled at him. "You were a bad boy," she whispered, then added, "but thanks for bringing the hunky guy to my door."

She brought the balloon inside and handed it to him. "Here you go. I hope she loves it." She gently eased the door closed. *Why did you send him away?*

Ben stepped back as the door closed. *You fool, why didn't you say something?* He walked toward the stairs and dialed his sister. "Hi sis, I'm just about at your apartment and . . . Oh, you're where? I see. Jason and you will be gone for a week? Uh, sure. Well, listen, just wanted to wish you a happy birthday. Have a great time and see you when you get back."

A giant smile flooded his face as he turned, marched back to Nina's door, and knocked.

The door opened to reveal a smile as bright as his.

"Seems Dove was right, this was meant to be yours," he said, handing her the balloon. "Can I buy you a cup of coffee?"

"Uh . . . sure," she answered, her smile growing even bigger. "Let me tell Dove he's got guard duty."

Ben watched as she walked out to the balcony, tied the balloon to the railing and then said something to Dove.

"Thanks," Nina whispered, then gently kissed the top of Dove's head before turning back toward the door.

Dove let out a loud "Coo, coo."

Finding Time

Christine L. Cunningham

I bagged the last of my pilled and pitted Target Ts, then paused to admire the nearly empty walk-in closet. Three days of nonstop bundling, bagging, and trashing twenty-five years of accumulation. I could hear the dog barking down the hallway, clearly tired of my preoccupation. *Remind me again why I agreed to get a dog?* Sweat pooled in the center of my lower back as I dragged the final load of unusually heavy clothing from one room to temporary quarters in another, filling three rooms total. The air conditioning was no match for the repetitive workout. I paused to consider whether something as simple as a newly designed closet could really organize years of total disorganization. The closet man was scheduled to do his magic first thing in the morning. By tomorrow evening, I will be transformed. The dog continued to bark. I needed a break anyway.

I stood surveying the empty closet for two, noticing for the first time my old jewelry armoire tucked against the wall. It had become an invisible part of the closet with the usual accumulation of clothes piled over it. I tossed the dog a treat, showed him a little love with a promise to return, then used what little energy I had to coax the four-foot-tall multi-drawer cabinet out of the closet and into the bedroom. No small feat as it turns out. *What's in this thing anyway?* It was much heavier than I thought possible. *Had my diamonds gained karats over the years?* I couldn't recall the last time I opened it, opting for the more casual jewelry kept near the bathroom sink.

I rocked and pulled the chunk of cherry wood causing the top to hiccup, exposing a long forgotten shallow compartment underneath. I stopped, lifted the lid, and was immediately startled by my reflection in its mirrored lining. I had forgotten that there was such a large mirror within. I had also forgotten that I hadn't put any make up on. But it was the contents of the compartment that prompted my hand to cover my heart, my eyes to soften. Beneath my reflection, staring back at me, was caricature me, drawn by my third-grade daughter twenty years ago. I had been chosen as the cover story for Time Magazine's "Mother-of-the-Year" special edition. Me, and every other third grade mom.

But more about me: Among the "most amazing" things about me back then, apparently, was my spaghetti sauce, my capacity for drinking massive amounts of cappuccino, my ability to drive our four kids around all day, and — my all-time favorite — that I have a "wonerful" husband whose name is Jim. I smiled, recalling an earlier Mother's Day gift highlighting that the best thing about me was my husband, whose initials "JC" pretty much summed up how my Catholic kids worshiped him. At least I had gained some significance since that Mother's Day with my spaghetti sauce, which was no doubt Ragu. I did get a shout-out as someone who is "loving, fun, nice, and caring," whose best advice has been to "always tell the truth." I guess that means that marrying Jim really is the best thing about me. Funny how kids think.

Among other truths listed, I easily set the World Record for drinking one hundred cups of cappuccino in one minute and hold the record for driving in the car all day. According to Time's young reporter, I am a "mother on the move" who "hardly ever rests," which must've impressed my precocious nine-year-old who added, "I don't know how she does it!" The Time Magazine article closes, describing me as a "full-time house mom" who "used to be a lawyer but she missed her kids too much." Nailed it. The truth is, I had missed them while I was working long hours as an attorney. I missed them so much that I wrote a letter to the person responsible for making me realize that taking care of them was more important than any client, any case, any paycheck, or any thing. I never once regretted that decision, as it was the best in my life. That, and marrying Jim — duh.

I looked back inside the shallow compartment where I had kept the twenty-year-old copy of Time Magazine and discovered several stained legal papers folded end to end and side to side underneath, origamied into a 4x5 inch rectangle of curiosity. What I found was a never-mailed letter from 1995 that changed my life.

Dear Dr. Laura Schlessinger,

I am a 36-yr. old lawyer, mother of three, ages 6, 3, and 9 months. As an attorney, I drive all over the county for court appearances, depositions, and scene investigations, which makes me a captive audience to your car radio talk show. I have been tuned in to you for over two years now, and find I agree with many of your "do unto others" opinions. However, when you pontificate about the evils of daycare and working moms, I find myself being very defensive. After all, my kids benefit from seeing Mommy as a lawyer and learning Spanish from our live-in nannies. How could an educated woman with a Ph.D. from Columbia University be so backwards in her thinking?

When I had my first child I was working at a "good ol' boys" law firm with no maternity leave policy in place. I was the only woman in the firm. As a young, aspiring, very pregnant associate, I worked beyond my due date, often appearing in court where people either stared at my girth or averted their eyes altogether. Pregnancy was not a common sight in court. In just five short weeks and still suffering scars of delivering a nearly ten-pound, 23-inch-long baby, I returned to work. The partners expected me to work weekends as well, which required schlepping all the necessary gear to transform my office into a nursery and take care of my baby as I tried to bill the requisite hours.

Despite my returning to work one week before the minimum time allowed for maternity leave, and despite having to drag my infant to the office on weekends, I was told by one of the partners that having a baby was "like pursuing a hobby" and that my time off would take me slightly off the partnership track. I left soon after and took a corporate position where the hours were more "family friendly." Because I felt more human again working without the pressure of billable hours, I had my second, then third child. There was no policy for part time work or job sharing, so I did my best to juggle family and clients within the flexibility allowed.

You were always good company on my forty-minute drive to Court, or during my lunch hour where most days I chose to eat in the car listening to your sage advice. I couldn't understand how I could agree with so much of your philosophy but disagree wholeheartedly on the issue of working moms. I remember arguing with you in the car as if you were opposing counsel in a precedent setting case. Then one day, I heard you read a fax from a woman who simply said "No" to her job and how extremely fulfilled she was as a result. That was followed by a psychologist who faxed a drawing by her daughter with, "I hate being alone," written below. She took the drawing to her employer the next day and quit. Wow, I thought. What courage. What conviction.

You and your listeners made me question why I was working at all. We could've gotten by on one salary, though not as comfortably, and I wasn't exactly helping anyone by defending big insurance companies. It was about me wanting the career I had worked so hard to get. I loved my job and loved being an attorney, but that was so insignificant compared to the love I felt toward our kids. Why wasn't I making them my sole priority? I went from feeling defensive to acknowledging that you were right. I traded in my car for a full-sized van, feeling steps closer to a decision to quit.

233

Lent began recently. My six-year-old, who was attending Catholic school, decided we all needed to give something up for Lent. Without making any correlation to Ash Wednesday or the weeks leading to Easter, I finally got the courage to quit work. The next day, my six-year-old announced to her first-grade class that her mommy, one of only two full-time working moms in her entire class, gave up work for Lent.

After announcing my leave, virtually every one of my female coworkers confessed how hard it has been to raise a family while working as a full-time lawyer. Two of them have given notice as a result, along with my male boss, who applauded my decision to choose family over work, who quit to spend more time with his grandkids. My skin is tingling with excitement that I will soon be home every day with my extraordinary kids. I am looking forward to the many trips we will be taking to the zoo, museums, parks and bookstores with me at the helm of our full-sized van that will one day sport the vanity plate: TYDRLRA.

Best decision of my life. Thank you, Dr. Laura.

I wiped my eyes contemplating all the time that would have been stolen from my kids had I not stopped working and returned the letter where I found it, ironically, under the crayon colored copy of Time.

Things Go Better with Coke

Paula Earnest

I wanted to buy the Seven-Up, but Helen insisted that Coke bottles spin better. Something about the curved shape and lines running down the glass. Ridiculous, I thought. Between the two of us, we had plenty of babysitting money saved, so we splurged and bought two 6-packs of Coca-Cola to take to Sally's party. Besides, the guys probably liked Coke better.

Sally Stack's parents never bothered to check on her when she had friends over. Sally could blast "I Want To Hold Your Hand" on the record player, and no one would pound on the door to the basement rec room and yell, "Turn that down!" It didn't matter if six or seven friends were over after school raiding the fridge, Sally Stack's parents simply didn't seem to care. And Sally was not someone you wanted to tangle with. In fact, she wore the "B-word" proudly, like her tight-fitting sweaters. The mutually-agreed-upon "avoidance rule" of parent to child worked well in the Stack family. There was no war, not even a cold one.

So, it was a no-brainer that the sleepover would be at Sally's house. And, OF COURSE the boys WOULD be leaving early, we all told our parents. When they dropped us off, we were all smiles, excited for the big sixth grade, end-of-the-school-year bash at Sally Stack's house. She was a girl who the boys said lived up to her name, even at twelve years old.

Our overnight Flower-Power suitcases bulged with just as much excitement, stuffed with a week's worth of clothes — Poor Boy tops, hip-hugger bell-bottoms, several day-of-the-week pairs of underwear, baby doll pj's, and, most important of all, our locked diaries with the key attached on a string. With all that, our parents would never think of looking at the bottom for our contraband of cigarettes, Ouija Board, and eyeliner secretly hidden.

And OF COURSE, Mr. and Mrs. Stack WOULD be there supervising the whole time, we told them. Pick up would be after breakfast pancakes tomorrow around 10. It was all just too easy.

~

At our lockers on the day of the party, Helen asked if the Coke bottle is full or empty when you spin it. I told her we'd have to wait till we got to the party—Sally would know.

"Oh, and guess who else is for sure coming tonight? Scott and Tim!" Helen beamed. I could feel my face getting hot.

"Really?" I said, turning the lock to open my locker, hoping Helen wouldn't see my fingers shaking. "Cool."

When Mrs. Bigalow, our science teacher, talked something about the Earth and Sun in class that Friday, not a single kid going to the party listened to a word. We were already on the Moon, counting the minutes till we could blast off to our darkly lit, starry-eyed, Spin-the-Bottle, best boy-girl party ever.

For the first half hour of the night, most of the partiers stood around the chip and dip and drinks table, talking and filling up on snacks. Mary-Jo, Connie, and Linda pinky-swore to each other they would be best friends forever and hoped they would be in each other's classes next year in junior high. Dave started joking about some boy who walked into English class that day with half a roll of toilet paper stuck to his shoe. And how Mrs. Vintelli went psycho on the class after some of the boy's friends started making fart noises when he sat down in his seat.

Helen kept complimenting Sally on what a good job she did hanging the streamers and helium balloons around her basement. Although the balloons came down early when Mikey and Dave thought it would be funny to suck the helium out of the balloons and talk with Munchkin voices. I admit, it was pretty funny.

Kevin and Tim arm wrestled in front of Mary-Jo. She watched and giggled and drank her Coke. Tim argued that Kevin cheated. Kevin laughed and called him a loser.

Tim said, "Rematch."

Kevin said, "Okay, Loser."

Mary-Jo almost choked laughing so hard when Kevin won again. No one sat on the couch yet.

Mikey kept the party pretty entertained with his high-pitched, helium-voiced impersonations, saying, "Auntie Em, we're off to see the wizard, and I'll get you my pretty."

Sally finally interrupted his performance saying, "Hey, I think we could have a lot of fun spinning this bottle," waving the empty Coke bottle above her head. That's when the room went quiet— all except for Frankie Valli who was singing, "Can't Take My Eyes Off of You" on the record player. A few brave teens started to form a circle on the braided rug. And pretty soon all twelve of us, six boys and six girls, sat facing each other on the floor. That's when Frankie's falsetto voice erupted in crescendo, professing his love for the girl of his dreams. Connie jumped up and grabbed the Coke bottle out of Sally's hand, and tried to do her best Four Seasons impression, screeching out the high notes into her fake mic. But she was quickly pulled back down by her two brace-faced girlfriends, Linda and Mary-Jo, and the three of them became a hugging pile of squeals.

When the song ended, someone flipped off the light switch. Only a slice of light from the outside streetlamp came through the small basement window, dimly lighting the room. But it was enough light to see the Coke bottle on its side, on the rug, in the middle of our circle. And although the beat of the music had stopped, I could hear my heart beating. I could hear everyone's heart beating. Not one of us moving, especially now, seeing the bottle there.

Then from out of the shadows, a sweet boy's voice cracked and said, "I'll spin first." A voice that I recognized. A voice that I liked the most out of all the voices in the whole world — Scott's. "Please God. Please. Let it spin to me," I silently prayed.

They say that you never forget your first kiss, or your first love. And they also say that "Things go better with Coke." At least that's what the commercial tells us. Who would have thought that a lucky spin of a Coke bottle could have been that "Thing."

A kiss. My first. In the dark. In Sally Stack's basement. Just one short kiss. The perfect one, that found my lips.

237

Ephemera

Erik C. Martin

The baby was apple-cheeked, cherubic.

"She's going to die someday," I said, talking to my friend, but speaking loud enough for anyone near me, parents included, to hear.

Stella took my arm and hurried me off. She looked stricken.

"It's true," I said. "Everyone is in denial of death; but none of *this* matters." I made a sweeping gesture to show I meant the whole of creation. "It's all bullshit."

Stella led me into Sunrise Coffee. She sat me down at the last free table. Most of the tables were four-tops occupied by lone millennials who were absorbed in their laptops and tablets. Stella reappeared in a few minutes bearing coffee and cake, just in time for my next rant.

"Look at all of these assholes," I said, again just loud enough to be overheard. "They're all here alone because they don't know how to socialize; they just swipe right. They go to college like it matters. But they're going to die. Their kids will die. And nothing they create will last." I paused and took a sip of my coffee; it was too hot. "The only thing that's forever is a student loan. But they probably all have rich parents who pay for their shit. Spoiled brats."

"Oh my God," Stella finally said. "You have got to stop."

I wanted to snap at her and call her a bitch or worse. Instead, I got up and put more cream into my coffee to cool it. When I returned, we were quiet for at least five minutes.

"Are you better?"

"I'm fine," I lied. "I just think that everything is stupid."

Stella set down her coffee and leaned forward.

"Is this a psychiatric emergency? Should I worry about you hurting yourself?"

It wasn't funny but I laughed.

"No. I'm not suicidal. The world is a joke, but I'm the only one who seems to realize it. Everything we do is going to be washed

239

away. Our lives are sandcastles."

Stella opened her mouth, then closed it. I'm sure she had been about to say something trite and uplifting but reconsidered.

"You should audition with me," she said instead.

Old me had liked theater.

New me said, "I can't think of anything more pointless than acting in a play."

"A musical. Les Misérables."

"How depressing. I don't have time to bust my ass for two months for something that runs for a week in some shithole theater in San Diego."

We said little for the rest of the afternoon. When we parted, Stella was at a loss. She hugged me.

"Bye, Sweetie, I'm really sorry about your mom. Call me if you want to talk. Or if you change your mind about auditioning."

I did not change my mind.

A month passed. I saw on Facebook that Stella won the role of Fantine. Once I would have called her with congratulations. Now the news made me vaguely angry.

I had more important things to do. I was busy cleaning up after someone's entire life — baby pictures, old report cards, prayer cards, magazines with little personal notes inside waiting to be found, rosaries, jewelry, a full set of religious statuary, a violin she'd tried but never really learned how to play, makeup, records, posters, clothes, letters, purses, and so much more. Everything she had loved and cared about.

Most of it was going into the trash.

Two more months passed. My attitude remained bleak. I went to work every day. I came home. Once a week, I went grocery shopping. And I worked hard to reduce my mother's life down to a few manageable keepsakes, while putting the rest of her life into the dumpster. Over and over again.

The invitation arrived in the mail. Paper. Not an e-vite. Not Facebook. Stella's play was opening Saturday. Inside of the card were two tickets.

Fine.

I called my sister. She liked the theater. She even auditioned sometimes, though she hadn't been in a show for a while.

Saturday night came. To see me, you would never guess that I was dead inside. I had decided to be appropriate. So on the outside, I was sparkles and sunshine. I denigrated acting, but I was the biggest phony in the theater when I met Stella, hugging

240

her and pretending to be interested.

The seats were in front. The houselights went out and the show began. The actor playing Jean Valjean was your typical community theater leading man; he'd probably been in show choir and drama club in high school. Good, but not great. Unfortunately, this likely salesman by day was the high point early on.

"The only miserable ones here are in the audience," I thought.

My sarcasm was in rare form right up until Stella's big moment.

She was front and center stage. The only illumination was a tight nimbus of spotlight.

She began to sing, "I Dreamed a Dream."

Stella was a good amateur, but in that moment, she vanished and Fantine stood alone. The voice of the woman whose whole existence was of loss and sacrifice was so saturated with despair, that it cracked through my malaise. Emotions that I had shut off for months flooded out.

I was crying when the song ended.

I pulled it together; my eye makeup looked too good for tears. I made it through the show, and even drinks afterwards with Stella and my sister.

I collapsed as soon as I got home. Three minutes of singing had shaken me, and I hated it. I tried to put the wall back up but the memories and feelings pent up over fifteen years poured out.

Death is made no less a surprise to know it is coming. Death shocks. And when death is brought by a long illness the hole left is greater, because of the attention the sickness demands. It consumes not only the life of the stricken but the lives of everyone close to that person.

How could there be a God who would let her suffer for so long, just to die in pain? What about all our work? The constant fighting? I had passed up jobs and opportunities. Now she was gone, and none of it mattered. How could anyone recover from that? If to heal meant that I could be hurt again, wasn't it better to stay broken?

There are only moments—fleeting moments flaring to life and burning out faster than a match. Songs or lives, it makes no difference.

I cried.

I cried until I could not breathe, and my chest and throat were knots. I yelled and cursed.

Goddamned *Les Mis*.

I spied my mother's violin, forgotten in the corner beside the table. It had been gifted to her a year ago by a friend who offered to teach her to play it. My mother was not doing well even then. She did not have a lot of time left. She knew that better than anyone.

And yet, she had started learning the violin.

I laughed at the absurdity.

She learned to play one song, not very well. But she kept trying until she got too sick to practice.

I took Stella out for coffee a week later.

"My show is over next weekend," she said. "But on Monday the fourteenth, in two weeks, there are auditions for a production of Wicked. I could be Elpheba and you could be Glinda, or vice versa. Either way. There are tons of good parts."

I smiled. "I haven't sung in public for years. I might have to get my feet wet in the chorus first. But it will have to be the next show; I'm taking violin lessons on Mondays."

Kitchen Help

Al Converse

The other day I found an old snapshot of myself and other folks working the kitchen in Paquette's Motel and Restaurant near Littleton, New Hampshire, in the summer of 1962.

As a nineteen-year-old freshman in college with no work prospects in my hometown in Massachusetts, I answered an ad for a dishwasher on the Boston University Student Aid bulletin board. I got the job and moved into a cabin on the motel's premises. The owner had replaced his "Cabins-for-Travelers" years before and built the motel complex. Room, board, and minimum wage for the summer — that was the deal. I could save all my pay for the next year at BU. It was before Vietnam, a turning point in my life. All things were possible. The yellowed picture brought the following slice of life to mind.

~

The waiter unzipped Penny's uniform dress all the way down the back as she stood before the salad man's counter arranging a diner's dish. The lush young waitress blushed, reached back, and zipped it up.

"Oh you," she said.

The grinning Unzipper glanced back over his shoulder, his tight trousers accentuating his effeminate-feline prance to the dining room entrance.

A flush washed across the baby-faced salad man's freckled face. The blond college student working on summer vacation stared at the waiter and frowned.

"Whatcha think you're doin'?" he said.

The second cook hustled to the pot washer and dumped a dirty bake pan in the skinny high school dropout's sudsy deep sink, glanced at Penny, and poked the dish washer, a college kid.

"Bet she does it like a mink," he whispered.

The chef, a stout man in his fifties with black heritage in his otherwise white skin, sweated behind the furnace-like bank of ovens, ignoring the event.

243

The forty-something second cook, bald and skinny with the red nose of an alky and sporting a sailor's white hat, zipped back behind the ovens.

"One dead fish," he shouted as he placed a rainbow trout amandine on the pick-up counter.

Cindy, the perky blond coed from Bennington College who had eyes for the salad man, grabbed the fish dish and bounced through the swinging doors to the dining room, her wiggling posterior not unnoticed.

Before the doors closed behind Cindy, the kitchen help caught a flash image of comfortable patrons. And the diners glimpsed only the never-used, shiny aluminum pots hanging above the pass-through counter.

And Then They Came

Anne M. Casey

Revelation
If all the dreams ever dreamed
Were collected in one place
Spread out in time,
Where the dreamers could meet
To collect those dreams

There would be
A place
A space
And a time
Where no dreams were unseen
Unfulfilled
Leftover
Unclaimed.

Early Autumn 2000 South Park, San Diego County: Scrape-brush-scrape. Scrape-brush-scrape. Heavy, strong, the steady tattoo pulsed. Loud and atonal, like a rusty ox-hauled plow on dirt-covered slate, the noise impinging upon my reverie seemed also to batter again the sides of my house. Two additional scratched measures of the cadence teased my curiosity. I raised the living room window blinds and squinted at the city canyon thirty feet below me. At 7:30 on a moonless autumn evening, it was impossible to identify anything moving through the darkness. Still, I hoped for a glimpse of the unimaginable canyon inhabitant that trespassed my solitude . . . Stinky, last year's skunk kit, is too small and careful for this.

Because this canyon and I share a history, I needed to know. Years before, pot-smoking teenagers carelessly strung themselves across the dingy black elevated sewer pipe that spanned this canyon between two alleys. I had imagined them crashing down onto oleanders, cacti and snakes, collecting battle scars on their twenty-foot descent.

As the scratching continued, I thought perhaps that Albert, the orangutan, notorious for his escapades, had sprung himself from the zoo again and come to visit. As my eyes adjusted to the deepening twilight, a vague figure appeared. It was The Vampire, my next door neighbor, so named because of his nocturnal habits. Middle-aged plus, slightly concave and wiry, The Vampire begins his construction projects at quiet evening hours. This, when one segment of the neighborhood is softening, his forays go on until midnight or more. Whining power tool sounds mingle and crash into the adjacent party group's nightly ten o'clock marimba serenades.

The Vampire has found joy in converting a private canyon into a garden retreat. He bulldozed, chopped down trees, hauled away truckloads of leaves and wood chips to create this municipal oasis. Along meandering paths, V and other transplanted urbanites decorate modern labyrinths with exotic vegetation, some of which will flourish in the San Diego climate. Some of it will also entice wild peacocks and parrots in to raise new families, Monarch butterflies to make a migratory stop over.

Mr. V's canyon monolith construction project began in late September. Commencing slowly with a few fieldstones placed on the lip of the canyon rim, he soon increased pace. Several wooden pallets, silvered from water exposure and seemingly placed by a lost helicopter, along with deposits of greyish stone and red clay pots, also appeared on the canyon floor. Scare crow heaps of bamboo stick curtains soon rested in pueblo levels from canyon rim to base to provide a shell for V's project design. He sifted rocks, stones, shards of crumbling concrete from the entire fifty by forty-foot gulch. He then proceeded to replace stones, one-by-one, from the top. Cascading from his second story porch to the canyon floor, the stones merge with odd debris, hint at a potential waterfall. *How inviting for the humming birds and doves! Alas.* The cemented rocks remain dry in the hillside. Embraced by red brick semicircles, these rocks now shelve Kim's (Mrs. V's) yucca and aloe vera-filled ceramic pots, V's bromeliad nursery, all shields for his true farm, marijuana.

Welcome yet fierce, winter rains originating in the Gulf of Alaska, began last week, turning V's carefully constructed hillside into a water slide. The V's, don't seem to understand the nature of southland canyons. No drainage tiles, no sprinkler system, no firebreaks, no cisterns are part of their design. This tributary of

246

Switzer canyon that K/V and I share is legendary for raging, hard-to-fight canyon fires and equally destructive monsoonal rains.

~

Where did the V's come from? Most Californians are transplanted, either by choice or necessity. Thus, conversations among neighbors often open with "Nice to meet you. Where are you from?" not "Nice to meet you. Didn't I see you at the market?" Running-to and running-from collide, barely obscuring any difference. Why did you leave Singapore, Izmir, Tucumcari, Beijing, or Appleton? Responses vary, yet the answer is the same. "I wanted to start again." Their non-English names and nicknames are Anglicized. Sasha, Berta, Shondar and Estaban become Alex, Robbie, Alex and Stephen. Adrianna, Chan, Malani, Farhi, Rham. They're all here. And in the process they import their home ports. Alex (Shondar) planted six types of hot peppers in this year's garden. Most are hot Hungarian varieties, straight from his father's stock in his Budapest childhood home. Berta and her family emigrated to the United States when she was twelve years old. She remembers Hungarian and Romanian languages even as she speaks unaccented American English. She misses the lilacs and chestnuts of Bucharest. "Chestnut trees are different here. Not huge like in Romania." And although she did find lilacs in Rochester, the lilac capital of America, they're not like her Romanian lilacs. America, she says, "just smells different."

Smells, sounds and touches forged into human memory construct mental blueprints, those indelible unconscious points in unique life histories. Fragrance triggers a time lapse, that one place where a rose, an onion, dew-washed grass or even sludge, corral an entire event. Recently, a young woman wearing a powder blue cotton dress crossed my path. Wind whipped the full skirt across her smartly moving legs. Instantly, it transported me to my youth on another warm, Indian summer day in Ohio, when I smelled the brightness of tomorrow in the promise of California. People occasionally leave California, realizing it's not the home they had hoped for. Some even long for their native lands yet know return isn't possible.

January 1992 La Jolla: Sasha had been completing a postdoctoral research fellowship in Canada when the government of the Soviet Union collapsed. He and his family were suddenly without a country, without passports, without a home. They became Canadian citizens. Through other connections, they made their way to the United States, obtained green cards, and he was accepted into a biomedical laboratory research program in Colorado, a place that will never be home to him or his family. I don't understand why people plant rocks, Sasha wonders why they stretch barbed wire fences across streams to claim property rights. "I feel like American Indian who could not understand white colonists who tried to buy land from them. Land, rivers, air belong to God, you cannot 'have' them," he said. He missed St. Petersburg, too. He feared that his son would be drafted to fight in Russian wars if the family returned there. "I can't risk it," he told me.

October 2000 South Park: V's project advances while the noise level increases from the steady round beat of a churning cement mixer on to the less rhythmic. Crash!

"Kim. Get down here. Something may be broken."

"Something on you?"

"Not yet. One of your clay pots fell from the ledge."

Her feet made scrambling sounds against twigs and rocks as Kim quickly slid her sixty-year old body toward the canyon floor. Picking through planter boxes, empty cement bags and generalized canyon debris, she selected the injured pot and tenderly held it to her chest.

"Naw. It's okay, John. Just a few scratches. I'll doctor it up with more blue paint. Probably should have been all blue to begin with." (*John??* V *now has a name!*).

A free-standing red ceramic fireplace, previously close to the back wall of their house, now rests on the canyon floor. Huddled nearby is a stunning San Diego red bougainvillea plant. Kindling and fire wood stacked near is ready for . . . what? Autumn solstice? Thanksgiving in California? Roasting the traditional bird in a pit? Other southern California shrubbery gradually appears. Inch by rotor inch, natural space metamorphoses into naturescape.

Last weekend, V (*he'll always be V to me*) and Kim added a steady snipping tone to our urban concert. At 3:00 a.m., K or V (it was too dark to determine which) began an earnest pruning of our shared jacaranda. First one small snip, then another. Delicate, slow, metal-on-brush sounds became a soothing cadence, like a wire stick brushing against stretched cowhide kettledrum. They work in patches, these two, as often with apparent planning and joint conference as not. A spot there — or here — like arranging a platter full of celery and carrot sticks or plumping sofa pillows.

248

Thick silence before spluush! Rain cascaded against my roof with fire hose strength. I was awake, listening to this determined storm add another dimension to the K & V canyon adventure. Steady rain wiped away both air allergens and dust from V's downward spiraled stone path. Rocks in our canyon are measured by the square yard, soil by the square foot. In 1979, the crumpled octogenarian man then living in V & K's house, stood with me on the chipped front sidewalk in front of our homes. Arm raised, as his palsied hand pointed northward, he traced for me the origin of my front yard. In the early 1920s commencing at Redwood Street, culminating at Juniper (our) Street, Switzer canyon had been plugged with mixed fill dirt for those eight blocks. Switzer's southern border is east of my house. Hence, K-V and I share the end of a canyon that begins nearly five miles south of our homes.

The winter rains have already floated V's light weight bamboo screens downstream. Kim's hand-thrown clay pots, detailed with her artist's concern for perfect, are perched within shallow rock ledges that portend their demise. It's only October. The rainy season has begun early. Pampas grass in assorted stone jars is the common denominator that helps K & V renew their lives with a blend of Midwestern Illinois and California Native American cultures.

~

Immigrant, migrant, vagrant, pilgrim, passing through. They arrive with snazzy mud flaps on their memory-stuffed camper shells or Mercedes spheres twirling on their sedans, carrying suitcases filled with portable hope. They move along, anywhere along. In frost-free southern California they plant Delicious apple and Bing cherry trees that crave a chill to bud. They assume that nurseries will only feature plants suitable to the climate. In reality, a seller sells what sells, and the immigrant buys a dream that will make home just like the home they left, wherever that was.

"Americans are not completely truthful," twenty-six-year-old Roberta noted. "They will tell you something's good when it's not, even when you know it's not. My mother is honest with me. If I make something that's not good, she'll tell me. How can people learn to do a good job if no one honestly criticizes them?"

Many arrive in America easily; for others not so. Michele from Singapore and Malini from New Delhi were easy transplants. Molecular biologists, they were both awarded research fellowships to study in American universities. They know which rules to keep and which to bend. Michele's mother knew and

249

smuggled Michele's favorite Oriental foods to her in San Diego by quadruple wrapping them to hide their pungent spice aromas. Michele would like to plant a durian tree — reminder of Singapore, but knows it won't survive in the San Diego climate. Malini readily finds Indian foodstuffs to prepare; she also has an Indian temple in which to worship her Hindu gods. Peaceful coexistence. Sasha misses the St. Petersburg culture, but rejoices in the religious freedom he has in America. Yet all admit to still being strangers in a distant home.

November 2000 South Park: Evening chill has settled into the canyon. Following two weeks of intermittent rains and a few lightning sparks, the K-V renovation pace slacked. Those floated bamboo curtains that earlier had attempted to barricade Switzer's southern-most end now stand at attention, a semicircular guard for an upended wheelbarrow, overflowing trash can, and several unplaced peeler logs that nestle on the canyon floor. Only a few more succulent-laden clay pots have appeared there in recent days. Perhaps K and V have gone to a Santa Fe ashram for the holidays or perhaps V's enthusiasm for the project has waned. Nevertheless, transplanted people need to be persistent.

January 1950, From Austria With Love: "Mitt füle Grüßen," with my love, she signed my birthday card. Barely literate, my maternal grandmother seemed to squeeze her person into each syllable. *Yes, Grandma, I love you, too.* Sitting back in time, I can feel her kisses placed on each side of my childhood cheeks. Many years later in high school German class, I learned to spell "viele Küssen," but those kisses weren't the same. Part of the wave of mid-Europeans who migrated to the United States in the early 1900s my grandmother learned English without formal instruction by listening to radio programs and reading newspapers and became an American citizen. She had crossed the Atlantic in steerage with the animals. Alien nationals use all means to reach their destinations. Flying, swimming, walking, sometimes crawling, they leave their native countries.

20th Century, Yugoslavia and Russia: Daily television portraits of families backpacking their few possessions tell the story. Onerous border crossings from Kosovo and Chechnya.

Mexico: Praying not to be caught, shot, or trapped in the mountains of snowy eastern San Diego County in winter, they illicitly course an imaginary line.

Far East and Caribbean. Securing contraband passage on Chinese boats and Cuban freighters, others beg refuge in the United States. Some, like Sasha, are in America almost accidentally. Others, like Alex, lived for the American dream since early childhood after Russian troops had invaded Hungary.

What is a rebel? A man who says no. – Albert Camus

October 1956 Budapest: Hungarian Freedom Fighters rebelled against Soviet Communist rule. For three days Hungarians were ecstatic, believing their Revolution had succeeded.

"I can't describe the feeling," Alex told me. The border to Austria was open and thousands of Hungarians fled across. He had no desire to leave when he thought Hungary was a free country. Alex's mother, Angie, and her two sons, thirteen-year-old Alex and sixteen-year-old Stephan, couldn't leave Budapest until December. When December arrived, the border had closed. The rebellion had been suppressed, making their passage into Austria treacherous. Lacking exit visas, the trio hid in the woods for one night, later in a frozen field. Twenty-five hundred other Hungarians died trying to leave.

"We were caught in the middle of plowed fields, thirty of us. Everyone got into furrow, December frozen dirt as deep as we could get in. A truck passed right by us. Looking back, it seems like a dream. My mouth was so dry I picked up dirt to wet my lips. One man came by in a truck and said he was sent to help us. My mother and others agreed something didn't seem right and wouldn't go with him. Finally, another man came, the one who was sent for us. We ran to get into the back of his truck and he took us across the border into Austria."

1960s Vietnam: *Where Have All the Flowers Gone?* Many of us sang along with Peter, Paul, and Mary during the 1960s. The flowers had gone to Vietnam to fight somebody's war. Some of them stayed, were buried, MIA, or captured in Vietnam while Vietnamese flowers replaced them on US soil. George, my brother, served on a US Navy ship in the Gulf of Tonkin as did his boyhood friends. Others, Navy and Army chaplain priest,s carried

251

packed pistols during their jeep rides through the jungle where they supplied sacraments and encouragement to the ground troops.

April 30, 1975 Saigon: Droves of South Vietnamese scrambled onto planes, boats, helicopters, any vehicle, to escape the country when North Vietnamese troops took control of Saigon. Early in the war, Dr. Trinh was drafted out of his medical practice to serve in the Vietnamese Navy. Throughout his service, he continued to see private patients who paid him in gold. Years later, that gold provided funds for his own family's escape to America. In San Diego, Dr. Trinh schooled his young children in English daily, drilled them in French and Vietnamese languages. They would remember, he vowed. But they also quickly learned about McDonald's and chocolate sundaes. The Trinhs remember Switzer Canyon too. It was adjacent to their first American home, a tiny Craftsman cottage behind my house.

November 2000 America: *Where Have All the Flowers Gone?* Some to Kuwait. Some to training accidents off San Diego's picture postcard coastline, some to Afghanistan, Germany, or the Korean DMZ. The flowers have gone to Washington to adorn politicians' lapels. Some, like my Marine son, came home and built a fence container for my cascading pink Dortmund roses. These same roses will shield my yard from the changes K & V are making to theirs.

December 2000 South Park, San Diego County: For two weeks, an odd silence has prevailed across the canyon. No thumps, crashes, buzzes have come from the east side of my property. I miss the mystery of V's next challenge. No changes, save one. Even in San Diego, adobe soil harbors seeds waiting to germinate. Small green tufts, some resembling young Bermuda and others cousin to St. Augustine grass, are sprouting around Kim's hillside pots. I'm a little sad for all of them — K, V, and the grasses. There's no way to cut the grass, impossible to keep it. Kim's pots languish in the advancing autumn weather. That seems an ignominious end to The Vampire's adventure.

V was last seen moving his bromeliads and K's potted white bougainvillea up the hillside to the front of their house. His marijuana plants were then carefully covered and placed beside the other plants in the bed of his silver Tacoma pickup. His own personal dispensary, the marijuana was used to quell the stomach upset of chemo and, later, the pain of advanced melanoma V suffered from.

January 2001 San Diego: *Where Have All the Flowers Gone?* They're here, second and third generation Americans. They're the ones someone's son or daughter died to liberate from foreign tyranny. They are the researchers who find new cancer treatments, create energy resources, write poetry, and build bridges across ravines and cultures. The flowers are the accented voices that will speak about the US Constitution on a near January day when they become citizens of the United States of America. In one refrain, the cadence might be uneven, inflections sing-song, soft or vigorous, they will be the new Americans.

What Am I Supposed To Do With This?

Christine L. Cunningham

I reached into the dirty laundry basket for the fourth high efficiency load of the day and pulled out a piece of contorted gray elastic lace. *What am I supposed to do with this?* I wondered, not fully comprehending my archeological find. I was used to washing laundry left behind by the kids' little friends — a stray tank top, a pair of running shorts, the occasional bathing suit top or bottom, but this was something I hadn't encountered in the piles of mostly red and navy plaid polyester Catholic school uniforms.

I unwound the tiny ball of elastic, thinking how an entire bolt of this fabric couldn't possibly weigh more than a potato chip. Was this a scrunchy? A hairband? A piece of gristle from last night's dinner? A narrow rectangular cream-colored tag popped out. Oh. My. God. I didn't know anyone named Victoria Secret.

Like one of those shrunken dehydrated sponges that only comes to life when water is added, this thing took form like lace dental floss with a small landing pad. A thong? What parent has allowed her thirteen-year-old to wear a thong? Which one of my daughters' friends left this and — ew — what exactly had I touched picking it up?

I showed it to my daughter, the oldest of our four kids, our athlete and part tomboy. "Elizabeth, whose is this?" I asked. "And why am I the one washing it?"

"It's mine. I bought it with my birthday money," she said, quite satisfied with herself.

"You mean the birthday where you JUST turned thirteen?"

"It's my money. You can't tell me how to spend it."

"Oh, really? Do you think Gramma and Papa gave you money so you could dress like a stripper? How many did you buy?"

"Only a few. Mom, all the girls are wearing them."

I bit my tongue to keep the words "so if all the girls jumped off a bridge" from escaping. "Are you telling me that all the seventh-grade girls in your Catholic school are wearing string as underwear beneath those pleated skirts (strictly hemmed no more than two inches above the knees)? A G-string? Do not tell me that 'G' stands for God. I don't believe it."

"Well, just ask Mrs. Lewis."

"The kindergarten teacher?"

"She's also Alison's mom."

"Are you telling me that Mrs. Lewis lets Alison wear a thong?"

"Mom, she wears them too."

"No way, she's my age. And how could you possibly know that?"

"Alison told me."

Elizabeth had been a skilled negotiator long before then. As a toddler, she chucked her hard, round poops at the daycare staff who put off changing her diaper, promising "Mommy would be here soon." Elizabeth wanted her diaper changed NOW. And, really, can you blame her? At two years old, she figured if they wouldn't change her diaper when it was an obvious need, then she would do it herself.

Elizabeth challenged things everyone else her age simply accepted. By five years old, she questioned the Monsignor, during a kindergarten class visit, about why women can't be priests.

"Because God meant for it to be that way," he responded, cloaked in the full authority of the Catholic church. When she continued to press him for a less ridiculous answer, he refused to take any more questions and announced it was time for him to leave.

It seemed like just yesterday she tried to negotiate with me to buy a pink Lion King sleeping bag for her for no particular reason. When I told her something like that was for a special occasion and not our weekly Costco run, she countered with, "Then I'll buy it with my own money." I had to admire her bulletproof confidence, so sure she could raise forty dollars in record time. She was six.

That weekend, during a family outing to the Del Mar Race Track, Elizabeth asked to place a two-dollar bet on a long shot. She didn't care that the odds were against her; she picked the horse because the jockey's pink jersey matched the pink Lion King sleeping bag she wanted. It was a sign. Naturally, the horse won. Elizabeth collected her fistful of winnings, turned toward me and

256

said smugly, "Now can I get that sleeping bag?" No amount of law school prepared me to negotiate with this child.

How quickly they go from diapers to gray lace. Elizabeth felt justified in continuing to purchase thongs based on the kindergarten teacher allowing her daughter to wear them. I threatened to throw them out if I found any more in the laundry, but she continued to buy them anyway with her debit card. I continued to throw them out. One by one, by one, by one. Ten in total. Ten dollars each—I looked it up. No arguments, I just threw them out. She continued to buy them. So, I closed her bank account. She blew a gasket.

"I warned you," I said, calmly folding her Little Mermaid bikini briefs purposefully plucked from the fresh laundry I had dumped on the kitchen table.

"You can't do that!"

I started to hum the Little Mermaid song, ignoring her outburst. In truth, it killed me to throw out one hundred dollars' worth of anything, but I was trying to teach her self-respect, respect for my authority, and not to follow the crowd. I was also trying to spare myself from the gross task of untangling something that had been buried deep in the crevices of Mount Butt. They really should come packaged with one of those squeeze-y pick up tools. A grab claw? Nifty nabber? How 'bout a thong thang?

That weekend, Elizabeth got a job bussing tables at the Pancake House earning tips. Cash tips. As in, not-tied-in-to-a-bank-account tips. This time, when I reached into the laundry, I uprooted a broad strand of purple lace. Target brand. Cheaper. Still a thong, but slightly more modest.

A truce? A compromise? *Stay strong*, I told myself. I pretended not to see it. I pretended someone else had done the wash, then quickly realized I must've been dreaming. Had she out-thonged the thong thrower outer? Had I been a tiny bit outsmarted by my teenybopper?

I "folded" the delicate thread into a neat two-inch square and placed it on top of her modest school uniform thinking to myself, *at least she's learning the value of money.*

There's a Method to Her Madness

Ruth Wallace

Louise smiled as she remembered telling Dr. Jackson during her job interview, "Sure, I can get things organized around here." She spit out her bubble gum and squeezed her hair back into the rubber band from the newspaper. *I wonder if he'll notice my new system today?* She settled in her chair, ready to greet the stream of patients arriving to see their psychiatrist.

Agnes was the first patient in the door that morning, her usual agitation plainly evident. *Got to get her settled in an examination room to keep the reception room calm. She'll get her second injection in the series today.*

Louise lined up the medical records to match the patients as they arrived.

Arthur labored his way across the carpet to sign in. *Last time he opted for pills instead of an injection.*

Next in line, Alexis shrugged and replied, "I don't really care," when asked if Arthur could go ahead of her, even though her appointment time was first.

Carl entered without looking around, signed his name without saying a word and sat down. He leafed through the *Daily Telegraph*, glanced at the *National Geographic*, flipped through *People* magazine, then started pacing.

Glancing at Eileen, Louise put the box of tissues on the counter in plain sight. *I wonder how long she can sit today without bursting into tears?*

Soon they were joined by Iris, who barked, "You have the very same magazines you had the last time I was here." She stomped to a seat and plopped down.

Then Mimi arrived. *She might not even remember Dr. Jackson's name, much less whether the magazines were the same or not.*

When Max walked in the door, Louise wondered, *Will he be "up" or "down" today?* Max approached the desk, signed in, and took a seat, not looking Louise in the eye.

The reception room filled with energy when Phil came

bouncing in with a big smile and flourished a small bouquet of flowers as he gave them to Louise. *What a change from the last time he was here and called me a moron.*

Louise snapped to attention when Pauline arrived. Leaning over the desk, Pauline whispered, "What's that big shaggy animal standing behind you?" Louise led her directly to the examination room they kept open for instances like this. "Let me get you a cup of water to sip while you wait," Louise said. She looked at her watch. *It takes Pauline's daughter about five minutes to park the car and get up to Psychiatry on the second floor.*

She indicated the corner chair to Sam after he checked in, knowing he would probably fall asleep while he waited. *Had he been "awake at all hours of the night" again?*

"Is he even here?" asked Suzanne, motioning toward the picture of Dr. Jackson hanging in the reception area. Louise just nodded. Raising her eyebrows, Suzanne pursued the issue, "Would you tell me if he wasn't?"

~

Running a little late after a full morning, Dr. Jackson came into the reception area. Leaning on the counter he asked, "How on earth did you manage to get all my vitamin B-12 patients scheduled for the same morning?"

The labels on the files weren't in view as Louise finished re-filing the morning medical records into her new system:

B-12 Deficiency

Agnes — agitation
Alexis — apathy
Arthur — anemia
Carl — concentration
Eileen — emotional instability
Iris — irritability
Mimi — memory problems
Max — mood swings
Phil — personality changes
Pauline — psychosis, hallucinations
Sam — somnolence
Suzanne — suspiciousness

260

A Flower

Dora Klinova

Good morning, everybody! Good morning, Sun!

Good morning, Sky! Good morning, Universe!

I am a new flower! I just opened my petals! I am here for you.

Look at me: I am so beautiful; you will never find such wonderful colors.

Each of my petals is a unique picture.

Smell me, breathe me, inhale my aroma in your chest, in your heart.

I am the best in this meadow!

You feel my elusive fragrance in the air.

Admire me, enjoy me. Don't postpone any moment of this delight.

You won't see anything like me, for nature never repeats itself.

Take me! I am the best gift!

I have the greatest power in the Universe, the power of love!

Give me to your loved one; I will make the vibrations of your love stronger.

Present me to your friend; the friendship will be deeper.

Bring me to your parents. I will illuminate them.

Put me in your girl's hair; I will transform her.

Give me to somebody who is already happy. I will take them to
the seventh heaven.

You will bathe in their emanation of happiness.

Take me to everyone who grieves; you will feel their appreciation.

If you lose your dearest one, bring me to his grave.

His soul will feel your sign of memory and love.

Give me to those who need support.

I will bring them joy!

Do it now, at this moment. Today I am fresh.

I am alive and my spirit is so strong!

Tomorrow will be too late . . .

The Path from Sorrow to Celebration

Dan Singer

I feel utter relief, yet a deep sense of loss and sadness; intense emotions that seem as polar as the power of opposing magnets pushing against each other. I'm struck by the total incongruence of my emotions, my reactions. It brings me guilt and disbelief. This loss is indelible; everyone around me is sad, distraught.

But no amount of sadness or sorrow on my part will help my friend feel better. My agony and darkness cannot mend his wounds nor bring him relief. His loving partner had been slowly dying for years. We all knew this day was coming. My best friend had even wished for the expediency of this day. Tired and emotionally spent by the act of being a full-time caregiver, full-time father of two beautiful teenagers, and the head of household, he would often lament that her departure wasn't coming quickly enough.

Now it has arrived. It is here. There is no turning back. It is permanent.

Still, were I to choose cheerfulness over sadness, I might alienate myself from those around me — those I love. They may see my brevity as callousness, my joy as heartlessness. I struggle to stay sad.

I want to celebrate her victories, her contributions, and her achievements. I want to laugh about her idiosyncrasies, her stubbornness, and her insatiable love of life. I want her children to remember all her qualities — her humanness — and cast aside the visual memories of her final days of torment, frailty, and delusion. I long to rid them of their anguish, to turn their grief into gladness. And then it happens.

That seminal, even inspirational moment, when I know everything — indeed everyone — will be all right. Her daughter, speaking to hundreds of mourners at the funeral, tells a story about her mother. It brings everyone to tears and laughter. The ice has been broken. Permission has been granted by the very person who has lost the most, hurts the deepest. Her story is about joy, motherhood, and unconditional love. If her children can stand before us, at their darkest hour, and proclaim their strongest memories of their mother — just as we all remember her, then I know it is safe to feel a sense of exultation. The path from sorrow to celebration has just been paved.

Since that day, I've been able to embrace the truth that there is polarity in everything around us — the yin and the yang. That euphoria can also be sadness. That hurt can also heal. Losing someone leaves us simply with thoughts and memories — memories that can enrich and enliven us. It is in this way, we continue to live life fully, even if a little less whole.

Kitty Genovese

Miriam Schraer

I awoke with a start on a cold autumn morning in 1963 to the loud alarm. I was living in my grandmother's apartment in the Bronx. In my freshman year at City College of New York (CCNY), every day at school was an adventure. College was my job and psychology was my major.

After eating a hearty breakfast for the burst of energy I needed for the hour-long subway ride to CCNY in the heart of Harlem, the five classes until lunch, the additional classes until 5:00 p.m., and the long subway ride home. I said goodbye to my grandmother and walked to the nearest subway station.

I spent an hour in the subway car reading my biology book and underlining the main ideas.

At the subway station at 125th Street in Harlem, I disembarked the train with a large crowd and walked up the stairs out into the crisp wind. Now came the long walk up the hill for blocks and blocks. CCNY came into view, its ancient gray buildings adorned with gargoyles. I stopped at the stoplight, waiting for the light to change.

When it turned green, I walked into the crosswalk, lost in thought. I slipped and slid, falling into the street, my books scattering all around me. Wide splashes of bright yellow paint streaked my faux black leather jacket and jeans. I looked around and saw a stiff folded sign just outside the crosswalk that read WET PAINT. I had slipped into a yellow crosswalk line that had just been painted!

Looking like a clown, but not being able to return home and change, I made my way to a large study hall, avoiding people's eyes so I wouldn't see their reaction to my clothes.

I took off my jacket — which sported gashes of bright yellow paint — turned it inside out, and spread it beneath me as I settled onto a couch against one wall of the cavernous room. I was soon entrenched in my biology book. Ten minutes later, a girl sat down next to me.

265

Three young guys ran into the large study hall, two of them shouting obscenities at the third. The two shouting guys looked like juvenile delinquents, in black leather jackets, black leather pants, black boots, gold chains hanging from their belts, and dark pompadours sitting like sculpted hills on top of their heads.

All three boys stopped in front of me, two of them still yelling at the third boy. One of the juvenile delinquents pulled all the books out of the arms of the third boy who had neat hair and was wearing khaki pants and a buttoned-down shirt.

My heart pounded. I wanted to help the boy, to stop this, but I felt glued to the couch. I couldn't stand. I saw my arm reach out and pull the top book from the juvenile delinquent's arms. The book slipped out of my hand and fell to the floor. Then, surprisingly, the nasty boy handed the books back to the scared boy, and the three of them walked out of the study hall without saying another word.

I sat there breathing heavily.

The girl sitting beside me turned to me and said, "This was an experiment for Sociology 101. We are doing this experiment because, as you probably heard on the news, Kitty Genovese was recently stabbed at night outside a large apartment building. Even though many people in the building heard her screams, not one person called the police, and she died. What was your reaction when you saw the boy attacked?"

I sat there in shock. Was this not the strangest day of my life?

"I can't believe this just happened to me," I said. "Right before coming into the library, while crossing a street, I slipped and fell in the street into a line of wet, bright yellow paint. Look at my clothes."

"That *is* weird," she agreed. "Well, what was your reaction when you saw the boys attack the student?"

I thought for a moment. "I was afraid of the boys who were yelling. I thought they might have a knife or a gun."

"What else did you feel?" she asked, writing down my response in a notebook.

"I felt angry that they were bullying the boy and afraid for him. I wanted to help him, but I felt paralyzed, like I couldn't stand. What if they hurt me? My heart was pounding. It still is."

"Anything else?"

"Yes, it felt like time was moving in slow motion. I saw my hand go out, almost like an out-of-body experience, and take the book out of the mean boy's hand. But my hand was so weak, I

266

couldn't hold onto the book, and it fell to the floor. I couldn't say anything. I felt frozen."

"Well, thank you very much," she said. "This has been helpful." She gathered her books and walked out of the room.

I sat there still out of breath. Why had this happened? Why had this happened to *me*? And why were my clothes covered with large swatches of bright yellow paint?

I thought about the two events all day and couldn't wait to get home to tell my boyfriend, Benny, about them on the phone that night. There must be some significance to this.

When Benny called that night, I raced through the two stories, and we laughed and laughed. We loved it when life jumped out at us this way, when it attacked us with its bright colors, sounds, smells, tastes. We loved having strong feelings, when life was heightened.

"Maybe I should sue the college for putting me through that terrifying experience without asking for my permission," I joked to Benny. "Or maybe someone is telling me bright yellow is my best color."

Why had this happened to me? Finally, I came up with an explanation for the two events. Even though I wasn't religious, and I knew almost nothing about Judaism, I was sure this was a sign from G-d. Maybe G-d wanted me to get involved and help if I ever saw someone being attacked. And the yellow paint was highlighting this message like a bright exclamation point. I would never forget this day.

I lived in New York and took the subway regularly, and I was tested not long afterward. Waiting on the platform near the tracks at the 125th Street station in Harlem for my train to take me home, I watched different trains roaring through the station in opposite directions.

A thin, elderly, grey-haired man in worn, dirty clothes was standing to the right of me and a well-dressed woman wearing a purse on her left shoulder was standing on the right side of him. Suddenly, I saw his hand slip into the purse. He pulled her wallet out without her noticing.

Instantly, remembering the incident in the college library, I pulled the wallet out of the man's hand. It fell onto the tracks, just as the book had fallen out of my hand and onto the floor in the study hall.

"Ma'am," I said, in a calm voice, "your wallet just fell onto the tracks."

"What?" she asked in disbelief.

"Your wallet just fell onto the tracks," I repeated, and she looked down at her wallet in shock.

"I'll get it for you," the elderly man said. "After the train leaves the station."

To the left of us, a train was roaring into the station. It stopped in front of us, the doors slapped open, a crowd poured out, another crowd rushed in. Then the doors slammed closed, and with a loud creak and gears crunching, the train slowly moved out of the station.

The well-dressed woman, the elderly man, and I were still standing there. The man nimbly jumped onto the tracks, picked up the wallet, climbed back onto the platform, and handed the wallet to the woman. Without either of us saying a word to the bewildered woman standing there in confusion with the wallet still in her hand, the elderly man and I both looked at each other for a split second, turned in opposite directions, and walked away.

That was the first of many tests.

Fables From The Atlantis Zoo

G. Raffe and P. Cock

Cy Roseman
(Technical assistance, research, and editorial review)

At an archeological dig conducted on the Greek island of Santorini, the last home of Plato, on December 12, 2031, an unusual discovery was made. The evidence on which Plato based his declaration of the existence of the lost continent of Atlantis was uncovered. In addition, this evidence was grounded in a verbatim transcript of discussions that had taken place several thousand years ago on Atlantis in its well-developed zoo.

This transcript offered a key source of knowledge long since lost to humans. It seems that many animals had, at that time, perfected the ability to communicate on an interspecies platform about fairly sophisticated subjects pertinent to "a higher understanding of the key elements in successful and joyous living." In short, discussions among the animals illuminated the special challenges in "living the good life." This transcript of these discussions, in effect, produced what could be called fables, comparable to those of Aesop, and perhaps, to the teachings of Jesus.

Here, then, is what we can now refer to as the Fables of the Atlantis Zoo, which is translated into English. For purposes of easier reading and greater entertainment value, liberties have been taken with this translation; and, to avoid any academic disputes over content and meaning of these commentaries, the original documents have been destroyed, making this the only version of the Fables available for human consumption. We hope that readers of these Fables will be enlightened and entertained, and that this process may go a long way toward improving the quality of life for humans.

Note: The authorship of these Fables has been ascribed to the two primary observers and commentators of the discussions which follow. In most cases they have attempted to offer the critical key ideas in the form of personalized dialogue. We can thank them for that, since it makes it much easier and more entertaining to read and think about.

Prologue: The Search for Authorship

At a recent meeting of the Atlantis's Zoo residents, it was determined that the reporting of discussions and the authorship of the final version of these Reports should be placed in the control of two residents, as it was established that no creature should have this important responsibility exclusively. Much consideration followed regarding who should be designated.

The first author identified was G. Raffe, in large part because his physiognomy, namely his long neck, which places his head — in particular his eyes and ears — far above the ground and the other residents. G. Raffe would be able to observe all residents and hear their discourses from above, much like a celestial god or creator. In addition, he was noted for his calm temperament, lack of aggressive behavior toward other creatures, and the steadiness of his behavior.

At the same time, it was clear that his expressed opinions and determined findings were likely to be rather dull and, in fact, probably boring to most listeners or readers. The work to be undertaken in the review, editing, and final presentation of the Reports would require, not only the somewhat academic objectivity and neutrality of G. Raffe, but also the creative spirit of his co-author who should be able to offer more dramatic expression of the findings in these Reports. The coauthor should manifest this creative, dramatic impact in his daily living, which would inevitably be expressed in his work on the development of the final expression of the Reports. Therefore, it was determined that the best candidate for coauthor should be P. Cock.

The issue then arose whether one author should be male and the other female, since this was likely to produce the most objectively neutral perspective on the Reports. After much review, it was determined that such gender differentiation, while it might produce objective neutrality between the two coauthors, would also likely generate considerable additional difficulties in communication between the coauthors because of their gender differentiation. This is not to say that all males easily agree between themselves as compared to the difficulty of agreement between any given male and any given female. But the probability

270

is that such gender differences would exacerbate the conflict in discussion between them and therefore should be avoided. (It was also noted in passing that male-female gender differentiation would not accommodate expression of opinion by species with considerable deviation of gender, i.e., LGBTQ tendencies. And, it was determined that it would be virtually impossible to represent all these "deviant" gender orientations.)

Now, as it turned out, representation of female gender on the part of both coauthors was in effect eliminated because it was clearly the male, P. Cock — not his female partner, P. Hen — that manifested the desired creative and dramatic effect in daily living by virtue of his ability to fan his glorious tail feathers.

What, then, of the difference between Mr. (bull) and Mrs. (cow) G. Raffe? The bull is taller and has bald horns. The difference in height is important not only for seeing over a greater area, but also because the bull is able to gather leaves from higher branches of trees to feed his family, thus eliminating one source of friction between bulls and cows in Raffe families. Since the female is not expected to engage in fighting, it would seem that the male would be better able to defend himself in arguments with his co-author.

So, it was decided that a male named G. Raffe and the male named P. Cock would be the coauthors of these Reports, and, at their first meeting, the coauthors discussed the issues surrounding said authorship. (This initial Report has been renamed Fable 1 for this translation.)

Fable 1 — How the Peacock Came
to Eat His Own Tail Feathers

G.R.: "Well, Mr. Cock, how do you feel about being named coauthor of these reports?"

P.C.: "Probably the same as every other creature who has finally been recognized as special or unique. Happy and proud. Probably the same as you feel. Am I right, G?"

G.R.: "I really don't know how to compare my feelings to those of anyone else's, since I don't feel their feelings. But my guess is I don't have the same pride of achievement that you do. I was selected for my height, which gives me a special ability to see others. In your case, Mr. Cock, you were selected for your tail feathers which, even if they do have eyes, cannot see. You are proud to be selected because of the way you look — not how you do things."

P.C.: "Isn't that the same as being selected because you are tall? Weren't we both selected because of the way we appear to others?"

G.R.: "I don't think so. You can fan your feathers and attract attention to yourself. I don't do anything, but be who I am. I don't get tall to attract attention. And, by the way, I use my height for this job in the same way a basketball player does who has an advantage because of his height. My height is very different than your good looks. Which, by the way, is very attractive to your hens. No Raffe cows are attracted to me because of my height."

P.C.: "I wasn't selected to be good looking. I was picked because I could be counted on to make the reports interesting to read. You are just SO dull; nobody is interested in reading your opinions about anything. I was picked to breathe life and vitality into the reports. And I know that I can do a better job at that than you can. Nobody wanted to see these reports go down in flames, because you present such bland pieces that they couldn't be sold to the public. Your reports are like used dish rags, piled high but going nowhere. With my fancy feathers, I can make the ordinary exciting. Your entire family looks like used dish rags piled high."

G.R.: "You certainly know how to insult ordinary creatures with ordinary looks. Like many movie stars, your ideas have nothing to offer readers, but provocative soft porn. How exactly do you hope to provide our zoo residents with enlightened perspectives on how to improve the quality of their life?"

P.C.: "I believe all creatures need to be inspired by the success stories of others, such as myself. They need to know that they can spread their tail feathers, just as I do, and attract attention to themselves; and, this is a common form of building successful charisma or, possibly, their own star power. Before they get rich, they may get famous. Do you have any comparable secrets on how they can be goal-driven in the future?"

G.R.: "Well, just as you make a terrible, awful noise when you open your mouth, so you have now revealed why your view of success is secondary to mine. Are you willing to challenge my rights as primary author and gamble your tail feathers on your contest with me over this issue?"

P.C.: "Yes I am ready to take that challenge. What will you put up if you lose?"

272

G.R.: "OK. Let's do it this way: if I win, you will eat your tail feathers, once a year, in molting season. To avoid any further feelings of hostility toward me, I will grant you the right to continue to wear your tail feathers and display them whenever you wish, to impress hens or otherwise. If you win, I will not argue with you about the advantages of achieving celebrity status, and you will be the primary author. I will be noted on the cover of these Reports as: 'with the technical assistance of G. Raffe.'

G.R.: "And, oh yes, you will be in complete charge of the promotion, marketing, or advertising of the Reports. I will not offer my opinion or advice to you about how to make the Reports a source of wisdom to the world-at-large. This should satisfy your unquenchable ego."

P.C.: "Does that last comment of yours imply that you have a very modest ego, one that does not look for recognition?"

G.R.: "Unfortunately, as I have listened to our discourse today, I realize that it is impossible for anyone, myself included, to be completely free of vanity and egotism. But it is one thing to revel in one's worldly recognition, securing ego gratification at every turn, and quite another thing to be aware of this trait as a character flaw — to be kept under control whenever possible.

G.R.: "The difference between us, Mr. Cock, is you tend to gravitate toward the former — vainly strutting around, full of pride — obnoxiously claiming credit for all good things, while most neutral observers would say my modesty and restraint of ego are important parts of my character."

P.C.: "Well, let's get back to the basic issue of who shall be the primary author, and how disagreement over this matter should be resolved. Why do you think you should be the primary author? And how do you plan to settle the question of who should come first?"

G.R.: "To answer your first question about primary authorship, I note that authorship should be determined by work performed, not personal attitudes and behavior. I believe the primary work of putting together these reports includes revealing the history and behavior of other Zoo residents, which involves gathering and constructing the transcripts, which offer the basic foundation for the reports. This work has nothing to do with author attitudes, behavior, or claims of superior understanding. I believe that I, G. Raffe, have a dedicated history of such activity — that I am better suited than you in reporting dispassionately the

273

behavior of other creatures. And I tend to avoid exaggerating for dramatic effect.

G.R.: "As for the second question, I assume that we will disagree about who should be primary author, and that we cannot settle this question nor decide the winner of the bet we made. I believe the settlement of this dispute should rest with the residents of the zoo. Do you agree with me, Mr. Cock, that we must alert the zoo residents to our differences? And that they must decide how the issue must be resolved?"

P.C.: "Well I think you're right that we have significant differences over who should be acknowledged as primary author. We must look to the zoo membership for settlement of our dispute and to make the determination of the winner of our bet."

A week went by while the respected elders of the zoo took this matter under consideration. Finally, they polled the membership, and it was overwhelmingly decided that G.'s primary status as author should be acknowledged. Thus, it was declared that P. Cock's tail feathers would be digested by him once a year in molting season. As G. Raffe noted:

> "... it is impossible for anyone ... to be
> completely free of vanity and egotism. It is one
> thing to revel in one's worldly recognition,
> securing ego gratification at every turn, and quite
> another to be aware of this trait as a character
> flaw — which must be kept under control ..."
>
> ~

The transcript of this dialogue shows how it came to pass that P. Cock could continue to show off his tail feathers while losing his bet, and yet retain his right to promote, market, and advertise the Reports or, what are now referred to as, **The Fables from the Atlantis Zoo**.

A Life of (In)Decisions

Dan Singer

Never in my wildest imagination did I think I would live to be 79. But here I am, still of sound mind, even if my body wants me to rest more than it allows me to blossom. An hour of gardening and running my fingers through the rich soils of the yard are just enough to exhaust me.

Yet despite my age, I can remember the day she walked into my life — like it was yesterday. A set of deep brown eyes drew me in like they were magnets, with an air about the way she walked — a confidence that I had yet to observe in a 19-year-old woman. Who was this mystery beauty? Would she even notice me?

It is easy to look back on life and see the milestones that clearly define who you are and how you got here. For me, my life was easy, and my decisions were of equal ease — get a good education; find someone who knows how to love unconditionally; commit to support, cherish and love them for the rest of your life; only have children once you are married; and, have a steady job. Be strong in the face of difficult decisions. Like a science book that lays out the formula for a perfect potion, my life was predictable. My decisions took me down roads that all proved to bring value to me and my family. Everything was good. That brown-eyed girl did notice me, and eventually, after I completed my education, we got married, settled in to start a family, and were surrounded by adventure, joy, and love.

How did I get so lucky to enjoy this life? Was it the smart, calculated decisions we made along the path of life, or was it the things I *didn't* choose that actually made the greatest difference? I didn't choose to let my affinity for a good drink interfere with what mattered in life, nor did I choose to succumb to the flirtations of that young attractive woman at that wine-tasting event. I didn't choose to move my family when my work moved me away from home, instead, spending years enduring a treacherous commute. And I didn't neglect the calls of our greater family circle when they were most in need.

But then, it was her non-decision, ten years ago, that changed my life forever — on that cold rainy night when she decided not to return from our mountain cabin. When the Sheriff called, he said they suspected some candles had caused the house fire that took her vibrant life, stealing her last breath. I choose to believe she never knew what happened, and never woke to suffer through the fear and horror of watching her life end in tragedy.

Aren't our non-decisions also decisions? Is there really a difference? Can we even know which options will result in the most favored outcomes and lead us to better endings? And do those choices define us or are they simply turns in the road? I don't know the answers. But I do know that for ten years, I've been stuck. I've made no decisions; I've chosen not to choose, not to decide, not to take action for fear of the consequences. And I've come to realize that fearing decisions or indecisions is no way to live my life.

So, I'm done deciding not to decide. Today I'll pack my sorrows away and choose to take control of my destiny, to live the rest of my life fully, to give — with everything left in my body.

But first, I'm going to spend a few hours gardening and feeling the soil between my fingers; for it is there, where my wife's ashes lay, I feel her spirit the strongest. And as I turn that dirt and cry my last tears, I know I will be nurturing the soil that will give life to new beginnings.

The Park Bench

Candace George Conradi

The sun felt warm; it was a relief to no longer feel cold. The winter had been a very long one, far longer than she had anticipated. The shawl she had worn was thrown casually over the back of the park bench; her arms rested beside her in a surrender. Relaxing, she closed her eyes and let the sound of the leaves dancing in the wind wash over her. The birds, how sweet their perfectly harmonized sound. For a moment she imagined they were singing her favorite tune from oh-so-long ago.

She did not hear him approach but only noticed his presence when she felt the bench bend under his weight. She knew it was him. Not so much from the aftershave he wore but from the scent of him. That warm essence floated through the air and wrapped its arms around her in a familiar embrace. Smiling she opened her eyes and met his loving gaze.

"Why did you go?" he asked, his voice moving over and through her, pulling at the tangles in her soul.

"You know why. It was just too much for me, too crowded. I used to love the crowds. You remember. I never shied away from the public. I guess after so many years it just seemed so loud. Or maybe it was so quiet, so muted? Maybe both. I don't hear like I used to. Does it make sense, a noisy void?"

He nodded in understanding but then shifted in his seat. The sound of weariness in her voice hit him hard, and realizing the inevitability of it all he buckled. Bending forward, he leaned on his knees for support.

"You haven't outgrown me? Have you?" he asked, tenuously.

"What do you think?" she asked, reaching over and squeezing his hand tenderly, earnestly. "Could I ever?"

He smiled.

"You and me? Why . . ." a sweet pause, and then, ". . . why, we are two puzzle pieces, you and me. We just fit together."

"I don't remember ever not having you next to me. Even when we were apart, you were there. I'd hear you whispering in

277

my ear, reminding me to say the right thing. Or I'd go to do something, make some decision, and you were at my side, reminding me that my decisions had impact. I can't feel you there now."

She sighed and moved closer to him. Reaching out she patted his hand in reassurance as he slipped his arm around her shoulder.

"When will they be here?"

"Soon, I think. Are the kids okay?"

"They are because they have you, they'll always have you."

"That's a nice thought. But honestly," and she leaned forward and he heard her laughter again, always showing up when she had a self-deprecating thought. "I think they get tired of having a crotchety old lady still telling them what to do. But I do so love each of them." She stretched and turned toward him, eyeing him in a soulful way. "I do love them equally, you know?"

He smiled and felt the warmth of her familiar body lean back again, into his shoulder. The air moved around them, interrupting the stillness. He reached across with his left hand and took her right, weaving their fingers together. The thought of letting go brought him back to his pain. He winced.

"You remember the day we met?" he asked.

She turned her face toward him, eyes sparkling in sweet remembrance, as she met his deep blue eyes with her own. "Lord yes. My heart stopped when I saw you walk in the room. I was certain you hadn't even noticed me."

"Well, truth be known, the whole room disappeared when I walked through that door and saw you standing there. It sounds so corny, but truly, the room emptied except for you. I didn't want anyone to notice how "flustergated" I was, so I excused myself and walked out to the back patio, just to gather my wits!"

Another giggle. "What kind of word is that?"

"It's the best one I could come up with to describe the moment. I was lost somewhere between flustered and flabbergasted." Now they shared their laughter. "Oh, how our minds play tricks. All this time I thought you were just running away from me!"

"I did, actually . . ." and a sideways glance brought out sighs from them both. He felt her soft breath brush past his cheek, so familiar and reassuring.

"Remember when Sarah was born?"

278

"You know I don't. I was away. I remember learning about the birth. I'm sorry I wasn't there."

"I knew you could not be. There was a war and a demand for talented pilots. You always were inclined to serve. Even me, your family. You've served us your whole life. It's in your DNA."

"Remember when we lost her?" he asked.

"The worst of the worst. I never really got over it. I never got over feeling the helplessness of it all. It impacted me for years. I had to fight down fear every time I watched our babies toddle out to our backyard until they moved out into their lives. I hope it didn't show."

"Sometimes it did. But I understood your pain."

"You did better than understand. You talked me through those dark days. Thank you for that. But I don't remember you sharing how you were feeling. How you coped. You just took care of me. Held me. Rocked me to sleep in the solitude of our bed, never demanding anything more than my presence."

"You have a selective memory my dear. We held each other and shared boxes of Kleenex. Maybe my war experience helped me with death. As soldiers, we were all helpless — bullets flying all around us. Sarah's loss was not the same, but I accepted it. We all have a date, you know? Damn it anyway, we all have . . ."

She squeezed his hand. "Well, we survived it. I couldn't have done it without you. I am always sad when a tragedy tears a family apart. We were lucky. We survived. But we're all just a little different, aren't we?"

Her hypothetical question was a rarity by her nature. He shook his head in agreement.

"Want to take a walk?" he asked. "It's a beautiful day. I think we have time. We won't wander too far . . ." His voice trailed off.

"I'd like that. Maybe take our stroll around our park. Think of the number of trips we've taken around this little patch of heaven. I would very much like to stop by the pond. I love watching the swans in and out of the water. So gangly on land, so graceful and elegant in water."

He rose slowly. Once stable he extended his hand and helped her to her feet. They stood there, rocking a little and then paused. Another giggle.

"Do you remember that party we went to at the Ridges when you were pregnant? We both had a little too much to drink. As we left the house, I remember we looked pretty much the same as today!"

279

"Oh my God, how could I forget! We fell into the Arb bushes, didn't we? All I recall is that it was a soft landing, catching us both. Good thing that ol' Arb bush was lush and tall, kept us from landing flat on our asses! Can you imagine that we drove home? Holy Mother of God, and I was pregnant with Alan. Maybe that's what's wrong with that boy?"

They both laughed again but he came to their son's defense. "There is nothing wrong with Alan. He just gets ahead of himself sometimes! He's successful enough, even if he forgets his keys and trips over things. You know he's your favorite."

"I told you, I don't have favorites." She squeezed his arm. "Except, of course, for you until you're not." She rolled her eyes. He understood.

As they rounded the bend and saw their bench, she put her hand on his chest, stopping them both in their tracks.

"I must go now. See? They've come and are waiting."

"Do you have to?"

She nodded her head.

Anxiously, he pled, "Will I hear from you soon?"

"I don't know, it's all a mystery to me." She reached up and touched his cheek. He felt her hand slip from his own as he watched her walk away.

~

Daylight called as he struggled to keep his eyes closed, to stay in the dream. His fingertips met the coolness on her side of their bed. Her pillows, fluffed and full, were propped up against the headboard. The blankets were empty and undisturbed. Reaching across the open space, he felt the cold objective tidiness of finality.

He reluctantly rose and went into their kitchen, made a pot of coffee and fed their dog. He moved slower these days.

The phone rang. It was their daughter.

"Are you ready, Dad?"

"No, but, yes. I will be."

"I'll be there to pick you up in about an hour. The caterers will be there and set up everything while we are gone. Do you need anything?"

"No. See you . . ." His words constricting his throat, he brusquely hung up before completing his thought.

Her photo was beautiful, everyone said so when they arrived at the reception. The minister had said all the right things. The eulogy was eloquent. The compassion was palpable. All the flowers had been transported back to their home and would soon

280

find their way to the hospital to be shared with the living. It was all so beautiful, so orderly, so hard.

The conversation and noise overcame him. He made his way to his den, invisible to the multitude of friends and family as he weaved in, around, and through them. From the solitude of his office he could see their park bench. Silent and alone, the bench and he were the same, both waiting. Placing his hand on the glass and leaning his head into it, he caught the wafting aroma of her perfume. Soft, with a light floral essence, it had always preceded her entrance into any room no matter how she had tried to surprise him.

Trembling he turned, expecting to see her standing there. He saw only the fulness of a life they had created together in the things that decorated their home. The pang of emptiness hit him, yet her perfume lingered. Deliberately turning back toward the window, he saw what he needed to do.

Silently, he slipped out the back door and made his way to her.

The Cellphone and The Cab

Laura Hoyt

A few weeks ago, I visited San Francisco. My mom was born and raised there. It's where my grandparents' home is, where I spent a lot of my childhood, and still do. Our family was fortunate to inherit this home where my sister now resides.

Hanging with my sister involves accompanying her while transporting her teenagers to their various activities. Driving to school or work in traffic. Delivering my nephews to their miscellaneous comings and goings, there's generally traffic. Sometimes they use the buses or driver cars. There are many vehicles and stop signs or traffic lights at almost every block. Thank you, cellphone, for the application which redirects to less congested routes. Somehow, someway, everyone reaches their destination in this busy city.

I love where we live because most often, I can leave the house without a car. I enjoy walking to numerous places to eat, shop, or play, all the while taking in the view of the Golden Gate Bridge and the beautiful bay. Up and down steep streets engages little used muscles and strengthens my lung capacity. Turning a corner is a sudden reminder of the icy wind that seems to go right through me until I change direction again.

Cooking is a passion and is requested when I'm there. I think my family enjoys my creations *if* I remember all the specific likes and dislikes. The most taxing chore is the grocery shopping. There is, however, a major market about six blocks away, which happens to be directly across from the scenic bay. Getting there is quite an enjoyable walk, but I have to get transportation back. This time I promised to bring back something delicious for my hungry nephew in about an hour.

~

Soon I had a checked-off list and a full cart. It was time to grab my cellphone to call for a driver car. Upon selecting the app, I viewed several available vehicles in the area. Easy. Of course, for some reason the line kept disconnecting. After a number of attempts, I went back into the market and tried again, hoping for better reception. No luck. Fortunately, this market offers customer service, and I requested a cab.

"You're caller number six. Please hold," said the recording.

After waiting quite some time, I was told the cab would arrive shortly. Appreciating this almost prehistoric assistance, I left to wait for my ride.

Twenty minutes later, and no cab, I had to call my nephew and inform him of my ordeal. Surprise, no service. Apparently, the network wasn't working in this area. Really? That's right, my husband recently changed networks. As usual, it was his fault. I decided to purchase a new cellphone and choose my own network when I returned home.

I reentered the market with my cart of groceries. The security guard looked at me and said, "Weren't you in here already?"

After I explained my situation, he kindly made another call for a cab.

"Three-minute wait," said the recording.

Does he have time for this? I wondered.

After a short wait, the security guard made the connection. To my delight, this cab was prompt. Grateful for the security guard's good nature, I packed everything into the trunk and was on my way.

~

Somewhat annoyed the cab driver held up his hand signaling to me he knew the way or, maybe, to stop talking?

Did I speak too forcefully?

"You said the street's right up here?"

"Yes," I replied sort of confused that he asked.

Upon reaching my destination, the cab driver slowly climbed out and proceeded to help with the bags. My senses told me something was strange. I moved quick, hoping to avoid his help. As I glanced over my shoulder, he was heading my way, swerving and unsteady on his feet, my groceries dangling at his sides.

Go figure, the guy was high. At least his ride was better than his stride.

Carrying my bags up the stairs with a chuckle and a sigh, I closed the door behind me. Another entertaining adventure in the City by the Bay.

Heroes Among Us

Sally Eckberg

Mom and I usually went for our walk in the early afternoon. Mom would always say, "Diego, I'll bet we meet your friend Lucy." I knew very well that we would meet Lucy, the female Doberman that lived down the block from us. Lucy and her Mom were at the end of the corner. We greeted each other with a little nose rubbing, and I admit I got somewhat excited. I did prance around just a bit. The moms walked together and talked and talked and talked. It seemed strange that they could talk so much when they had just seen each other yesterday.

When we got home from our walk, I noticed that Mom called Dad at his office. They chatted for a few minutes. I heard Mom say okay, and then she hung up. I spent the rest of the day herding the chickens and then napping out of sheer exhaustion.

When Dad came home, Mom met him. I knew something was up because she had a nice dress on and had a coat over her arm. The doorbell rang, and I ran to answer it, but was shooed out of the way. It was Lucy with her mom and dad. Oh, then I got it. They were going out, and Lucy and I were staying home. Not a totally bad situation.

Lucy and I romped around the yard for a short time, and then I showed her how to open the door to the chicken coop. Of course, the chickens made quite a racket, but we managed to edge over to the nest boxes anyway. I showed Lucy the pretty colored eggs and encouraged her to help herself. Then we slipped out of the coop and pushed the lock closed.

We feasted on the eggs which complemented our kibble and then played a game of hide and seek. The porch was a bit chilly, and Mom left the back door unlocked. We decided to find a comfortable place in the house. We looked around and chose a spare bedroom. Lucy and I jumped up on the bed and settled in for an evening nap.

We must have been asleep for a few hours when we both heard a crash. I jumped off the bed and went into the hall to see if

Mom and Dad were home. I was surprised to see a strange person sneaking around the room. He was picking things up. Sometimes he put the item in a bag, and other times he put the thing back.

I did not recognize anything about the stranger, so I growled in my low voice. By this time, Lucy was standing behind me and she also growled. The stranger looked in our direction and said, "Nice doggies, be good doggies now."

I thought how insulting could he be. Canines of our stature are definitely not "doggies." We are well behaved canines. But we are not to be trifled with.

The stranger walked slowly towards the door and I followed him. I was on him before he got off the front step. He stumbled but recovered and started to run. Not fast enough. I jumped on his back. Down he went with me, Diego, right on top of him. He struggled, but Lucy had taken a position in front of him, and she generously showed him her beautiful white incisors. He stopped moving and lay very still. Each time he tried to move, Lucy and I reminded him that he might not want to argue with us about his situation. It worked.

After a short time, Mom and Dad came home accompanied by Lucy's parents. When Dad saw me sitting on the stranger, he hurried to assess the problem of the intruder who was weakly calling out for help. However, Dad was too smart to fall for the innocence charade. He immediately tied the stranger's hands with a leash. Then he called the police who quickly arrived on the crime scene.

The police examined the bag that the stranger was carrying and promptly put him in handcuffs. They also commended Lucy and me for being such brave watchdogs, scratching both our heads. Truth be known, the stranger was no match for one of us, let alone two.

The following day, Lucy came back to my house followed by several men with cameras. They all seemed excited and wanted to pet and scratch Lucy and me. Usually, petting and scratching is a plus but I had not had my kibble yet, so I was only mildly interested.

Dad put Lucy and me in a "sit" position. Then a policeman walked over to us and put a gold medal on a red ribbon around each of our necks. The other men took pictures. Everyone chattered loudly, mixed with some laughter. I was not into the whole scene because I couldn't stop thinking about my kibble.

The next morning, Dad banged out on the porch disturbing

286

my early morning nap, yelling, "Hot Dog." He was swishing the newspaper at me and I was not sure if he meant to swat me with it. But no. There on the front page was a photo of Lucy and me wearing our gold medals and looking smart. In large print above the photo were the words: Hero Dogs Catch Neighborhood Burglar.

She Found the One

Peggy Hinaekian

Samantha was bored.

She had discarded her latest boyfriend who had turned out to be a loser. She did not like ordinary men and Steven was ordinary personified. Not to start with, though. His ordinariness manifested itself after a couple of months. He was charming and amused her at times, but his conversation got to be monotonous. His jokes were repetitious. She let go of him gently, as she did not want to hurt his feelings.

"Steven," she said, "I don't think we are really suited to each other. You are a great guy, but I am just not the girl for you. I am too complicated."

He stared at her, puzzled. "I think we are getting along fine. I don't see anything unsuitable. I don't understand what you are talking about."

"No, Steven, I don't have the same sentiment, so let's just be friends. I hope you are not upset." And with that said, she left him, after having had a last dinner together. He accompanied her home, gave her two pecks on the cheek, and pleaded with her.

"Are you sure you won't change your mind, Sweetie?" he asked her hopefully, holding her hand and not wanting to let go.

It broke Samantha's heart to see the pain on his face, but she was adamant.

"Yes, I am sure." she said. And that was that.

Now, it was time to hunt for a new man. She had never gone more than two weeks without a man friend, ever. It had always been easy for her. There were numerous specimens around. She attracted them like fruit flies. However, it was the fourth week now and, so far, the terrain was barren. She was becoming restless. She craved masculine company.

Samantha had been told by several men that she was a temptress. She liked that. She was also called a seductress, comparing her to Cleopatra. Lately, however, she was not meeting "doable" men. A dependable man. A charming man. A passionate man. And one with a good job, of course. She liked being wined and dined, expensively. She liked exotic vacations. She wanted to find a "Leopatra," as she called it. She knew that would be a real challenge. Although she liked macho men, they had to be tamable, flexible enough to suit her needs. She did not like to feel dominated, but she did not want a guy who was docile as a lamb either. She was relentless in her pursuit, but her plans did not seem to materialize. Time was galloping fast, and she was still looking almost all over Paris, with no possibilities in sight. She had scoured the health clubs, the tennis clubs, the golf clubs, everywhere that men frequented.

Nada.

"What's happened to eligible men? Have they evaporated from the face of the earth?" she asked her best friend, Diana. They were having their usual coffee together, one morning before heading off to work.

"The whole dynamic has changed, my dear," Diana replied. "Men no longer chase women. Forget about the old days. We are in an electronic age."

"Sure, I know. Men are now in the passive mode, with all the women offering themselves on match sites. But those sites are not my scene. They post an old picture of themselves, and half the stuff they say is not true. They can be married and want to fool around. It's time I take some serious action."

Samantha was invited to a cocktail party at the posh Plaza Athenée Hotel on Avenue Montaigne, one of the best places to meet new people. The host, Ben, a gay Italian interior decorator, happened to be a good friend of hers. He was launching his new business and had invited all sorts of people — affluent people.

The venue was seductive and glittered with candles strategically placed. Ben liked the mysterious. At the grand piano, the pianist played some smooth melodies, the type that could put you in the mood for romance. *Romance with the right person, of course,* she thought.

Samantha surveyed the glitzy crowd. *Looks promising.*

"Hello, darling." Ben greeted her. "You look like one sexy bitch, *mia cara*," he continued, brushing his cheek against hers. His cologne was overwhelming. She winced unnoticeably. It must be "Man in Black" by Bulgari, she presumed. Every man seemed to be using that scent nowadays.

Samantha, dressed to kill in an off-the-shoulder tight black dress that showed off her curvaceous slim body, felt empowered.

She knew she stood out. She worked hard to keep her body trim, tight, and tempting. She swam for one full hour every day at the Sports Club and tanned only long enough to keep her bronze glow.

Her entire ensemble was a fashion statement. She had donned red, spiked sandals that made her unsteady; but they were the latest fashion—and fashion was her bible. As a flirty touch, she added short lacy gloves—red, or course—cut off at the fingers to show her matching manicure. Her luxurious raven hair was gathered to one side and cascaded down to her bare left shoulder, showing off her smooth, tanned skin. And her dark doe-like eyes—her most prominent feature, and what some would say was the "mirror of the soul"—sparkled with anticipation, eager for the hunt.

"No partner?" Ben asked.

"No, Ben, I hope to meet new prey here. I do hope you have invited eligible candidates for me. Otherwise, my evening will be lost—totally *kaput*—sweetheart!"

Again, Samantha surveyed the crowded hall. The flickering candlelight made it difficult to determine who was worth meeting. A man had to catch her eye at first view before she would determine how to ensnare him. While sensual and appealing, the dimly lit atmosphere was a challenge. All the men looked the same in their dark colored suits or tuxedos and some more elegant than others.

Samantha sauntered around the hall with a champagne glass in her hand. She saw some old men huddled in a corner talking to a couple of older women. She immediately disregarded those. They would be the drooling type. She ignored the young studs. They would be too narcissistic (she knew this by experience). She needed a man between 35 and 45, just the right age for her. She was only 30; she had not yet consumed her childbearing years.

She kept walking slowly. Looking above the rim of her glass, straining her dark, heavily mascaraed eyes, she saw him. A tall, attractive man hanging at the bar with a rather flashy woman. At first, she did not think they were together. But then she saw the movement of her hand on his arm, trying to capture his attention. By the look on his chiseled face, lit by a single candle on the bar, he looked bored and not very interested in what she was saying. The man in question was broad shouldered, had dark brown hair with a streak of gray and a facial stubble, also sprinkled with gray. He was not beautiful, but he was handsome and exuded strength.

Samantha's eyes lit up. *This is the one,* she told herself. She was definitely attracted to him. She was determined to snatch him away from that woman, whether she was a mere acquaintance or his lover. Samantha did not give a hoot. Her self-assuredness propelled her to make a beeline towards the bar where they were standing. She made herself trip right in front of him and fell on the floor at his feet. Her glass slipped from her hand and shattered.

"Damn!" she cried out.

The man turned. He immediately came to her rescue.

Good. First contact.

"Here, let me help you," he said softly. His deep baritone sent shivers up her spine.

She looked up at him with her sultry signature look and thanked him. Their eyes locked.

The woman was staring at them and did not seem to like what she saw — her partner trying to help an attractive woman off the floor.

"I hope you haven't hurt yourself," he said, looking concerned.

"No, I think I'm fine."

"Let's get you on a chair somewhere and I'll take a look at that ankle."

She feigned pain and helplessness.

"You're so very kind," she said in a soft, sultry voice.

He helped her up, made her sit down on a chair against the wall, and knelt down in front her. The woman who had not moved from her place at the bar was still staring — and not in sympathy.

Samantha rubbed her ankle and grimaced in pain — all phony acting.

"Let me look at that ankle," he said.

She looked down at him with a surprised look on her face.

"I'm a doctor, an orthopedic one," he said reassuringly.

Samantha tensed. *Oh, oh, I hope my game is not up. If he finds out that there is nothing wrong with my ankle, I will be extremely embarrassed.*

She looked gingerly at her ankle and saw that it was, in fact, swollen. Uttering a sigh of relief, she thought how lucky for her to have stumbled (literally) in front of the right person.

"I'm taking you to Urgent Care for an X-ray," he said.

She liked men who took charge without hesitation.

He turned to the woman at the bar. "Sorry, I can't continue our conversation."

She glared at them both, her mouth agape. Samantha noticed that she had some lipstick on her upper teeth. *So unappealing,* Samantha thought, running her tongue along her own perfect teeth to be sure that she didn't.

Meanwhile, the doctor, held Samantha close, making her lean against him. Her "chevalier servant" escorted her out of the party to his waiting midnight blue BMW.

Samantha allowed herself a little cat-like purr at the feel of his strong arms encircling her. She liked everything about him—his voice, his stubble, and his faint after shave. *So manly.*

Samantha settled back into the plush leather seat and felt instantly at home. She had been lost—but now, she was found. The seductress had been seduced.

This was THE ONE. His name was Dominic.

The Heat of the Moment

Ty Piz

Biting my lower lip as I bounce through mounds of dirt and sand, the bitter metallic taste makes me nearly throwup. I'm forced off the track. I recover balance, quickly spin her around, and get back onto the racing surface, to begin my hunt for the demon racer that ran me off the track.

Steam rises; psyche is stirred. My mind boils with aggression, overtakes me, spurring me on. The strong wind shakes me side to side. I lower my head behind the windscreen of this thoroughbred Yamaha race bike and shift her to a higher gear, pursuing more speed. Only three corners and the front straight remain before the finish line. The adrenaline pump is wide open causing my right foot to shake feverishly upon the peg. Now, with teeth grinding, the fierce "Tiger" inside me enters attack mode. Going hot into the braking zone, tires chirp from the pressure exerted upon them. I regain forty feet of the critical real estate lost.

Leaning my body to the inside of this slim rocket ship, right knee-puck skims along the steaming asphalt, I aim toward the apex of this fast sweeping left-hand turn. Only two corners remain. With engine screaming at red line, my heart pounds as I charge after the same demon racer that nearly crashed me into a heap of flesh and twisted metal.

I close in tight, keeping watch as my archrival's wrist rolls off the throttle. It's a battle to the checkers! My rival relaxes his fierceness for a millisecond. That opens the door for me. I accelerate deeper into the corner and move into his draft. His technique is solid, yet he does run a few inches off the ideal racing line, and that single flaw leaves a small gap. I make my move. I overtake him. He immediately swerves his bright yellow motorcycle over and slams the door in my face.

I shout, "You punk!"

With the final corner merely eighty feet away, he holds the good inside line. There's no option for me to get around.

Oh crap, what now?

My front wheel is within centimeters of his extended knee. We both exit the corner strong, our front wheels loft skyward from the power exerted to the rear tire. I pull out of his draft. It's a drag race to the finish line. As the RPMs climb, we match shift for shift. My bike is pulling stronger and I inch closer to the lead. Side by side we reach a hundred-and-thirty-five miles per hour. We're closing in on the race official who's stepped to the center of the track with the checkered flag in hand.

Exhaling, I push my head down behind the windscreen to be more aerodynamic. We cross the thick white strip and I sense a brief flash of light as we break through the infra-red beam that reflects off the timing transponders mounted on our machines. In that instant, with the large crowd of spectators cheering us on, bright colored flags waving in the breeze, and steam radiating off the tarmac, I fly on past — my vison blurred by the official directly in front of me jumping in the air as he waves the black-and-white checkerboard flag.

My heart sinks. I'm half a wheel short of reaching my goal. This maniac beat me. My head drops and tears stream down. It's over. Second place today.

I've lost the race!

~

My mind races backward, scrutinizing every clip — like a video of the moves I should have made, and those I shouldn't have. I recall the twenty-eight minutes of aggressive back-and-forth riding between four racers, as we exchanged the lead, several times, every lap.

I see the awesome dual of Lap 17 — while I was in first place, railing along the back straight at top speed, when two riders draft passed.

Suddenly, I found myself in third place. With engine's revving to redline, we darted into the ultrafast sweeper, still nervous from the elbow-to-elbow exchange of position, I hesitated slightly, and, just as quickly, another rider drove on by. Icy shivers shot through my trembling hands, I sat up and held her steady. I was faced with another opportunity to duplicate this trail-braking skill. I applied maximum braking and zipped through the quick right-hand turn that descends over this blind curve.

My body felt what I had read about in the master riding manual: "Under extreme braking situations the rider's wrists are exposed to Three-Gs of negative force." That amount of pressure, once, makes a significant impact upon the body, let alone out on

296

the racecourse where this concentration to push the limits of the tires and personal strength happens in nearly every one of the fifteen corners, for seventeen laps around the demanding Mid-Ohio Road Course.

After the momentary hesitation, I scrambled to recover my race pace. My charge for victory resumed as the intensity of this very close battle between professional athletes raged on, and we diced hard for each position.

I chose the section of the circuit with the most dramatic change of elevation, the hills of the "Roller Coaster," to make my move. This section of track unsettles the chassis of the machine and the nerves of the racer. Riding a lap at speed here is a thing of beauty, like a symphony of relaxing melodies.

Yet, racing an AHRMA National event with forty other champion caliber riders in full-on race mode, is nothing short of a dog fight. The dream of experiencing the pleasure of standing on the top step of the victory podium ended. There was not enough time to catch the demon racer today.

~

Head down, dejected, I down shift to forth gear, then to third, as we make the fast corner under the bridge for turn one.

Corner workers and spectators scream and shower us with waves of joy and optimism.

Turns two, three, and four pass by, as we rail up the mountainside. More shouts of "Good job" and cheers of "Yahoo" can be heard. Speeds mellow as we descend the far side of the course and cruise along the back straight-a-way.

Now, as I ride beside my rival, we wave to spectators and salute corner workers to show respect. Our eyes meet, and the rage I have inside my heart for this racer returns. We approach turn nine, and the bright red uniforms of the safety crews grab my attention — their smiles and waves bring a beam of serenity to my heart. Anger mellows and shifts to acceptance, then to appreciation, which allows me to remember why I am here to begin with. *They love us and I love them!* Awe and tranquility overshadow the fierceness of the battle. Heads turn and our eyes meet. We ride in close. Give high fives to one another. We part and continue the cool down lap.

Amid trials, temptation, and thrills, I discover the meaning of this last lap as we journey around one of my all-time favorite tracks. So, we don't go back to the paddock with anger spewing and get into a battle with one another. Sure, it's important to allow the engine and tires a chance to cool down. But really, it's a period for the riders to chill and appreciate what we just accomplished, and all the amazing people in our corner, and all the hard work it took to get here. As the shadows from the pedestrian crossover bridge fall on the Mid-Ohio racetrack, I begin to load the trailer for the 32-hour drive to Colorado — our impassioned gamble for the ultimate goal remains a dream.

~

There is a constant struggle inside the heart of the athlete to reach this level of competition — seeking time in the gym to be fit and finding space in the tight schedule for precious moments with family and friends. No one who arrives at an AMA National event for the first time can expect to compete at the front of the pack. Maybe the second or third year, as they learn the twists and bends of the unique track design as well as the proper gearing and suspension setups, maybe, they'll have a chance. I realize, even though it's my first time here, reaching the top step of the podium is still my dream.

To be competitive, the rider needs a team of mechanics, a host of sponsors, and the input from a bank of computers to navigate this treacherous circuit quick enough to win. It takes all of this — and so much more. A rider must have the presence of mind to remain focused in the moment, confidence in himself and his machine, an understanding of the precise line of the track to carry the most speed, and the nerves to contend with the pressure of competition to reach the final goal.

When I was a teenager, I was dedicated to my sports. I embraced the 1970s film, *Tribes*, also known as *The Soldier that Declares Peace*. Those scenes now flash through my brain. I recall a scary scene where the platoon of Marines stood in the hot sun. Every man held two buckets filled with sand, their arms extended parallel to the ground — bodies shaking, hearts pounding — as the Drill Instructor screams, "Hold em' up soldier." It was hard for me to comprehend how someone, on the same military team, could torture his own men like that. Then, my thinking shifted. I pictured it as a wicked form of discipline — to build stamina in a young athlete.

I was reminded of my own training.

Of course, I had tough coaches from youth football league who pushed us beyond fatigue; the highly structured basketball teams that pressed our values; the sweaty wrestling practices and hours in the sauna to lose weight for the match on that Friday; the encounters with big waves while water skiing; and, skiing the huge moguls in the snow — all challenging our need for the essentials, like food and water. Rock climbing also taught insight into the finesse required to remain calm under pressure while putting it all on the line.

Even with all this rigor to become a fighting machine, I was determined to stay focused on the part of the motorcycle sport I loved, and to keep it fun.

Motorcycles came into my life at seven, and by thirteen years old, I began racing moto cross. The next step up the ladder of extreme speed was flat-track racing with their quick transitions from side to side — learning the art of pitching the thing sideways to scrub off speed on the fast dirt tracks. Riding street bikes soon took shape with a group of high school buddies carving turns through the canyons of the Rocky Mountains. As I progressed through a couple of speedway races, I learned how skilled a rider must be to shift their weight forward to back and side to side to maintain ultimate traction while not upsetting the balance of this single purpose motorcycle.

I even had the opportunity to participate in a few contests of low speed techniques at trials events, where — during these actions of balance over all sorts of obstacles — I learned how to gain a feel for the friction zone of the clutch and how important it is to use just a tiny bit of front brake to change the steering of the bike.

Still, the greatest race challenge of them all, for a young man, is this hunt for a connection in life. Just as racing maneuvers require skill, the answers from this hunt arrive in many forms. For me, I've been fortunate to ride a variety of motorcycles throughout my career. Mainly, I'm blessed to still be alive and healthy enough to be on another ride with my great group of friends.

Last Sunday I had one of the most memorable rides of all, a play day in the Rocky Mountain National Forest with two good buddies. This was not the powerful force of a race weekend. No. Rather it was a good pace in a relaxed atmosphere en route to the crest of the continental divide at 11,500 feet. The air was brisk, a light sheet of fresh snow covered the ground and there was plenty of fall colors to stimulate the imagination.

Do not underestimate the need for complete concentration as we rode through the wilderness on the sides of mountains with sixty-foot drop-offs over sharp cliffs on one side and the steep incline with evergreen trees on the other. Bouncing our dirt bikes around and over massive boulders, we finally reached the threatening descent of The Devil's Staircase to the icy river below. With front wheels lofted upward, we crossed the river to the other side only to discover a slippery bank of clay, with a challenging field of jagged rocks and more tree roots in our path. Roosting a cloud of dirt from our rear tires, we traversed onto fire roads at a quick pace. Suddenly, we faced other groups of riders approaching from the opposite direction. To avoid a bad situation required quick reflexes from all riders sharing this trail.

Colorful Colorado. There's nothing like the feel of riding a motorized two-wheeler on this planet — it was another epic ride for sure!

So, really, it's not about being super aggressive and jumping with all my might to twist the throttle wide open really fast that counts — it's finessing the technique that works best to slowly dial up the throttle. It's like gently rolling on the rheostat to brighten up the room or diming the lights for a romantic dinner. It's regulating the situation — that's what counts, just as it does in the day-to-day world.

There's a time for racing — to experience that exhilaration of being in the heat of the moment, side-by-side with the unknown element of danger. As racers, we push ourselves, the machines, and each other beyond the usual limits of riding solo. There is also a time for the casual pace of a trail ride with the gentleness of nature all around and an opportunity for refreshing body and soul—with a cool dip into the quiet solitude beneath the water's surface of the Blue River near Yampa, Colorado.

For each of us, it's finding that sweet harmony between these two extremely different worlds that's the real challenge — living in the heat of the moment and finding that sweet spot that restores serenity to the soul.

The Wizard of OZ
A Learning Curve for Life

Laurie Asher

I once read that L. Frank Baum got the idea for the name of his classic book by looking at a nearby file cabinet. There was **A-N** and an **O-Z**. Whether it's true doesn't really matter to me. We all take a bit of poetic license, and that's what writers are supposed to do—find the unique meaning in their stories. And here's mine.

The movie version starts out in stark black and white with a big tornado heading toward Any Town, USA. Already I'm starting to get the connection here. Bad things happen to good people. The difference, I guess, is how we handle the crisis. I'm still a young girl at the time, confess to being inquisitive, but not terribly knowledgeable about anything—except maybe how to grow delicious cherry tomatoes.

I'd like to step over to another sound stage for just a second to illustrate: In *Gone with the Wind*, Melanie is ready to give birth, and Prissy is supposed to help deliver her baby. But when the time comes, she panics and screams, "I don't know nuthin 'bout birthin' babies, Miss Scarlett." I learned early—Don't be Prissy. Be prepared for anything. **Life Lesson #1: Constitution.**

But back to the tornado. It would seem ridiculous to shoot at a big tornado heading your way. And running away from it will only result in a nice view looking down at it from the heavens. Finding shelter if you can, is always the best option. **Life Lesson #2: Think carefully first, then act.**

Dorothy, the focus of the movie, is separated from her beloved canine friend, Toto, and several human friends and family members. She has a serious accident, blacks out, starts hallucinating, and is taken to a very scary place. Looking back, this scene felt suspiciously like my teenage years. But was this the kind of life I wanted? **Life Lesson #3: Choices.**

In a parallel universe, Dorothy is wandering through the countryside and comes across a genial, but dunderheaded scarecrow who wants a brain. She wonders how she can help him. She's alone and wouldn't mind a companion, or, for that matter, acquiring a few new brain cells herself, so off they go.

Next, we meet the Cowardly Lion. And, at this point, I think *Does he represent all of my fears, weaknesses and faults? Am I really that terrified of life?* But he's an important part of this journey. Yup, he's irritating, but I better take him along. **Life Lesson #4: Courage.**

And finally, we spot the Tin Man. He's just as rigid as he can be. He needs to be oiled to soften him up, and he has no heart! Sometimes I felt just the same. It's hard enough taking care of *myself* at fourteen, and now I'm supposed to make time to love and help all these other strangers, too? Please! Since being self-centered was not a quality I wanted to be known for, I dragged him along as well. **Life Lesson #5: Compassion.**

Just being alive has its inherent risks, and sometimes I was a bit cloudy on what good judgement was—and here's where my mind went: *Are we the Four Horsemen of the Apocalypse, or the Three Musketeers, plus D'Artagnan? Was I ready to find out?*

My great, great, great uncle and Vaudevillian star, Harry Lauder, wrote this in his autobiography: "The optimist looks at the donut and the pessimist looks at the hole." So, who doesn't want the donut?

They all move on. But first, a message appears in the sky—written plain as day: **"SURRENDER DOROTHY!"**

She's still wondering what this means. Glynda, the Good Witch, had appeared earlier and suggested a path that Dorothy should follow, along with her newfound friends. This meandering path does feel rather safe for now, and she instinctively trusts Glynda. But there's lots to absorb while skipping along those yellow bricks. And she'll need some time to sort things out, as they are on their way to the Emerald City to meet the all-powerful "Wizard of Oz."

I'm right there—gamboling along with Dorothy in my mind's eye. Maybe, for now, I can't answer all the questions posed either, and I will just need to continue down this Yellow Brick Road and trust a Higher Power. But, like that road, real life has lots of meandering twists and turns. Some wonderful, some scary as hell. But at least I'm willing to give it a try, and I'm currently wearing sensible shoes.

Dorothy is pensive and considers the messages. But soon enough, she's taken hostage by Glynda's evil sister—reliving that dark, dangerous place in her mind—and she realizes that if something doesn't change soon, deep in her soul, that hourglass she calls her life is going to run out of sand fairly soon. She gets a glimpse of her old life in a crystal ball, and in good time, she is able to escape with the help of The Lion, The Tin Man, and the Scarecrow — her three pillars — her true friends.

And off they go, searching for the "answers." She and her alter egos take a few unfortunate detours along the way, just like we all do! They run into some pretty weird and unsavory characters, as well. There's flying monkeys and little folks with cute, harmonic voices, violent talking fruit trees and people flying through the air — not unlike my old drinkin' buddies. And, there are all those temptations along the way. Oh, that Poppy Field!

But in a newfound sense of serenity and purpose, something's starting to feel better about this journey. It's calming. And now everything is in color. Greens are greener. Reds seem brighter, like rubies. Blues are brilliant sapphires and Yellow is definitely shinier. The dreary black and white surroundings have been vanquished. Everything now is so vivid! It's almost impossible not to smile out loud.

The old Wizard is very helpful in many ways — like a good friend who is willing to tell you the truth and help you discover things you never recognized about yourself. I read a quote somewhere that "a good friend stabs you in the front, and an enemy stabs you in the back." It may sound a bit cruel, but it's apt, and she does lose some of her initial fear. She begins to trust. But when Dorothy first meets the Wizard, he doesn't initially see a rational solution for her as he seems to have found for the others.

She *believes* she's coming into being, that her heart and mind are starting to work together in tandem. But Dorothy is still frightened and confused. Instinctively, she knows there aren't really purple horses — green and yellow with polka dots, maybe. She's willing to accept them, for now, and to pay close attention to her surroundings.

Does she have what it takes deep within her? When her new, beautiful mentor, Glynda, comes back and points out that she's had it inside her all along! She just needed to "click her heels together" — perhaps a metaphor for getting her "*stuff*" together?
Life Lesson #6: Believe.

And at the end of the movie, just like a country-western record that's played backwards, she gets her dog back, gets her friends and family back, and that wicked old Elvira Gulch is gone. Dorothy gets a new, refreshing look at life, her heart and soul stronger, with the ability to love honestly, and all emotions back intact — plus plenty of room for expansion.

Dorothy probably won't forget these experiences, and she'll be telling this story more than once — to those seeking their own Yellow Brick Road. People just need to believe in her.

It's a simple message, really, but not an easy-breezy one.

~

"Life is not easy for any of us. But what of that? We must have perseverance and above all confidence in ourselves. We must believe that we are gifted for something, and that this thing, at whatever cost, must be attained." Marie Curie

Life Lesson #7: I'll leave that up to you. Blessings from a survivor.

Still Looking

Invisible Coyotes

Erik C. Martin

His co-workers tried to discourage him from walking.

"It's too cold," one said.

Jerry chuckled. It was almost sixty degrees.

"It's raining," protested another.

But the rain had stopped. The only moisture falling now was that which was dripping from the tree branches.

"It's dark," his boss said. "We walk around the parking lot at night. Management thinks it's dangerous. Renee saw a coyote last month."

Jerry laughed outright.

"I can take care of myself. I'm not scared of coyotes. Animals avoid people."

Jerry walked during all of his breaks. Just because he was working a night shift for once was no reason to forgo exercise. His route was a half mile out, turn, and then a half mile back; a straight but hilly shot past the neighboring businesses.

Jerry took a deep breath. He smelled fall. The rain had stirred up the odor of decaying leaves, eliciting scents rare in Southern California. Jerry never missed Ohio winters, but he missed fall. He walked next to the dark street, down the hill, away from work. He closed his eyes and pretended that he was back in Cleveland where fall was a firm statement, not a mere hint.

He was making good time. The cool weather helped. He loved how desolate and quiet the street was at night. His head on a swivel, Jerry drank it all in — the faint mist rising off of the ground, the lights of the distant freeway, his shadows projected on the front of a white-faced building, trees swaying in the push and pull of the evening breeze. If he was lucky, he'd see some of those animals his coworkers were so afraid of.

He plodded ahead.

Something nagged at him.

Shadows?

He had two shadows.

A lone light from the Otis Elevator Company across the street was the only illumination. Clouds blocked the starlight. The moon was new. One light source meant one shadow.

He looked at a tree ahead. One shadow.

Jerry glanced right. Two shadows.

Weird. I must be missing a light.

Jerry walked on. For a moment, he thought he heard footsteps behind him. He stopped and turned.

Nothing was there.

Of course not; I'm alone.

He glanced at the nearest building. Two shadows.

One started at his feet. The second shadow was about a yard behind and didn't quite meet his feet. Jerry raised one arm. Both shadows raised an arm.

Was the second one slower? No, that was crazy.

Jerry's heart pounded. He walked faster.

Again, he heard footsteps out of sync with his own. *An echo?*

He glanced at the shadows. The rear shadow was still there, following at the same distance. Was the second a little taller and thicker than the first?

He heard a low chuckle. He began to speed walk.

Get a grip. You're imagining things.

The lamp post that marked his turn around spot loomed closer. Jerry's breathing came heavy. From behind was a faint but unmistakable scrape, like a sick dog's dry pad on the sidewalk.

The darkness was thick here. To his right was a canyon wall overgrown with sharp, scrub foliage. Across the road to his left were empty businesses.

He had to make a choice. Would he turn and start back when he reached the turn around? Or?

His eyes said nothing was behind him. His brain said he was being stupid. His pride made him think of the people who had told him to stay in the parking lot. But his gut said to keep going, to run. Maybe a cleaning crew was working late in one of the buildings across the street.

He reached the lamp post.

Jerry stopped.

He turned around.

The light was coming from almost directly above; the shadows were minimal. But there were definitely two, his and the other, three or four feet away. Both were completely still.

A sickening odor of mildew hit him like a punch.

He heard the deep chuckle again, more like a growl.

His knees felt like soup, but he took a step forward as rationalization and ingrained behavior overrode the survival instinct.

Nothing is there. Nothing is there. Nothing is there.

The second shadow didn't move.

Jerry stopped right before it. He heard raspy, amused breathing. He smelled mildew and carrion. What was it? What was it waiting for?

Jerry barely registered a light growing brighter down the road. He choked on a fetid wave of hot breath. Something cold and rubbery touched his hand and the back of his head gently, as if to embrace him.

And then it showed itself, perhaps as consolation to prey that had played the game and lost. Jerry looked up into big nocturnal eyes and a grinning mouth that was wide and full of saws.

"No!" he screamed.

Energized by fear, Jerry pushed against it. The teeth cut his face and sought his neck. The thing was too strong.

The headlamps of a car cast the growing light. The beams shined in the monster's pale, saucer eyes. The creature winced and Jerry was suddenly free. He stumbled into the road as the car arrived. The driver stomped the brake pedal. Tires squealed on the wet pavement and the car began to slide. Jerry felt the impact as the car hit him. Then there was only blackness.

He was in and out of consciousness when the ambulance came and took him to the hospital. Jerry's legs were broken, among other things. But he was alive.

The distraught driver told the responding police officer that she had seen something attacking Jerry just before he'd run into the road.

"It was big and white, like a hairless polar bear."

"We don't see many polar bears in San Diego, hairless or otherwise," the officer deadpanned. "Maybe you saw a coyote."

Later, loathe to report what had actually happened, Jerry confirmed that he had indeed been attacked by a coyote. This led to a dozen of the wild canines being shot and tested for rabies.

Jerry spent over a week in the hospital. Many of his co-workers came to see him. Everyone was sympathetic. No one gloated or said, "I told you so."

When he went home, his insurance paid for a physical therapist to come by daily, and for an aide to help with meals and such.

On the third day, he heard the door open. He had left it unlocked because it was hard for him to get up, but they had knocked before. He glanced at the clock. They were twenty minutes early.

"Hello?" he called.

Jerry heard scraping footsteps in the hall. He smelled mildew and death.

City Planner

Elizabeth Duris

In our backyard
the emerging spring
powers its way
through gopher mounded grass

It's a subway down there,
with multiple metro stops
that expand and extend the grid
each season.

These diligent rodent miners
continue to outwit
the best anti-gopher warfare
man can offer.

"Plug the holes."
"Suffocate them!"
A resounding *HA!*
is heard down under.

They *welcome* the newest *sonic plug in*

They *cool themselves* with the *whirring wind tunnel*

They *evade* the sure-thing *buried trap*

They *side step* the ever ready *power hose*

All failures.

Complete failures,

against the subterranean metropolis

of the energetic city planner below.

Kamikaze Bees

Amy Wall

I have arthritis in my left toe joint. The big one. The one you need for balance, and I *need* balance. Not just the hippy Southern California kind of balance, like in my life, but the kind of balance that you need to do adult gymnastics. In my infinite wisdom, I've traded the injuries that come with a running career for a sport with far fewer injuries — gymnastics. I need my big toe to work properly and I need it to work quickly so I can get my standing back tuck without a spot.

Here's the problem: I found out it might be scientific that bee stings can help arthritis.

I'm a sucker for this kind of thing.

I'd swung from putting my trust into doctors to putting my trust in homeopathic medicine. That was then. Now I've hit a happy medium where I go to the doctor once a year and, if they insist I need antibiotics, I take the script. But I don't fill it (unless one day I discover I've contracted a flesh-eating bacteria — and even then, a good portion of flesh will have to be gone first).

As far as homeopathy is concerned, I'd taken their magic potions, flower petals, and smelly scents, and they didn't work. So there you have it. I've decided I need some science behind what I put in my body.

Consequently, finding out there is a scientific study that shows bee stings have given relief to arthritic joints is *so* my thing. Thank you very much Dr. Suzana Beatriz Verissimo de Mello. Thank you and curse you. Why couldn't you have discovered rubbing daisies was the cure? It is so much more aesthetic and far less painful.

~

313

Arthritis is no fun and, sometimes I feel like I'd do anything to make it go away. Careful what you wish for because now I'm thinking I might want to let myself get stung by a bee. On purpose.

The day I read the study, something crazy happened. My friend randomly told me that her uncle finds bees at her mom's house for his arthritis. She was using it to outline how crazy he was, but that was beside the point. The point was, it was a sign. I know *that* isn't science, but just give it to me.

I knew I had to do it, but I also know how much I hated needles and anything sharp. I especially hate bee stings. I mean, I don't expect to be judged here, I'm pretty sure most of us don't like bee stings. I was going to have to convince myself it was worth the trauma to have arthritic relief.

Casually mentioning it to my family at the dinner table resulted in a room full of eye rolls and comments like, "Here we go again." No respect.

Clearly, I was going to have to figure this out on my own. The first step was to solve the major conflict that arose in my head—my hippy Southern California tendencies also mean that I love and embrace all living things. This is in direct conflict with a bee sting because the poor little insect dies. Aren't we lucky that if we express our discontent with something we don't automatically die? It's a bee design flaw really.

The science on *this* hasn't been published, but I'm assuming old dried up venom isn't going to work. So I made the logical assumption that I need a bee that just died and has a belly full of fresh venom to inject into my toe. Additionally, the bee can't have died from a bee sting because the fresh venom I need would have been wasted on an innocent victim. A non-arthritic victim most likely.

What I needed was a bee that dropped out of the sky in some kind of kamikaze death move. It would tick off all the required boxes—just died so I wasn't senselessly killing, and still had fresh bee juice.

Because my kids would never give up the opportunity

to go on a hunt for dead bees, I sent them to find a kamikaze bee.

What they came back with was possibly a flying insect. It was hard to tell given it had been smashed by a wheel of the trash bin being dragged back to the house, so it wasn't completely intact. I do have some standards. All I could picture was trading arthritis for a flesh-eating bacteria.

At that point, my criteria list got longer. I not only needed a bee, but I needed one that lived a clean life *and* had a clean death.

Deep down inside, I was secretly relieved that the kids didn't find the right bee because I knew it would mean that they would sit there and watch me try to push the stinger into my joint. I would have to act like I knew what I was doing, which I didn't. It also meant I couldn't scream and cry like a school girl if it hurt.

The day that I found the right bee *did* finally come though. Thankfully the kids were out of sight. I found a dead bee on our footpath on the side of our house, just after walking past that same spot, so I knew it was fresh. It was fully intact and looked as though it should have been wearing a kamikaze bandana, the one with the red sun and thick rays stretching across the front. Perfect.

This is where a doubled-edged sword takes on a whole new meaning. The search was over, which meant I had to consider what came next—shoving a dead bee stinger into my toe, then having to squeeze it somehow to get the toxins far enough into my joint to actually do something.

I pulled out a container of alcohol, poured it onto a cotton ball and wiped my toe, emulating a nurse about to administer a shot. I even considered wiping the bee's butt with it, but I wasn't sure if that might compromise the stinger.

In a quiet spot in the living room, I sat down, feet in front of me, and carefully placed the bee on my toe. I let it sit there for a while so I could try to figure out how to sting myself. Do I grab it and quickly shove it in? Do I balance it on its back end and slowly push down?

It was at this time I started to get nervous. When I'd been stung by a bee in the past, it came as a surprise. I didn't have a chance to think about it or psyche myself up, or in this case, psyche myself out. I never thought I would appreciate the shock of a bee sting, but I kind of needed it at this point.

I sat there for probably three or four minutes and was snapped back to the circumstance by the sound of my husband's footsteps up the stairs.

Thankfully he went into the bedroom and didn't stand over me while I was attempting my bee stabbing. However, he was within earshot. Why hadn't I done it sooner?

"I don't know if this thing even still has its stinger," I blurted louder than I needed to, verbally positioning myself for potential failure that obviously had *nothing* to do with me chickening out.

I slowly and gently pushed on the bee, but strangely I didn't feel any pain or anything that indicated it was going in.

"Yep, I'm nearly positive the stinger is gone."

I pushed slightly harder, but probably not with the force a live bee would have to exert to break the first layer of skin. Again, I felt nothing.

"No stinger," I concluded, announcing it to whoever would listen.

"This one is clearly no good," I said as I threw the dead bee in the trash.

~

I've decided that I might need a live bee to do the job for me because I have no experience in stinging. I'm still trying to figure out how to get the live bee to sting in the exact spot I need it to and nowhere else — definitely nowhere else. Of course, I am still conflicted about killing a living being for my own benefit.

How about this: I look for a dying bee, but not one dying from a disease that can be passed on from bee venom. I still need one that isn't dying from having stung someone else. It needs to be healthy looking — besides the fact that it is dying, of course. Maybe one with a broken wing that would otherwise be left to a bird? I could give it one last chance to do something very bee-like. It would be like a mercy stinging.

It's been a few months now, and I haven't found a bee that fits my criteria. But I'm still looking. I'm gonna do it, people. I'm GONNA DO IT.

Collision

Jenna Benson

Alone, I gather the flowers strewn on the side of the highway.
I scramble to save every petal.

What I can't carry I'll replace along the way.

It may have been a bad crash,
the worst you've ever seen,
but you survived.
We survived.

We must endure.
Even when taking a breath seems absurd.
When you smell the gas leaking you have to run away.
We have to save ourselves.

Starting over is not the end,
although it may seem that way now.
Push the pedal, flatten it to the ground;
after a few miles you will realize your folly in wanting to stay.

Nothing will ever be the same.
Only while driving away,
glancing in the rearview mirror,
can your restless heart realize that,

perhaps,

this is the best part of all.

The French Episode

Gary Winters

I was taken to a castle (well, it had a turret) in France by a woman I met during the running of the bulls at Pamplona in Navarre province, northern Spain. We drove across the French border at night with no border check. She wanted me to come to Brittany where she lived on land reclaimed from the ocean by her grandfather who had built walls in the sea. But I did not speak the language and decided to fly back to the Costa del Sol in Spain.

Getting out of the country was a whole different story. I was detained at the airport and ushered into an office where four customs officials gazed at me with stern looks. It seems I was in the country illegally. A crime.

I told them I had entered France with a bunch of drunken bull runners and didn't know I was in France. I whipped out my red bandanna and slipped it over my head. Proof! I was allowed to make my flight, but not before receiving a lecture on how I needed to obtain a proper visa to enter France. The customs man actually shook his finger at me.

Gin & Tonic, Please —
Hold the Stirrups

Christine L. Cunningham

Most women see their gynecologists once a year. I have the awkward pleasure of seeing mine all the time — at parties, in restaurants, on the church pew directly across from me, or on a golf course with my husband. Looking back at my gynecological experiences over the years I wonder: *Is there a conspiracy to expose me? Force me to open up so to speak?*

I was eighteen when I had my first OBGYN appointment. Dr. Kharti was from India. Or maybe he was Chaldean. All I remember is that I was a little embarrassed by such an intimate appointment with a total stranger. After ten minutes, he officially knew me better than anyone, including myself.

A few weeks after my appointment, I attended the wedding of the sister of my friend, George. I had known George and his sister since middle school. Her fiancé was George's best friend. Their union was a Chaldean mob dream come true, celebrated by hundreds of guests with a full orchestra, premium bar, filet mignon, and flaming baked Alaska.

Just before the wedding, George's uncle took me into his study of crimson leather chairs and tobacco-tainted tapestries to proclaim through pulls on his Cuban that he wanted me to marry George. The head of the family looked directly into my eyes, exhaled a contrail of spiciness, and in his raspy Brando voice stated, "I want you's two to be married."

Was I being ordered to marry George? Could he even do that? I wasn't sure of the rules.

"Uncle Eddie," I whispered leaning forward, a little embarrassed. "I'm only eighteen. I'm not looking to marry anybody right now."

"Well, you let me know when you're ready, sweetheart. Georgie's a good man. Remember that," he challenged, gesturing with his cigar.

"There you are!" George said, relieved to have found me. Not nearly relieved as I. "What are you guys doing in here?" He glanced toward his uncle then back at me. "What's going on?" He smiled.

"Oh, nothing much. Uncle Eddie was just proposing to me for you."

"Really? Well how about we get through this wedding first. Come on, I want you to meet some people."

George ushered me out of the room into the receiving line. And there he was. My gynecologist. Apparently, the extended family's gynecologist. Oh, my God, one OBGYN appointment and I'm prepped to marry the mafia.

"This is Doctor Kharti."

"Hello, doctor," I said shaking the hand that had been halfway up my body weeks earlier, wondering if he was still looking at me in that way. "Actually, George, Dr. Kharti is *my* doctor. He knows me better than you do."

Twenty-five years and four kids later, in a state three thousand miles away, I visited my current OBGYN who was called out for an emergency C-section just as I had checked in. His staff asked if I would mind having a nurse practitioner do the exam.

"Not at all," I responded, having taken the time to lose a couple pounds and up my grooming game specifically for the appointment. She was female, about my age, and very friendly.

"So, where are you from?" she asked, placing my feet in the stirrups.

"Well, I've lived in San Diego for a while, but am originally from Michigan."

"What part?" she asked, peeling apart the purple gloves while searching for the lubricant.

"I grew up in Birmingham but then we moved to Clarkston. I went to school in Ann Arbor."

"Really? So did my husband. What high school did you go to?"

"Seaholm." In goes the hand.

"Seaholm? My husband went to Seaholm. What year did you graduate?" Her hand reaching for my uterus.

"19-ugh-77." She must've found it.

"No kidding. My husband graduated in 1977."

"No shit," I said, feeling more uncomfortable than I thought possible, wondering if she was still looking in me. "What's his name?"

Not only did I know him, but he was also one of George's good friends. I was certain that my vapid vagina became the topic of some hypothetical conversation that evening. So much for doctor/patient privilege.

More recently, however, I attended a fundraiser where I was greeted by my 6'8" OBGYN, the one who was called out for an emergency C-section. I immediately felt naked. And not a good naked; an aging, spotted, sagging skin, estrogen-deficient kind of naked. After all, I had just seen him a few months earlier for my annual check-up. The appointment went something like this:

"How are you?" Big hug. "You look great. How are the kids? How's Jim?" He said, reaching for the stirrups hidden under the table while recalling a recent golf game with Jim.

"Everyone's doing great," I said leaning back, dutifully placing my heels in the stirrups, pleased with my recent pedicure, feeling the goose of cool air as my knees parted.

"So, I hear Jim is retiring from council," he said while gently sliding his eight-inch fingers into my private underpass, oblivious to my fabulous feet.

"Yeah, bittersweet for him, though," I replied, chewing on the inside of my cheek as his fingers seemed to search for a missing baby. *Or was that my esophagus?*

"Do you know you have a tilted uterus?" he said for the twenty-fifth time, once for every year I've seen him.

"Yes, it's to help balance my oversized breasts." I laughed, knowing he would soon be typing on my miniature breasts with his fingertips looking for mysterious tissue (or any tissue for that matter), wondering if he was still looking at the tilt of my uterus.

Without warning, he slipped—a thumb, was it? Into my, well, . . .you know. Was I expected to control the sudden assault on my sphincter? It was as if he pulled the pin on a grenade. Would I explode? Would a Brussel sprouts bomb launch anytime soon? *Please, God, not today.*

"Well, we'll miss seeing Jim on council. He has done so much for this city," he said, burrowing deeper. "My wife and I are actually good friends with one of the other councilmen. Our son used to date his daughter," he continued as if we were at a cocktail party.

Did he *not* know where his thumb was? Did he *not* fear for his life? Seek shelter against impending doom? Fortunately for us both, the exam ended without casualties. I still had my dignity along with my undigested Brussel sprouts.

I tucked our mostly one-way conversation away until we walked into a councilman's poolside fundraiser some months later.

"Hey, look, there's Kevin," Jim pointed out.

"Why would my gynecologist be here?" I asked, still looking, scanning the party.

"I don't know, but there he is."

Suddenly, every lounge chair sported stirrups, every dish of dip offered lubricant, the serving utensils resembled pap smear tools. I could feel my uterus tilting, my sphincter tightening, my breasts blushing, my mind racing with all the private things discussed. Our conversation about him knowing someone on council came flooding back.

"How's my favorite patient?" he smiled, arms extended.

"Thought you knew the answer to that," I joked.

"You remember my wife, don't you?"

I couldn't help wondering what would it feel like to be the wife of a man who looks at, up, and through vaginas fifty times a week for over twenty-five years, who palpates breasts much younger and more voluptuous than women our age. I quickly calculated, stopping at 65,000, reaching for her hand.

"Of course. Hi, Nancy. Great to see you again."

"You, too. I love what you're wearing."

Was she looking at my outfit or my lady parts, picturing her OBGYN husband reaching for my uterus? Was it her turn to feel awkward or mine? Still looking for a way to escape, I took a long sip of my gin & tonic, thinking that gin really should be spelled with a "y," intended for just such moments.

326

The Case for Short Words

Richard Lederer

When you speak and write, there is no law that says you have to use big words. Short words are as good as long ones, and short, old words — like *sun* and *grass* and *home* — are best of all. A lot of small words, more than you might think, can meet your needs with a strength, grace, and charm that large words do not have.

Big words can make the way dark for those who read what you write and hear what you say. Small words cast their clear light on big things — night and day, love and hate, war and peace, and life and death. Big words at times seem strange to the eye and the ear and the mind and the heart. Small words are the ones we seem to have known from the time we were born, like the hearth fire that warms the home.

Short words are bright like sparks that glow in the night, prompt like the dawn that greets the day, sharp like the blade of a knife, hot like salt tears that scald the cheek, quick like moths that flit from flame to flame, and terse like the dart and sting of a bee.

Here is a sound rule: Use small, old words where you can. If a long word says just what you want to say, do not fear to use it. But know that our tongue is rich in crisp, brisk, swift, short words. Make them the spine and the heart of what you speak and write. Short words are like fast friends. They will not let you down.

The title of this piece and the four paragraphs that you have just read are wrought entirely of words of one syllable. In setting myself this task, I did not feel especially cabined, cribbed or confined. In fact, the structure helped me to focus on the power of the message I was trying to put across.

One study shows that twenty words account for twenty-five percent of all spoken English words, and all twenty are monosyllabic. In order of frequency they are: *I, you, the, a, to, is, it, that, of, and, in, what, he, this, have, do, she, not, on,* and *they.* Other studies indicate that the fifty most common words in written English are each made of a single syllable.

For centuries our finest poets and orators have recognized and employed the power of small words to make the straightest line between two minds. A great many of our proverbs punch home their points with pithy monosyllables: "Where there's a will, there's a way." "A stitch in time saves nine." "Spare the rod and spoil the child." "A bird in the hand is worth two in the bush."

Nobody used the short word more skillfully than William Shakespeare, who's dying King Lear laments:

> And my poor fool is hang'd! No, no, no life!
> Why should a dog, a horse, a rat have life,
> And thou no breathe at all?...
> Do you see this? Look on her, Look! Her lips!
> Look there, look there!

Shakespeare's contemporaries made the King James Bible a centerpiece of short words: "And God said, Let there be light: and there was light. And God saw the light, that it was good." The descendants of such mighty lines live on. When asked to explain his policy to parliament, Winston Churchill responded with these ringing monosyllables: "I will say: it is to wage war, by sea, land, and air, with all our might and with all the strength that God can give us." In his "Death of the Hired Man," Robert Frost observes, "Home is the place where, when you have to go there, / They have to take you in." And William H. Johnson uses ten two-letter words to explain his secret of success: "If it is to be, / It is up to me."

You don't have to be a great author, statesman, or philosopher to tap the energy and eloquence of small words. When I was an English teacher, I asked my ninth-graders at St. Paul's School each year to write a composition composed entirely of one-syllable words. My students greeted my request with obligatory moans and groans, but, when they returned to class with their essays, most felt that, with the pressure to produce high-sounding polysyllables relieved, they had created some of their most powerful and luminous prose. Here are submissions from two of my ninth-graders:

> What can you say to a boy who has left home? You can say that he has done wrong, but he does not care. He has left home so that he will not have to deal with what you say. He wants to go as far as he can. He will do what he wants to do.
> This boy does not want to be forced to go to church, to comb his hair,

or to be on time. A good time for this boy does not lie in your reach, for what you have he does not want. He dreams of ripped jeans, shirts with no starch, and old socks.

So now this boy is on a bus to a place he dreams of, a place with no rules. This boy now walks a strange street, his long hair blown back by the wind. He wears no coat or tie, just jeans and an old shirt. He hates your world, and he has left it.

— Charles Shaffer

~

For a long time we cruised by the coast and at last came to a wide bay past the curve of a hill, at the end of which lay a small town. Our long boat ride at an end, we all stretched and stood up to watch as the boat nosed its way in.

The town climbed up the hill that rose from the shore, a space in front of it left bare for the port. Each house was a clean white with sky blue or gray trim; in front of each one was a small yard, edged by a white stone wall strewn with green vines.

As the town basked in the heat of noon, not a thing stirred in the streets or by the shore. The sun beat down on the sea, the land, and the back of our necks, so that, in spite of the breeze that made the vines sway, we all wished we could hide from the glare in a cool, white house. But, as there was no one to help dock the boat, we had to stand and wait.

At last the head of the crew leaped from the side and strode to a large house on the right. He shoved the door wide, poked his head through the gloom, and roared with a fierce voice. Five or six men came out, and soon the port was loud with the clank of chains and creak of planks as the men caught ropes thrown by the crew, pulled them taut, and tied them to posts. Then they set up a rough plank so we could cross from the deck to the shore. We all made for the large house while the crew watched, glad to be rid of us.

— Celia Wren

You too can tap into the vitality and vigor of compact expression. Take a suggestion from the highway department. At the boundaries of your speech and prose place a sign that reads "Caution: Small Words at Work."

Some Good People in the World

Wayne Raffesberger

It was flat, all right. He could stare at it all he wanted, and the tire was just as flat. There was no other choice, so he left the Little League field on foot, pushing the Huffy bike. The flat tire flapped rhythmically in time with his steps.

Bobby thought it had enough air when he left home. It looked bad, but he was so anxious to watch his school buddies play a game that day he risked it anyway.

"Darn it," he said aloud, "why didn't I fix this yesterday when it was already low?" He knew the answer, of course. He didn't know how to fix a flat tire. Dad fixed them for him many times, but Dad wasn't there. He was gone again. "On business," Bobby was told.

Pushing the bike meant he'd have a very long and slow walk home. Up the big hill he didn't like riding and hated walking. As he started out, his leg flapped a little like the flat tire. By the time he reached home, he would be dragging the leg behind him.

The disease left that leg shrunken and weak. Surgeries and therapy made walking possible, but not done well. It was the bike that freed him from the stares of strangers, the occasional taunts, and the shame of inadequacy. On the bike, he moved like any other kid, with freedom. He was normal.

And on the bike, he could escape them. The apartment buildings across the street from the field were the first problem. Mean, hard people lived there. Whenever he passed by, it seemed as though someone was yelling. Bobby wanted to be on the other side of the street, except there was no sidewalk. He moved past without incident and continued up always busy Lemon Avenue. That wasn't a good place for him, either. Too many cars whenever he had to walk it. Sometimes older boys in a car would slow down just to yell insults when they saw his awkward gait. Bobby always wondered why. He didn't even know them, yet they felt the need to scream an insult while driving by.

Today was a good day. There were no passing cars. He made it to the quieter cross street, which wasn't pleasant even without traffic. Too many dogs barking and charging him, and he didn't know anyone on those blocks. At the end of the street, though, was the reward of the Junior High School with its empty ballfields and frontage road usually blocked from traffic.

There he could continue the long march home alone. Unless they saw him. They might be there, waiting.

When he made it to the end, Bobby scanned the vacant fields anxiously, and felt the usual dread while trying to walk quickly. Quickly really wasn't an option, but he scuttled along as fast as possible. There was no sign of them yet. Maybe he could hustle just a little more and escape notice this time.

He approached the outdoor equipment area with growing optimism. This was going to work; another glance at the fields revealed nothing. Two more blocks and he would be safely back in his own neighborhood.

Suddenly, there they were, emerging between two buildings. It was a pack of boys, maybe five or six. They headed to the pull-up bars, yelling and joking. As each one took to the bars, taunts from the others rang out over who could do the most.

Bobby froze with fear, hoping they wouldn't notice him. Where was his big brother? Big brother could take on all of them, Bobby just knew it. But he was alone, and running was out of the question. Head down, he started to move, very slowly.

"Hey, is that the cripple? That Bobby kid?"

"Yeah, I think it is. Let's mess him up more than he already is."

Bobby was quickly surrounded by the pack. One grabbed at his Huffy, then thrust it back, disgusted. "It's got a flat tire, just like him." The others roared with laughter.

The biggest boy moved in and gave Bobby a shove. "Whatta ya doing here, anyway?"

"I'm, I'm t-trying just to, just to go home," was all he could choke out.

"So, what if we stop ya from going home? Whatta ya gonna do about it?" he said, shoving Bobby again.

Another boy reached in and knocked Bobby's ball cap from his head just as the first rock crashed down on the leg of the boy in the rear. That boy screamed in pain, clutched his leg, and fell to the ground. The group spun around in panic as another rock

332

thudded at their feet. One more granitic missile slammed into the biggest boy's thigh, who crumpled to the ground, crying.

Bobby looked up at the thrower, and right away recognized Corker. The bad older boy with the fabulous arm who had been kicked out of Little League a few years before.

"Leave him alone," Corker bellowed. They looked bewildered, some still whimpering. "Leave him alone," he yelled again, launching more rocks. When they hit at their feet, all the boys turned and ran down the frontage road. A last missile skittered on the pavement between their legs.

Bobby wanted to yell his thanks, but he couldn't breathe. He tried again to shout "Thank you," and no words came out, so he just waved and waved. Corker made a casual half wave back and disappeared behind a building.

His limp didn't slow him now as he almost skipped up the hill. He had a purpose, there was something to share. When he arrived home, his mother was working in the front yard.

"Hi, Bobby, how was the game? Bobby, are you ok? Your face looks flushed."

"I'm good, Mom. I'm really good."

"Well, you're excited. So, it was a good game, huh? Bobby, your tire's flat. How long has it been flat?"

"Since the ballpark."

"You walked all that way home? That must have been a tough walk. We'll get that tire fixed so you don't have to walk so much, ok?"

"No, no, it was pretty easy. I didn't have any big problems. But, Mom?"

She turned away. Bobby could tell she knew there had been another incident.

"Yes, Bobby?"

"Mom, you know, there are some — some good people in the world, right?"

"Yes. Yes, Bobby, there are."

You Got the Right

Rivkah Sleeth

Daisy walked over to check the huge table already set for dinner and glanced at the group standing in the corner. She began. "We declare these truths to be self-evident, that all men are created equal, that they are endowed by their Creator with certain unalienable Rights, that among these are Life, Liberty, and the pursuit of Happiness."

She picked up a dish, inspected it, laid it back down. Shaking her head and walking to the water basin, she said softly, "Don't nobody deserve to eat on a dirty plate." She squeezed the extra water out of the washing cloth and walked back to the table.

Each man and woman, eight in all, stood still as statues, unsure what to do. Their eyes darted from the uniformed man at the fireplace to the woman speaking.

As she picked up each plate, wiped the front and back, and replaced it on the table, Daisy continued. "Now what that first part means is — what it says. Don't nobody gotta figure out this truth part. It's a truth. Somethin' that even the simple ones can know." She stopped and smiled, watching the sunken faces staring back at her.

"That's what self-evident means. It esplains itself. So, I don't have to esplain to you why these truths are true. They just are."

She put the last clean plate back on the table. She turned toward the fire, throwing the washing cloth over her shoulder.

Even the men flinched at the sudden motion.

"George, these plates are good to put the food on now."

George, Chief of the local fire brigade, carried several platters of fried fish and grilled vegetables to the table. The aroma was almost a meal in itself. On his last trip to the table, he brought serving utensils for each platter.

Satisfied that everything was in place, Daisy said, "Sit down, now. Make yourself comfy. You is safe here." She could see they were half-starved, and she didn't want them to have to wait much longer.

335

Looking from one to the other, at the Chief, then Daisy, the skittish eight shifted their chairs away from the table. As each one claimed a seat, George filled the plate with steaming food. Within minutes, all were perched on their chairs, eyeing the feast before them.

Daisy took the corner of her apron and wiped the streams of sweat off her shiny dark forehead and her glistening upper lip. "Everybody got food on they plates?"

The eight heads at the table nodded.

"Good, good." She paused for a second. Looking up towards the ceiling, she closed her eyes and prayed. "Thank you, God, for all You've done for us. We trust You'll continue. That fish sure smells good." She peeked at those surrounding the table, smiled, and went on. "We know that You gives us life. And You count on us to do somethin' meaningful with that life you gives us. We'll do our honest best. Amen."

She waited. Opening her eyes, she lowered her gaze and looked at those seated at the table. "I said Amen. Do I hear an Amen?"

"Amen!" George's voice boomed into the quiet.

Eight heads jerked up—their wide-eyed faces focused on the huge white man who followed their hostess's instructions.

She could barely hear the two amens that came back to her. Shaking her head once again, she said, "Well, let's get on with the eatin'. Maybe after that, you'll have 'nough energy to say a proper amen." She laughed out loud as she took her place at the table.

Joining Daisy in laughter, George lumbered across the room and sat at the other end of the table. When Daisy picked up her fork, he gave a great sigh, picked up the serving spoon, filled it, and loaded a generous portion onto his plate. "Now. Let's eat," he encouraged the other guests, as he picked up his fork. "Daisy's the best cook around and getting an invite from her sets my mouth to watering." Grinning at Daisy, his fork poised and loaded with fish, he added, "Eat up! You won't be sorry!" He plopped the food into his mouth and announced his appreciation with "Mmmmm, mmmmm, mmmmm."

Daisy returned his smile and skewered a piece of fish.

The room erupted into a cacophony of metal on pottery, devoid of human speech.

Halfway through the meal, Daisy drank deeply from her water glass and resumed her lecture. "So, like I was sayin' earlier,

336

them truths just are. They is true. So now, le's talk about each one of them truths. Anybody remember 'em?"

She looked around the table. Every head was lowered. Each appeared to be staring past their nearly empty plates into a void, as if searching for the answer within the pottery.

This was going to be a tough group to work with. Daisy had heard the stories. Most of them had been beaten into submission, tortured, threatened with the death of their families—some had already lost most members of their families. There were just too many similar tales to doubt a word of the horrors these people had faced. It was going to be hard.

"This ain't no test," George said in his gravelly voice. "You can even take a guess." His scarred smile looked more like a grimace. "She's a good woman."

Daisy grinned at George. His eyes told her he was confident in her abilities. She squared her shoulders and repeated, "Anybody remember them truths that are self-evident?"

Silence.

"Well, the way I count, there be two of 'em. One is that all men are created equal. I'll just add that what they meant by that was all mankind, not just men folk. They meant all human beings, of which each of us is."

Daisy smiled, but no one noticed. They were still looking through their plates.

She went on. "And two: that they—meanin' each of us human beings; are endowed—meanin' He done give it as a matter of course; by their Creator . . ." She stopped.

No one looked up. All eyes were focused on their plates.

Daisy picked up her spoon from the table and held it over her head.

No one reacted.

She grinned at George. He was already choking back a laugh. She dropped the spoon onto her plate. The sound of the metal on the pottery crashed into the silence of the room. Every head jerked up, each with wild-eyed fear on their faces.

Daisy smiled warmly at each one. "We're all friends. You don't have to hide. There ain't nothin' to fear here." She picked up the spoon and placed it next to her plate. She stood and walked around the table, stopped behind George.

Their gaze followed her every move.

She had their attention now. "We just want you to know what you have. What they tried to take away from you, but couldn't. It be yours. You can give it away, but no one can take it from you."

George nodded.

She smiled again, fixing on each one, until she saw several faces ease into a slight grin. As she moved back to her seat, she continued talking.

"So, as I was sayin', the Creator done give all us human beings some unalienable rights after creatin' us all equal. We'll come back to the equal part later. Right now, I want you to understand what you have."

Daisy stood behind her chair, holding onto it. She slowed her pacing, taking time with each phrase. "You have the right to Life. Right now, you are breathin' and eatin' and listenin' to what I'm sayin'. That means you got life. And this life you got belongs to you. Only God can give it to you. It's precious. You gotta take care of it, do somethin' with it."

She looked at each face, searching for some glimmer of understanding, hope, anger, confusion, anything. The blank faces stared back at her.

She sat. *At least they aren't looking at the floor anymore.* She persisted.

"Next, you got the right to Liberty. That means you're free. Free to think for yourselves. Decide for yourselves. Choose what you gonna do with your life. I don't know if you ever thought about what you might do if you could choose." She waited for any response. Getting none, she continued. "Well, now's the time to be thinkin' about that. 'Cause now, you can choose."

Frowning, one of the men pushed his chair back from the table, folding his arms across his chest.

Seeing that she was getting through, she added quickly, "And lastly you got the right to pursue Happiness."

The man's frown changed to anger. He glared at Daisy.

"Let me emphasize here. They said Pursuit. We got the right to pursue it. But it's up to us to find it and keep it."

Anger changed to fear, then sadness.

"Now I just gotta say, happiness looks different to different folks. Mostly, I figure that the goin' after it part means way more than the arrivin' at it part." She paused for a full minute, took a sip of water, and stood. Every face remained focused on Daisy.

338

She chuckled. "I find for myself, I'm happiest when I be doin' somethin' for somebody. Or makin' life better for my chil'ren. Or just workin' in my garden. Or . . ." She laughed.

George joined in. "Daisy has shown me that she's happy just about most of the time. Just as long as she's busy."

The three women seated at the table smiled timidly. Daisy rewarded them with a huge grin.

The men looked at George.

George said, "I'm most happy protecting people. From fire or anything else that ain't right." The men seemed to visibly relax.

"Do you realize you already used your unalienable rights?" Daisy continued. "By riskin' your lives? To gain your freedom? To pursue your happiness?"

She paused intentionally long. She wanted the thought to take hold. She sat down. "Now. Just take a minute to think about what might make you feel joy."

The ever-changing facial expressions around the table spoke of uncertain excitement. There seemed to be a new light dawning in their eyes.

"I know it might sound crazy. But try. Just lean on the thought." She closed her eyes, leaned back, and rested her head on the chair. Almost in a whisper, she asked, "You people just risked everythin' to get your freedom from the life you been livin'. Now that you have that freedom, what'cha gonna do with it?"

CONVEYANCE

Irene Flynn

Which streetcar would you
rush to my desire
on?
My arms open for warm embrace,
Your presence to anticipate
The tension of my passion
attendant
On your arrival.

Meet the Hightowers

Lawrence Carleton

I woke on a crisp autumn day, the morning after my retirement party, and observed, mostly to myself, "Walter 'Dubby' Down, you've made no difference to the world. There's nothing notable in all you've done that has your name on it."

Pat mumbled, without rolling over from her side of our bed facing away from me, "I've heard this before. And you've done plenty."

"Nothing that anyone can identify as mine."

"Well, you've written several short stories, and your novel is actually published." Pat sighed, rolled onto her back and sat up, bracing on her pillows.

"Two of the four copies I've sold on Amazon were bought by personal friends. Fifteen of the nineteen copies I've given away for free were given in the hope someone would post a review. So far no luck."

"Maybe you could write something that would interest other people, not just yourself." Pat yawned. "Well, now I'm awake, and hungry. Feed me!" She rolled out of bed and shuffled off to the bathroom.

I knew I was living a life most people would consider successful. I'd taught philosophy in several universities, but after wearing out my welcome at each of the institutions of higher learning in the area by bringing up questions uncomfortable to the resident authorities, I found sanctuary as a technology writer for a large software concern. That paid the bills. Meanwhile it allowed us to stay here so Pat could pursue her career in biotech.

Still, I wanted to have something to say in The Great Public Conversation, so I started to write short stories — usually of some social significance but sometimes just good stories — and send them off to relevant publications. One story had grown, pretty much on its own, into a novel.

"Anyway, remember I signed us up for the Homecoming this Saturday," Pat noted.

343

Ah yes. Peninsular Christian. "Old Insular, the last place I'd teach."

"My alma mater. You go there with me and be nice. I still have friends."

"I'll get your breakfast now."

~

Saturday came and we went.

A cool breeze ruffled the banner at the campus entrance. I read it to Pat: Peninsular Christian University Homecoming 2013 — 60 years of Excrudescence."

"That's *excellence*, Dubby. I'm warning you, be nice!" Pat hissed.

Peninsular was the last place I taught and was kicked out of. Pat had gotten her BA there before she knew me, and she was fondly remembered — which probably helped me get that position when I did. It likely helped our son Burton get his scholarship too. (He left the nest for grad school up north at Palo Alto three years ago this fall and as usual wouldn't be back for our local festivities.)

The alumni breakfast went smoothly enough.

After the breakfast Pat took off for her reunion. Curious about the state of Insular philosophy after all the years, I wandered over to the designated meeting room. It was not a large room. It had five rows of chairs set up facing a lectern accompanied by three stools. People I didn't know stood in clusters waiting for the presentation to start. My former colleagues, Dwayne Leporello and Milton Fudge, stood near the lectern. Dwayne's face turned to mild disdain as he searched his memory and slowly came to recognize me. "Dubby?" he acknowledged. "What are you doing here?" Milton suppressed a little gasp, waited a beat, and blurted, "This is a blast from the past! What've you been up to?"

"Just curious to hear what's changed. I see from the program that you now have a Center for Combating Consequentialism."

Dwayne replied. "Yes. When Peter Singer justified animal rights on the basis of utilitarianism, we knew we had to restore godliness to the discussion. Fundraising was a snap, and then in no time Professor Zverkov had the center up and running."

Zverkov! Enemy of true inquiry! Partisan for enforced fundamentalism in the schools.

"He's going to be the main speaker tonight," said Dwayne.

Milton remarked, "You used to be a utilitarian. Are you still, or have you outgrown that?"

344

"Still immature," I replied. "What can I say? It seems to me you reject consequentialism because of its consequences. So, you're still evaluating a belief system on the basis of the results you get following it. The key to choosing a belief system is the question of whether following it leads to results you can accept.

"For a utilitarian, you get the best results by considering the results in the first place. For other systems, the question of, say, whether making a rule of the activity you're considering leads to the best results, or following a list of commands does the trick is key to evaluating the system. But in the end, 'by their fruits you shall know them.'"

"Same old bullshit," someone grumbled.

"There are problems in applying utilitarianism," I continued. "It's often hard to tell whether you've calculated all the consequences, especially when there are long lasting or far reaching effects. Should you honor a dying wish? Well, the dead guy isn't around to experience disappointment if you choose not to. But are you figuring in the potential unhappiness of observers who might want to declare their own wishes?"

"It's not for you to know these things. God knows. It's for you to obey."

It was Zverkov.

"Ah, Professor Jerkoff. What does God know, Leo? The total consequences for happiness?"

"God knows what He wants. Not necessarily for you to be happy."

"Especially not for me to be happy."

"Think of me as God's little helper where that's concerned. I thought we'd gotten rid of you."

Dwayne announced that it was time to get the presentation started.

I took a seat. Introductions began. There was a difficulty getting the projector to work, so they declared a recess while they called for help. A technician arrived. I idly scanned the room while he applied himself. Sitting a couple of seats to my left was a vaguely familiar figure — neatly dressed in a dark blue business suit with a short skirt and a silk scarf, greying but still reddish hair tied back in a tight bun. She turned to peer at me over black-rimmed glasses, smiled, and asked, "Is that you, Dubby?"

It was me. She scooted over to the seat next to me.

"Liza Hightower, it's been a while."

345

"No kidding. What have you been doing with yourself since leaving here?"

"You first, Liza. What's happening in good ole Insular Christian?"

"Well the Big Three . . ."

"Stooges . . ."

"Be nice. The Big Three are pretty much what they were when you left. Dwayne publishes anthologies of other people's ideas and uses his connections to get on committees, but so far," she leaned in and whispered, "nothing original on his part." She straightened again. "Milton's thing is an early morning interview hour on public radio, guests are visiting philosophers and professors from other schools' philosophy departments. You'll know all you want from Leo when the projector works. I'm still trudging away in philosophy of science, cranking out monographs. Also I'm the local designee for women's issues now. For fun, I do the occasional book review in the popular press. The three faculty here are, I think, the ones you know. Your turn. What became of you after your tar and feathering?"

"Well, I'd used up all the local schools. I could have dragged my wife off to Utah or Minnesota to wear out my welcome in other parts of the country, but she had a position she liked working among friends at a biotech company here in town. What was a good utilitarian to do? I wangled a tech writer position at Cybergers, a local startup, and have been there since."

"Poor Dubby. Done in by your philosophy."

"Well, for a while I tried contributing to the journals and going to the conferences in philosophy and cognitive science, but you really need connections to get anywhere. Now in order to have something to say I'm cranking out short stories which bring attention to this or that social issue I care about."

"Maybe you should write a book."

"Interestingly, I have. Still, I feel a little guilty telling myself I'm doing this for the common good and not just burnishing my self-image. I'm not sure one can be an egotist and utilitarian at the same time."

The projector was fixed, the recess over. After the presentation, time for questions. Surprisingly (not), I didn't get called upon. Time to go.

Liza tapped my shoulder, and when I turned, she asked for my contact information. I gave her the card I'd made up to advertise the book.

346

At the picnic we ran into some more of Pat's old classmates. At the football game, no one got hurt.

The following Friday, Pat answered the house phone, and told me, "It's for you. A Liza Hightower?"

"It's an old colleague from the phil department. We ran into each other at the presentation at Homecoming."

"Hightower, yes. I met her husband at the reunion. Never knew him back then, but we were in the same graduating class. Seems very nice. They have a daughter at Stanford."

"May I have the phone?"

"Oh, right. Here you go." Pat handed me the phone.

Liza said, "Have you checked out your book on Amazon lately? You have more than four sales now."

I logged in.

"You have a review now, too."

I skimmed Liza's review. It looked pretty good. "Imagine if you will 'Notes From Underground' but written by Laurence Sterne instead of Dostoevsky . . ." She'd captured the essence of what I'd done.

"Thank you," I acknowledged. Sales were up. "Just the thing to goose sales. This is very good of you."

"You're welcome. By the way, you can also hype your book indirectly by being a reviewer of other books, in a newspaper or magazine, and signing off as an author. I can get you a gig with the Trib. Interested?"

It did sound interesting.

"Can you drop by my house tonight? Seven? That'll give me time to arrange things."

I asked Pat whether she'd like to go with me.

"That'd be a distraction, I think. You're a big boy. You can do this on your own."

"Seven it is," I agreed.

Liza gave me her address. It was walking distance, just down the street.

~

At seven, Liza's husband met me at the door and led me into the living room. Liza was seated on a sofa behind a coffee table.

I took a seat across the table from her. She told me what she'd arranged for me with the Trib. She called out to her husband, who'd retreated to the study, asking him to bring the book she'd left on her desk. "Walden, it's the one with me on the cover."

347

"You wish," he laughed. In a few minutes he materialized with the book. "I'm going out now, sweetie. Don't wait up."

"I won't. May even turn in early." They nuzzled, and he left.

She moved me to the sofa and handed me the book. Its cover featured a revealingly attired redhead standing, hands on hips, in front of a diversified coterie of obviously interested men. *Riding Herd* was its title.

"It does look a little like you," I remarked.

"Flattery'll get you everywhere." She smiled. "Take a look inside. Do you have time? See what you think. I'll leave you to it. Back in a while."

The book was a picaresque adventure in the vein of Fifty Shades but with multiple men and more self-deprecating humor.

Apparently, the novel was more interesting than I remember it. I hadn't noticed Liza sit down next to me. Suddenly I was aware of one superbly toned thigh gliding across my legs. Before I could react, I found myself straddled by two perfect thighs, with two perfect lips zeroing in on my mouth. "You know you want it," they breathed.

It didn't seem to matter at all what I wanted. I struggled to my feet but with her legs wrapped around me I couldn't achieve stability. I staggered and spun until I fell forward on top of her on top of the coffee table.

"Yes, yes, Dubby yes," she shrieked, "Take me now!"

I pried myself loose and hurried to the front door.

She followed.

I turned to her and tried to think what to say. I stared into her eyes. At last I said, "I don't think I can review that book objectively."

"Perhaps a different one."

"Perhaps."

"Think about it."

I let myself out. I'd taken a few steps when the door opened again. Liza stood in the entrance, dangling my keys from her hand.

I took the keys.

"Standing offer," she smiled, and giggled.

"Yes, it will have to be standing."

She smiled.

I left.

~

Pat laughed when I told her about my adventure. "Still, you've been a good boy all along. Maybe you're entitled to a fling in your declining years. Is she hot?"

"I have to say the flesh is willing but the spirit . . . isn't. You're no slouch either, my dear. I'm a one-woman dog. I know a good thing when I have it."

"So, I'm a thing you have, eh?"

"You're a goddess and all I want."

"Well, I'm just saying. You could get away with an indiscretion maybe once. Ms. Hightower can help you get your book sales to improve. It wouldn't hurt to visit her again. Anyway, I know you're going to be up late and toss and turn in your sleep, and I'm already tired, so I'll take the guest room tonight." Pat planted a peck on my cheek and toddled off to the guest room.

In the weeks to come I visited Liza several times. I did book reviews, a radio talk show, a local book fair. Sales of my book improved, though it's never going to be a best seller. That's all right. People know the book is available and they can read it if they want. This is my identifiable accomplishment.

These visits were always on a Friday night, and Walden always left for a night out when I arrived. My guess was that he had some regular thing to do and I was Liza's amusement for the otherwise empty time.

Pat and I fell into a pattern when I got home from these soirées. I'd report on my visit, Pat would give me a peck on the cheek and take off for the guest room.

I did notice her being more enthusiastic and adventurous in our lovemaking, when we did it. Then one night she blurted out, "Wally, yes!"

"Hello, I'm 'Dubby', dear."

She gasped. "Dubby Dear, did I just call you 'Wally'?"

"Yes, you did, Patricia."

She paused. "Well I was just thinking. It's time you graduated to 'Wally' for 'Walter.' You've been 'Dubby' for 'W' since you were a kid. I've been thinking of you more as 'Wally' these days."

"So, I'm Wally now . . ."

"Yes, dear. And I'm tired. Let's sleep."

Next Friday, as visiting time rolled around, I asked Pat, "Going fishing on Walden Pond again?"

"Uh oh. Busted."

"Well, you've been good all these years. Maybe you're entitled to a fling while you're still hot."

Pat admitted that, now that the affair was in the open, it would be less exciting. The assignations continued for a couple of weeks, but in the end Walden and Liza had to agree that with the loss of secrecy the whole thing was deflating for them as well.

The Hightowers' girl, Virginia, was due home for school break any day, our son Burton should already be home, but no word yet. We knew he had arranged to share a ride with a fellow student. The four of us agreed to suspend our farce at least while the kids were in town.

When we returned to the Hightowers' from our celebratory dinner at Domingo's, Virginia's car was parked outside. "We can go in for a final toast, but Ginny's probably asleep, so everyone quiet." We went to the living room and waited while Walden obtained the wine and glasses. "Here's to separate lives," he declared. "Good-bye and good luck."

"Cheers."

"Cheers."

"Cheers."

"Cheers."

We touched glasses and sipped in silence. We all heard it then. Was it the wind? No, the sounds of some activity were coming from the study: "Yes Burton yes! Omigod! Yes!"

When Ted Met Chris

Penn Wallace

The Greyhound neared the bus station just off I-90 at
Royal Brougham way. Eighteen-year-old Ted Higuera had
never traveled away from home by himself. Sure, he'd taken
many football trips with the team from Los Angeles'
Garfield High, but never by himself and never to such a
foreign land as Seattle, Washington.

The bus traveled up I-5 through great cities and miles of
farmland.

Ted had no idea that there was so much unpopulated
land in the world. Growing up in the barrios of East LA
afforded him little chance to view the outside world.

Behind him he heard excited chattering in Spanish. He
felt a little more relaxed. His family spoke Spanish at home.
In the outside world, he spoke English. He desperately
wanted to be seen as an American.

Growing up, there wasn't a day went by that he wasn't
called "wetback," "dirty Mexican," "spick," or "beaner."
Racial tension was just part of everyday life in East LA.

The big bus exited the freeway and crawled through the
city streets to the terminal. Ted disembarked and looked
around as if he'd just landed in Oz.

The terminal wasn't that different from the one in LA.
Long wooden benches, ticket counters, a greasy-spoon
restaurant. But it was different. Torrential rain poured down
outside. Everyone was bundled up in overcoats and parkas.
Many people wore boots.

He stood with the rest of the riders waiting for his bags
to be disgorged from under the bus. He finally saw a large
purple duffel with a golden "W" on it and the picture of a
Siberian Husky. A gift from the coach of his new team.

351

He thought back to his high school days. Small for a running back, he was lightning quick. He juked and ran past defenders to all-time LA high school rushing and touchdown records. His coach and advisers said he would have his pick of colleges.

It didn't happen. He got a couple of offers from Division II schools but was devastated that none of the major colleges were interested. Coach told him that his dream school, USC, said he was too small for big time football. He wouldn't last through four years of constant battering from three-hundred-pound linemen.

He picked up his bags and headed for the exit. A line of taxis waited outside.

"University of Washington, please," he said to the turbaned man as he got in.

The yellow Toyota Prius pulled away from the terminal and headed back to the freeway.

Ted watched in wonder as the tall buildings of downtown appeared. His heart was beating with excitement as he saw Seattle's landmark, the Space Needle. They took the express lanes under the city and came out looking down at Lake Union. The gray September sky reflected in the gray waters of the lake. They crossed over the Ship Canal Bridge and he saw numerous sail and power boats heading one way or the other.

In LA, no one would be out on a day like this.

At 45th Street, the cabbie exited the freeway. "Where you want to go?" the heavily bearded cabbie asked.

"McMahon dorm." That was where all the freshmen football players lived.

The cab pulled into the circular drive and the cabbie helped Ted unload his bags. After a fruitless search for a tip, Ted finally checked in with the reception area and a junior fullback showed him to his room.

"Higuera, huh?" the full-back asked. "I don't remember you on any of the recruiting charts."

Ted looked at the floor and spoke in a soft voice. "Coach Harper came to Garfield to scout a couple of our wide

352

receivers. He saw me and liked me, but Coach didn't want a little running back."

"So, how did you get here?" Tony opened a door marked 316. "Here we are."

Ted looked at Tony. He seemed like a nice enough guy. *How much should I tell him?*

"I . . . ah, . . . when Dawson decided to go to Illinois, they had one running back scholarship left. Coach Harper managed to convince Coach to give it to me."

Tony held to door open for Ted to enter. "Second choice, huh? I guess you'll get a lot of time on the practice team."

Ted stepped inside the room. It was a sitting area with a flat screen TV mounted on one wall, two couches and a couple of fabric covered chairs near the opposite wall. A large window looked out to the south. Ted could see the ship canal with a bunch of rowing shells on it. They looked like bugs making their way swiftly across the water.

Beyond the canal, Mount Rainier stood in all its glory. One of the highest peaks in the Cascades, it towered over the other mountains with its permanent cover of snow and curving clouds over its head.

"Wow. Some view. We ain't got nuthin' like that in LA."

Tony held out his hand. "Tony Adams. Fullback. We don't have anything like that in Waco, Texas, either." He looked at his clipboard. "You're in room C." He pointed with his clipboard. "I'll leave you to unpack."

Ted dragged his constantly heavier bags to the door and stepped into room C.

He checked out the room. The walls were plain beige. A bed against one wall and a long Formica desk extending from the bed to the opposite wall comprised all the furniture. Six drawers under the bed, a large closet and two bookshelves over the desk. Lots of storage. Ted didn't have much to bring, so everything would fit in nicely.

"C'mon Dad," Ted heard voices in the living room. "I can't wait to see my room."

"Take it easy, Slugger." This was a more mature male voice. "Help me with the fridge."

Ted moved to his door to see what was happening.

A tall, blond, god helped his son—also tall, blond, and god-like—move an apartment-sized refrigerator into the room next to him.

Behind them, two other huge human beings, one white and the other black, carried boxes.

Linemen. The only people that big on campus had to be linemen.

"Where do you want these, Mr. Hardwick?" one of the linemen asked.

"Set them down in the living area for now. We'll sort them out later. Just go down and bring up the rest."

Ted stepped into the main area. "Ted Higuera." He extended his hand. "I'm from LA."

Mr. Hardwick took him in in a glance. Ted felt like he was in an x-ray machine in the airport.

"Harry Hardwick." His grip was firm. "This is my son, Chris. He'll be your roommate." He flipped a hand towards the two linemen. "Charles McChord and Thomas Winslow. Both offensive linemen."

Ted shook each hand in turn.

"I'm from Mobile, Alabama," the black lineman said. "Call me Charlie."

Thomas offered his hand. "Tom Winslow, Eugene, Oregon. I'm a physics major."

Whew, no one would guess that. He must have a big brain inside that big body.

"Good to meet you."

The third young man stood with his arms folded, sizing Ted up. Finally, he moved toward his new roommate. "Chris Hardwick. I don't know what the hell I'm doing in this dorm. I don't play football."

Ted looked up at the tall guy. He had to be at least six inches taller than Ted's five foot eight. Wearing a tank top and shorts, Ted could see he was thin, but well-muscled. He had what his sister, Hope, would call bedroom eyes.

Ted returned to his room and finished unpacking. He heard Mr. Hardwick's voice through the door.

354

"Anyone want to go to the North Lake for Pizza?"

"Sure."

"Yeah."

"Me too."

Ted put down the cardboard box and headed to the door. "I'm in," he said to an empty room.

~

"Dad, I'm not sure I feel safe with a gangbanger living next door. The guy has 'sketch' written all over him."

"You can't choose your roommates. With Charlie and Tom here, you shouldn't have any problems."

Ted rolled over in bed and looked at the alarm clock. Two fourteen a.m.

The conversation went on.

"I mean, I'm not prejudiced or anything, I just didn't like the vibe I got from that dude."

"Son, if there's one thing I learned in business, it's that inside, we're all the same. I've had a number of Mexican-American clients, and they're just like everybody else."

"I don't know . . . Something just feels off."

"Well, sleep on it. I'll talk to you tomorrow."

Ted heard the door closing.

Jesus, Jose y Maria. What've I got myself into. A racist roommate?

~

It was still the week before school started. Ted was exhausted. The two-a-day drills sucked every bit of life out of him. He sat by himself in the cafeteria and played with his meatloaf. *Not like Mama used to make.* He stirred his mashed potatoes. *What I wouldn't give for one tamale.*

Voices rose a couple of tables over.

"Hey, Lord Fauntleroy, how come you're roomin' with the real men?" A large young man stood over Chris Hardwick.

Chris ignored him.

"Too sissy to play football. Why don't you find a tea-and-book-club dorm, Nancy?"

Chris stared into his tormentor's eyes.

355

"Hey man, I'm talkin' to ya." The big guy shoved Chris's chair.

Chris stood to face his tormenter. "Look, I didn't ask to be here. I guess my dad pulled a few strings to get me here. He wants me to bask in his legacy."

The tough kid got right in Chris's face. "You think just cuz your dad was some kinda super stud, you can hang out with the team? It ain't goin' to work." He gave Chris a shove in the chest.

Ted's senses went into hyperdrive. Everything seemed to be in slow motion.

Chris staggered back a couple of steps, then charged the big guy.

The tormentor's two friends stepped up, and each grabbed one of Chris's arms.

Chris struggled to get free, but they were too strong.

"Here's a little present for your dad." The tormentor slugged Chris in the stomach.

Chris let out an "Ughh" and all his breath.

"Want some more, Nancy?" The big guy asked.

Ted didn't stop to think. He was up and running toward the slugger before he knew what he was doing. The smaller man smashed into the tormenter's solar plexus with his head at full speed.

The slugger sat down on his ass on the tile floor.

Before he had a chance to get up, Ted delivered an upper cut to his jaw that laid him out on the floor.

The two friends dropped Chris's arms and stared.

Ted stood over his opponent with both fists clinched. "You mess with my roomie, man, you mess with me."

~

Author's Note: When *The Inside Passage* was published, Ted and Chris had just graduated from the University of Washington and were twenty-two years old. In *The Chinatown Murders,* Ted turns thirty. Ted now owns a private investigation agency, and Chris is a partner in his own law firm. They have now appeared in eleven novels together and continue to grow in each book. Our boys will

356

continue to age with their adventures and, hopefully, become wiser and smarter as they go.

Enigma Stroller

Gary Winters

In Baja, California, an Indian woman sits cross-legged on the sidewalk selling pottery, pine needle baskets, ironwood carvings, whatever her tribe produces. It is all spread out on a cloth. An infant sits on the ground close by.

Everything is fine until a flash sandstorm kicks up. The kind that can strip the paint off your RV in mere minutes. One minute is more time than the Indian mother needs to catch up the four corners of the ground cloth, tie them up, grab her child's left arm with her right hand, and sling him over her left shoulder. The child squeals with delight — this is some ride — clutches the woman's long black hair with tiny fists and buries his face in mom's hair. Mother whips out a length of cloth and flings it around the little body. She ties the ends in a big bow under her chin and moves out with offspring and merchandise heading to a safe haven.

I told this story to a yuppie father in an upscale San Francisco bar, comparing the simplicity of it with a modern eight-wheeled chrome and plastic stroller complete with hoods and umbrellas. He explained how he was ever so happy when he found a collapsible baby buggy that was easy as pie to open. Noticing my skeptical look, he insisted I come out to his car and see the engineering marvel. We saunter out into the cool San Francisco evening. He pops the trunk and yanks out a collapsed tangle of metal and cloth. For the next ten minutes he tries to get the thing to open up, all the while assuring me he could do it. I left him standing there mute, fog rolling in, intensely gazing down at the mechanical monstrosity like it was some enigmatic thing from another planet.

Still Waiting

Olga Singer

My first live, in-person encounter with him was at the LA Live Nokia Theatre in 2008. But really, it started when I first heard his signature hit, *Waiting On the World to Change*. I've been in love with him ever since. And thirteen years later, that love is still going strong. He has brought me to the *Edge of Desire*, where I've daydreamed of *Slow Dancing in a Burning Room*, only to find *My Stupid Mouth* always wrecks the fantasy!

Side note to John: If you're out there reading this, know I'm not some crazy fan out to stalk you—just someone who is thankful your music was introduced to me, years ago, by my then teenaged son.

Here's how it all started. The first time I heard his voice, I was busy in the kitchen rolling tortillas and prepping tuna enchiladas for dinner. My oldest son, a freshman in high school, had a new artist playing on his iPod speaker. The lyrics drifted into my brain, and I began to hum along to the beat.

"Who is that?" I asked.

"John Mayer," he responded.

"I like it," I said.

A few days later, I heard the song again. My son was sitting at the kitchen table doing his math homework.

"I know you told me, but I can't remember. Who is that again?" I asked, interrupting his grumblings.

"John Mayer."

"And what's the name of the song?"

"*Waiting On the World to Change*," he said a bit exasperated.

Did I write it down? Of course not—but I could feel myself slowly starting to fall in love with this new artist.

A few more days went by before I heard the song again. Jack was getting ready for school and filling his backpack. I hesitated before asking, but I couldn't help myself. "Don't kill me, but tell me again, who is that?" I could hear his younger brother laughing in the hallway, knowing all too well how this would play out.

361

"Mom! I've told you a million times, it's John Mayer," retorted Jack. "Maybe you should download his album on iTunes. It's called *Continuum*, and it's really good." He replied, a bit annoyed at me, as he grabbed his backpack and headed out the door with his brother.

And so, that's how my love affair with John Mayer began.

As soon as the boys were out the door and the house quiet, I went online. I googled John and downloaded his current album — and the two previous ones, *Room for Squares* and *Heavier Things*. And so began the constant melody and sound of John's voice as his music filled the house 24/7! It didn't take long for my family to start resenting me, and John. (Sorry John. It's not you . . . my family really loves your music. I think they were just getting sick of hearing it ALL the time.) Meanwhile I continued to grow more and more in love him.

I thought back to the pre-teen crush I had on Donny Osmond. My room was plastered with his photos, including an oversized poster of his dazzling smile and his adorable face pinned to my ceiling. *Puppy Love* became my all-time favorite song. And that was also about the same time purple became my number one color. Imagine that? Donny and I both liked purple! I wondered what John's favorite color was. Maybe I should I google it?

As a forty-something woman, I quickly realized I was starting to behave like that star-struck teenager who had fallen for Donny.

But alas, I digress. I have been to four of John's concerts, including that first one taking place at the Nokia Theatre in LA. Two years later, I experienced his incredible guitar playing talent and his bad boy charisma at the Staples Center, followed by two back-to-back concerts at the Paso Robles Fairgrounds in Northern California. But LA is where it all began.

Much time has passed since I first heard John's melodic voice that long-ago day in the kitchen and I am somewhat embarrassed to say he still rocks my world at fifty something! I now own all of his albums, and I still play his music a lot. My love affair with John Mayer continues to this day. And although it is one-sided, it suits me just fine, even if we never meet, dear John, just know that *You're Gonna Live Forever in Me*!

362

Is Age 72 Really the New 30?

Frank Newton

Because my last birthday certified that I had indeed reached six dozen years of life on earth, it's not surprising that a particular news headline recently grabbed my attention — *72 is the new 30!* It turned out to be a study of age-based mortality rates — or what scientists indelicately call "age-specific risk of death."

The study was thick with mathematics and scientific verbiage which boiled down to this: 10,000 years ago, a 30-year-old hunter-gatherer had a five percent chance of dying before reaching age 31. The scientists said that, nowadays, our likelihood of dying within one year is usually less than one percent, and our risk doesn't reach the caveman's five percent until we are 72 years old.

Evidently, this gift of 42 extra years speaks well of advances in housing, food, and medicine over the last 10 millennia and, also, to the fact that there are fewer saber-tooth tigers trying to eat us. But the scientific study does not indicate whether or not we've made wise use of this precious gift of longer life.

Despite phenomenal gains in extending our life span, it seems some of our attitudes about aging are still rooted in caveman days. Americans still glorify all things young, while they deprecate growing older. Worse, long-lived seniors have increasingly become a lightning rod for dire predictions about the world's future. In Europe, for example, some governments are buckling under the cost of pensions for retirees. While in America, pundits and politicians wail that Social Security, Medicare, and other "entitlements" are going to bankrupt our nation.

But I ask, "Do older adults necessarily have to be a burden and the scourge of our society?" I would love to see public discussion about changing social attitudes and practices so that older adults would not be the problem and, instead, become part of the solution.

To head in this more positive direction, we first need to stop the innumerable pejorative expressions for older folks — like "old fogey" and "over the hill" (and far worse). These sayings legitimize negative stereotypes. If you think eliminating such expressions is impossible, remember how public opinion put a damper on "moron" and "Polish" jokes.

Second, businesses should remove their age blinders and biases about older workers. Too often, people in their 40s and 50s are regarded as unemployable which, in my view, is raw bigotry. Instead of treating workers like paper towels that are used up and tossed away, American businesses should enable mature workers to continue using their practical wisdom, job expertise, and solid work ethic. One good step would be to change the 40-hour work week requirement, allowing older workers to reduce their hours while still being productive.

Next, we should honor the positive qualities that come with growing older. In particular, seniors embody cultural continuity, as their memories and experiences help to preserve history and cultural traditions that enrich our society. We should also appreciate the wisdom that comes with age.

Instead, we act as if our life span is like a bottle of Coca Cola, where the flavor and bubbly refreshment come only when you pop the cap; then, it goes flat and tasteless over time. Maybe a better image is fine wine that grows richer with flavor and quality as it ages.

I also feel that youth glorifies immediate experience, quick success, and personal gain. Along with age comes a longer-term perspective on issues and a greater concern for the common good. I'm convinced we need the wisdom of seniors because they are wary of short-term fixes and, instead, are guided by the legacy they will be leaving their grandchildren.

I can't claim to have all the answers, but I would urge people to start thinking about how to reframe our cultural attitudes and practices to make use of the contributions of seniors. We need to view seniors as a resource — not a burden. Instead of pushing seniors aside, instead of making them feel discarded, we need to be asking how seniors can participate and help our community. It would be wonderful if our political and business leaders would promote such changes. But I believe, it is seniors themselves who will have to step up and be more vocal in promoting their own worth.

The silver tsunami has already begun to sweep over America, and it will inexorably impact every facet of American life.

The sooner we begin reframing the role, meaning, and value of older adults, the better for our society and our economy, both now and in the future.

At Twelve Thousand Feet

Janet Hafner

Hot Tibetan air slaps me as I exit the plane. *Ridiculous. Can't breathe.* Pushed from behind, I pick up my one carry-on bag and navigate the steps. *Oh my God, the heat of the airfield could scorch the soles of my shoes.*

Emptiness . . . barren hills flanked by bleak mountains. *What happened to the snowy, inaccessible village perched atop a cliff, reachable only by parachute or yak?* This is "nothingness" — I rush to get to a miniature terminal.

Our party of seven — all related — husbands, children, grandchildren, cousins, in-laws, and out-laws. We struggle to fill our lungs with thin air. *So, this is high altitude.*

We stop before entering the building.

I look up. A glorious sky. Azure — embodying every hue within its color from the darkest of the deepest ocean to a tint so light it's as if winds blew all the color clear over the Himalayas into Nepal. The mountains stand alone — naked in a vacant sky. *Same sky as in San Diego, or New York, or Paris, but it isn't . . . it's unique.* I feel it touching my cheek. No pollution — no blemishes — just one expanse of blueness.

~

"Hello, my weary travelers," says our guide and driver. "You'll find oxygen in your rooms. Use two or three pillows and keep your head high. Drink water. I must know where you are every moment of your journey. The government doesn't want you to become too familiar with the Tibetans." *How strange...our guide, a laid-back smiling Tibetan with Oakley sunglasses.* "And one more thing — you can call me Harrison." He leaves us with his back, and the yellow group flag is raised above his head.

~

Harrison takes us on a slow walk through Barkhor, Lhasa's medieval town. One giant marketplace. We shuffle forward, following throngs of pilgrims.

"Everyone is so short," my cousin, Stan, says. "Janet, you look like a giant." Our laughter punctuates the humming, chanting crowd whose sounds blend with the whirr of the spinning prayer wheels.

"I thought I had a California tan," I say, "but compared with the native Tibetans, I'm a 'mighty whitey.'" Skin surrounding us is dry, wrinkled — prune-like. Natives are baked.

Moving forward, we come to a giant intersection looking like one of San Diego's roundabouts with one significant difference. Hundreds of Tibetan pilgrims wait to cross this main thoroughfare.

"Stay together, folks. Don't want to lose anyone," Harrison calls. We wait — our eyes fixed on the pilgrims. Some have a twirling prayer wheel in their right hand. Ten steps into the street, then to their knees, arms slide out in front of them, faces touch the street, back up on their feet, another ten steps, down, stretch out, mumble a prayer, up and so it goes. Cars, taxis, buses, bicycles, carts all stop. Nothing moves until the mass completes the journey across the street and reaches the other side. Only then does traffic move. *I can't imagine how this would work in LA.*

~

Harrison announces, "Potala Palace is our goal today. Hope you got a good night's sleep." No one responds . . . a telling sign.

It's a staggering sight. No photo I had previously seen prepared me for the scale and beauty of the palace. Harrison says, "Built in 1645 with one thousand rooms, it housed the successive Dalai Lamas. It's a long uphill trek. Ready?"

The wide cobblestone incline stretches before us. We climb, we stop, we continue, we pause, we gasp at the air molecules. We put one foot in front of the other. Far above us is the palace.

"We have a long way to go before any shade," he tells us.

"Can we sit and rest a while?" my voice shakes. "If we come across a bench, I'll be the first one on it," I shout. No benches . . . not even a low wall to perch on. Gasping and moaning, all fight to advance.

A doorway — a dark cavern. Steps quicken . . . and then we're inside.

"That was grueling. Anyone want to go back?"

"Nope. This is a once in a lifetime adventure," I answer.

"Is everyone here? It's easy to get lost in here. Follow my yellow flag," Harrison says.

Darkness welcomes us. *Nowhere to sit. Damn.*

"What's that strange smell? Don't recognize it. Yuk," I say. I pinch my nose.

Harrison tells us, "You're close . . . not yuk, but yak — it's yak butter — made into candles. The Tibetans use it for tea, candles, incense . . . like it?" Silence. My nostrils keep my tongue from forming words.

A twenty-foot white jade Buddha rests on a two-foot tall pedestal adorned with semiprecious stones, coral, turquoise, agates, jade — each as large as an emu egg — the magnitude of the statue and the stones stuns me.

Before the Buddha, rows and rows of yak candles twinkle at us. The pungent odor bathes us. Pilgrims crowd around a wooden box. Their fingers let go of the valuables they've brought as offerings. Barley, water, milk, money and yak butter.

I drag my feet along the cobblestone floor. Can't rush. So much to take in. Many half-smiling Buddha faces peer down at me from behind glass. In some of the display cases, a crouching monk holds a small dish of gold leaf, which he painstakingly applies with a small paintbrush to the waiting, smiling Buddha who anticipates a new glorious finish.

"They'll use kilos of gold to cover the tower in the next room," Harrison says. I have no way to compute the value of what I see.

~

Time ceases to be. Don't know if it's daylight or evening. Doesn't really matter. A totally new mysterious world has wrapped itself around me.

Monks, young and old, chant, sit in meditation, and pray, when they are not maintaining the statues.

~

From the dark chambers, we emerge into cool evening air. *I can breathe.*

Harrison smiles at our weary bodies and says, "Stay right here. I'm going to see if there's room for all of us in the next chamber."

"Oh my God — a bench," I call out. Like a flock of pigeons, we dive onto the five-foot long plank and squeeze together for a moment of rest. My eyes close out the sights.

I feel a hot hand on the back of my hand. My eyes spring open. A pair of jet-black eyes set in a woman's weathered face peer through me. I feel my lips part, but sound doesn't spill out. I stare into the black pools.

369

Our hands are locked. She pulls me to my feet. I hesitate but follow. She doesn't drop my hand. I am compelled to move with her. Her hair is coiled into ropes, wrapped around her head, and decorated with coral, turquoise, and brightly dyed wool. I follow. She moves quickly. We stop before a Buddha in a niche in the ancient wall. She mumbles prayers and makes gestures with her hand. She turns to me and nods. I mumble a prayer and copy her gesture . . . we're off. We climb fifteen steps and stand once again in front of a different deity. Her grip is like a vice. The ritual is repeated. She looks eighty and walks like sixteen. I can barely keep up. This time twenty steps. Another mumbled prayer.

I hear my husband's voice. "Where are you going? He doesn't want anyone getting lost."

I don't answer. I'm on a marathon. Now we've entered a covered pathway — more steps, more alcoves, more bowing. I'm wheezing. Can't keep up. I look back — no one's there. *Where am I? Where's my family?* "Where are you taking me? I don't want to get lost," my voice pleads. The woman doesn't answer.

Again, and again, I perform — then stop — that's it. No air. I collapse on the steps. The black pools wash over me. I feel tears spilling onto my cheeks. The vice grip loosens, and my hand lands on the step. She bows deeply and peers into my soul. With unequaled energy she leaps up the steps like a young gazelle. She disappears. *Where am I? Where's Pai? They'll never find me.*

~

I don't remember how long I rested on the steps. *Where are they?* The words chase each other in my head. I wait. The sun shifts. *It's going to be dark soon.* Stomach churns, as I mumble a prayer. *Stay calm, don't panic.*

Voices . . . familiar voices. My group appears.

"Thank God."

"You found me," I whimper.

"What happened?" My husband's eyes search for my answer. His face is strained. "Where did you go with that woman?"

"She climbed . . . I climbed . . . we climbed until . . . "

I don't know why she chose me. I'm still trying to understand what happened at twelve thousand feet. I guess I never will.

The Crumpled Note

Sarah Faxon

Late night at the side of a seaport was no place for a young academic. The cool, salt-laden breeze was enough to invigorate the souls of seamen, but for the student laden with balancing books in one arm and constantly correcting his bifocals with the other, the smell was sickening. He was looking green. However, this lad's business had nothing to do with the tall ships that lay with their anchors planted in the deep waters of the marina. The business of young Thad was to meet with someone he had never seen, to deliver the books beneath his arms. The crumpled bit of paper in his tweed jacket pocket revealed an address to which he had never visited.

The burly sailors that passed by were far too intimidating for the young man to question. Instead, Thad scooted along, clinging to the books, as if they were a bastion between his pocket watch and pickpockets. A low hanging streetlamp shone in the evening mist; Thad moved into it and reached for the paper in his pocket. Adjusting his spectacles to better see the crumpled note, Thad leaned against the light post and read: Gormhook R.A., 127 Pearl.

Thad sighed. He knew, by the crooked signposts lining the port, that he had reached Pearl Street, but none of the red-bricked buildings appeared to be number 127. He stood in the precise middle of number 126 and number 128. There was no other building behind him, and this appeared to be an even-numbered street. Yet, the street on the other side of Pearl was marked as any other with odds and evens exchanging on either side. This task, assigned by his professor, seemed hopeless. *Is this a test?*

~

From the standing post on his slip, Rear Admiral Gormhook watched with great interest as the young academic paced to and fro, passing countless men and the occasional gal who could have easily pointed him in the right direction.

Taking in a deep drag from his cigar, the Rear Admiral watched the young man traveling like a pendulum across the way.

All Gormhook wanted were the books clutched in the academic's arms, detailing the tales of sailors long lost. He considered how long he would let the young lad continue in this way. Perhaps he would wait until the timid boy passed out from fright at being so far away from everything he knew, or, maybe until he gave up without once asking for aid.

The man chuckled to himself, thinking that all the lad had to do was turn to look at the long wooden slips that stuck out from the pier where he stood, all of which, were clearly numbered. The Rear Admiral was even standing directly beneath the numbers of his slip, but the boy seemed to refuse to look his way.

Shaking his head, Gormhook said to the spirits of the ships that surrounded him, "That's the trouble with students these days — they're lost beyond the library."

Three Times a Year

Laurie Asher

Here we go again. Report Card Day. I was always happy with my progress reports. There was usually very little change from the last one, three months past. Being in the fifth grade was more fun than the fourth grade, and more interesting than the third.

I excelled in every subject but arithmetic. Always straight As, even in math, for the first six grades. Somehow, I was able to fake it for this long. But I was quickly exposed in the 7th grade, when I entered Junior High.

The section on the report card about "plays well with others and doesn't run with scissors," (*my* interpretation) was always marked satisfactory or above.

Most kids my age would be proud of themselves and couldn't wait to get home to share the report card with their parents. But I wasn't. I did try to tell myself that maybe it would be different this time. But that didn't happen. Or did it?

~

Three months ago, as usual, my mom asked us to place our report cards on the kitchen table. She didn't look at, or even touch them. They just sat there for an hour doing nothing, waiting to be reviewed — but only by my father when he got home from work.

There was one thing different, though. My two aunts, my mother's much older sisters, who lived close by and visited often, were over that day to visit us, with bags of oranges, lemons, and peaches from their fruit trees. They were present to watch the drama play out.

My dog, Miss Aubrey, let out a low, but not unfriendly, bark. We knew this meant my dad's truck was pulling up outside. He came, in his dirty work clothes. His hands were always filthy, and his routine was to wash them at the kitchen sink, with a soap called Lava.

My mom told him it was report card day, and he picked up my brother's report card first. It was, as usual, pitiful. Out loud, he

373

read Ds, Fs, and an occasional C-minus. The shouting started from both parents simultaneously.

"What the h*ll are you doing all day?"

My brother stood with his head down, having nothing to say to defend himself, and the shouting continued.

I saw my mom pick up my report card, take a cursory look inside, and set it back down. And then, she grabbed my sister's. She fared a bit better. One C, one B in PE, and the rest Ds, no Fs. She handed it to my dad. But the yelling was the same, nevertheless. She couldn't defend herself either, but she kept her head up in defiance.

"Go to your room," my mother scolded them. I followed out of the kitchen and went to my room, as well. My parents were now arguing with each other, and, within a few minutes, I got up from my bed to take my dog for a walk. It was a good time to leave quietly. My aunts beat me out the front door.

They both hugged me at the same time and noticed the tears in my eyes. One aunt handed me her silky handkerchief. They understood how I, once again, processed the familiar scene. If you make good grades, don't expect to get any positive attention for doing well. If you are practically a failure, at least they say *something* to you. Message—bad behavior gets attention. I was starting to believe that any attention, even negative, was better than none at all. I didn't want to think this, but it made perfect sense at the time.

Auntie Kay said, "We're very proud of you, honey. You got straight As, and that's very impressive." Each aunt slipped me a five-dollar bill, and Aunt Billie said, "Keep this between us. Go buy yourself something nice."

I cried even more. Ten dollars, back then, was really something! It was a fortune to me. I quickly forgot to keep crying and feeling sorry for myself. I was happy they recognized my achievements and I hugged them both—thanking them, over and over.

I waved goodbye and, smiling ear to ear, skipped up the street with my dog.

When I returned home, my report card was laying on my dresser bearing my mother's signature. The yelling had stopped, and dinner was served. We had chicken pies and cottage cheese—usually reserved for our regular ol' Sunday night dinner. We didn't ask why. No one spoke a word.

~

This time, three months later and another report, I found what, I thought, was a clever solution. Coming home on report card day, I told my mother I accidently left my report card in my locker.

She asked, "Did you get good grades?"

I lied and said yes, because I had started Algebra 1A this semester, and the C looked so awful amongst all the As.

She said, "OK, just go ahead and sign my name and turn it in."

That was easy.

The Party — And Marilyn:
A True Story

Dale Combs

In 1968, 16,899 young Americans died in Vietnam. Before that senseless war would end, we would loose 58,220 lives, or more than half the total enrollment of the University of California system at that time. A year later, I was 20 years old. The draft lottery for young men between the ages of 19 and 26 would be held. There are 365 days in a year and the lottery ball with my November birthday would come up as the 66th number selected. That became my first recollection of advancing to the top 20% of anything.

It is winter, and I am a first-year architecture student at Cal Poly San Luis Obispo. I'm here because I want to become an architect — not because my full-time enrollment afforded me a good reason to not join the military. As a student, I was granted a deferment from the draft. Even with that perceived protection, there always seemed to be a cloud that followed my thoughts, a weighty reminder of what might be if my path varied. On this evening, that particular cloud forgot about me.

On a cold and very rainy Saturday night, clouds of a different sort were proving problematic. I was with my roommates, pushing a stalled yellow Volkswagen bug up Santa Rosa Street. We were outside the car trying to nudge the vehicle and its cargo uphill. The rain was loud and relentless, as each drop crashed against the car in an increasing drum roll. The water, rushing down the street's concrete gutter, was being diverted by the car tires up over the curb in a perfect and continual wave of runoff onto me and my partners in crime. We were completely soaked.

However, at this point, there was not a thought of protecting ourselves from that evening's onslaught of wind and rain. We needed to transport our cargo to its destination. The cargo we were in custody of was the keg of beer for that night's party. For the record, soaking wet and pushing a car uphill in a monsoon, I was underage—but one of my roommates was not.

By anyone's definition, I was not a party person. But I do think young college students are vulnerable to herd mentality. On this night, we were hosting the party at our place, an off-campus dorm, with a shared public room large enough for the anticipated crowd. Each member of the herd was to bring a date. I was an introvert, shy, had no girlfriend, and relied on one of my roommates to fix me up.

My date was Marilyn. She wore a conservative dress, had long curly brown hair, and was very pretty. She was quiet. She came to the party with her friend, my roommate's girlfriend.

In a now-crowded room with the deafening background beat of Steppenwolf's "Magic Carpet Ride," Marilyn and I found some standing room and tried to talk. Attempting not to spill, we each held a cup with beer. Our conversation was more like a verbal multiple-choice test. She asked a question, and I would shout back what I thought was the right answer.

I asked a question, and, after deep thought, she would shout above the noise, "What did you say?" I would ask again, and with a slight smile, she responded with a very detailed two-word answer. We were learning very little about each other, beyond our majors and our shared dislike of rain. She was there, talking to me, standing by me, but at the same time, she wasn't really there. I was trying to have a good time but could tell she was not.

We continued our exchange of quiz questions for a very long hour, at which point Marilyn announced that she needed to leave. There was a break in the storm, and she told me her roommate would walk her home. She did not want me to come. I did not expect to see her again.

It seemed very clear to me that, as a date for this function, I was a complete failure. I was quiet enough naturally and, I thought perhaps, too self-absorbed in my own failing as a conversationalist. I moved on and chose not to dwell on that evening's disappointment. However, fate sometimes has other plans for us, and something happened that would change that night's memory.

Two years passed. It was a warm spring afternoon on campus, with students randomly shuffling with apparent purpose off to their next classes. I could sense a very slight breeze feeling its way inland from the ocean. It seemed to enhance the top of the hour chimes emanating from the old administration building tower.

Thankful for recent rains, the hills that served as the campus

378

backdrop for Cal Poly were already showing off that central California emerald carpet, highlighted by a scattering of oak trees. It was a perfect cloud-free day with the sun looking for a high point. As I was traveling to my next class, I stopped to talk to a friend, when I heard a woman's voice speak out behind me.

"Excuse me, is your name Dale?"

I turned to see a pretty girl with curly brown hair. It was Marilyn, now wearing jeans and a loose tie-dyed top. Surprised and fumbling for my words, I responded with an awkward, "Yes, hi."

"Dale," she said, "I owe you an apology for that night we dated." She continued. "You see, I had been married. The year before our date, my husband had been killed in Vietnam. I was not myself, or good company, for a long time."

I stood there, dumbfounded, feeling a little small and unable to react. I didn't know what to say beyond, "I'm so sorry."

She stood there a moment more. "I just wanted you to know." She turned quietly and walked off to her destination.

I never saw Marilyn again.

Looking back to that rainy night, and the spring day that followed years later, I feel somewhat guilty for being overly concerned with trying to have a good time on a date at a college party. Now, I do reminisce about my friends who were serving in South East Asia at that time. They can look back and relive the concerns they had about living to see the next day. I expect many of them try very hard to forget.

From time to time, my cloud returns, when I think about that night and the lost soldier that was hers. Although I never knew her husband, I do know that I will never forget Marilyn.

Please Post in the Want Ads

Laurie Asher

I'm not skinny,

I'm curvy.

I'm not shy.

I'm nervy.

I'm no stranger to trauma,

But far away from the drama.

I'm very good at many things,

But not so great at most.

Always trying to get much better,

But never one to boast.

I try to be entertaining,

But sometimes require explaining.

Often witty, but style all mine

If you sometimes don't get it,

Just give me a sign.

I love my doggies and my family, as well.

Maybe we'll connect

Only time will tell.

 I enjoy new acquaintances, too,

So maybe I will fall for you.

Contributors

(Numbers in parenthesis reference author's contributions.)

DIANA AVERY AMSDEN, PhD, (103) has an academic background in anthropology, archaeology, architecture, and art history. Among her scholarly and popular works are poetry, an index to Ayn Rand's *Atlas Shrugged,* and, currently in progress, a multigenerational family story, *The Stained Glass Woman.* Recently interviewed by Marilyn Moore of the Atlas Society, she discussed growing up in a family of archaeologists in northern New Mexico, six degrees, her discovery and critique of Ayn Rand, her experiences at the first Libertarian Party convention, working in Hollywood, her *Atlas Shrugged Index,* and ideas for an *Atlas Shrugged* miniseries. To view: https://atlassociety.org/commentary/commentary-blog/6318-member-spotlight-diana-amsden.

LAURIE ASHER, (301, 373, 381) currently serving as Secretary of the SDWEG board of directors, acquired her street smarts on the beach/boardwalk in Venice, CA. After retiring from Real Estate, she began her writing career, including short stories and poetry; she is currently working on her certification as a memoir writer. Her work has been performed onstage at the Memoir Showcase in San Diego, has previously been published in the Guild's Anthology, and includes one currently unpublished children's book — in honor of her nephew. She is currently working on two other novels. A product of the California Public School System, Laurie says she never mastered grammar or punctuation skills and will always require excellent editors. Her favorite "literature" quote is by Dr. Seuss, "Everything stinks until it's finished." She read *Green Eggs and Ham* for the first time in the 9th grade and thought it was pretty darn good.

KELLY BARGABOS (71) lives and writes in San Diego, CA. Her memoir, *Chasing the Merry-Go-Round: Holding on to Hope & Home When the World Moves Too Fast,* was a 2018 Nautilus Book Award Silver winner and a finalist in the National Indie Excellence Awards. Her award-winning work has appeared in literary journals, anthologies, and news publications; she holds a certificate in Creative Nonfiction from the Downtown Writer's Center in Syracuse, NY.

GERED BEEBY's (43) suspense-thriller of industrial espionage, *Dark Option* (2002), was nominated for a PMA Benjamin Franklin award in the category, Best New Voice-Fiction (2003). Author of two screenplays, *The Bottle Imp,* a deal-with-the-devil story based on Robert Louis Stevenson's 1892 classic tale, and *Dark Option,* he has contributed short stories and essays to *The Guilded Pen* anthologies since its first edition in 2012. He is a Past President (2003) of the San Diego Writers and Editors Guild and remains on the Board as a Director-at-Large as Official Greeter. A registered professional engineer (PE), Gered serves as a Subject Matter Expert for the California engineer licensing Board, and, in this capacity, he performs detailed analyses for the Board's technical advisory unit.

ROBYN BENNETT (155, 225) lives in Blenheim, on the South Island of New Zealand, has five published fiction and non-fiction works, and is an avid reader, reviewer, beta reader, blogger, and guest blogger on several web sites. She and her writing partner, Bob Boze, are collaborating on several novels, short stories, articles, and other works. They offer a variety of editing, proofreading, and business services including lectures, workshops, and speaking engagements at writer's conferences, public or private events through their business partnership, Writing Allsorts: https://writingallsorts.com/

JENNA BENSON (41, 67, 319) is a substitute teacher and freelance writer currently living in El Cajon, California, having moved three and a half years ago to be closer to her family (and the beach) and to focus on her craft and passion: writing. Originally from Las Vegas, Nevada, and graduated from the University of Nevada-Reno in 2014 with a bachelor's degree in English (Writing) and Sociology, she has been writing creatively in different facets for over a decade. Her writing includes poetry, fiction, nonfiction, technical writing, short stories, and newspaper columns. Jenna has been a member of the San Diego Writers and Editors Guild since May 2018 and has learned much from the community. Her hobbies consist of reading books from her ever-growing "to be read" pile, binge watching the latest shows, working on her upcoming novel, practicing yoga and meditation, and attempting to train her beloved cat, Oliver.

BOB BOZE (225) lives in the south bay area of San Diego and is a diverse author with eight published fiction and nonfiction works, including an entry in last year's SDWEG Anthology. He is an avid reader, reviewer, beta reader, blogger, and guest blogger on several web sites. In addition, Bob and his writing partner, Robyn Bennett, are collaborating on several novels, short stories, articles and other works. They offer a variety of editing, proofreading, and business services including lectures, workshops, and speaking engagements at writer's conferences, public or private events through their business partnership, Writing Allsorts: https://writingallsorts.com/.

MARCIA BUOMPENSIERO (105) is the author of *Sumerland*, winner of the 2017 San Diego Book Award, Best Published Mystery. Writing under the pseudonym "Loren Zahn," Marcia also publishes the Theo Hunter mystery series: *Dirty Little Murders* (2009/2017), *Deadly Little Secrets* (2015), and *Fatal Little Lies* (2018). *Deadly Little Secrets* received a "highly recommended" rating from the SDWEG Manuscript Review Board and was a finalist in the 2015 San Diego Book Awards unpublished manuscript division. She writes nonfiction magazine articles about the history of San Diego's Little Italy. Marcia serves on SDWEG board of directors as Treasurer and has been the managing editor of *The Guilded Pen* anthologies since 2013. SDWEG recognized her efforts to further the impact of the Guild in the writing community and honored her contributions by presenting her with a *Rhoda Riddell Builders Award* in 2018. She is the founder of Grey Castle Publishing: www.greycastlepublishing.com.

LAWRENCE CARLETON (85, 343) has published or otherwise presented scholarly work in philosophy, cognitive science, and software development, thereby putting to some use his advanced degrees in computer science and philosophy, and his post doctorate in cognitive science. He took up writing when Parkinson's disease ended his hobby as a jazz trumpeter, and currently amuses himself and, he hopes, others, by writing short stories with interesting characters in unusual situations. A contributor to several anthologies including *The Guilded Pen,* he's particularly proud of his book, *I'm Not Roger Blaime and Other Curious Phenomena*, which contains twelve of his best stories. lrcarleton@gmail.com Facebook: Lawrence Carleton.

ANNE M. CASEY (245) asks which came first, the writer or the reader? For Anne, the desires to read and to write seemed concurrent. She created the usual child's pencil squiggle stories on envelope backs which were related to her doll house family and paper dolls on long winter days in Ohio. She continues to write on paper scraps which rival in number her book collection. Anne has contributed to the SDWEG Anthology, written training manuals, and edited college theses. Her current writing projects are the long in-process Hungarian recipe book, *First You Steal One Chicken;* a memoir, *The Juniper Street Lemonade Stand;* and, a poetry book tentatively titled *Myriad*. She is past editor of the Writers Guild newsletter, among others, and served as an at-large member of the SDWEG Board. Following retirement from UCSD as a medical/scientific secretary, she finally obtained a degree in Literature/Writing at UCSD. She and her fluffy white cat, Marlin, live in San Diego with family very, very close by.

DALE COMBS (377) is a practicing architect calling San Diego home since his graduation from California Polytechnic State University, San Luis Obispo, in 1972. His architectural practice specializes in the design and planning of custom residential and waterfront hospitality projects. Those designs have been noted for their creativity and some published nationally. He and his wife have raised three wonderful children and are now blessed with seven grandchildren. Dale's interest in writing has been brought about by a desire to share some of his life stories with his family.

CANDACE GEORGE CONRADI (153, 277) is a published author and founder of Writers Inner Circle and Storytellers Edge, a live mic forum for writers/authors. First published in 2006, she has since written and published her books independently. For six years, she worked privately with writers, many who completed their manuscripts and successfully Indie published their books. She has since returned to her own writing. Conradi received a 2013 Professional Women of the Year Award from the National Association of Professional Women. She has been featured on the Padres Station and Channel 6 Morning Show, is a recognized author by the San Diego Public Library for her contributions, and an honored participant in the Gallery 4311 Artists and Authors Series. She has also been a featured guest on numerous talk radio shows and podcasts focusing on the importance of women's issues and life purpose. Her books can be found on Amazon.com.

AL CONVERSE (243) is a 1965 graduate of Boston University, served as a Naval Officer in the Vietnam War 1965-1968, earned an MBA from the University of Connecticut (1969), worked many years in the finance industry, and retired as Chief, Finance Division, US Small Business Administration, San Diego District. Since retiring, he has published seven novels, *Bitch'n, Die Again, Boston Boogie, Baja Moon, News from the East, Flagship,* and *Hornwinkle Hustle.* His short stories, "Warrior's Stone," "The Marble Game," "Drippy Pants," "The Woods," "The Wake Up," "A Rose for Mrs. Delahanty," "One Soldier," and "Old Kim" have appeared in different editions of the Guild's annual anthology.

JANICE COY (23, 113) is the award-winning author of five suspense novels, a scuba diver, a hiker (successfully reaching the summit of Mt. Kilimanjaro), a runner, and an animal lover—all elements that enrich her stories. Her most recent novel, *The Water's Fine,* opens on a scuba dive boat on the Sea of Cortez. Her third novel, *The Smallest of Waves,* is a suspense finalist at the SDBAA. Her fourth novel, *North of Eden,* received the Indie Reader stamp of approval. A former journalist, Coy has always been curious about people's motives. "Now I get to create motives for my characters," says Coy. Her books can be purchased through her website www.janicecoy.com or on Amazon.

CHRISTINE L. CUNNINGHAM, (231, 255, 323) a lawyer and mother of four, enjoys writing about humor in everyday life drawing inspiration from her kids, her husband of over thirty years, and her former life as a bartender and ballet dancer. Christine is a member of the San Diego Writers and Editors Guild, currently serves on the Board of the Southern California Ballet, is acting President of the Poway Veterans Park Committee, and is a founding member of the Just Write Society. Originally from Michigan, she now resides in the San Diego area.

C. H. "SCOTT" CURRIER (213) was born in Pasadena, CA in 1954. He attended Pasadena City College and Mesa Junior College. In 1979 he was accepted into Cal Poly San Luis Obispo where he graduated with a BS in Ornamental Horticulture. He returned to San Diego and worked in the landscape and nursery industry for forty years until retiring in 2015. His wife, Lynne, and he have two daughters, Corinne and Michelle. He is currently completing his first book titled *Where the Ashes Fell*, a historical novel based on stories his grandfather wrote in 1933. He has been a member of the writer's support groups The Writer's Connection of Rancho Bernardo and Linked in Ink. He owes any successes in writing largely to their tutelage and encouragement. He thanks his mother, Liza, who could turn a yarn. Scott's passions are traveling, politics, and classic cars.

BOB DOUBLEBOWER (143) was born in Philadelphia, raised in the southern New Jersey town of Lindenwold, and attended Villanova University where he received a bachelor's degree in Civil Engineering. Beginning his engineering work with Bechtel Power division in Washington, DC, his career has taken him to Colorado, Arizona, Virginia, and, finally, California where he now maintains a consulting engineering practice, Regional Shoring Design, in San Diego County. Bob has been published in *The Guilded Pen* since 2012 and is currently working on a horror novel, *The Circling Bench*. Bob is past president of the SDWEG board of directors and currently serves as vice president.

ELIZABETH DURIS (69, 205, 311) is a mother of six and a former high school teacher with a master's degree in English Literature. She treasures her three book clubs and two writing groups, where she enjoys seeing the world through the prism of the writer. A founding member of the Just Write Society, she has written fiction, nonfiction, and poetry.

PAULA EARNEST (13, 29, 235) is a former high school English and drama teacher who loved inspiring her students in writing, public speaking, literature, and acting for thirty-five years. She directed high school plays for over fifteen years, coached speech and debate students — competing in tournaments throughout California, held a directorship for an experimental theatre group in San Diego called "Actors for Actors Theater Company," and is currently freelancing as a professional speech writer. Paula enjoys her morning hikes, writing poetry, drinking champagne with her writing group, and spending time with family.

MARTY EBERHARDT (55, 77) is a retired botanical garden director and nonprofit consultant, and has resumed writing poetry and fiction, right-brain activities that disappeared in a life bursting with work and family obligations. She has published two prose pieces and ten poems, in the publications *The Dragon Poet Review, The Wilderness House Literary Review, The Twisted Vine Literary Arts Journal, A Year in Ink, Vol. 11,* three volumes of *The Guilded Pen,* and *The Silver City Quarterly Review.* She has two novels being considered for publication. She divides her time between Silver City, NM, and San Diego.

SALLY ECKBERG (161, 285) says, "I was born and raised in a mortuary, I had to learn to play only quiet games. Therefore, I became quite addicted to reading and drawing. This, I am sure, had a great effect on my career choices." Sally's first major in college was Speech Therapy. After working in a clinical setting for a short time, she decided to get teaching degrees in both regular and special education. She started out teaching multi-handicapped children and then decided to concentrate on deaf education. Sally's love of reading and storytelling greatly affected her teaching. She tried to make her lessons in English, reading, and history as creative as possible. Her students wrote and acted out historical scenes. They wrote alternative endings to stories as well as taking on the persona of literary characters to act out scenes in a book. Sally says she has always loved to make up stories and her students were the perfect audience.

CHLOE KERNS EDGE (209) is currently teaching creative writing at OASIS in Escondido and working as a ghost writer. Her works include *Birdcage Review* (1982) and *Maize, Volume 6* (1983); a published book, *Tattoo (1988)*, for women in prison; poems; nonfiction; and, has been published in *The Guilded Pen* (2012-2019). She is currently working on a memoir.

SARAH FAXON (141, 203, 371) has completed fourteen full-length original novels, with seven more in the works, and has written countless short stories. S. Faxon is currently an administrator at an internationally acclaimed museum in San Diego. In her previous career, she was an administrator in a human rights advocacy nonprofit at Columbia University, where she assisted in regional-political, social development programs in countries throughout the world. Sarah received her master's degree in Government & Politics, with a certificate in International Law and Diplomacy from St. John's University in New York, where she served as an adjunct professor. Sarah's first published novel, *The Animal Court*, is available in paperback and e-book format on Amazon. To learn more about Sarah's creative projects, visit her website at www.sfaxon.com.

DAVID FELDMAN (135) spent thirty years as a copy editor at *The San Diego Union-Tribune*, fifty-five years working as a reporter and editor on newspapers, including *Stars & Stripes* in Europe and the *Honolulu Star-Bulletin*. He taught journalism in colleges for thirty-four years. For the past six years, Dave faithfully copy edited *The Guilded Pen*, and has been published in it since 2012. Dave served on the SDWEG board of directors and tinkered with classic cars. In 2018, Dave published his autobiography, *Irreverent Forever, True Tales from a Newspaperman's Outrageously Rewarding Life*. It is a candid look at some of the world's zaniest people — newspaper men and women — and their tales from the old days, filled with rapscallions, inebriates, and a few decent souls. Visit Dave's website: www.feldysworld.com.

IRENE FLYNN (17, 31, 341) was born in Cleveland, Ohio, and raised in its suburb of Willowick, just the other side of The Twilight Zone's train stop of Willoughby. She says, "I spent 3.3 years of my life in a semi-cloistered convent — years I like to refer to as my life of Pi. I completed my bachelor's in communication with an emphasis in writing from Notre Dame College in South Euclid and, not too long after, moved to Key West, where some of my feature articles were published in the local newspaper. Thank God, I moved again, to what I consider my heart-home of New Orleans. I simply wallowed in the vibrant culture there that inspired me to write for some future, unmapped goal. I graduated from the University of New Orleans in 2002 with a master's in arts administration and, eventually, was blown to San Diego through the influences of Hurricane Katrina. Since then, I have simply worked and worked only to find myself now striving to make good on those earlier aspirations of publishing poetry and short stories."

ROBERT GILBERG (81) is a retired semiconductor executive, holding patented designs for computer and communications microcircuits, with thirty-five years' experience in the industry dating from the earliest days of transistorized computers to today's world of digital High Definition TV and the connected home. His team received an Academy of Television Arts and Sciences Emmy Award for digital television anti-piracy systems. Robert is the author of four books: his memoir, *The Last Road Rebel and Other Lost Stories*, and the novels, *Alice Chang, A Simple Twist of Fate,* and *Starvation Mountain.* A career with multinational corporations took him around the world. With Nikki — his wife of fifty-two years, a travel expert, and consummate traveling companion — he has added many exotic locations to his resume. The couple loves theater and music, sharing a life mission of seeing the greatest musicians of the generation and the finest theatre in San Diego. Two dogs, a canary, and Coco, the African Grey parrot, complete their family.

JANET HAFNER (367) has loved words from an early age. She taught how to use language to achieve goals, and later, used it to obtain grants. Her professional career included teaching English as a Second Language, Spanish, training teachers in effective techniques for second language acquisition, and coaching corporate managers and supervisors to overcome linguistic challenges. *Conversemos*, a televised Spanish course, is offered throughout the United States. Her published children's novel, *Eye of an Eagle*, aims to show how easy it is to misjudge people. Janet's memoir essays appear in anthologies, and she has been published in *The Guilded Pen* since 2015. She serves on the board of SDWEG, is a member of The Society of Children's Book Writers and Illustrators, San Diego Writer's Ink, and has published essays in the Oasis Anthology 2017. Janet enjoys art and ballroom dancing. She is an all-the-time optimist who loves to laugh and knows the value of tears. Visit: jrhafner.com or jrhafner19@gmail.com.

MARGARET HARMON (19) is a fabulist and humorist, author of *The Genie Who Had Wishes of His Own: 21st-century Fables* (with a blurb from Ray Bradbury), *The Man Who Learned to Walk In Shoes That Pinch: Contemporary Fables,* and *A Field Guide to North American Birders: A Parody.*

389

Over 300 of her humor pieces, fables, features, and Op-Eds have appeared in local or national publications, online, or on National Public Radio. Her fables, taught in literature and oral interpretation courses, are also analyzed in a French doctoral dissertation at the Université d'Aix-en-Provence. Awards include "Best of the Best San Diego Writers" on NPR's "San Diego Journal" and San Diego Book Awards Association's "Best Anthology" and "Best Fun & Games." Her website is www.margaretharmon.com.

PEGGY HINAEKIAN (79, 289) is of Armenian origin, born and raised in Egypt. Her paternal grandfather owned the largest private library in Egypt and introduced her to books in three languages at a very young age (English, French, and Armenian). Raised in a cosmopolitan environment, she became an avid reader, has kept a journal since age twelve, was editor of her high school magazine, and has written short stories and essays, which have been published in the SDWEG anthologies since 2016. Her debut novel, *Of Julia and Men,* was included in the *New York Times Book Review Magazine* under "Discover New Titles — Great Stories, Unique Perspectives." The novel is almost entirely fictional except for the international settings, which Peggy drew from her lifetime of world travel. Peggy is an internationally recognized and well-established artist, living and working in the United States and Switzerland. The illustration on the cover of her book and the twenty-six images inside are her own artwork. View it on www.OfJuliaAndMen.com. Visit www.peggyhinaekian.artspan.com to see Peggy's art and bio.

LAURA HOYT (283) describes herself as a visual person with an art and design background, enjoying reading and writing poetry and essays since she was in high school. Song lyrics have always attracted her. Laura says, "Reading was difficult as a child, but I eventually discovered other outlets for expression. A film study class captivated me and sparked my writing enthusiasm. Dissecting classic movies through essays helped me develop critical thinking using examples of my thoughts and ideas. In martial arts, I composed several disquisition-type essays as part of earning rank. Now, experiences are becoming stories, and I find myself here again. Thanks to the inspiration of a recent writing instructor and fellow students, I am working on a fictionalized memoir." Laura's goal is to continue having fun learning and telling stories through the beauty of writing. Her hope is that interest in the lives and stories of others will encourage compassion.

DORA KLINOVA (73, 197, 261) is an award-winning writer and poet. In 1992, Dora emigrated from the Ukraine and left behind her profession as an engineer-designer in the movie industry. America recreated Dora. Her thoughts flooded onto paper like a rushing stream. To her surprise, the torrent of words was in English, not her native Russian. In March 2003, the International Society of Poets presented Dora a Merit Award for her poetry. Dora's works have been published in newspapers and magazines, performed in many theaters in San Diego, and were published in three anthologies: *Hot Chocolate for Seniors, Hot Chocolate for Senior Romance,* and *The Guilded Pen, 2018 Anthology.* Dora wrote three books, all of which have achieved worldwide success. Her first book, *A Melody from an Immigrant's Soul,* is a collection of heartfelt stories. Her second book, *The Queen of the Universe,* is translated into Japanese. The novel, *Did You Ever Have the Chance to Marry an American Multimillionaire?* is Dora's personal story. www.doraklinova.com.

MELODY A. KRAMER (207) is an innovative lawyer, freelance writer, speaker, and author of Amazon best-seller, *Lawyers Decoded,* an exposé on how lawyers think and act. She loves playing with words, whether writing hard-hitting journalistic pieces, colorful story lines, or the occasional poem. When her writing muse goes silent, a long, barefoot walk on one of San Diego's many beaches seems to bring him back. Melody launched her legal career in Lincoln, Nebraska, and now runs a business law practice in San Diego, California. Her company, Legal Greenhouse, is committed to creating innovative solutions in the legal space, changing how lawyers and clients interact, and making lawyers more useful to their clients. Melody lives in San Diego with her teenaged daughter and two precocious kitties. She is a founding member of the Just Write Society: www.thejustwritesociety.com. Visit her website: www.melodyannkramer.com.

LEON LAZARUS (1) was a rebellious child growing up in Apartheid South Africa. Recognizing the brutality of the regime at a young age, he arrived at Rhodes University in 1986 as an anti-apartheid activist. By the start of his second year, Leon had formed an eleven-piece non-racial band, destroyed student radio with a show called *The Hallucinogenic Wasteland,* and published three controversial student magazines. He graduated as a journalist in 1991. Leon has spent the intervening twenty-eight years in marketing and communications and has held senior positions in both corporations and agencies. Today, Leon consults on projects that interest him, but writing remains his first love. He has written and illustrated four children's picture books with more on the way. Leon also has a new middle grade chapter book in editing, and looks forward to completing *Barking At Dogs,* a collection of creative non-fiction short stories that describe a life similar to his in Apartheid South Africa. Leon devotes part of his time to volunteering as a second grade reading tutor and producing a podcast featuring South African music and musicians at TuneMeWhat.com.

RICHARD LEDERER (327) is the author of 50 books about language, history, and humor, including his best-selling *Anguished English* series. He has been profiled in magazines as diverse as *The New Yorker, People,* and the *National Inquirer* and is founding cohost of "A Way with Words" on KPBS Public Radio. Dr. Lederer's column, "Lederer on Language,""appears in newspapers and magazines throughout the United States, including the *San Diego Union-Tribune.* He has been named

International Punster of the Year and Toastmasters International's Golden Gavel winner. He was awarded the Guild's Odin Award 2019. Website: www.verbivore.com.

TOM LEECH (163) is the author of several books covering a variety of topics. His most recent is *FUN ON THE JOB: Amusing and true tales from Rosie-the-Riveters to Rocket Scientists at a major (San Diego-based) aerospace company.* Garnering attention is Tom's book, *On the Road in '68: A year of turmoil, a journey of friendship,* about his travel experiences during that wild year, fifty years ago. His years as Forum Editor for *San Diego Magazine Online* led to his book, *Outdoors San Diego: Hiking, Biking & Camping.* Other current books include *Say It Like Shakespeare: The Bard's Timeless Tips for Successful Communication,* 2nd ed. and *The Curious Adventures of Santa's Wayward Elves,* with coauthor and wife, Leslie. His AMACOM book, *How to Prepare, Stage & Deliver Winning Presentations,* is in its 3rd edition and has been acclaimed by many relevant publications. His poems have appeared in many anthologies and journals.

CHERYL LENDVAY (167) was born in Oklahoma, raised in California, has lived on the east coast, and is a member of the Osage tribe. Writing under the pen name, C. Big Eagle, she is composing a fact-based short novel set in the Tall Grass Prairie region of Osage County, Oklahoma, during the "Reign of Terror" and Great Depression. Also underway is a collection of personal essays, *Life with Jack. Flying by the Seat of our Pants.* "Shark Island" is one in this series. A world explorer, she has traveled to 142 countries and territories and is a member of the Travelers Century Club. Her goal is to visit eight additional countries by the end of 2020. She is retired from a thirty-eight-year career in aviation and lives with her husband and a ginger cat on Mt. Helix.

VALERIE E. LOOPER (33) is a patent attorney and chemist, with an appreciation for high literature and low humor.

SYD LOVE (187) has self-published two historical novels and two collections of short stories. Over 250 magazine and newspaper articles — mostly about places and people of South America, Mexico, and Spain — and a hard-cover San Diego history book have been published. He is still at it.

ERIK C. MARTIN (131, 239, 307) was born in Ohio, spent the first two years of his life in San Diego, and moved back to Cleveland for the next three decades before bouncing about and ending up back in San Diego. His writing has appeared in *A Year in Ink, Frontier Tales,* and *Coffin Bell,* as well as three novels published for Young Adult and Middle Grade readers. Erik is a member of the SCBWI, SDWEG, and San Diego Writers, Ink. He was prepared for the rejection inherent to a writer's life by being a lifelong Cleveland Browns fan. When not writing, Erik enjoys reading everything, wearing costumes, playing tabletop games, and sharing life with his wife and partner, Toni.

MICHAEL J. McMAHON (117) was born in the East Wall area of Dublin, Ireland, and has been writing since he was ten years old. He has many poems and short stories in his portfolio, two completed novels, *The Sea Has No Dreams* and *The Cloud Above The Platanos*—book one of a projected trilogy, and is currently working on book two. He has countless musical performance credits to his name and has received many awards for acting performances in plays ranging from Chekhov to Shakespeare. Since retiring from his job as a structural steel and masonry inspector, he has embarked on a full-time writing career. He has made San Diego home for the past thirty-one years.

FRANK NEWTON (363) was, for most of his working life, a national leader of Hispanic-American affairs in journalism and public policy. He was founding director of both the National Association of Hispanic Journalists and the National Hispanic Leadership Agenda. A writer, editor, and publisher in a variety of capacities, he edited the Smithsonian's *New World* publication about the Columbus quincentenary, published the *Silver Wave* newspaper about older adult issues, and edited newsletters for various nonprofit organizations, including the SDWEG newsletter, *A Writer's Life*.

YVONNE NELSON PERRY (63) was born, raised, and educated in the Hawaiian Islands, and is of Polynesian descent. Yvonne's first book, *The Other Side of the Island*, is a collection of short stories set in a timeless Hawai`i. Although she didn't start writing fiction until her 60s, she had been a columnist, and has had forty-nine short stories published in literary journals, magazines, and anthologies. An editor for years, she held creative writing classes in her home. A unique writers conference Yvonne staged in Balboa Park to prove conferences don't need to be so expensive had well-known writer volunteers sitting under trees, teaching the craft of writing like Aristotle and his disciples. For nine years, she participated in Long Beach's "A Living Author in Every Classroom" program and continues to be invited to read her work in San Diego schools. She teaches at the world-class Santa Barbara Writers Conference, now twenty-five years and ongoing. Her work-in-progress is another collection of short fiction set in the Pacific Rim. Her stories are about conditions of the human heart and evoke strong emotions. Yvonne is the recipient of SDWEG's Odin Award for her many contributions to San Diego's writing community.

TY PIZ (295) raced Motocross and Flatrack from 1972 through 1979. In 1980 he switched to road racing until retiring in 2004. He has won three regional championships, and twice finished Top Ten overall in the AMA Superbike Series onboard a Yamaha TZ-250 Grand Prix motorcycle. Ty is a Paraeducator, working in the public-school system with high school students that have a wide range of special needs. He feels great to share his passion for life with these loving, caring young people. He has been published in *The Guilded Pen* since 2012.

FRANK PRIMIANO (129, 177) retired from academic and industrial careers, in which his writing was required to be strictly nonfiction, and has given free rein to his imagination. Except for the occasional, creative, memoirist episodes, he concentrates on fiction, some of which have appeared in local anthologies, including *The Guilded Pen* (annually since 2015). He has been a finalist in the San Diego Book Awards' Unpublished Novel and Unpublished Short Story categories. Frank is a Philadelphian who lived for over thirty years in Cleveland, Ohio. He and his wife, Elaine, moved to San Diego in 1998 in search of the sun.

WAYNE RAFFESBERGER (331) has been writing for decades. As a trained lawyer, most of his work has been commentaries on public policy, including work on issues of general interest, and numerous travel articles, published in many different newspapers and magazines. In recent years, he has been writing fiction, finishing several short stories — one published in an anthology and another recognized as Honorable Mention in the Lorian Hemingway Short Story Writing Contest. He is currently working on his first book. He resides in Point Loma with his wife, Kaye, and their polydactyl cat, Ernie.

ARTHUR RAYBOLD (139) has penned *Home from the Banks*, a poetry collection, and *The Trip Home*, a memoir. In process is an historical fiction for young readers about King Philip's War, circa 1662.

CY ROSEMAN, PhD, (269) is rounding the turn into his third career as a writer, his first, a university professor and his second, a financial advisor and retirement planner. While he continues to satisfy financial clients and has never really given up on being a professor, he is now increasingly engaged as a writer, focused primarily on drawing Fables out of his searching soul. Cy says, "To be a writer is, first and foremost, to have something philosophically important to say; second, to be drawn to storytelling as an art form; and, third, to execute the assignment in the same way a baker fashions his pastries and breads — using tools and techniques to generate an appetite for delicious morsels." Cy is currently engaged in combining a baker's artful presentation with the confectioner's talent for stimulating salivary expectations.

MIRIAM SCHRAER (265) grew up in the Bronx on a wonderful block in which three generations of Italian or Jewish families lived in each house. She describes those days as being very happy. At age eleven, Miriam, her parents, and her sister moved to New Rochelle, where she graduated from high school. She received a BA in psychology from City College of New York (CCNY) in 1968 and attended the masters creative writing program at San Francisco State in the early 1970s. In Berkeley, she directed a drama program for children called The Strawberry Playhouse. Miriam spent years advocating for her sons who have ADHD and learning disabilities, and was successful in getting services for them. In

1986 she and her husband moved to San Diego, where they raised their three sons. She is a copy editor for her husband's legal briefs.

MARDIE SCHROEDER (57, 165) published her debut novel, *Go West For Luck Go West for Love*, in 2015, and republished it in 2018. Her contributions to *The Guilded Pen* appear in the 2014, 2015, 2016, 2017, 2018 and 2019 editions. She serves as president on the SDWEG board of directors. Website: www.mardieschroeder.com.

DAN SINGER, (263, 275) a public servant in local government for over twenty-seven years — most recently as City Manager of the City of Poway, is now serving various communities as a consultant. Dan began his career after receiving a master's degree in Public Administration and in Political Science from Syracuse University, and, throughout his public-sector career, has been an active writer, penning hundreds of staff reports, memos, studies, and analyses. More recently, Dan has begun to appreciate the value of reading and writing more creatively. In the past three years, he has written several articles focused on employee engagement, risk taking, and personal growth. He looks forward to exploring further opportunities to write and learn. Dan currently lives in northern San Diego County with his partner, Olga. Together they have two adult sons. Dan enjoys reading, travelling, cooking and sports.

OLGA SINGER (101, 111, 361) would not describe herself as a writer in the traditional sense and hesitates to use that label to describe what she does. Journaling is where she hones her writing craft. When she found herself in a new town, not knowing a soul and struggling with empty nest syndrome, journaling became her solace, her outlet, her "safe" place. Her days are filled with many creative outlets: designing logos, websites, book covers, and layouts. She and her sister own a small graphic design firm servicing clients in the Southern California area. Creativity colors everything in her world and she wouldn't have it any other way. Writing reflects both her humor and perspective on the comings and goings of ordinary life, sometimes made extraordinary.

RIVKAH SLEETH's (335) first short story, "To Be Determined," was published in *The Guilded Pen* in 2017. She is currently working on an American historical fiction series set in the early 19th century, serves on the SDWEG board of directors, and serves as Assistant Editor of the SDWEG 2019 Anthology. Also a member of San Diego Writers, Ink and the Historical Novel Society, Rivkah is a voracious reader and historical researcher. In her spare time, she is a willing storyteller and a very involved grandmother.

AMY WALL (39, 313) believes putting pen to paper is like sprouting wings — anything is possible. She loves when her writing makes someone laugh or smile, whether it is a children's story, essay, or humorous story. Her published works include an essay in *Chaleur Magazine* in December 2018 and a fictional story in *Inlandia Literary Journal*. When not writing,

Amy can be found at her day job in M&A, traveling with her family (nearly thirty countries and counting), backpacking, running, or in adult gymnastics. After eight years in Australia and New Zealand, she finally settled down in sunny San Diego. Amy is a member of the Just Write Society, www.thejustwritesociety.com, and can be found at www.amywallauthor.com, or on Facebook, Twitter, Instagram, or LinkedIn.

PENN WALLACE (351) is a happy-go-lucky, Hemmingwayesque adventurer who lives on his sailboat as he sails around the world and is the author of the Ted Higuera and Catrina Flaherty series. penn@pennwallace.com.

RUTH LEYSE WALLACE, PhD, (259) retired from clinical practice in dietetics and self-published *Linking Nutrition and Mental Health*. A second book, *Nutrition and Mental Health*, was published later by Taylor and Francis. She contributes to the Behavioral Health Nutrition dietetic practice group's newsletter and educational webinars. Ruth has been published in *The Guilded Pen* since its inception in 2012 and has served as Assistant Editor of the anthology. She served as president of SDWEG and edited *The Writer's Life* for five years. While president, Ruth initiated the SDWEG Marketing Support Group and Open Mic Night. She is currently developing a collection of short stories as a nontraditional means of teaching nutrition.

GARY WINTERS (127, 321, 359) authored *The Deer Dancer,* a novel about a Yaqui boy in Mexico, which won the silver medal from UC Irvine for the Chicano/Latino Literary Prize, was runner-up in the San Diego Book Awards, won Best Novel 2010 Mensa Creative Awards, and received the bronze 2011 Book of the Year award for Multicultural Fiction in *ForeWord Reviews Magazine.* The book has been in the curriculum at Southwestern College, where *Poets & Writers Magazine* awarded Gary an honorarium to speak. *The Deer Dancer* is currently used in writing classes at San Diego Juvenile Hall and is in local Indian and county libraries. Winning awards for short story and photojournalism, he has won international and national awards for his poetry including a Mensa global contest that published his work in a hundred countries. His fiction and poetry have appeared in numerous anthologies and in such diverse publications as *Whisperings, A Literary and Visual Culture Magazine; The Caribbean Writer,* a literary journal of the University of the Virgin Islands; the San Francisco-based experimental/alternative multimedia journal, *Free the Marque*; and, *BEAT-itude: National Beat Poetry Festival 10-Year Anthology,* dedicated to the preservation and promotion of Beat poetry. His poem, *Cantina Dog,* has been included in *The Walt Whitman 200th Birthday Poets to Come Anthology.*

KEN YAROS, DDS, (89) is an alumnus of Albright College and received his DDS degree from Temple University. He spent six years serving with the US Air Force and seven years serving with the Connecticut Air National Guard, attaining the rank of Major. Now, semiretired after forty-five years of practice and teaching dental hygiene, he has turned his hand to writing short stories, both nonfiction and fiction. He has been a contributor to *The Guilded Pen* since 2013 and was published in the national OASIS Journal 2014. Ken often writes under his pen name, KAY Allen, and is putting together an anthology of short stories for Kindle publication. Ken serves as a Director-at-Large on the SDWEG board.

SANDRA YEAMAN (59) spent the first twenty years of her life trying to figure out how to get away from Minnesota. She spent the next forty years living in twelve countries, as she worked first as a teacher, then as an engineer, and finally as a diplomat. While she thought those exotic locations and occupations would provide her with plenty to write about, she finds the topics she draws from most often in her writing are her childhood and her home state.

Made in the
USA
Lexington, KY